Perfect Recall

New Stories by

Ann Beattie

Scribner

New York   London   Toronto   Sydney   Singapore

SCRIBNER
1230 Avenue of the Americas
New York, NY 10020

SCRIBNER and design are trademarks of Macmillan Library
Reference USA, Inc. used under license by Simon & Schuster,
the publisher of this work.

Designed by Kyoko Watanabe
Set in Aldine

Manufactured in the United States of America

10 9 8 7 6 5 4 3 2 1

Library of Congress Cataloging-in-Publication Data is available.

ISBN 0-7432-1169-3

For Ruth Danon

Contents

Perfect Recall

Hurricane
Carleyville

———

CARLEYVILLE left late because of the rain. That morning the phone had finally been disconnected, after a ridiculous argument with the phone company, when the supervisor he was finally connected with agreed to disconnect after asking a series of questions he could not possibly answer. With his credit card, his "code" was his mother's maiden name, but what security precaution had he come up with a year before for the phone company? What had happened to this country, that a citizen needed a magic word to turn off the telephone? Finally the woman had settled for his social security number, information about other occupants of the house (none, unless you counted the animals), and his assurance that he would put his request in writing and fax it to her before the end of the day. He had a fax, but the thing wasn't working: it spewed out page after page of blank paper for every incoming page, all marked with a deep black line. The broken machine would be Daley's problem now.

Hitched together, his moving home was a wonder: truck pulling trailer pulling horse carrier. The cat, Adventure Kitty, rode in the truck's cabin with Carleyville. That gave Coon, the dog, the use of the trailer—the space shared with the birds and the two chickens, all of which were suspended in a cage he'd improvised from the laundry basket and some nylon netting that hung above the floor, away from Coon's restless tongue. Secretly, Carleyville hoped that the ride would shake up the birds' insides enough that they'd stop laying eggs. He'd left two birds with Daley for Daley's daughter—a sort of early Christmas present—and lost two more, with not bad timing, when they poked their heads far enough outside the cage to peck the paint on an exposed pipe and died (he presumed) of lead poisoning. He and Daley had disposed of them in a backyard burial a few days earlier—Daley had done the digging, because Carleyville was trying to sort out the insurance company's failure to pay for X rays he'd had taken months ago when, walking across a street in the dark, he'd broken his ankle in a hole down which Alice could have easily tumbled into Wonderland. As the two bird-stuffed Styrofoam cups with plastic tops (left over from Chai tea to go) were lowered into the ground for a decent burial, a rather amazing thing happened: birds making an early migration passed overhead, the long line uninterrupted until they passed directly above, the birds in back suddenly slowing, as if the gap conveyed a symbolic good-bye, a respectful enactment of emptiness, for their fellow birds. *Two less critters for Coon to bark at,* Daley had commented. And then commented, again, *bark at,* because in spite of the holistic remedy Carleyville had insisted he try, he still suffered from echolalia.

At the end of the street, where the school bus turned around, Carleyville made his final swing, missing a maple tree by a fraction of an inch, settling for letting the horse bounce around for a few seconds. He was always too attuned to her mental state. The guy who ran the organic farm at the end of the road was nice enough, but a worrier: the whole rig might bust apart, he'd said nervously, inspecting it the night before; the horse could move around enough to get hurt, in his opinion. Finally, he and the guy had exchanged firm handshakes and Carleyville had reminded him that undiagnosed hypoglycemia could cause both sweating and anxiety—Malcolm Curry was a sweatbox, winter and summer—and Malcolm had kidded Carleyville one last time about the pumpkin suicide—a reference to the time a really *enormous* pumpkin had fallen off the back of a truck in front of Carleyville, providing months of what Malcolm called "punkin' postmortems": pumpkin soup, pumpkin flan, manicotti stuffed with pumpkin, pumpkin spice cookies, and of course traditional pumpkin pie. Being a farmer, Malcolm had respect for Carleyville's appreciation of vegetables. Carleyville would miss him, but not his wife, who stood looking grimly out the kitchen window.

Dangling from the rearview mirror was a tail feather from a bluejay the cat had mauled in the front yard—the yard whose lawn was now much healthier as a meadow—and two or three other trinkets or memorabilia, whatever you'd call them, from moments of adversity that Carleyville had triumphed over or, just as important, had come to terms with. These little mementos included the rubber finger his former girlfriend had left on the bathroom counter one morning, along with her note saying good-bye (was he ever right about not marrying her!), along with a splash of watery ketchup and a big knife from the kitchen, the sight of which almost made him faint . . . yep; more than once he'd picked a real crazy. Imagine doing that when things were going fine between them simply because he'd told her there would be no engagement ring on her finger. Imagine waiting two days, purchasing the finger (apparently), never telling him how angry she was, plotting all the while. This was in June, too: not around Halloween. So good-bye to all that: good-bye, Christie, good-bye, phone company with its sky-high rates, good-bye, landlord from hell. He and the feather and the finger would sustain each other on the ride to Maine, on the way to Jimmy and Fiona's house.

The truck lost significant power on hills, but that was to be expected. As were the assholes behind him. What did they think? That their flashing lights would send photoelectric vibes, causing the rig to clear the road by ascending directly into the universe, on the principle of *The force be with you*? Let *them* try to drive a rig like this. They'd end up a big metal turtle on its back, while he had experience guiding his slithering snake. He had experience, he knew what he was doing, so horns and flashing lights be damned.

He was miles away when he remembered the fish. How had he forgotten it? Probably trying to struggle out with the dog on its leash and his computer in the other hand, plus various odds and ends clamped under his armpit. His thumb had been in the fishbowl, but apparently he had forgotten to pick it up again, once he set it down to close the door. He patted his pocket and felt the cheesecloth he'd brought to put over the top of the fish-bowl, and the rubber band—damn! He'd thought of the rubber band in the middle of the night, then forgotten the whole fish-bowl. Though the maleficent landlord would no doubt be around immediately to find excuses not to refund the security deposit (he'd probably cut the grass himself and deduct a hefty sum), so, sensitive soul that he was, he would doubtless take the fish.

The force of the rain would not be good for the fish, though if he'd left it under the overhang, everything would be all right. If not, the fish could spend some time dancing in a watery disco.

He used the gauze to wipe the inside of the window, which had fogged up in spite of the defroster being on high. In front of the truck, a squirrel dashed across the road and made it to the other side. Seeing it reminded Carleyville of the days when he and his friends had hunted gophers in Texas, where his grand-father lived: the high-powered slingshots they'd fashioned; the metal bottlecaps—in those days that was all there was; metal, not plastic—launched from slingshots. When his foot suddenly plunged into a gopher's hole—the same damn foot he broke

again, wouldn't you know, crossing the mothering street—
Carleyville's slingshot had misfired as his friend Timmy turned
to see what all the noise was about, bull's-eyeing Timmy in his
right eye. Timmy—wherever he was now. Wherever so many
of his buddies were.

Thirteen hours later, Carleyville was so tired he could hardly
keep his eyes open. If the radio worked that would have helped,
but only the darkened scenery of Erie, Pennsylvania, was there
to keep him awake, and it wasn't exactly tantalizing. Since it
was time to let Coon out of the trailer anyway, he pulled into a
rest area and hopped out, leaving the window half-down on the
passenger's side because the rain that had chased him from
state to state was making sure that the truck windows stayed
perpetually fogged. It was colder than he expected, and his legs
were stiffer than he thought they'd be. Getting out, he knocked
over the water jug he kept next to Adventure Kitty's cage. He
thought he'd screwed the cap back on, but no such luck. Water
splashed into the cat's cage and produced a shriek he had never
before heard, and this cat was big on histrionics. "It's just
water," he said. He lifted the cage and tilted it slightly. Adventure Kitty slid forward. Water splashed to the floor. The cat
seemed to be soaked. One paw clawed the mesh of the cage.
Time for some TLC. He opened the glove compartment and
pulled out one of the catnip sticks he'd made after drying the
year's catnip crop and poked it into her cage. The cat did not
sniff the catnip; she only glared at him.

What happened next he had no explanation for: he was
reaching for the water jug, its cap silver-dollar bright as it lay on
the floor, when he got a stitch in his side and jerked forward, his
ribs pressing into the cage. It was like pleurisy, though he no

longer had pleurisy. But still, it was that same searing pain. He took a few breaths, then forced his body to right itself, though in the process he knocked over the jug again. He cursed Adventure Kitty—despised her for making what were already pain-filled, unbearable moments even more excruciating. The cat was capable of sending up a sound like a skill saw. Sweating, he kept his hand clamped to his ribs and slowly, awkwardly, bumped out of the truck, lowering one leg, the distance to the ground seeming interminable. As he finally stood on both feet, another car entered and swept over him with its headlights. He turned to block the glare, and as he raised his arm he felt the pain shift into his groin. What the hell! He walked tentatively, the pain gradually easing, toward the cinderblock bathroom. Inside, he glanced in the mirror and saw that he had forgotten to shave. The wasp bite on his cheek gave him the look of a half-painted doll—one of those cutesy crafts fair specials with apple-red cheeks and marble eyes: Grandpa with his mouth puckered like an anus. Those junky crafts fairs where Christie used to try to sell her stained glass—those all-day, exhausting gatherings, where people looked and exclaimed and did not buy, and afterwards you spent too much money consoling yourself with expensive roadside food.

So who should he have been involved with? A lady stockbroker?

He sat on a toilet in one of the stalls, but the pain had passed. Try explaining that to a doctor: sudden, unprecedented pain, and then nothing. Not even a crap. They'd put you through every test in the book. That, or write you off as mental. He decided it had been some bizarre muscle spasm, probably the result of days of packing and hauling cartons to the van, aggravated by tension when the water tipped over. The last of his spring water was now soaking the floor of the truck. Time to get some water to the horse and the dog. Enough of impersonating *The Thinker,* with his pants around his knees.

Outside, a kid with a white skunk streak in his black hair asked him if he had a match. The kid was sitting on one of those folding stools, like an old-timer at a parade. What the kid thought the spectacle might be, outside the restrooms when it was almost midnight, he couldn't say. "No, sorry, I don't smoke," he said, but the last word was not entirely out of his mouth before he tripped. Too late, he saw in the dark the narrow end of a black guitar case. He stumbled badly but kept himself upright, though for a moment he was almost nose-to-nose with the kid, who looked at him impassively and said nothing. No apology, nothing. Just one of God's children, out for a pleasant evening of putting invisible obstacles on the ground. Mothering punk: just set up outside a rest area bathroom, kick back with some Absolut Kurant, some Absolut *Asshole,* stretch your feet. If the guitar case doesn't do it, maybe the big Nike'd foot will. "You got a problem?" the kid said. Punk, with his dyed hair and his "Just Do It" shoes. Kids were a new breed now: purposeful, in spite of their mock passivity; unflinching. Everybody had become a malcontent with attitude, a *mock marine.*

He went back to the truck and let Coon out of the trailer. Coon had been staring at him out the window, his golden eyes glinting like a hologram as Carleyville approached. There was a dog with dignity: none of that scratching and whining. He'd had a bad life, had a leg that had healed so poorly after a break he'd gotten before Carleyville found him that he'd saved up and gotten him an operation, wondering whether that experience wouldn't traumatize the poor beast even further, but Coon had come back from the vet's a new dog. His loyalty to Carleyville even intensified, though he'd still had to work on him for a year to get the dog to make eye contact.

"How you doing, old boy?" Carleyville said. The dog jumped out of the trailer and ran to the trash receptacle and peed for a long time. Carleyville sensed that the punk was watching, but it was too dark to see and he was too tired to get himself more agitated. If sodas didn't cost a dollar a pop (a pun!) he would have bought himself one, his throat was so dry, in spite of the fact that they screwed up your metabolism. With the dog at his side, he went back toward the restrooms, where there was a water fountain.

"Hey, pooch," the punk said, as if nothing had previously transpired between them.

Carleyville got a drink from the fountain and put his hand to his throat as he swallowed. It was almost as if the water was hot, it burned so going down. Carleyville tested the fountain with his finger: cold water. Okay: so another unsolvable mystery. Something made him go into the bathroom a second time, to check in the mirror; when he did, he saw that his Adam's apple was swollen. Allergies, maybe, if he was lucky. Again, he regretted not shaving, but what did it matter at this hour. When he exited, he saw the punk in a sleeping bag, under a tree. He flashed forward to Coon running up to him, raising his leg to piss the last few drops. The fight that would ensue. Then he shook his head—thank God Coon had good sense—and trekked to the rig to begin tending to the horse. She was lucky to be Coon's best buddy, rather than his dinner. A horse like Cleopatra would have been shipped off to the slaughterhouse if not for him—if not for Malcolm telling him she was about to be Alpo'd by people two farms over—so in spite of the rocky ride, she should still thank her lucky stars. He had a sack of food for her to eat in the trailer, but the dishes were all packed, and there was no telling which box contained the bowls. He took a guess, but the tinny sound he'd heard inside one box turned out not to be metal bowls, but Christie's trophy cups: trophies she'd won playing golf, that he'd felt bad about leaving behind. Eventually he'd ship them back to her. He settled for scooping food into the dish drainer, which wasn't boxed. Some fell out, but most of it made it to the ground, where he set it down. For the third time he returned to the restrooms, filling a bucket he *had* left accessible as the dog salivated at his side. "Hey, what am I thinking of?" he said, setting the bucket on the floor of the bathroom. "Thinking of Cleo and not about you, hey, old boy?" The dog lapped up the water until its head was almost stuck in the bucket. "Hey, we don't want you pissing a river in the trailer," Carleyville said, lifting the bucket. He refilled it and headed back. He noticed that the punk was no longer under the tree. A thought went through his head that amused him: maybe it had been a space alien, not a real person. Maybe that was why he'd been so strange, perched on his stool outside a bathroom, with his surliness and his skunk hair. There'd been some skit on *Saturday Night Live* years back about questions to ask to find out if somebody was a space alien; if they couldn't answer, you knew they were. There was some hilarious scene with one of the actors cornering his mother-in-law, firing off the names of bands, about which, of course, she was completely ignorant. The Butt Hole Surfers. That sort of thing.

Getting ready to spring the horse's door, he went into a spasm of coughing, with his damned dry throat. It had been Christie's opinion that he was allergic to animals, but that was just because she didn't like them. In any case, he was taking an antihistamine.

The chickens had set up a real ruckus as soon as he stopped in the parking lot. The next morning he'd get some food for them—they'd been fed once, for God's sake. For the moment, he began to assist in the backwards exit of Cleo the Horse.

He awoke before dawn, coughing his way to consciousness, and decided to get a jump on the day. The Martian never reappeared—probably off passing for a New York City cop, or whatever it was Martians did to be puckish these days. Carrying a bomb into a stadium, maybe. Cleo had backed right over his hand the night before and it was badly swollen, his knuckles gray-blue with contusions. The hand—wouldn't you know it would be his right hand—was half again its normal size. If he knew where the contents of his medicine cabinet were, he could bandage it, but there was no chance of finding them. All his possessions, for the umpteenth time, somehow eluding him.

The day before he'd forgotten to send the fax he'd promised the telephone lady, though he'd awakened during the night, smugly proud because he'd dreamed he'd sent it. What would she have done but lose it, anyway. She was probably no longer even working there. If you talked to somebody one day they'd be gone an hour later, and you'd be back to square one, spelling your last name and playing the *as in* game: the new, monotonous world of "B as in Boy." Then, when the deaf moron had that down, you could start touching your toes, or whatever else they wanted you to do.

He did a few jumping jacks to jazz up his system. The finale was too enthusiastic and made his hand hurt. Though he'd more or less given up caffeine, the idea of coffee still floated across his mind some mornings—although today was not a day he'd want to pour a hot beverage down his throat. Could it be strep? He watched Coon run around sniffing things, then clicked his fingers for the dog to come. Back in the cabin of the truck, Adventure Kitty clawed at the cage. He got the leash he'd fashioned for her out of a bandanna made ropelike with knots and a length of leftover sailcloth he'd been saving for another project and opened the top of the cage. She stared at him, just on the verge of hissing, though she did not. He slipped it around her neck—nasty swipe from her paw; just what his sore hand needed—and slid his other hand under her belly and lifted her. Probably busting with piss, so maybe it would come out her ears if she pulled her usual shit and wouldn't do it while she was on the leash. He was too smart in the ways of living with cats to let her walk around unleashed on the grass outside a rest area, that was for sure.

On the grass, the cat gagged, dislodging a small ball of fur. The cat proceeded to stand there, wouldn't even walk, let alone pee. After five minutes of tugging her forward in increments he decided to put her back in the cage. He told her to remember that she'd had her chance. And let the damn horse stay in its carrier until they got to Maine; it would have what it wanted soon enough. Lucky not to be dog food. He'd stop for some food for the chickens—maybe something he could get for himself that they could share.

But the engine wouldn't start. How do you like that? Is that good? Just click-click-click. And, for good measure: click-click-click-click. Still interested? Then click-click-click-click-click. He'd traded his redwood lawn chairs for Daley's extra battery only a week before. What he needed was a jump, but the rest area was deserted. He'd either have to hike out and see if there was a gas station or wait for somebody to pull in, and then you could bet that person would either be a woman, and therefore too afraid to even roll down her window, or some macho truck driver who wouldn't have the inclination, so he'd claim he couldn't take the drain, himself. And who knew: maybe Jesus Christ would pull in and have all the time, and all the good inclinations, in the world. That's "J as in Joker."

He got out of the truck and slammed the door, leaning back and staring into space, trying to keep calm—and, having thought of Jesus Christ, made a bargain prayer: If you get me out of this parking lot in the next ten minutes, I'll send the phone lady a fax *and* a bunch of roses.

And so it came to pass. In the form of a woman, all right, but led into the lot by a guy on a motorcycle. Dawn just breaking, and there was this pale little blonde thing driving a little white Toyota, Harley thundering in front of her with a Wonder Warthog guy gripping the handlebars. "Use some help, bro?" the motorcyclist shouted.

He nodded. This was happening: no dream. "Weak battery," he said.

"Cheryl," the motorcyclist shouted into the Toyota's now open window, "back it up a little."

The Toyota rolled backwards.

"I've got cables," Carleyville said.

"Got my own right in the trunk," the man said. Cheryl switched off her engine and got out. She smiled faintly, hurrying toward the bathroom.

"We'll get 'er goin'," the man said.

"Thanks for the help," Carleyville said. The last word didn't make it; it came out a painful croak. He opened the hood. The man was already dragging cables toward the car. "Yeah, anybody moves around without these, he probably don't know to bring a beer cooler, either," the man said. "And that would be *some stupid.*"

Carleyville nodded. The man was taking charge, placing the clips. His hands were greasy, as if he'd been doing this before. "Get in," the man said, gesturing with his elbow.

Right. Carleyville had forgotten the part about being inside, turning on the ignition.

It started right away. Hummed like new. As he gave the thumbs-up, he noticed that the overhead light was on. Could he have slept all night with the light on, after he'd turned it on to check the map before doubling up the sleeping bag on top of the cat's cage for a pillow?

"I'm no good with thank-yous," the man said. The look in his eye let Carleyville know he shouldn't insist on any further exchange. It was a look Adventure Kitty might have if he'd left her in the cage for a month. Carleyville nodded and gripped the man's hand, which was difficult to do, since he had to shake left-handed.

He was on his way again. It took him a while to realize that he shouldn't obsess about sending roses to the phone lady, because he wouldn't know where to send them. People who answered the telephone never used their real names, so who was she, really? Even if he remembered her name, it would have been a made-up name, her work address one he wouldn't know until he unpacked and found a phone bill with the address on it. Of course, he could call and ask—but that might begin to seem like he was hassling her. Roses probably cost too much, anyway, and his credit card was pretty much maxed out. That, however, was a thought he did not want to dwell on.

The house was right where Jimmy circled the map: on the corner of Battsbridge Road and Route 91, four miles from the highway. Or he supposed it was four miles, since it seemed a good stretch. The odometer was broken. He'd overshot, at first, and finding a place to turn around had taken him a couple of miles out of his way.

Fiona, pulling weeds in front of the big brown house, stood slowly, frowning at the caravan pulling onto their street. She looked so much like the birds—she held her head at such a birdlike angle—that he cocked his own head, taking it in. Fiona was adorable. A worrywart, but cute. He tapped the horn, but to his surprise, the horn didn't make a sound. The sun glinted off the window, which must have been why she couldn't see him waving. It was murder trying to round the curve and get the horse carrier off 91; expressions of friendship were going to have to be momentarily put on hold.

He sideswiped their mailbox, but it didn't go down; only minor damage had been done to the pole. Cheap metal thing, anyway: he'd fashion them a better one.

"Nelson!" he heard Fiona call. Shrill voice: that was the downside to Fiona.

Fiona rushed to the rig. And the damned window would hardly go down. He had to settle for saying hello through a three-inch crack at the top.

"Is that really you?" Fiona was squealing. "You said September."

"I had to get out of there," he said. "Mr. Rogers was having a breakdown." He smiled at his new nickname for the landlord.

"Where will you park this?" she asked, more hushed than shrill.

Across from Fiona was a dirt road cutting through a field. Jimmy had described their five acres accurately: not much land where the house stood, but a nice amount of acreage across the way. Carleyville jerked his thumb to the right, pointing to the obvious. Fiona nodded. How the rig was going to make the turn onto such a narrow road was another matter . . . but suddenly Jimmy, in sweatpants and tee-shirt, was rushing to Fiona's side, so he threw open the door to give his old buddy a hug. In fact, the door flew open too quickly, but Jimmy jumped back in time. Fiona had to steady him. Carleyville hopped out and embraced both of them—a mistake to squeeze with his right hand; he let Jimmy's back thump pass unreturned—telling them, all at once, about how he'd thought he might be broken down for good in a rest area parking lot, but that he'd gotten out by making a silent promise to God concerning a woman he'd never met.

Jimmy said to Fiona: "That's Carleyville—saved, every time, by his incurable romanticism."

Two days later, clouds were gathering and an impressive wind was blowing up. Jimmy had gone out at daybreak to join two of the guys he worked with, who were racing against the impending hurricane to finish a roof. The rig was going to be fine. There wasn't a tree for a hundred yards. At Fiona's insistence, Adventure Kitty had the run of the house, and the birds were hanging in cages inside the garage. Both of the chickens ran off the day they were put in the pen he'd made for them, and Jimmy had told him—straight out; no nonsense—he'd seen one pancaked just up the road. From Fiona and Jimmy's living-room window, he could see Coon curled up outside the trailer. Coon would never run away or otherwise cause trouble like Adventure Kitty by being piteous and gagging and staggering in the presence of a fairy-tale lady who could rescue her and put her inside her big, beautiful castle, where she served *sardines*. Coon would have disdained being renamed *Precious Little One*.

"It's the waiting that gets to me," Fiona said. "I can't stand simply waiting around."

"It's better when you don't have the television on," he said. "They're in the business of exciting you."

"I know, but I'm just all jittery, waiting."

"You'll feel better when you have some lunch," he said. He was chopping vegetables. Already missing Malcolm's organic carrots and turnips and beets. "You drink so much coffee, you could do with a B complex, Fiona. Coffee leaches vitamin B right out of your system."

"But I just don't believe in all these vitamins, Nelson. Too many can be worse than not enough."

"You're a Brit," Carleyville said. "Why aren't you drinking tea, in the first place?"

"Let's not have any harmful stereotyping," she said.

She had started chopping with him. She chopped vegetables the way hopeless girls threw softballs: tentatively, and entirely without will.

"Did she get a job?" he said, knowing Fiona would know whom he meant.

"Right away. She said there was a terrible shortage of nurses. She could have been at work while the ink was drying on her signature."

He spent a few seconds trying to imagine Christie—wash-and-wear, no-nonsense Christie—writing with a fountain pen. Though considering the bad business trades she made, maybe she'd traded a stained glass lampshade she'd worked weeks on for a fountain pen. Outside, trees were swaying in the wind. Fiona said: "Well, we've got flashlights and candles, plenty of candles. I suppose if we lose power we can still have light."

"You know," he said, "after lunch I think I'll go over and pitch in on that roof."

"Oh, I think you have to have insurance. Be insured, I mean. I don't think—"

"Well, maybe my good intentions will get rained out," he said.

The lights flickered. He finished scooping vegetables into the wok and ran for the front door, to get Coon. But Coon was already headed his way, he saw, when he threw open the door. He clicked his fingers, urging the dog to speed it up, though

Coon always pretty much moved at his own pace, even with a hurricane brewing. His clicking fingers could not be heard anyway, because of the force of the wind.

"You know, I can't get that story out of my mind that you—look at it out there! Where do you think Jimmy is? Hello, Coon. You come right into the kitchen and stay safe with us," Fiona said, patting his side. She started her sentence again: "That story you told about forgetting the goldfish. I mean, you *are* funny. Though I'd never tell such a story on myself."

"Fiona," he said, "don't you know that old ploy? If you're really self-loathing, no one will listen to you. So you tell them little things, you point out the road markers, rather than talking about the big wreck on the highway."

"Oh, you can't be serious," she said. "You're teasing. I mean, I think it's *terrible* you forgot the goldfish. I really do. But one doesn't know what to do but see the humor in it."

"I tell things for laughs. I want people like you to fall into the trap. It's a skill of mine, very self-serving. Not everybody's Jimmy, who can act like whatever happened the second before never happened."

"Oh, he's haunted. That's all talk, and you know it. He's seen psychiatrists half a dozen times, you know that. He has night sweats. He could use with a little of your ability to back off from the unimportant things, and see life as a comedy." She looked at him. "As a mixture of comedy and tragedy," she amended.

"It isn't. Jimmy's right, and we're kidding ourselves."

She shook her head, disagreeing.

"Tell the truth," he said. "That time I went to bed and forgot I'd left the pressure cooker on. You were furious, weren't you? You didn't think how funny it was the plum puddings were on the ceiling, did you? You were as mad as I've ever seen you."

"Well, I'm not proud of my reaction. You can't take a compliment, Nelson. All I was saying was that your perspectives can be helpful. Especially when a thing's already happened."

Lightning seared into the trees at the back of the property. There was a deep rumble of thunder.

"Times like these you think you might be missing your cue and the special effects are there to help turn you into Frankenstein," Carleyville said, staring out the window. "But Jimmy and I have already done Frankenstein, so now we spend the rest of our lives figuring out an encore."

She looked at him, frowning. Finally, her voice more gentle than her eyes, she said: "I know how politically incorrect this is to say, but it still surprises me that a woman wrote that."

"To me," he said, interested in his thoughts, "every day is special effects. Except that there's no transformation. It rains, it snows, it's sunny, there's a hurricane—it's like background music in a movie to create emotion, but the movie's over and there was no plot. Fiona, I ask you: Is there any reason I should be alive, and other people should be dead?"

"That's an unanswerable question, and you know it," she said. "The war is over, Nelson, and you've moved on."

"To your field."

"You're just visiting," Fiona said. "You can be so scathing about yourself. You've only come for a visit."

He thought he detected the ripple of a question in her voice. It was mean to be cynical with Fiona. Truth was, she thought of him more, did more for him, than Jimmy did.

Rain lashed the house as another burst of thunder thudded from the sky.

"I'd think he'd have been back ages ago," Fiona said.

"Maybe I should drive over and see if there's a crisis, or something."

"Oh, Nelson, *of course not.* We're having a hurricane. It's bad enough *he's* not back."

The stove was gas-burning, so there would be no trouble cooking lunch. He decided to start, to distract her.

"Where did the cat go?" she said, as if snapping out of a fog.

"You know what the cat did one time?" he said. "She got in the tub and curled up right over the drain. Nobody would believe a cat ever did that."

"The tub?" Fiona said, getting up. "You think she could be in the tub?"

She came back a few minutes later, Adventure Kitty curled in her arms. "She was on a shelf of the linen closet," she said. "Someone left the door ajar."

"I hope a handful of kittens didn't follow her out."

"Oh, Nelson, really! You had her fixed, didn't you?"

"I was going to, but I had to put the money into truck repairs."

As Carleyville sautéed, the delectable odor of onions and carrots began to permeate the kitchen. He reached in his pants pocket and took out a small plastic container of dried mint, placing it on the counter. He stirred for another minute, then added green pepper and mushrooms. On top of this he placed shrimp to steam. With his favorite lacquer chopstick, he stirred everything together, gave it another thirty seconds, then reached in the bag and took out a big pinch of what looked to Fiona like anemic mouse shit. "What is that?" she couldn't resist asking.

"Lecithin granules," he said. "Lowers cholesterol."

"Well, I hope there's no harm in it: I mean, half these natural food things, there's—"

"It's good for you," he said. "Here I am optimistic about something and you try to make me skeptical." He opened the other container and sprinkled mint on the food.

With the next clap of thunder, the cat jumped from Fiona's arms, landing on the dog, who sprang up, scaring the cat even worse.

"Oh!" Fiona said.

Carleyville did not respond to her, but to the scrabbling animals. "Remember this, you assholes," he shouted. "Every cat and dog must take responsibility not only for himself, but also for his buddy."

They were without power that night and all the next day. In the morning it was still sprinkling rain, and there were enough gusts of wind to have blown Cleo's blanket off, although it had been secured with two belts. Carleyville and Jimmy took a walk to assess the damage. A big tree had gone down across 91 and was being worked on by a yellow-jacketed work crew who stopped cutting to call out that they should be careful because of downed wires. The wires were obvious, like spaghetti dumped on top of drumsticks. Like a really bad meal in a really bad restaurant. Nice of them to pipe up, but, Carleyville thought, he and Jimmy had experienced a few worse dangers.

The second-floor shutters of a Victorian had fallen to the ground. "Made pickup sticks out of those," Jimmy said, gesturing through the rain. The glass on a downstairs window also seemed to be cracked.

"Hey, there's live wires around the bend," a red-faced man in a telephone truck stopped to holler.

"Okay," Jimmy said.

"Why don't we walk down and take a look at the river?" Carleyville said. He hadn't seen the river, but Jimmy had told him it was there.

"Yeah, good idea." He and Jimmy sank to their ankles in

somebody's wet lawn, sidestepping the downed wires. Someone had put a flashing light near the tangle. A car approached, stopped, and went into reverse, taking the only other option: a fork in the road.

"'But took the other, just as fair,'" Carleyville said.

"Fair? What's fair?" Jimmy said.

"No, I said, 'took the other, just as fair,'" Carleyville said. "Just to let you know I'm not some schmuck out walking around, I'm an educated man."

"Never doubted that," Jimmy said.

What? No return wisecrack? "You can be my Boswell," Carleyville said. "'Of a pile of fallen telephone wires, Dr. Johnson was said to have observed . . .'"

Jimmy continued walking. He said: "There weren't any fucking telephones then, Carleyville. No fax, no e-mail, no Dr. Johnson@aol.com."

The roses. He had never sent the fax or the roses.

"Why don't you go back and finish your degree? Stranger things have happened to old guys like us," Jimmy said. "Fiona and I were talking about that."

"Hey, Jimmy, you know me: I'm not too big on the concept of going back." Carleyville inspected a dead snake on the road. "Going back is more or less a concept useful for scaring you in science-fiction movies."

"I like the ones that catapult you into the future."

"Most of them do both," Carleyville said. "That way, they spook you with either thing you fear. Sound familiar?"

"We'd have been lucky if that had just been a science-fiction movie," Jimmy snorted. "Then that wall in Washington could have just been the credits rolling."

Jimmy joined him in looking at the snake, until his attention shifted to a big house beside them, and another set of shutters that had been blown to the ground. "Maybe it's God's will that people redecorate," Jimmy said.

Around the bend, Jimmy gestured for Carleyville to take off his hiking boots—Jimmy himself had worn Top-Siders—so they could cut through a marshy field. They immediately sank a foot deep into the mush. Jimmy hopped one-legged to roll up his pants. "Muddy clothes make Fiona batshit," Jimmy said.

"She told me you told her I was spinning out," Carleyville said.

Jimmy picked up the pace, to get back to Carleyville's side. "We worry about you," he said.

"So what you've come up with is the idea that the prodigal son should go back to school?"

Jimmy looked at him. "We're the same age," he said.

The house they were passing, an acre or so behind a larger house that faced the main road, was a barn that had been renovated by yuppies. A gravel road led to it. They'd done a nice job: redwood shutters, front door with leaded glass. Lucky that sucker didn't blow out in the hurricane, Carleyville thought. He wasn't up for the maintenance of a house anymore. The leaded glass reminded him of Christie's stained glass, and he wondered what her life was like as a nurse in Montana. There was someone who did believe in the concept of going back—she'd bailed and then gone back to her previously despised career.

They were soaked, except for the areas the rain parkas protected—though Carleyville hadn't zipped his until it was too late. More of a wind was coming up. Out in the middle of the field was a muddy dress or robe or something that had blown away. It looked like the most out-of-place thing in the world—or, at least, Carleyville imagined it would to anyone who hadn't already seen plenty of things out of place, including arms and legs.

Ahead was the river. They were coming at it across people's backyards; as they moved closer to the water the fields tapered into suburban lawns. A few had docks. The damage varied: only one seemed to be intact. For whatever reason, some people had left their boats moored in the harbor, though most must have either gotten them to land or transported them to a safer place. He looked at a sailboat with a broken mast. Who would worry so little about damage that they'd just leave the thing out there? Maybe people who were away. People who already lived in a vacation spot, who were off taking a vacation elsewhere.

Jimmy began doing a sort of dance, lifting his muddy feet in something that resembled a Scottish jig and t'ai chi at the same time. He couldn't help smiling. Jimmy was shedding the parka, pantomiming that he'd let it fly away to join the dress or whatever it was that kept getting airborne behind them. But then he hung it from the branch of a tree—maybe he was going to let the wind decide for him—and Carleyville understood Jimmy's odd dance. Of course; it was the most logical thing in the world: a swim in the river. In a minute they were bobbing around like mad—strange, strange sensation—wearing only their underwear. Carleyville quickly shed his, figuring that this was the perfect opportunity to discard his overload of clothes. Clothes crept up on you: no one needed as many clothes as he had.

As they drifted toward the bridge, a woman stopped her car and her son got out to look. An enormous truck was coming from the other direction, so the woman backed her car off the bridge and then, when the truck passed (UPS! You had to admire them), joined her son at the rail, cupping her hands over her eyes as if the sun shone directly in them, though there was no sun. Carleyville left it to Jimmy to pantomime that they were okay. Jimmy stuck out his tongue, one hand raised to make a corkscrew curl by his ear. Though he smiled, Carleyville could see that the woman did not, as the tide caught them and they shot under the bridge. They went with the flow until they managed to latch onto the roots of a big tree that Jimmy gestured to in front of them. If Jimmy thought it was stopping time, why not? Carleyville swam toward shore, and the snaggled roots, to join his buddy.

Lips pursed, Fiona was putting dinner on the table. Carleyville had contributed the spinach-tofu dish she removed from the oven. The refrigerator wasn't working, but she thought that since the dish did not contain meat, it would be safe to eat. Jimmy had set the table, putting all the silverware on the napkin, which drove her mad.

"Fiona, this is not something he could help," Jimmy said. "This is the sort of thing that could happen to anyone."

"Jumping into a river during a storm?"

"Okay, we might have restrained ourselves, but the rest of it was only bad luck, Fiona: bad luck to get cut by some rusting-away trash can some jerk threw in the water."

"Perhaps better not to jump in at all, when the water is churning and *a person can't see.*"

"Boys will be boys?" he said.

Her jaw was set. "At least he got diagnosed," she said. "Imagine the pain he must have been in with his thyroid gland burning up."

"That's just a figure of speech. 'Burning out'—overactive—was actually what the doctor said."

"So go get him! I've called him twice!"

Adventure Kitty rubbed against Fiona's ankles. She had just finished a meal of canned chicken, to which Fiona had added cream.

"You're nice to his pets, Fiona. Have a little patience with him."

"He has no sense of time. I do everything I can. I tell him an hour before the meal's being served, and then I remind him a second time. Then just when he's supposed to come down, I hear the bathwater being drawn."

"I'll get him," Jimmy said. He turned and, taking a flashlight, walked upstairs. Behind him, the kitchen was lit by an oil-burning lamp.

"Carleyville," he said. "Haul your ass outta there or she's gonna bust a gasket."

"Oh, sorry, dinner," Carleyville said from behind the closed door.

Jimmy shone the light in front of him, heading back downstairs.

"And I want you to bring up the phone call," Fiona said. "You must, Jimmy. I don't want to be involved, though heaven knows, I should know better, by now, than to pick up my own phone."

As soon as the phone service was restored, they had gotten a call from Daley, who had made a good guess where Carleyville had gone. Daley had been none too happy, and had been sarcastic to Fiona, which had made her angry at him, at Carleyville, and at her husband, for knowing both of them.

"I hardly know that Daley person," Fiona added. "Really, except for coming upon him pissing in the bushes at a picnic, I have no memory of him at all."

"That'll do," Jimmy said.

They sat down without Carleyville. Fiona had left the oil lamp glowing in the kitchen and lit three candles on the table. Fiona began to dish up the tofu. When she was done, instead of handing her plate to Jimmy, she purposefully put it down in front of her and began to eat. Jimmy stood and dished up his own dinner without comment.

"I do feel sorry for him with his thyroid burnout, or whatever it is," Fiona said, after a couple of bites. "I'm sure we would never have gotten him to the hospital if it hadn't been for the cut. And imagine him wanting to sew it up himself, left-handed. It boggles the mind. Jimmy—*it really does.*"

"He's not going to like hearing about money problems," Jimmy said. "He feels awkward about our having paid cash in the emergency room. That's why he's hiding upstairs."

"Well, but he's been called to dinner," Fiona said. "What does he think? That we're going to try to collect, three hours later?" She added: "It makes no sense that you two would have gone into the river. None at all."

"Give me your dream scenario. He passes up the swim and he . . ."

"Disappears from earth," Fiona said. Though he could tell from her tone of voice that she didn't mean it.

"Hello, everybody," Carleyville said.

"Hello," Fiona said, when Jimmy said nothing. "Did you take one of those codeine pills the doctor gave you?"

"Yeah," Carleyville said, sitting down. Fiona looked at him, skeptically. His eyes did not meet hers. Fiona pushed her chair back, and dished up some food for him.

"Because there's no reason to suffer, if some medicine will make you feel better," Fiona said. Her voice softened. "How long did your throat—"

"It was nothing," Carleyville said. "I just thought that as long as I was paying the guy—"

"Well, it's good you brought it up. To have your thyroid malfunctioning and not—"

"It wasn't like I was losing my leg and I didn't get myself to the hospital," Carleyville muttered, head still averted. "It was activity inside a gland."

She was staring at him. She said: "You might have lost your leg in the river, but you escaped with only twenty-five stitches and a tetanus shot. Just a minor matter, I'm sure."

"'Nothing is, but thinking makes it so,'" Carleyville said.

"The river *is* churning and *is* filled with debris, which anyone knows," Fiona shot back.

"We got a phone call from Daley," Jimmy broke in. "He wants us to try to get you to accept responsibility for the failure of the business. He also wants to be reimbursed for cleaning up what he said looked like a 3-D Jackson Pollock. It seems you left behind a bunch of birds that flew around the office shitting all over everything. According to him."

Carleyville put down his fork. "The phone's working?" he said.

"I don't feel that this involves me," Fiona said. "I want to say that I think he was overstepping his bounds to call us."

"You've got no head for business," Jimmy said, with a shrug. "So apologize to the guy about the birdshit and send him a check." He did not add: *If you've got any money.* "The failure of the business you can sort out later."

Carleyville reached for the salt. His arm brushed the candlestick, knocking the candle to the tabletop. Carleyville grabbed for it, but it rolled onto the rug and Carleyville had to stomp out a small fire.

Fiona jumped up. "What is it?" she said. "What is it that makes everything so *precarious* if you're anywhere near it? You walk into a room and you knock over a table. You turn to pick it up and you step on the cat's tail. I've never seen anything like it! I understand *completely* why Christie left. We ought to send *you* outside and let the damned *hurricane* in." Fiona turned and walked quickly out of the room. She toppled nothing. The cat was not nearby.

They stared after her. The rain had ended, but outside, trees still swayed in the wind. There was a moon; otherwise, even the outlines of things would be difficult to see.

"She's a little worked up. Believe it or not, it was the thyroiditis diagnosis that put her over the top. Concern for you, I mean."

Carleyville folded his hands on the table. He looked at Jimmy.

"Listen, Daley's not gonna stay mad at you forever," Jimmy said. "Send him a check. Put your finger in the dam. That stupid vitamins-by-mail stuff was never gonna work. You've got to have a movie star to promote your friggin' vitamins, nowadays. Newsletters about double-blind tests . . ." He couldn't continue.

Carleyville pretended to have a better view of the trees than he did. He could see some leaves, occasionally, highlighted in the moonlight. When lightning lit up the sky, though, he saw something else: the outline of his truck, much lower than he expected. He stared until lightning flashed far in the distance, then realized what he was seeing: everything had begun to sink in the sodden field.

"If I just don't move, everything will stay the same," Carleyville finally said. "Very important, magical thinking. You must have done it yourself. Everybody did. If I run fast enough. If I make it to the tree. If I zig left and right and agree that my mother can die. My wife. Anybody."

"She's gonna be sorry as hell she jumped down your throat. You know she already is," Jimmy said.

"But she was right."

"So in the future be more careful. Come on—she's all to

pieces because she thinks you're self-medicating and doing it all wrong. You saw how upset she got at the hospital. It was actually sort of funny, that young intern seeing her taking it so hard that you had a thyroid infection. 'He doesn't tend to anything!' I forget I'm married to a Brit half the time, and then she comes out with, 'He doesn't tend to anything!' like you had a flock you were supposed to tend."

"I do. It's part of my traveling road show. The birds; my former chickens; the cat; the dog; the horse. Fiona's appropriated the cat, so I won't have to think about her anymore."

"Well, man, you're just going to have to simplify. That menagerie would be too much for anybody. You're like a magnet for other people's problems, which often take the form of having paws and hooves and being covered in fur." Jimmy got up and took a second helping of food. "She's upstairs trying to figure out how to apologize," he said. "Trust me. Fiona is your friend. If she wasn't, she wouldn't have gotten so bent out of shape at the hospital."

"Codeine makes me funny in the head. I didn't take it," Carleyville said.

"I didn't suspect for a minute you did." Jimmy shifted in his chair. "Listen, if it's a matter of writing Daley an apology . . ."

"He had all his money in the business. He doesn't care about birdshit."

"Well, you didn't twist his arm and force him to put his money in the business."

"It was my idea."

"He was interested. He talked to me about it. He thought it was a good idea."

"The war's over, as Fiona always says, but I convinced Daley to do magical thinking, anyway," Carleyville said.

"Stop blaming yourself. Magical thinking, bargains with

God—if you want to think that's what it was, fine. It worked.
But in peacetime, you've got to have a different m.o. You've got
to realize you can accomplish things through your own efforts,
not because you've got the right incantation or because you've
held your breath until the wheel stopped spinning."

There it was: Jimmy's insistence on the future. And maybe
it was wallowing, to go back to the time when he had avoided
booby traps because of his ESP, moved through minefields like
a gazelle. Back then, he'd moved in a protective bubble of
blessedness. The bubble had stretched over him Trojan-size,
making a big prick out of him—that was funny: a medic as a big
prick; a big, animated schlong coming at you in what might be
your last few seconds . . . in the end, the bubble was so tight he
thought he'd suffocate, but then he was saved: the last time
into the field, the last maneuver accomplished, helicopter hovering for an immediate, absolute, final evacuation—that helicopter, like a big asterisk that could eventually footnote the
whole friggin' war: *This all made no sense.* Though it might have,
if you believed in colossal, malevolent jokes. Years later, the
time had still not come to lean back and have a good laugh. He
had once been fleet. Fortunate. He had lived, and certain other
people—Daley's kid brother among them—had not. Then
began the revenge of the ordinary world, and of inanimate
objects: the corner of a table nicking his thigh where he'd once
been grazed by a bullet; falling on ice, the simple contents of
his grocery bag raining down on his head—the ignominy of
being pounded by bananas and grapes, instead of artillery fire.
During the war, he had escaped friendly fire, though Fiona's
helpful criticism might be seen, now, as a new, benign form of
that.

It was true: he was still back there, running—was there any
lesser speed?—making his bargains, hedging his bets, endor-

phins in a race with adrenaline. He'd made it across the finish line, arms flung high not in surrender, but in victory: a lucky sprinter pulling the ribbon, instead of his intestines, with him.

Fiona was standing in the doorway. She had on a blue terrycloth robe and silly slippers that made it look as if she'd plunged her feet into armadillos. She looked chagrined. She was back-lit from the oil lamp, and with her enigmatic gaze she looked vaguely Madonna-ish: the real Madonna, not the dyed blonde money machine who dangled a cross.

Jimmy held out his hand. She walked forward, and took it. Jimmy said to her: "Nobody ran faster. Nobody did it better. *He* did it better long before the James Bond theme song. Nobody was faster, or braver, or more inventive than Carleyville. But everybody's only got a particular ration of luck, and to be perfectly honest, I think it might pretty much have run out in his case."

Fiona looked at Carleyville. "I apologize for losing my temper," she said.

"You could do me a favor," he said.

She looked surprised. "What?" she said.

"Do you know a good florist?"

She half smiled, suspecting the beginning of some joke.

"I know it exasperates you to hear my notions about karma, but I owe somebody something, and until I deliver, my karma's going to stay jeopardized."

"Flowers?" she said.

"Right. Getting some roses to a woman I was supposed to send a fax to. A woman who works for the phone company."

"Who is that?" Jimmy said.

"Some woman who helped me out," Carleyville said.

"Well, actually, I have a catalogue from a place that delivers very nice flowers," Fiona said. She turned and left the room.

Good, Carleyville thought. That left only the question of what her name was . . . if he'd written it down. . . . . Her name, her alias—and then the address to send them to. That would be something he could call and ask, since he wouldn't know where to begin looking for an old bill.

It seemed destined not to work; he didn't require ESP to figure that out. "Scratch that," he said suddenly. "Scratch the phone lady. I know what to do."

Fiona reappeared with a catalogue. He flipped through, stopped when he saw an interesting flower. *Birds-of-paradise;* maybe she'd see the significance in that. More amusing than roses. An improvement on the roses idea. A little pricey, but his credit card wasn't maxed out yet. He went to the phone—the miraculously working phone—and dialed the toll-free number. Twenty-four-hour flowers—great. Always open, like a hospital. Like a church.

He gave the operator the information: Birds-of-paradise were to be sent to Christie Cooper in Billings, Montana. Her address (he fumbled) was written down on the top of a traffic ticket he'd gotten for parking approximately ten seconds too long at some voracious Pac-Man parking meter, the day before he left. He'd jotted down her address just in case. On the off chance he might decide to get in touch. In extracting his wallet, though, half of the inside of his pants pocket came with it. What next? Scarves? A rabbit? Adventure Kitty brushed against his leg from behind, and he kicked reflexively. The cat scrambled backwards, mewing loudly. He felt awful, actually apologized to the cat, but in moving toward her, the phone toppled to the floor. The cat dashed from the room, and Fiona rushed after her. Only Jimmy was still there, looking at him with willed composure.

He gave the operator his credit card information—good

thing he'd never notified the credit card company to change his billing address—and felt much better, as if the bad black karma cloud had lifted, and lo and behold, it was only a gray day. "Sign it, 'Forgive me, Carleyville,'" he said softly.

"C as in Calm?" the operator said.

The Big-Breasted Pilgrim

OUR HOUSE in the Florida Keys is down a narrow road, half a mile from a convenience store with a green neon sign that advertises "Bait and Basics." Lowell's sister, Kathryn, called to get us to arrange for a car to drive her from Miami. She considers everywhere Lowell has ever lived to be Siberia, including Saratoga, New York, which she saw only once, during a blizzard. TriBeCa, circa 1977, was Siberia. Ditto Ashland, Oregon. In all those places, Lowell had what he now calls "The Siberian Brides": his first and second wives, who gradually became as incomprehensible to him as foreigners: Tish, who lived with us in Saratoga and later in TriBeCa; Leigh Anne Leighton—a name so melodic he always speaks of her that way, even though it seems inordinately formal—who lived with us for a month in Ashland before flying to Los Angeles for her grandfather's funeral, from which she never returned. This was no case of riding forever 'neath the streets of Boston, however: she got a Mexican divorce and remarried a youth Lowell and I recently saw on *Late Night with Conan O'Brien,* playing soprano sax with a group called Bobecito and the Brazen Beauties.

My own life is nothing like Lowell's. The joke is that I am his Boswell, and to the extent that I used to take dictation in Lowell's precomputer days, I suppose I have been a sort of Boswell—though I doubt the man, himself, ever scrubbed down a shower with Tilex, or would have, even if shower stalls—to say nothing of the excessively effective cleaning products we have now—existed. Nor, say, did we mistake Ashland for the Hebrides, though Lowell and I have inevitably arrived at pithy pronouncements as a prelude to packing up and leaving place after place.

I, Richard Howard Manson, was an army brat, living in thirteen different locations by the time I started high school. The one good thing about that was that it made me pretty unflappable, though at the same time, it's given me a wanderlust I've tired of as I've aged. Lowell makes fun of me for trying to decondition myself by accepting vicarious travel in place of the real thing; I subscribed to almost every travel magazine, and view cassettes of foreign cities, or even silly resort promo tapes, almost every night before bed. Lowell calls this "nicotine patch travel." Passing in front of the TV, he'll drag hard on an imaginary cigarette, then toss the phantom cig on the floor, grind it out, and slap his right arm to his left bicep, exhaling with instant relief. As it happens, I quit smoking—I mean real cigarettes—cold turkey. The travel addiction has not been so easy to break, but since I like my job, and since my employer is terminally itchy, he has often been pleased to take advantage of my weakness. The way wheedling wives have talked husbands into second and third babies, Lowell has persuaded me to give a month at the Chateau Marmont, or a few years in a rented Victorian in upstate New York, a try. He never claims we're staying, though he doesn't present the trips as vacations, either. When he had a larger network of friends—that period, about ten years ago, when everybody seemed to be between marriages—our ostensible reason for going somewhere would often be that we were on a mercy mission to cheer up so-and-so. Once there, so-and-so would be found, miraculously, to have cheered *us* up, and so we would stay for a longer infusion of friendliness, until so-and-so became affiliated with the next Mrs. So-and-so, who would inevitably dislike us, or until that moment when a blizzard hit and we thought of being in the sun, or when summer heat settled like an itchy, wooly mantle. In most of the places we've lived, there have been constants, Kathryn's visits among them. Other constants are a few ceramics made by a friend, a couple of very nice geometrically patterned rugs, and our picture mugs, depicting each of us sitting on camels in front of pyramids. There's also the favorite this, or the favored that—small things, like jars of home-grown herbs, or the amazing sea nettle suntan lotion that can be ordered by calling an 800 number that relays a request for shipping to the apothecary in St. Paul de Vence. Our Barbour jackets are indispensable, as is a particular wine pull, no longer manufactured. When you travel as much as we do, you can seem to fixate on what looks to other people to be trivia. I make it a point to be casual about the wine pull, letting other people use it whenever they insist upon being helpful, though I often awaken in the night, convinced that it has been thrown away during the cleanup period, and then I go downstairs and open the drawer and see it, but return to bed convinced that I have nevertheless had an accurate premonition of its fate following the next dinner party.

Lowell is a chef, and a quite brilliant one. He has one of those metabolisms that allows him to eat anything and remain thin. I, too, can and do eat anything, my diabetes having been miraculously cured by a Japanese acupuncturist, but unlike Lowell, everything I eat increases my weight. At six feet, I am two hundred and seventy pounds—so imposing that the first time I hurried inside to pick up some items at our "Bait and" convenience store, the teenager behind the counter raised his hands above his head. This has become a standing joke with Lowell, who sometimes imitates the teenager when he and I cross paths in the house, or when I bring the evening cocktails to the back deck.

Lowell and I met more than twenty years ago, when I was driving for my cousin's private car company in New York City. Lowell was in town, that evening, to be a guest chef for the weekend at the short-lived but much admired Le Monde d'Aujourd'hui. I picked him up at La Guardia in a downpour, and on the way in—he was coming from a birthday party for Craig Claiborne, in upstate New York—we talked about our preferences in junk food, rock and roll, and—I should have been suspicious—whether any city that was a state capital had any zip to it. But this gives the impression that we chattered away. We spoke only intermittently, and I had little to say, except that I liked Montpelier, Vermont, very much, but that was probably because I'd only visited the state once, during a heat wave in New York, and it had seemed to me I'd gone to heaven. This brought up the subject of gardens, and I heard for the first time, though others no doubt knew it, the theory of planting certain flowers to repel insects from certain vegetables. On the streets of Brooklyn, you didn't hear about things like that—Brooklyn Heights being the place I had settled when I was discharged from the Marine Corps. I was living in my uncle's spare bedroom, driving for my cousin's car company, making extra money to help support the baby that would be born to Rita and me—that was going to happen, whether she left me or not, as she was always threatening to do—though less than four months from the day I picked Lowell up, my twenty-two-year-old, in-the-process-of-becoming ex-wife, as well as the child she was carrying, would be dead after a collision on the Merritt Parkway. In the years following the accident, this has never come up in conversation, so even if I'd been able to look in a crystal ball, I would still have chatted with Lowell about Sara Lee chocolate cupcakes and the extraordinarily addictive quality of Cheetos. I do not care to discuss matters of substance, as

Kathryn has correctly stated many times. Both she and Lowell know the fact of my wife's death, of course. My uncle told them, the time they came to a barbecue at his apartment, six months or so after I met them. By that time, I was in Lowell's employ, and he was working on the second of his cookbooks, trying to decide whether he should take a very lucrative, full-time position at a New Orleans hotel. I had become his secretary, because—as it turned out, to my own surprise—I seem to have a tenacity about succeeding in minor matters, which are all that frustrate the majority of people, anyway. That is, after some research, I would find the telephone number of the dive shop in Tortola that was across the street from a phoneless shack, where the non-English-speaking cook had used a certain herb mixture on the grilled chicken he had served to me and to Lowell that Lowell felt he must find a way to reproduce. (Not that these things ever struck him in the moment. He often has a delayed reaction to certain preparations, but his insistence in deciphering the mystery is always in direct proportion to the time elapsed between eating and doing the double-take.) My next step would be to send Chef Lowell tee-shirts to the helpful salesman in the dive shop, one for him, his wife, and their two children, and—FedEx's ideas about not sending cash in envelopes be damned—money to bribe both salesman and chef. It was a minor matter to get a friend of a friend, who was a stewardess, to use her free hours before her flight took off again from Beef Island to take a cab to the dive shop and pick up a small quantity of the ground herb concoction, which chemical analysis later revealed to be powdered rhino horn (one could well wonder how they got that in Tortola), mixed with something called dried Annie flower, to which was added a generous pinch—as Lowell suspected—of simple ginger. Of course I see these small successes of mine as minor victories, but to Lowell they seem a display of inventive brilliance. He describes himself, quite unfairly, I think, as a plodder. He will try a recipe a hundred times, if that's what it takes. But to me that isn't plodding; it's being a perfectionist, which, God knows, too few people are these days.

Tonight, before Kathryn arrives, Lowell's new love interest will be arriving for drinks. She has no idea that he is a famous chef who has published numerous cookbooks, writes a monthly column for one of the most prestigious food magazines, and teaches seminars on the art of sautéing in St. Croix, where we are put up annually at the Chenay Bay Beach Resort. I have met this woman, who has a name like something out of a cheap English romance, Daphne Crowell, exactly once, when I stumbled into them—literally—on the back deck. It was a moonless night, exceedingly dark, and the two of them had gone downstairs to observe our neighbor's speedy little boat coming around the point with another load of drugs. She had been wearing *my* bathrobe, which she simply helped herself to, after taking it from the hook on the back of *my* bathroom door. There she was, leaning against the rail at the edge of the deck like a car's hood ornament, when I awoke from slumbering under a blanket on a chaise longue just in time to see her untie the sash and pull off the robe, giggling as she held it forward to flap in the breeze—*my* robe—like some big flag at a parade. I'm sure the silly gesture was equally appreciated by our neighbor, whose own "secretary" wears night goggles for land-to-shore vision, in case the police are waiting in ambush with their panthers, or whatever intimidating beasts they currently favor. Anyway: Daphne is a fool, but nobody ever said Lowell didn't like to waste his time. A recipe he will fret over forever, but any woman will do—particularly on a night when Kathryn, whom he is still intimidated by, is arriving, all big-city bluster and Oh, how are you doing out here in the boonies? Since starting a graduate program in writing at the New School, she treats everyone as interesting material. She has been trying for years to see if she can make me mad by insisting that I read *The Remains of the Day,* which—I have not told her, and will not—I have, in fact, viewed on television. I understand completely that she wishes me to see myself as some pathetic, latter-day servant who has wasted his life by missing the forest for the trees. If she thinks I live to serve, she's wrong. I simply live to avoid my previous life.

"Everything ready out here?" Lowell calls. He has opened the French doors and is propping them open with cement-filled conch shells. Everything ready, indeed: he's the one who set out the cheese torte, under the big upside-down brass colander. All I had to do was bring out the gallon of Tanqueray, the tonic, and some Key limes. My Swiss Army knife will do for slicing, and even mixing.

"Are you going deaf, Richard? Half the things I ask you, you don't respond to."

He's mad at me not because I haven't answered, really, but because I refused to drive to Miami to get his sister. The ride wouldn't have bothered me, but two and a half hours with Kathryn in a car would be more than I could take, by approximately two hours and twenty-five minutes.

"Richard . . . is there a possibility that not only do you not hear me, but that you have no curiosity about why I'm standing here, moving my lips?"

"I thought maybe you'd just had something tasty," I say.

A pause. "You did hear me, then? You just chose not to answer?"

"What's the point of these random women?" I say.

He walks toward me. "I don't know why it upset you so much that she borrowed your robe," he says. "Anything that smacks of exuberance, you insist upon as seeing as drunken foolishness."

"Remember the Siberians," I say. "And the one you picked up in South Beach, who wanted to sue for palimony after one weekend."

He looks at my knife, open to the longest blade, next to the bottle of gin. "This was your idea of a stirrer?" he says.

"She's so spontaneous and uninhibited," I say. "Let's see if she doesn't just use her finger."

As if that were a cue, we hear the crunch of gravel under Daphne's tires. Since today is Friday, she will have spent the day making fruit smoothies for tourists. On Monday and Tuesday, the only other days she works, she has been substituting for a dentist's receptionist, who was mugged in Miami during her ninth month of pregnancy. Six weeks after the mugging, the woman has still not given birth. If nothing happens by Monday, they are going to induce labor—though apparently what the woman is most afraid of is leaving her house. I know all this because Daphne phones the house often, and when I answer she always feels obliged to strike up a conversation.

Much ooh-ing and aah-ing at the front door: such a lovely house, so secluded, such beautiful plants everywhere. The unexpected delight of seeing roses growing in profusion in the Keys, blah blah blah.

She has brought me—the absurd cow has brought me—a plastic manatee. She has brought Lowell three birds-of-paradise, wrapped by the flower shop in lavender paper, which she pronounces "coals to Newcastle." But the manatee . . . we don't already have one of those, do we? No, we don't. We don't even have a rubber ducky to float in the bathwater. We're so . . . you know . . . old.

Behold: she has on gold Lycra pants, gold thong sandals, and a football-sized shirt with enormous shoulder pads. The material is iridescent: blue, shimmering gold, flashing orange, everything sparkling as if Tinker Bell, in a mad mood, applied the finishing touches. The sparkly stuff is also in her hair, broken lines of it, as if to provide a passing lane. All this, because she put a heaping teaspoon of protein powder into Lowell's smoothie, gratis. I see Lowell slip his arm around her shoulder as the two of them walk to the edge of the deck. I go into the house to get glasses and ice.

When I return, with the three glasses on a tray, she is in midbanality: the loveliness of the sky, etc. Well: Kathryn's pathetic butler would bow out at this point, but in our house, the servant drinks and eats with the employer. The employer has no real friends except for the servant, in good part because he is given to sarcasm, periods of dark despair, temper tantrums, and hypochondriacal illnesses, alternating with intense self-appreciation. Similarly, the servant has been co-opted by a life of leisure, a feeling of gratitude. Lowell is far easier to take care of than a wife, certainly easier to care for than a child, much easier to look after than the majority of dogs, by which I mean no disrespect to either party, as a dog was the one thing I ever had a strong attachment to and deep admiration for. The Marines, I found out, were sociopaths. Imagine the days of my youth when I thought I would prove my manhood and patriotism by outdoing my army lieutenant colonel father by joining the Marines. *Sir, yes, sir!* And Lowell thinks there might be a problem with tracking down a particular herb mixture? I could kiss his feet. Though I settle for shining his shoes—or did, in pre-Reebok days.

Lowell and Daphne have decided to take a ride in the kayak, tied to the end of the pier. This may leave me alone to greet Kathryn, who should arrive in twenty minutes or so, if everything goes according to schedule. Lately, I have begun to think that she is angry because she has had to pity me for so many years. The choked-up version my uncle gave her of the event that ostensibly ruined my young life registered so strongly with her that she has never been able to put it aside. The sheer misery of what I went through gets superimposed, I suspect, on her desire to be competitive with me, makes her back off from trying, more tenaciously, to solve the puzzle that is me: a street kid who gradually became educated (nothing else to do those four long, cold years we lived in Saratoga), only to shun those with similar education—to shun everyone, in fact. What she doesn't know is that I knew almost immediately my marriage was a mistake, I never wanted to become a father—the accident was my way out, not only from the situation, but for all time. Daphne could have spooned so much protein powder into my fruit drink it would have had the consistency of sawdust, and I would only have paid her and walked away. I've faltered a bit, from time to time; Kathryn would love to know with whom, and when, but my uncle spoke so graphically to her, years ago, that he managed to instill even future shame—that's the way I think of the service he inadvertently did for me—so that she still can't bring herself to ask outright what the story is with some hulking street kid who has no girlfriend and no friends, who is aging companionably, in the lower Florida Keys, with her bizarre, neurotic brother.

They descend into the kayak. Daphne has found something, already, to giggle about. She has left one shoe on the dock, it seems. I am summoned to help. Once seated, Lowell doesn't want to risk toppling the boat, I suppose. I don't play deaf; I respond to his entreaty, and at the edge of the dock I bend and pick up her gold flip-flop, for which she thanks me profusely, and then Prince Charming and Cinderella set sail. Which leaves me with the four-cheese tortes with rye saffron crust that I don't mind being the first to cut into, taking out a neat wedge with the knife and admiring its firm, yet creamy consistency. It is flecked with rosemary and ground pink peppercorns: the appetizer other chefs have been stealing and altering almost from the minute Lowell invented it. What none of them have guessed, to my knowledge, is the presence of the single simmered vanilla bean. I bite off a tiny piece, chew slowly, and consider the possibility that anything as ambrosial as this might be interchangeable with love.

The Triple J Cab pulls into the drive as the sun is setting. Kathryn alights from the front seat—wouldn't you know she'd be so ballsy, she'd sit up front. She seems to have only a small bag with her, which means, thank God, she won't be visiting longer than she said. But then, from the backseat, a skinny woman emerges, holding her own small bag, wearing a beret and a long white scarf, which matches her white shorts and her white tee-shirt, over which she wears a droopy vest. "Paradise!" she exclaims, throwing back her head and enthusing, as if the sky were awaiting her verdict. Yes, indeed—but who is she?

She is Nancy Cummins—Cummins without a "g"—who is en route to a *bris* to be held in a suite at the Casa Marina Hotel, in Key West. She is an acquaintance of Kathryn's from New York—a highlighter whom Kathryn arranged to meet at JFK, when it turned out the two women would be taking trips at the same time, almost to the same destination ("Highlighter"—meaning that she paints streaks in rich people's hair).

I carry their two small bags. Inside one, it will later turn out, is a narcotized kitten.

"Where's my brother?" Kathryn asks. Rushing to also ask: "Did he forget I was coming?"

"He's in a kayak with his girlfriend," I say.

"See?" Kathryn says to the highlighter. "No one meets anybody in New York; you come to Siberia, and *bingo.*"

"Bingo," I say. "I haven't thought of bingo in a million years."

"They don't play games. They read books," Kathryn says to the highlighter, as if I'm not there.

"You know," I say, realizing I'm about to make a fool of myself, but not caring, "when she said you were a highlighter, I thought at first she must mean of books. Those yellow markers you underline with. You know: highlighters."

The highlighter says, "I've always stayed as far from school as I could get."

I put their bags on the kitchen counter. It's only then that the highlighter unzips her bag and removes what I take, at first, to be a wad of material. It is a six-week-old black kitten, sleeping what looks like the sleep of death, though the thing does twitch when she puts it on the counter.

"Isn't it adorable?" Kathryn says.

Oh, absolutely. Now we have a cow, a manatee, and a kitten.

"Did he chill my favorite wine, or did he forget?" Kathryn wants to know, pulling open the refrigerator door. In the shelf sit four bottles of Vichon Chardonnay, with two cans of Tecate at either end, seeming to brace the bottles like bookends. Kathryn plucks a bottle from the shelf and closes the door. I open the drawer and silently pantomime that I would be happy to extract the cork. But no: she's a liberated woman, none of that harmful stereotyping of the helpless female allowed. Flip forward until two A.M., when I'll have the anxiety dream.

The highlighter opens the door and seizes a Tecate.

"Key lime?" I offer, reaching behind the slightly quivering kitten and extracting one from a basket.

"What do you do with it?"

"You squirt some in your beer," Kathryn says.

"I hope . . . I hope it isn't too much trouble, my just, you know, *coming here,*" the highlighter says, as if the idea of limes used to enhance the flavor of drinks has just defined some complexity for her.

"Look at this! Next Sunday's *Times Book Review*—by subscription!" Kathryn says.

"Yes. We alternate with our reading of *The Siberian Daily.*"

"Didn't I tell you he has a clever comeback for everything?" Kathryn says.

As if this weren't a put-down, the highlighter extends her hand and says, "I can't believe my good fortune in being here. I mean, it's very generous of you to have me. Because what a coincidence, my flying to this part of Florida—I *guess* I'm in the right part of Florida!—just when . . ."

I shake her hand. It is what we might have done from the first, if she had said immediately how happy she was to be where she was, and if Kathryn hadn't plunked the two bags in my hand. Does this happen to other people? This finding oneself suddenly greeting someone, or introducing oneself, long after things have gotten rolling? Roger Vergé once introduced himself to me on the second day of his visit, following his dinner of the night before, and after preparing lunch, for which he'd had me shop earlier that morning. Does some strange, sudden formality overcome people, or is there something I do that makes them feel so immediately a part of the family that they forget social form? I've asked Lowell, and that is his explanation. Just as his sister would never miss an opportunity to express skepticism about me, Lowell lets no opportunity pass when he can reassure me of my worthiness, by putting a positive spin on things. Leaving aside those periods when he is too depressed to speak, that is.

"And so you . . . you stay out here and create recipes together?" the highlighter asks.

"That sounds so domestic," I say. "No, actually. I have nothing to do with composing the recipes, and now that Lowell has mastered the computer, I sometimes don't even—"

"Tell her about tracking down the powdered rhino horn," Kathryn says, stroking the collapsed kitten.

"She's talking about my tracking down an herbal mixture Lowell had interest in," I begin.

"Did you go to jail?"

"Pardon?"

"For importing the rhinoceros."

"I didn't. . . . I didn't import a whole rhinoceros."

"The drug smuggler around the corner would probably be willing to do that for a price," Kathryn says.

The highlighter looks at me, wide-eyed. "She told me about the guy who runs drugs."

"And did she tell you that we disapprove, and that we're spying on him for the federal government?"

"No."

"Only kidding. We don't care what out neighbors do."

"For one thing, you'd have to be delusional to live here on the edge of nowhere and think in terms of having a neighbor," Kathryn says.

"I know everybody in my building," the highlighter says. "Of course, there are only four apartments."

"Apartments," Kathryn muses, strolling onto the back deck. "Can you stand here and imagine one going up across the way?"

"No," the highlighter says.

"We've left places because of equally ridiculous scenarios," I say.

"Kathryn told me that you two have lived just about everywhere."

"She did? Well, as an adult I've only—"

"Rhinoceros," the highlighter says. "Isn't that an aphrodisiac, or something?"

The wall phone rings, sending a short spasm through the kitten, who has dragged itself almost underneath it, before collapsing again.

That is what we were doing, what the three of us were talking about, when a chef whose name I faintly computed called from Coral Gables, in quite a dither, wanting me to inform Lowell that George Stephanopoulos would be calling momentarily.

The president, it seems, is a lover of mango. He has recently sampled Lowell's preparation of baked mango gratinée—usually served as an accompaniment to chicken or fish—at the home of a friend, who prepared it from Lowell's newest cookbook. The president loved it, as well as the main course, which was apparently prepared out of the same cookbook. Furthermore, Mrs. Clinton has become intent upon sampling some of Lowell's newer dishes (*but no chocolate chip cookies,* goes through my mind) and wonders if they might recruit Lowell to cook for them during an upcoming weekend at a friend's borrowed home in Boca Raton. Mrs. Clinton will call herself, to confer about the menu, which would be for ten people—three of them teenage girls—whenever it is convenient.

I cover the receiver with my hand and whisper: "When can you talk to Hillary?"

Kathryn, from the back deck, maintains this is all a prank.

"Any time," Lowell whispers back.

"Would Mrs. Clinton be able to talk to Mr. Cartwright now?"

"Probably she would right after the Kennedy Center performance," George Stephanopoulos says. "Give me five minutes. Let me get back to you on that."

The phone doesn't ring for an hour. By the time it does ring, the kitten is upright and spunky, chasing after Key limes rolled across the kitchen floor.

"George Stephanopoulos," the voice says. "Are you . . . there's a landing field in Marathon, correct?"

"Yes," I say.

"Big planes don't come in, though?"

I see the dinner slipping away. "No," I say.

"Is there a roasted pig?"

"I'm sorry, sir?"

"Not at the airport. I mean, is there a recipe for roasted pig?"

"Prepared with a cumin marinade, and served with pistachio pureed potatoes."

"The Clintons have left for an evening performance, but if it wouldn't be inconvenient, I think Mrs. Clinton would like to call when they return. It might be eleven, ten-thirty, or eleven—something like that."

"Mr. Cartwright stays up until well after midnight."

"I'll bet I'm interrupting your dinner right now. Tell me the truth."

"No. Actually, we've been watching what has turned out to be an incredible sunset and we've been waiting for your call."

"Sunset," Stephanopoulos says, with real longing in his voice. "Okay," he says. "Speak to you later."

"This is *amazing*," the highlighter says.

"Sting and Trudie Styler rented a house in Key West last winter," Daphne says. "Also, David Hyde Pierce, who plays Frasier's brother, took a date for dinner on Little Palm Island, and he tipped really well."

Since the moment they were introduced, Daphne and the highlighter have gotten along famously. They're sitting on the kitchen floor, rolling limes around like some variation of playing marbles, and the kitten has sprung to life and is going gonzo.

"When would the dinner be?" Lowell asks.

"They're going to call around eleven," I say. "You can ask."

"You ask," Lowell says. "I'd make a fool of myself if I had to talk to Hillary Clinton."

On the deck, Kathryn plucks a stalk of lemon grass growing from a clay pot, puts it between her two thumbs, and blows loudly. The kitten slithers under the refrigerator.

"Reminds me of certain of the doctor's patients," Daphne says, watching the kitten disappear. "You know, what really drives me crazy is that when they call, they give every last detail about their problem, as if the dentist cares whether the tooth broke because they were eating pizza or gnawing on a brick."

The kitten emerges, followed by what looks like its own kitten: a quick moving palmetto bug that disappears under the stove.

"Jesus Christ," Lowell says. "Where's the bug spray?"

Antonio, the chef from Coral Gables, calls back. He wants Lowell to know that since the president will be having lunch at his restaurant, he is not at all offended that the president wishes to dine with us. Every effort must be made, however, not to duplicate dishes. He asks, bleakly, if we have had any success in finding fresh estragon in southern Florida.

"If this were *Frasier,* Niles would run out and buy a speakerphone before the president called back. He'd hook it up, but then in the middle of the call it would blow up, or something," Daphne says.

We all look at her.

"I always watch because I like my namesake," Daphne says.

"That's what he said?" Lowell says, pouring chardonnay into his glass. "He came right out and said the president liked my potato-mango gratinée?"

"What do you think he'd say to lead into the subject that Clinton wanted to come to dinner? That the president had been very depressed about the Whitewater investigation?"

"No mention of Whitewater!" Lowell says.

"It's like: don't think of a pink elephant," the highlighter says.

Kathryn comes in from the back deck. "The bugs are starting to bite," she says.

"Also, where are we going to seat them?" Lowell says.

I say: "At the dining room table."

"Twelve, with the leaf up, but fourteen? Where will we get the chairs?"

"You can probably leave that up to someone on his staff."

"This isn't going to happen," Kathryn says. "You really think the Clintons are going to come bumping down that dirt road like the Beverly Hillbillies?"

"Gravel," Lowell says. "But you're right. We could easily get it paved."

"Remember when Queen Elizabeth went to Washington, and they took her to the home of a typical black family, or whatever it was, and the woman went up to the queen and gave her a big hug, and all the newspapers had the photograph of the queen going into shock when she was touched?" the highlighter says.

"A good suggestion: a simple handshake with the president and first lady will suffice," Lowell says to the highlighter.

"If I had to talk to them I'd probably piss my pants," the highlighter says.

"We could mention to Hillary that treatment for adult incontinence was not often covered under current health insurance policies," I say.

"We could say that *yellow water* was better than *white water,*" Daphne chimes in.

"I just realized: I didn't put the carpaccio out," I say, going to the refrigerator.

"Let's spray ourselves and knock back some more wine out on the deck before we eat," Kathryn says.

"Yes, but . . . *we won't swallow!*" the highlighter says.

Well before eleven, we've run out of jokes.

"This is *the* most strange and exciting day I have had since Madonna came in to get her roots retouched after closing. There she was, looking like a little wet dog, with her hair shampooed and the handkerchief-size towel behind her neck, and she wouldn't speak to me directly, she said everything to her bodyguard, who relayed it to me: all of a sudden, instead of touching up her roots, I was supposed to dry her hair, set the dryer on low and give it to him, actually, and let him dry it, and I was supposed to highlight her wig, instead. And then we had a blackout. The whole place went dark, and do you know, her bodyguard thought it was deliberate. It wasn't Con Ed fucking up again, it was a plot to kidnap Madonna! He kept lighting this butane lighter he had with him and looking incredibly fierce. She was smoking a cigarette and talking to herself. She was dabbing at her neck and saying that she wished she could be somewhere else, and then, in almost no light, the bodyguard kept telling me to hurry up with highlighting the wig."

"What did she name that baby?" Kathryn says.

"LuLu," Daphne says.

I correct her. "Lourdes."

"He reads the tabloids in the food store," Kathryn says.

At eleven-thirty, George Stephanopoulos has not called back. After Letterman's monologue, we decide to skip Burt Bachrach and call it a night. The kitten has been sleeping on its back, like a dog, for quite a long time. The highlighter casually reaches for it, as if it were her evening bag.

"You're sure it was George Stephanopoulos?" Lowell says to me, as Kathryn volunteers to lead the ladies to their rooms.

"It had the ring of truth about it," I say.

"I bet the president would have liked the dinner we had tonight, and then he could have played *Last Year at Marienbad* with the three of us!" Daphne giggles, as she follows Kathryn toward the stairs.

I am amazed that the twenty-something highlighter doesn't ask, "What's *Last Year at Marienbad*?"

Then she does, pronouncing the last two words so that they resonate amusingly. The words are "marine" and "bad."

The mere idea that I might have thought to take down George Stephanopoulos's phone number provokes merriment at breakfast (frittata and an orange-coconut salad; two-shot *con leches* all around).

Antonio, his wife informs me when I call, is spending the day fishing off a pontoon boat. She will have him return my call when he returns.

"Maybe he decided McDonald's was easier," Daphne says.

"Impossible. His wife was going to be along," Lowell reminds her.

Someone who is driving from Miami for the *bris* will pick up the highlighter at the discount sandal store ten minutes from our house, and give her a lift to the Casa Marina. I'll give her a ride out to the highway in another half hour.

"You'd think they'd call," the highlighter says.

We sit around, like a bunch of kids nobody's asked to dance. In a little while, when I go out to sweep the deck, the highlighter follows me.

"Are you guys gay?" she says.

"No," I say, "but you aren't the first to wonder."

"Because you're hanging out in the Keys. And you've been together so long, and all."

"Right," I say.

"What kind of tree is that?" she says, stepping around the pile of leaves.

"Kapok. It doesn't always drop its leaves, but when it does, it does."

"So listen," she says. "I didn't offend you by asking?"

"No," I say.

"Because if you're not a couple—I didn't think you were a couple—but I mean, since you're not, I'm going to be at that Casa Marina place for a couple of days after Izzy gets snipped, and I wonder if maybe I could take you out."

It's the first time a woman has ever invited me on a date. I haven't been on a date in years. I only vaguely remember how to go on a date.

"There's a private party in some place called Bahama Village. Gianni Versace's sister invited me. It's some house where they took out the kitchen and put in a swimming pool. He's given her a bunch of ties to give out. Not that you'd want a tie," she says.

"No particular use for them," I say.

"Doesn't seem," she says. Then: "So. Would you like to do that?"

"To swim in someone's kitchen?"

"If you'd rather we just—"

"No. No. Party sounds fine. I should come around to the Casa Marina, then? What time?"

"I think the party starts at ten."

"Little before ten, then."

"Great," she says.

"See you then," I say. "Of course, I'll also see you in about five minutes, when we should leave for the sandal store."

She nods.

"Like to sweep for a few minutes?" I ask.

That drives her away.

The next day, there is still no word. Could the potato-mango gratinée have been a moment's passing fancy? Antonio knows nothing, except that the Clintons will be arriving at his restaurant February 11, and that the restaurant will be closed after the first seating on February 10, when it will be secured by the Secret Service. The following day, they will watch Antonio and one assistant prepare all the food. He worries aloud about finding good quality estragon.

Just as I am about to step into the shower, the phone rings. It is George Stephanopoulos. He is apologetic. The president has been put on a new allergy medicine, which had unexpected side effects. Mrs. Clinton has been preoccupied with other details of the trip, and only realized that morning that further communication was needed from her. She is prepared to talk to me in just a few minutes, if I'm able to hold on.

I hold on. To my surprise, though, it is the president, himself, who comes on the line. "I'm very glad to talk to you, sir," the president says. "Hillary and I have greatly enjoyed your recipes."

"Actually, Mr. President, Mr. Cartwright is the person you want to talk to. I'm his assistant. I'm afraid he's out, right now, kayaking."

"Kayaking? Where are you all?"

"In the Florida Keys, Mr. President."

"Is that right? I thought you were in Louisiana."

"We're in the Florida Keys. A bit short of Key West."

"I see. Then where will we be having lunch before we come over to you?" the president asks.

"I believe you'll be lunching in Boca Raton, which is about three hours by car from where Lowell—Mr. Cartwright—lives."

"We're going to be coming to your restaurant that evening? How are we getting there, George?"

A muffled answer.

"I see. Well, that's fine. Wish I could take the time to do some fishing. But your restaurant—it's not a fish restaurant, is it?"

"Oh, no sir. It's . . . the thing is, it's not a restaurant. It's"— Is this going to screw the whole deal, somehow?—"It's where we live. Mr. Cartwright prefers to have favored people dine with us in his home. The view of the water from the back deck is splendid."

"A house on the water?" the president says. "Has George registered that?"

More muted discussion.

"I'm sorry," the president says. "I get caught up in logistics, when it's better to leave it to the experts."

"*Water,*" I hear George Stephanopoulos hissing in the background.

"You know, I'm a chef's nightmare," the president says. "If I had my way, I'd eat a medium hamburger with extra mustard and go fishing with you guys." He says: "Isn't that what I'd do, George?"

"Papaya," Stephanopoulos hisses. Is he hissing at the president?

"Hillary got all excited about that papaya dish," the president says. "I'm going to let you speak to the boss about this, but if there's one thing I might request, with the exception of shrimp, I'm not overly fond of seafood."

"No seafood," I say.

"Well, yeah, that kind of cuts to the chase," the president says. He clears his throat. "Just out of curiosity, how far is the airport from where you are?"

"Less than an hour, sir."

"That's fine, then. George and Hillary will firm this up, and we're looking forward to an exceptional meal."

"Mr. Cartwright will be so sorry he missed your call."

"Fishing in the kayak?" the president asks.

"Just paddling around with a friend," I reply.

This seems to cause the president several seconds of mirth. "Quite different from my plans for the afternoon," the president says.

George Stephanopoulos cuts in: "Thank you very much," George Stephanopoulos says.

"We look forward to making plans," I say.

"Good-bye," George Stephanopoulos says. "Thanks again."

I am standing there in my barracuda briefs, preparing to shower and go on my date. I fully realize that when Kathryn finds out, she will raise an eyebrow and say something sarcastic about my having a date. She will no doubt see my going into Key West as analogous to the butler's going off to find the former housemaid: a sad moment of self-protective delusion. Like him, I also won't be bringing her back. I'll be swimming with her at some party. Then, if we have sex, it can very well be in her room at the hotel. Simple white boxers are almost always preferable to the barracudas, when one is disrobing for the first time. The tangerine sports shirt that is my favorite is probably a bit too tropical-jokey; slightly faded denim seems better, with a pair of new khaki trousers.

"I'm going into Key West," I say, coming upon Lowell, pouring glasses of iced tea at the kitchen counter. "See you tonight."

"Why are you going into Key West?" he says.

"Date," I say.

"You have a date? With whom?"

"The highlighter."

"She just left," he says.

"Yesterday."

"I see," he says.

"Mrs. Clinton, or her secretary, will be calling. I spoke to the president briefly, and he doesn't want seafood."

"You spoke to the president? When?"

"Just before I showered."

He looks at me. "You've cleaned up beautifully," he says.

"Thank you," I say.

"Nothing else you want to tell me about anything?" he says.

"She asked if we were gay and I told her we weren't, and that seemed to provoke her to ask me out to a party."

"I meant, was there anything else you wanted to report about your conversation with the president," he says.

"If you get to speak to the president himself, tell him about kayaking," I say. "When I mentioned it, the idea seemed to please him."

"Maybe we could borrow a couple of kayaks and take them all for a predinner sail."

"Right. They can bring in the Navy SEALs."

"You're saying that would be too complicated," Lowell says.

"I suspect."

"You should leave before Kathryn begins to cross-examine you."

"Good idea."

"Be sure to fill the gas tank to the level you found it at."

I turn to look at him. He does a double-take, and raises his hands above his head. "Joke," he says.

The party is at a house with crayon-blue shutters. Broken pieces of colored tile are embedded in the cement steps. A piece of sculpture that looks like a cross between Edward Munch's *Scream* and a fancy can opener stands gap-mouthed on the side lawn, but the lawn isn't a lawn in the usual sense: it's pink gravel, with a huge cement birdbath that is spotlit with a bright pink light. Orchids bloom from square wooden boxes suspended from hooks on the porch columns. A man who makes me look like an ant to his Mighty Mouse opens the door and scrutinizes us. Nancy—I am thinking of her as Nancy, instead of as the highlighter—reaches in the pocket of her white jacket and removes an invitation with a golden sun shining on the front.

"That's the ticket to ride," the man says. "Party's out back."

We walk through the house. Some Dade County pine. Ceiling fans going. Nice. The backyard is another story: a big tent has been set up, and a carousel revolves in the center, though instead of carousel animals, oversized pit bulls and rottweilers circulate, bright-eyed, jaws protruding, teeth bared. One little girl in a party dress rides round and round on a rottweiler. In the far corner is the bar, where another enormous man is mixing drinks. Upon close inspection, I see that he has a diamond stud in one ear. Wraparound sunglasses have been pushed to the top of his shaved head.

"I guess . . . gee, what do I want?" Nancy says. "A rum and Coke."

"The real thing, or diet?"

"Diet," Nancy says, demurely.

"A shot of Stoli," I say, as the man hands Nancy her drink. He pours me half a glass of vodka.

"Thank you," I say.

"Nancy!" a woman in a leopard print jumpsuit says, clattering toward her in black mules.

"Inez!" Nancy says, embracing the woman. She turns to me. "This is, like, absolutely *the* best makeup person in New York."

"Did you make friends with Madonna?" Inez asks.

"No," Nancy says. "She didn't like me. It was clear that I was really a menial person to her."

"She didn't know you," Inez says.

"Well, you can't meet somebody if you won't speak to them," Nancy says.

The woman disappears into the growing crowd, and Nancy sighs. "I didn't do a very good job of introducing you," she says.

"Can I be honest? I'll never see these people again, so it really doesn't matter to me."

She squeezes my hand. "I'd like to think that maybe there's a chance that I'll see you again, at least," she says. "Maybe sometime you'll want to come to New York and check out what's new in some restaurants there."

"Maybe so," I say. "That would be very nice."

"It would," she says. "There are hardly any straight men in New York."

Two ladies in hats are air kissing. One holds a small dog on a leash. It's so small, Nancy's kitten could devour it. On closer inspection, though, I see that it's a tiny windup toy. I overhear the woman saying that she's bringing a nonpooping pet as a gift for the hostess. People begin to play Where's-the-Hostess.

"I think it's so exciting you're going to meet the president," Nancy says. "Hillary, too."

"Are you talking about my friend Hillary?" the woman who'd been talking to the woman with the toy dog says.

"Nothing detrimental," I say quickly.

"Priscilla DeNova," the woman says. "Pleased to meet you both."

"I'm Nancy," Nancy says. "This is my friend Richard."

"Richard," the woman echoes. "And do you know George, if you know Hillary?"

"I've only spoken to him on the phone," I say.

"Oh. What were you discussing with my friend George?"

"The president's coming to dinner," I say.

"I see. Is he going to drop by to fish, first?"

"He did mention the possibility. But no. He's just stopping by to dine."

"Conch fritters?" the woman says. She seems very amused by something.

"I think we can do a little better than that."

"What he really likes is burgers," Priscilla says. "I guess anyone who reads the paper knows that." She tosses back her long hair and says, almost conspiratorially, "Tell me the truth. Have you been having me on about Clinton coming for dinner?"

"No. The whole family will be coming."

"You must either be a fascinating conversationalist or quite a cook," she says.

"Or quite delusional," I say.

"Yes, well, that possibility did cross my mind." She looks around for someone more interesting to talk to.

"Tell us how you know George Stephanopoulos," Nancy says.

"My sister cleans house for a friend of his," the woman says. "She was a brilliant teacher, but she ruined her mind with drugs, and now about all she can remember is *Get the vacuum.* George has always been very kind to her. He gave her a ride once when she got stuck in the snow. He has a four-wheel drive, or whatever those things are. One time he saw us out hailing a cab, and he dropped us at the Avalon and came in to see the movie." She looks down, considering. "You know, I've never gotten straight on whether George, himself, goes on some fishing expeditions—so to speak, I mean—or whether Clinton gets some idea in his head, and then it just disappears. What I mean is, I wouldn't get my hopes up about them coming to dinner." She looks around, again. "Though if Hillary's involved, I suppose it might happen."

She drifts off without saying good-bye.

"Would I scare you off if I said that part of the reason I came to a *bris* in Florida was because a psychic told me that on this trip, or the next trip, I'd find true love?" Nancy says suddenly.

"You don't mean *me.*"

"Oh, of course not," she says, straight-faced. "The woman who just walked away."

"You did mean me," I say.

"Yes, I did. I don't mean that right this moment I'm in love with you, but you do seem like a real possibility." Her eyes meet mine. "Come on: you must have had some interest, or you wouldn't have come tonight."

I smile.

"And you have such a nice smile," she says.

"Excuse me for interrupting, but have you seen Gianni?" a small man asks. He has on a Gianni Versace shirt and black pants. He might be five feet tall, he might not.

"I'm afraid I don't know him," I say.

"But he's about to meet the president," Nancy says.

"The president of what?" the short man says.

"The United States," Nancy says.

"I'm Cuban," the man says. He walks away.

"So maybe it would be more fun at the Casa Marina," Nancy says. "Did you bring your bathing suit? There's a hot tub there."

"It's in my car," I say. "But didn't you say there was a pool here, in the kitchen?"

"Oh, right. I almost forgot," she says. "Let's find it."

We make our way back into the house. Two women are making out on a sofa in the hallway. The bouncer looms in the doorway, checking invitations. We take a left and find ourselves in a Victorian parlor. We turn around and go in the opposite direction. That room contains a stainless steel sink, where two women are washing and drying glasses. Nothing else that resembles a kitchen is there: no refrigerator; no cupboards. An indoor hot tub bubbles away, with several men and women inside, talking and laughing. There is a mat below the three steps leading to the hot tub. It depicts a moose, and says, in large black letters: WELCOME TO THE CAMP. The people in the hot tub are all speaking Italian. At the sink, the women are speaking Spanish. From a radio above the sink, Rod Stewart sings.

"Bathroom?" one of the women at the sink asks us.

"No, no. Just looking," Nancy says.

"Mr. Loring," the woman says, puckering her lips excessively to say "Loring." She looks at Nancy. She says: "He went to the bathroom."

Nancy considers this. "Thank you," she says.

"*De nada,*" the woman says.

"I think it would be more fun at the Casa Marina," Nancy says.

"Welllllll," Kathryn says. "Somebody got home *very* late."

"Refill the tank?" Lowell asks.

"Just imagine me blushing deeply," I say.

"But at least somebody thought to bring the *New York Times.* Good, good, good," Kathryn says.

"If you like all these things so much, why do you leave New York?"

"To check the level of depredation," she says.

"Any update on the president?" I ask.

"You'd better not be responsible for my favorite hair highlighter of all time leaving New York City to live in the boonies," Kathryn says.

"Don't worry. I didn't ask her to marry me."

"You don't have to. Sex with a straight guy is enough to drive them over the edge."

"Quiet," Lowell says. "I don't want to hear the two of you sniping at each other before I've even had a cup of coffee."

On the counter, the coffee is slowly dripping into the pot.

"We went to a party," I say. "Gianni Versace was there, but he was peeing the whole time. We left and got into the hot tub at the Casa Marina. We watched *Grand Hotel* on the tube and had room service deliver a steak."

"It's love," Kathryn sighs.

"Well, don't sound so despondent about it, Cruella," Lowell says.

The phone rings. Lowell ignores it, resting his head on his hands. Kathryn is fanning herself with the travel section.

I answer the phone.

"George here," the voice says. "I just found out there was a screwup, and that no one from Mrs. Clinton's staff got back to you. My apologies for that. I didn't awaken you, did I?"

"No, not at all. You'll want to be speaking to Mr. Cartwright," I say.

"Well, actually, if you could just relay the message that things are pretty much on hold at this end, I'd appreciate it."

"Of course," I say.

"I hope we can do it another time," George Stephanopoulos says.

I don't know what makes me do it, but I say, "You know, last night I was at a party—Gianni Versace and some other folks, down in Key West—and I met a woman who knows you. Apparently her sister cleans house for a friend of yours. Does this ring a bell?"

"What?" George Stephanopoulos says.

"Nice-looking woman. From Washington. With a sister, who—"

"Oh, sure. You're talking about Francine Worth's sister Priscilla."

"Yes," I say.

There is a pause. "What about her?" George Stephanopoulos says.

Lowell and Kathryn are staring at me. The dripping coffee is making deep, guttural, sexual sounds.

"The party wasn't that much fun. You weren't missing anything," I say.

"Is that right? Well, a lot of the time I feel like I am missing something, so maybe I'll feel better now that I know I'm not."

"It wasn't so bad, I guess. I haven't been to a party for years. Not on a date, either, to tell the truth. So last night was quite out of the ordinary for me."

"I guess so, then," George Stephanopoulos says, after a slight pause.

I can't think what to say. I realize that I'm being watched from one end, and listened to carefully at the other.

"Well, we'll see if this can be worked out sometime when things are less hectic," George Stephanopoulous says. "Just think of me stuck at the desk the next time you step out."

"Oh, there isn't going to be a next time. She's going back to New York tomorrow." I add: "Priscilla had only good things to say about you. Your kindness in giving people rides, I mean. Very generous."

"Yeah, I caught a movie with them one time. Seems like that was in another lifetime."

"I often have that same feeling of disorientation. I've lived so many places. Thailand. All over France, at various times. Le Moulin de Mougins, when the cooking was still brilliant. In the U.S., there's a place called Lava Hot Springs. Lowell and I went there when he took part in a steak barbecuing competition, I guess you'd call it. A very nice place. And the country is full of places like that."

"I know it," George Stephanopoulos says. "Man, you're making me chomp at the bit."

"You should come here and fish and have dinner, yourself, if you ever take a couple of days off. We're right on the water. Plenty of room."

"That's very nice of you. Very nice indeed. Certainly be easier than trying to get everybody together to caravan down there in early February, Mrs. Clinton converging from one place, the president with no idea what time his meeting is going to conclude. And you toss into that three or four teenage girls, some of them who'll back out at the last minute because some boy might call, or something."

"Feel free to call us," I say. "Some of Lowell's uncollected recipes are his very best. The Thai-California fusion dishes he's been working on have really come together."

"My mouth is watering," George Stephanopoulos says. "Think of me, when you're having some of that terrific food."

"Will do," I say.

"And thanks again," George Stephanopoulos says. It doesn't seem like he really wants to hang up.

"See you, then, maybe," I say.

"I'll keep that in mind," he says. "Good-bye."

Kathryn is the first to speak. She collects her cup, and her brother's, and pours coffee, giving me a wide berth to indicate her skepticism. She's jealous; that's what it's always been with Kathryn. She's very possessive, very set in her ways. In spite of passing judgment on anything new, she's still trying to come to terms with things that are old. How many years have I been around, now—years in which I've been pretty decent to her—and she still wishes that she had her brother all to herself? Kathryn says: "The new effusiveness."

I say nothing.

"Well, for God's sake, would you mind letting me know the outcome of your little chat? Am I correct in assuming that the president is not coming, but that George Stephanopoulos might?" Lowell says.

I nod.

"What is this? Twenty Questions? The president is not coming . . . why?"

"Some meeting is probably going to run late, and Mrs. Clinton would be rendezvousing with him from wherever she was, and Chelsea and her friends apparently drive him mad, because they're so unpredictable."

"He didn't know this when he called?" Kathryn says.

"How would I know?"

"Don't you two start in on each other. Think about me, for once. What about my feelings, when I was prepared to be cooking for the president and suddenly he decides to blow the whole thing off because some meeting might run a little late?"

Kathryn and I take this in. I get a mug and pour coffee. We all sit at the table in silence.

"I'm not sure it quite computed with me," I say. "The president visiting, I mean."

"I wonder if the bastard's still having lunch at Antonio's," Lowell says.

"Read the *Times*," I say. "Would you like me to make you some toast?"

"No thank you," Lowell says. "But it's nice of you to offer."

"I'll be on the deck," Kathryn says. She picks up her mug and half the paper and walks outside.

"Still," Lowell says. "Not everyone gets a call from the president." He looks at me. "Remember a few months after we met, when we had that barbecue over at your uncle's?"

"Of course I remember. He was a great guy. Never charged me a nickel for room and board. A totally generous man. 'Never get too big for your britches that you turn your back on your family,' my uncle used to say."

"You never did," Lowell says. "You sent him food every time we went somewhere exotic."

"Pistachios from Saudi Arabia," I say.

"And I've taken his advice, too. Which means that Kathryn will tyrannize us forever," Lowell says.

Back in Key West that evening, on impulse, I'm almost giddy. I go to the Green Parrot and have a cold draft before going over to the Casa Marina to meet Nancy and her friends in the bar there. Some bikers are at the Parrot with their girlfriends. Somebody who looks like a tweedy professor, except that he's got on pink short shorts as well as the tweed jacket with elbow patches, so he might be just another unemployed oddball. He's playing a game of Nintendo while sipping some tropical drink through double-barrel straws.

I am thinking about what I might have said to the president if he came to dinner.

But then I think: he no doubt already knows the marines are a bunch of dangerous psychos. He always had better sense than to truck with any of that stuff.

What would Nancy say if I suggested moving to New York with her?

Probably yes. She dropped enough hints about the lack of straight guys in Manhattan.

What do you get when you fall in love?

You get enough germs to catch pneumonia.

What happened to all the great singers of yesteryear?

Replaced by Smashing Pumpkins.

"You hear the one about this guy's girlfriend, who's leaving him?" a skinny guy in cutoffs and a "Mommy and Daddy Visited Key West and All I Got Was This Crummy Shirt" tee-shirt says, sitting next to me on a barstool.

"Don't think so," I say.

"The girlfriend says, 'I'm leaving you. I'm out of here.' And the guy says, 'Whoa there, can a guy even know why?' and she goes, 'Yeah, I've heard something very, very disturbing about you.' He says, 'Oh yeah? What's that?' She says, 'I heard that you were a pedophile.' He says, 'Hey, that's a pretty big word for an eleven-year-old.'"

Today I have spoken to this unfunny jerk, and to the president's assistant, George Stephanopoulos. Also to my employer, who is depressed, because the president was going to come to dinner and then suddenly he didn't want to, and to Kathryn— the sarcastic Kathryn, who always brings both of us down— though soon I will be talking to the lovely, though fleeting-as-the-breeze Nancy. Somewhere in the middle of these thoughts, I manage a strained "ha-ha." I ask for the check and pay the bill before the guy gets wound up again.

I drive on Duval, to check out the action. A bunch of middle-aged tourists, who wonder what they're doing in Key West, a lot of tee-shirt shops, quite a few kids beneath the age of consent, not yet at the age of reason, who have never even heard of the Age of Aquarius. Duval looks like Forty-second Street, although maybe by now Forty-second Street looks like Disneyland.

I meet Nancy and her friends—both women—where she said they'd be: at the beach bar. The women give me the once-over, and the You-Might-Hurt-Her-Permanently squint. Nancy flashes bedroom eyes, but only gives me a discreet peck on the cheek. "There's another party, in a condo over by the beach. But first Jerri has to go back to the photo place where she works, because she needs to double-check that the alarm is activated," she says.

"Nobody has a car. Would you mind driving?" Jerri says.

"Not at all," I say.

"Some customer left a bottle of champagne for the owner, but he's in AA, so he just gives me those things. If you want, we could take that out of the fridge and drink it."

"Mmmm," Bea, the other woman, says. Bea looks like she might eventually forgive me for being a man.

"This new alarm system has been screwing up in a major way," Jerri says. "It will take me ten secs to make sure it hasn't deprogrammed itself. And to round up the bubbly."

"So," Bea says. "I hear you're the assistant to a famous chef."

"Yes, I am."

"Do you cook, too?"

"Just help out," I say. "I'm not innovative, myself."

"So how does somebody get a job like that?" Bea says.

"Lowell and I became friends when I picked him up for a car service I used to drive for. It was back in the days when you'd meet somebody and check them out, and basically, if you liked the person, you never minded running some strange proposition past him."

"What was the strange proposition?" Nancy says.

"It wasn't so strange in and of itself. But there I was driving for a car service, and basically, he wanted to know if I had any interest in coming to work for him. Letting the other job go."

"Did he talk about money? I had two job interviews last year and it turned out they didn't want to give me any money at all. They wanted me to take a full-time job as a volunteer!"

"He didn't mention money, now that you mention it. But people went more on intuition then, I think. I figured he'd pay me a decent wage."

"So where did he get a name like Lowell?"

"I'm not sure."

"Everybody who meets me wants to know absolutely everything about me," Jerri says. "Full disclosure, even if I'm, like, trying on a pair of shoes. I wouldn't get out of the store without saying how much I pay in rent. Though I suppose people in Key West are obsessed with that."

"They are? Why?" I ask, grateful that something has come up that I can ask about.

"Because it costs so much to live here," she says.

"Oh. Right," I say. I open the car door, and everyone gets in.

"Guess what I pay in rent?" Jerri says.

"I wouldn't have any idea."

"It's a one-bedroom, and the bedroom isn't mine. It's on the top floor of a house on Francis that has a separate entrance. I share it with the landlady's granddaughter, who's not all there, if you know what I mean. She's forty years old, and all she does all day is read gardening books and drown all the houseplants so they die."

"When she moved in, they gave her a mattress that used to be the dog's bed," Bea says.

"God," Nancy says. "Things were never that bad back in New York, were they?"

"Oh, I didn't *sleep* on it," Jerri says. "But it was really depressing, because all these little fleas were using it as a trampoline. You could see them jumping up and down."

"I suppose you're going to tell me that the rent costs a fortune," I say.

"One fifty-five a month," Jerri says. "Take a turn here. The next street's one way."

"Isn't that reasonable for Key West?" I ask.

"Yeah, it's reasonable, but I had to buy my own mattress and box spring, and the granddaughter insists on keeping lights on in every room, all night."

"You couldn't find another place to live?" I ask.

"For *one fifty-five*?"

Jerri indicates that I should take an empty parking space. I park, and we lock the car and start down the street. From a clip hanging off her belt, Jerri removes a keyring. She opens two locks with two different keys and flips on a light inside the back of the shop. We walk in behind her. She looks at a panel, flashing a number, on the same wall as the light switch. "Whew," she says. "Okay, this is cool." She pushes a couple of buttons and walks to the small refrigerator in the corner, from which she removes the bottle of champagne. She reaches up on a shelf and takes down a tower of upside-down plastic glasses. She counts out four and puts the rest back on the shelf.

But my attention is drifting. In the back of the shop there are life-size cardboard cutouts with cutout faces. One is Marilyn Monroe, with her skirt blowing up. Another is Tina Turner, all long legs and stiletto heels and micro-mini skirt with fringe. There is the *American Gothic* couple, and there are a couple of Pilgrims, complete with a turkey that retains its own face. There's Donald Duck, and Donald Trump with Marla Maples, who also has her face; Sylvester Stallone as Rocky; James Dean on his motorcycle. There is also Bill Clinton, arm extended to clasp the shoulder of whoever stands beside him. Jerri has walked over to the figures; first she becomes Marilyn, then Tina Turner. Her young, narrow face makes her unconvincing as either. Nancy is the next to wander over. Champagne glass in hand, she tries her luck as Rocky. She motions for me to join her. I do, and together we peer out from behind the Pilgrim couple. Behind the cutouts she passes me her glass, and I duck back to take a sip of champagne.

"I look at this stuff all day long. It doesn't seem so funny anymore," Jerri says. "And what's really not funny is when some guy who thinks he's a real stud comes in to be Stallone, or when some guy who smells like a brewery wants his girlfriend to be Marilyn. *Really* wants her to be Marilyn."

"I notice they don't have one of Ike with his gun," Jerri says, sticking her face through Tina Turner's highly teased hair.

"Too bad there's not one of your good friend, George Stephanopoulos, just his flunky," Jerri says. "Nancy was telling us about that before you came over."

Nancy smiles, mugging from behind the female Pilgrim again.

"Well, we all know Nancy. Nancy's only interested in the rich and famous. Or in people who hang with the rich and famous," Jerri says.

"That cowboy she lived with was hardly rich or famous," Bea says.

"You were always so jealous you couldn't see straight, because somebody followed me all the way from Montana to New York," Nancy says. "It really made you crazy, didn't it, Bea?"

"Oh, look who's talking! Like you didn't call my old boyfriend the day he moved out!" Bea says.

"I called him to get my canvas bag back."

"Listen to her! She called about eight hours after he moved into his new place because she needed a bag back!" Bea shrieks.

"You are so sadly misled," Jerri says. "I mean, fun is fun, but this is one time I've got to defend my friend Nancy. She always thought your boyfriend was a *jerk*!"

It's as if I'm not there, suddenly. While they continue to go at it, I wander over to the plastic glass of champagne that's been poured for me and take a long, bubbly sip. So she lived with some guy who followed her all the way to New York from Montana. When? How long were they together?

"And you look so much like him!" Bea suddenly says to me. "If you were, like, fifty pounds lighter, and if you wore cowboy boots some armadillo gave its life for instead of those goony shoes, you'd be a dead ringer for Les."

"*Jesus!* I can't believe you're so jealous I've got a date that you're insulting him about his weight!" Nancy says.

"Oh, sit on it," Jerri says. "Both of you."

"Bea has really got it in for me!" Nancy says to Jerri.

"*I've* got it in for *you*? Nancy, you need to ask yourself why, every time somebody says something that's true, but maybe you don't want to hear it . . . you should ask yourself why you

find it necessary to say that that person is *crazy.* I mean, fuck
you!" Bea says. She pushes past Marilyn and storms out the
back door, crushing her empty plastic glass.

"Je-*sus,*" Nancy say. "What is *wrong* with her?"

"Well, don't get on your high horse," Jerri says. "You didn't
have to tell her how mean and spiteful she was."

"I didn't say that. I only said she was jealous of me and Les."

"Who's Les?" I ask.

"I don't see why we should be talking about this now,"
Nancy says.

"You mean, you thought we were having a conventional
date?" I ask.

"No, I didn't . . . I mean, we're going to a party, aren't we?
We stopped by here because Jerri had to check the damned
alarm."

"She wanted an excuse to say mean things and run off," Jerri
says. "It pisses her off that Nancy and I can discuss things and
be really honest with each other, because she introduced the
two of us, and she's got some weird thing about how each of us
has to have her as our best friend, so we're not supposed to care
that much about each other."

"I can't follow all this. Maybe we should go to the party,"
I say.

"I feel bad," Jerri says. "I should have tried to cool her out."

"Why should you feel responsible for Bea's state of mind?"
Nancy says.

"Let me get a picture of you two," Jerri says. "Souvenir of
our wonderful evening, so far."

She goes to a safe and turns the combination lock. When the
door swings open, she takes out a Polaroid and fiddles with the
camera. I'm still wondering: Who's Les? How long has he been
gone? And: What constitutes goony shoes?

Nancy seems quite shaken by Bea's exit. She is fighting back tears, I see, as Jerri gestures for us to make a choice: for a couples shot, it's either *American Gothic* or the Pilgrim couple. Nancy, sniffing, moves behind the Pilgrims. I stand beside her, crouching so my face peers out where it's supposed to.

The camera spews out the photograph. We both converge on Jerri, to watch it develop.

"Let me get you with the president. Go on," Jerri says, gesturing for me to stand next to Clinton.

"You know, she can really be a terrible bitch," Nancy says. "But now I feel like everything's all messed up."

The flash goes off. Jerri takes the first photograph out of her pocket and nods approvingly. The second photograph—the one she just took—begins to quickly develop. There I am, probably closer to the president than I'd ever have gotten if he'd come to the house, and obviously on much chummier terms. Probably just as good as meeting him, the photo op being interchangeable with real experiences in recent years.

"You're mad at me for dragging you into this," Nancy says. Tears are rolling down her cheeks.

"No, it's just one of those things that happened," I say.

"One of those things that happened?" she repeats. She seems confused. "You mean, you think this was okay? It's okay if somebody insults you and if the person you slept with the night before turns out to be in love with some other guy?"

It takes me a minute to respond. "I didn't know until now that you were in love with him," I say.

"I am! And I think that if the mere mention of his name, by that bitch, can make me this upset, maybe I should swallow my pride and go out to Montana and get him. He didn't hate me, he just hated New York."

I raise both hands, palms up.

"That's fine with you?" she says.

"What can I do about it?" I say.

"You know, I think that once again, I've found an apathetic jerk," Nancy says. "I guess it's all for the best that this happened, because this way you and I won't waste any more time with each other."

"I cannot believe this," Jerri says. She puts both pictures in her shirt pocket. She walks over to the safe, shaking her head. She replaces the camera in the safe and shuts the door. "Lights out, kids," she says, tiredly.

"Yeah," Nancy says. "I think I'll be the first off to dreamy dreamland. I think I'll just spend the night alone with my fabulous new scenario."

We watch her go.

"I suppose I should have gone after her, but I couldn't see the point in it. I think she meant everything she said. So why would I go after her?" I say.

"Is that really a question?" Jerri says.

"Yes," I say.

"In my opinion, you did the right thing not to," she says.

"Thank you," I say.

"You don't have to thank me. I wasn't trying to flatter you. I was just saying that I think you made the right decision."

"What do you say, if you don't say thank you?"

"You don't have to say anything."

I consider this. "I think I'll drive home, but if you'd like a lift anywhere . . ."

"You know, you really didn't deserve that. You really seem like a very nice man."

"With dorky shoes," I say, extending my foot.

"Top-Siders are dorky? Millions of people wear Top-Siders."

"But I can see that they aren't exactly cool."

"We're not teenagers anymore," she says. "I don't think any of us will perish if we don't have the exact newest thing."

"No," I say.

"Thanks for the offer, but I think I'll just walk over to a friend's house."

"Fine," I say. "I'm sorry about all this, too. It's a lame thing to say, but I sort of appreciate the fact that at least one person is still talking to me."

She shrugs. "You take care," she says.

I'm out the door when she says, "Oh, wait. Take your pictures."

I turn around, and she puts the photographs in my hand. For the first time, I see that they're joke Pilgrims: the woman excessively big-breasted, the man with his fly unzipped. Stallone, of course, you wouldn't dare joke about. And Marilyn is almost a sacred cultural icon. People who don't like James Dean would nevertheless realize that he was the embodiment of cool. But the Pilgrims, I suppose, have become so anachronistic that there's no harm in joking about them. I hand that photograph back to her. "Two turkeys and one big-breasted babe," I say. "I think I might as well pass on that one."

Then I'm out on Duval, going around the corner to the street where I parked the car.

A guy in dreadlocks walks past, bouncing on the balls of his bare feet. On the steps by a guest house, a man lies sprawled on top of a coat, a small pile of clutter next to him. He's wearing a beret, shirtless, and almost trouserless. His pants are down around his hips. He's lying on his side, mouth lolled open. I walk past a store selling silk-screened bags with tropical birds on them. I stop to admire a traveler's palm in someone's front yard, spotlit. As they pass by, a middle-aged woman says to the man she is walking with, "So what part of town did they film

Key Largo in?" In a shop window, I see a verdigris crane, flanked by gargoyles in graduated sizes. Just as I get near the car, someone's light sensor is activated by my presence and floods the street with light, and I feel embarrassed, as if I've been caught doing something bad. Or as if I've unnecessarily caused some commotion. But the light blinks out after I pass, and the whole block—surprising, this close to Duval—is eerily quiet. It gives me more time than I want to hear the voice in my head telling me that I've done everything wrong, that years ago, I took the easy way out, that if I think I'm indispensable to Lowell, that's only a delusion—like the delusion that I'm a nice-looking man, or at least ordinary, wearing inconspicuous clothes and conventional shoes. What must it be like to be the president? Pictures in the paper of you jogging, sweating, your heavy legs caught at a bad angle, so they look like tree trunks? Cry at a funeral, and they zoom the lens in on you. "It's love," I hear Kathryn saying sarcastically. Well, no: it certainly isn't, and apparently wasn't going to be. But what version is Nancy going to give Kathryn, back in the great city of New York? On the other hand, what do I care? What do I have to be embarrassed about?

I get in the car, not much looking forward to joining the weekend traffic exiting Key West. It seems that half the world is intent upon getting to the southernmost point, and half the world is intent upon fleeing it. Half an hour up the Keys, there's a police roadblock. A cop standing in the street is motioning cars over to the side, but thank heaven: I was feeling so sorry for myself, and so preoccupied, that I was creeping along, barely going the minimum. Once past, I turn on the radio. The tape deck has been broken for weeks. I fiddle with the dial and find Rod Stewart, singing "Do you feel what I feel/Can we make it so that's part of the deal," which reminds me of the party the night before, which reminds me of afterwards, at the Casa Marina. Bad luck, I think. Bad timing, bad lady, bad luck.

"A Whiter Shade of Pale" comes on, which really takes me back. I'm probably among the few Americans who first heard that song in a bar in Tangier. I think about returning to my room, my VCR, my travel tapes. It seems a pleasant notion. And if I'm lucky, there will be leftovers to eat while I take the nightly imaginative voyage.

Then I see it: the police cars in the driveway. Police on the front steps. Police standing by the rose garden, writing whatever they're writing. The grating noise of their radios seems to stab the quiet of the night. I catch Kathryn, like a stunned deer, in my headlights. Then, suddenly, she is on her way back to the house, accompanied by a policeman. Lowell. Something terrible has happened to Lowell.

"What?" I say to the first cop I see. I only say that word; I can't manage a full sentence.

"Who are you?" he says.

"Lowell's assistant," I say.

"His assistant? You live here?"

I nod yes.

"There was an accident," he says. "The gentleman fell out of a tree."

"Fell?"

"Fell," the cop says, his shoulders going a little limp and his knees slightly buckling as he slumps toward the ground. "From a tree," he says again.

"What happened to him?" I ask.

"He was airlifted to Miami," the cop says. "I wouldn't want to speculate about the extent of his injuries."

"He's alive," I say.

"He might have broken his neck," the cop says. He swivels

his head and puts his ear as close to his shoulder as it can get without actually touching the shoulder.

I go in the house, where every light is on.

"They wouldn't let me on the plane," Kathryn says, turning toward me in the glare. Then she collapses in tears. "That stupid whore you've taken such a liking to, with her mangy kitten. She just turned it out and then . . ." Tears interrupt Kathryn's story. Then she pulls herself together, or tries to imitate someone who's pulled herself together. She looks into my eyes. "You knew she left the God damned thing here, didn't you? It got away, and she just left it. She told me to find it, like I was her servant, or something." She stops. "I didn't mean that the way it sounded," she said. "I didn't mean anything personal. Oh, God, if he lives, I'll never be awful again. I really won't. All I'm saying is, why am I supposed to find some scrappy cat and get it back to her in New York? That's something perfectly normal to expect, like she left an earring here, or something? She didn't even tell you any of this, when the other morning it was such a crisis I thought she was going to jump out of her skin if the ratty thing didn't come back?"

I shake my head no. This can't be happening. Just a few hours ago, everything was fine.

"It's impossible," Kathryn says to a cop who passes by. "This morning we were talking about the president coming here for dinner."

I reach in my pocket and take out the photograph of myself with Clinton. I stare at it, as if it's evidence of something.

"Hey! You and President Clinton!" the cop says. He's young. Blond with blue eyes. He looks like he's barely more than a teenager. But can he really be so unobservant that he doesn't know it's a joke photograph? My head begins to pound.

"It's my fault for ever bringing her here," Kathryn says. "She let her cat go, like it was a dog that would come back from a walk." She turns to me. "He was fixing dinner, and I saw it. It ran up a tree, like a squirrel. Lowell was inside. He turned off the stove and went out on the deck, and eventually we got the ladder and put it up. Lowell was trying to coax it down from the kapok tree. Then he started to climb, and the next thing I knew, he was in the water, but he wasn't moving. I thought he didn't move right away because the fall had stunned him. I waded out and got him. Otherwise, he would have drowned. You don't live where there's anyone who can help you in any emergency. I could have screamed my head off, and nobody would have come. He went after that stupid cat, and now they think something horrible happened to his spine."

The young cop has listened attentively to this avalanche of information. Finally he turns to me. "Was he also a friend of the president's? Should someone let the president know?" he says.

Is he possibly making some bizarre joke? I look at the photograph again, as if I might be the one who's missing something. Clinton, in a gray suit, stands smiling, his arm, with its inexactly cutout hand, too stiffly extended to really appear to be clasping anyone's shoulder.

Words tumble through my mind, as I imagine the letter I might send: *"Dear George, I enclose a photo that's as close as I'll ever come now to the real thing. This evening Lowell was airlifted to Miami, with serious injuries: quite probably, a broken neck. Which leaves me wondering—if things go as badly as they seem to be going at the moment—what a person who has always been a maverick in this country is supposed to do when the comfortable life he more or less stumbled into unexpectedly disappears out from under him. The first woman I dated in years turns out to be in love with another man. . . ."*

I open the kitchen drawer. There is the wine pull, foolish

contraption that it is. An item guaranteed to be puzzled over if found years hence in a time capsule.

"How you doing, big guy?" a cop I haven't spoken to before says to me.

"This is a joke," I say, removing the Polaroid from my pocket and holding it out. "You see that, don't you?"

"Sure," he says slowly, as if I'm playing some sort of parlor game. He studies my face. "I had a picture taken of myself one time in one of those fake stockades. Used it as a Christmas card. One of those 'From Our House to Yours' things. Turned out pretty funny."

"Thank you," I say, so quietly I can barely hear my own voice. I put the picture back in my pocket, clamping my right hand over it as if it might fly out and disappear. As if I were a boy again, in one of the many schools I attended, dutifully reciting the pledge of allegiance. Those days when life consisted of ritual, wherever we lived; ritual was the one constant, as predictable as my father's patriotism, as inevitable as my mother's church-going. I would get away from all that, I vowed. And I did—researching hotels and restaurants around the world, booking flights, arranging for any necessary letters of introduction, Lowell and I greeted by interesting and important people wherever we journeyed—people with whom we drank wine and dined. And now, it seems, that travel has concluded in the Florida Keys.

The note—the note in response to the letter I do eventually write to George Stephanopoulos—is very brief. It is addressed to Lowell, naturally enough, not to me. It concludes, in a heartfelt, yet predictable way, yet in a totally sincere way, if you know George: *"You are in the president and first lady's prayers."*

Mermaids

T HOUGH they usually spent Christmas with James's relatives in Pennsylvania, this year they had decided to see the family at New Year's and had taken a last-minute trip to Key West. James was finally going to enact his dream of spending Christmas Day fishing. Miles Hetherly was driving three hours south to get aboard the charter boat with him. She planned to spend the day by the pool of the Hilton Hotel. It would never have occurred to her to tell Hetherly that they'd be in Key West at the same time he was visiting his relative, but it *had* occurred to James. Later, he swore he'd just said it out of nervousness— that he never knew what to talk to Hetherly about on the phone. Hetherly was her friend. She was not all that good at keeping friends, so their contact over thirty-some years had been more his doing than hers. Hetherly had never forgotten that she had written him during the time he was in Vietnam. That she alone, among their friends, had been the only loyal correspondent. She still cringed to think that she had sent him copies of the very antiwar *SoHo Weekly News,* as well as cocktail napkins from trendy restaurants she had gone to on dates. All that seemed so ludicrous, in retrospect; it had been rather insensitive, though the truth was, she'd been engaged and she had no more idea what to write him than her husband had now about what to say when he talked to him on the phone. It was a source of some amusement between them that neither could say exactly what Hetherly did. James maintained—only half jokingly—that he must be a spook.

Hetherly had jumped at the chance to drive down the Keys

early Christmas morning to get aboard the boat. James had not actually invited him, but logically enough, Hetherly had assumed that James had brought up the trip for that reason. Passing through the room, she had overheard James saying that, well, if Hetherly wanted to start driving in what amounted to the middle of the night, then sure: he'd be welcome aboard the 7:30 A.M. departure of *Treasure Trove*. For her part, she was going to sun and swim. She would see James and Hetherly— she supposed they would have a big Christmas dinner at the hotel—upon their return.

"He's always been a little in love with you," James said, as they settled into their room.

"No he hasn't," she said. She had thought about it before, unprovoked, and the answer, she was sure, was that he was not a little in love with her. Indebted, perhaps. Appreciative. But more than that? No. "Thank you for pretending to be jealous, though," she said.

"And you might be a little in love, too, except that I know how much you disapprove of men who shirk their responsibility," he said.

"It's not so much that I disapprove. I only think it's sad." Years before, Hetherly and his second wife, Maude—she had never known his first wife, because they'd eloped and separated after the first few months of marriage—had pursued adoption, even though it was clear their marriage was rocky. And what had happened but that twin boys were found—not one child, but two—and in exchange for his not having to support the boys, his soon-to-be-ex-wife's lawyer had gotten him to agree to say nothing about the divorce to the adoption agency. So really, it was hardly her concern, if that was what Hetherly had felt comfortable agreeing to, and if it was what Maude wanted, as well. She supposed James might think she disapproved because she so often changed the subject when Hetherly mentioned the boys. He hardly knew them, hardly saw them at all—but her disapproval was not so much because he'd dismissed his sons as an intolerance for people who pretended. He didn't care about the children. He never had. So why should she *ooh* and *aah* about their crayoned pictures? Why feign interest in their hobbies and preoccupations, when Hetherly, himself, knew only what his ex-wife reported?

"You have your face set in that I'm-hard-hearted-and-proud-of-it look."

"Give me a break," she said, turning away from the sliding glass doors that led to a tiny balcony. In the distance, she could hear sirens. "The sun was in my face."

"Sun is what you came for," he said, crossing the room and putting his arms around her.

"Give me a break," she said again. "On my back, with a hat brim over my sunglasses—not blinded by light glinting off the gulf."

The next morning, she didn't hear James leave the room. When he left early, he was kind enough to shave with a razor, instead of the electric shaver. Though there was a coffee maker in the room, he had obviously decided to spare her the burbling and to find his morning caffeine elsewhere. It was after ten when she awoke, startled into consciousness by the wail of sirens somewhere near the hotel, and ten-thirty by the time she'd washed her hair and showered. It was not until then that she saw the little piece of paper by the bathroom sink: a note telling her that Hetherly's aunt had come with him, and that she would be at the pool. How rude, to put her in the position of spending Christmas with someone she had never met. She could hardly believe Hetherly's nerve. She could also not think what to do except to have some breakfast and then go to the pool. It was Christmas, after all: one of those days on which you were obliged to be nice. She was in the elevator before she wondered how she and the woman would recognize each other. Having her coffee and croissant, she became preoccupied with the question. Perhaps his aunt would be the oldest person at the pool. But, if so, how could she march right up and say hello? Wouldn't his aunt figure out how she'd been recognized? Or perhaps he'd described her to his aunt. Yes; it seemed likely he would have. So that left her wondering how she'd been described: middle-aged? Dyed brown hair? A little too smiley, too sure of herself? She'd heard that one more than once, sometimes disguised as a compliment, sometimes as the insult it clearly was. The *nerve* he had, bringing his aunt, uninvited. Though she supposed if he'd asked, she would have found it difficult to say no. It *was* Christmas. She finished her breakfast and asked the waiter how to get to the pool. He smiled: a trim, dark-skinned man with a slight paunch, wearing khaki bermudas, a white shirt, white socks, red sneakers, and foam antlers on his head. He gestured behind her: through the restaurant, into the courtyard. She was very close to the pool.

The hotel's courtyard was a pretty area, rectangular, trees in the garden strung with lights, though in the daylight, of course, no lights were turned on. The hurricane that had come through Key West had apparently done little damage, though here and there when you saw something odd, you suspected the hurricane was the explanation. The trunk of a slanting palm tree, minus its fronds, protruded five feet or so from the ground and had been wrapped in silver, tied with red bows. Atop it sat a plastic reindeer head, on which someone had plopped a Santa hat. Protruding from the base of the trunk

were two hooves that looked very real. They might even have
been something provided by a taxidermist. She looked away,
not wanting to think about it.

A woman about her age, wearing a white bikini, waved, and
her eyes widened with surprise. Then she realized that the
woman was waving at a blond boy behind her, struggling to
carry three cans of Coke. At the far end of the pool, she saw a
cabana with a man inside, dispensing towels. Around his head
he wore a furry headband with bells dangling from it. "May I
give you one or two towels?" he asked, as she approached. She
asked for two. "Room number?" he said, picking up a pencil
with a Santa head where the eraser would normally be. She
reached in her shirt pocket for the key. "Two-eleven," she said.
"Ah," he said, and reached behind him to a clipboard, from
which he took a folded piece of paper. He held it out to her. It
was a note from Aunt Rose. It said: "It would be pleasant to join
you at poolside, but I realize that this is your vacation, so perhaps tea later this afternoon would be best." She read it, frowning. The poor woman had gone down to the cabana but had not
stayed, because she thought she might be intruding? Suddenly,
her heart went out to her. She asked where a house phone was,
and the man reached beneath the counter and put a cordless
phone in front of her. The phone was white and had no Christmas decorations. She dialed the hotel operator. After being told
the person's name, and that she was at a Hilton Hotel, and
wished a Merry Christmas, she was asked, rapid-fire, how her
call should be directed. It was only then that she realized she
did not know Aunt Rose's last name. But of course she must be
registered under the name Hetherly. She and her nephew must
be sharing a room. It was so obvious that she was shocked when
the operator said there was no Hetherly registered. Confused,
she spelled the name. No; there was no person by that name

registered. "They checked in early this morning. Four hours ago. Something like that," she said. The person on the other end said that the computer had just been updated, and that no Hetherly was registered. She was wished a happy holiday.

"They say the person who left me this note isn't registered here," she said to the young man in the cabana. "How am I going to find her?"

"I don't know, ma'am," he said.

"Did this lady stay by the pool, earlier? Did you see her?" she asked.

"That would have been before my shift," he said.

She nodded. It wasn't his problem. It shouldn't be her problem, either. Before she got any more upset, she decided to spread a towel on a lounge and enjoy the sun, while she thought about what to do. She walked on the opposite side of the pool from the mother and the blond boy, because the boy was pretending to dive-bomb all the lounges on that side with whatever he held in his hand. She picked a lounge near a little table and put her suntan lotion down, then took off the denim shirt she'd worn over her bathing suit, lifted the suntan lotion, and put the folded shirt underneath it. She hadn't wanted to have to visit his aunt, so why was she so perturbed? Because everything was so inefficient, these days; inefficient and inconclusive. American Express was investigating a charge on her latest bill for a magazine she'd never subscribed to (or received); she had called the bank twice, asking for a copy of a canceled check, and it still had not been sent; she'd ordered a funny present for her best friend from a catalogue in early November, and it wasn't until the day before Christmas that she got a postcard saying the item was out of stock and wouldn't be shipped for another three weeks. Her own mother was alone at Christmas; her brother had said he and his fiancée would visit her, but he had come down with a cold and canceled their flight. Christmas, itself, was a rather inconclusive holiday: it seemed to mark the end of the year that had passed, though it was not yet New Year's. She put some suntan lotion on her throat and face, careful to pat, rather than rub. Even as a small child, her mother had given her hints to avoid aging: never scrub; always pat gently. Pat, pat, pat. She always felt like she was roughhousing with herself if she put a towel around her body and pulled it back and forth. She rearranged her other towel under her feet and leaned back to soak in the sun. From speakers hidden somewhere, she heard bells ringing out a tinkly "Santa Claus Is Comin' to Town." Sure. Maybe in the biplane flying overhead, advertising some seafood restaurant. Or maybe he was inside the hotel, bending the concierge's ear. That might be what was occupying the concierge. ("Whaddya mean you don't have a Hetherly? Ho ho ho.")

She surprised herself by falling asleep so soon after arising. When she awoke, it was almost an hour later. Two teenage girls in bikinis were sitting a few lounges away, talking about the best way to apply nail polish. Apparently, it should be done just the way you'd imagine, but afterwards you should stick your hands in the freezer for sixty seconds. Across the pool, she saw the cabana boy opening an umbrella, trying to crowd three lounges for a family underneath. She got up and asked the cabana boy, when he returned, if she could use the phone again. He handed it up silently. She dialed the concierge. A man's voice answered on the third ring, wishing her a Merry Christmas. She cut him off before he could tell her his name, and where she was staying, etc., etc., by asking, in a louder voice than his, if he could help her locate a "Ms. Hetherly. H-e-t-h-e-r-l-y." He said he would transfer her call to the operator, but she said that no, she had tried that, and for some reason, they hadn't been able to find the room number. "You're sure this guest is registered here?" he said. "Yes," she said, although she was less and less sure. "Checking H-e-t-h-e-r-l-y, I'm sorry that no one is listed by that name. Is there another name the guest might be registered under?" Well, yes, her own name, clearly, but she didn't know what that was. "There's no way you could check by looking at first names, is there?" she said halfheartedly, instead of answering the question. That elicited a clipped "No there isn't. I'm sorry." Okay: she would wait to be found.

She swam. She ordered lunch and ate a Caesar salad with shrimp and was amused when some croutons blew away in the breeze. A large seagull swooped and got them almost immediately. Between swimming and eating she had gone into the hotel to get a newspaper. After lunch she read it, thoroughly, reapplying suntan lotion and putting on her shirt, in case she was getting too much sun. The biplane buzzed across the sky and, as she watched it pull its ripply message, she saw, in the corner of her eye, a parasailer. She wondered if she'd ever have the nerve to parasail and decided it was unlikely. Stocks were down, but they'd finished high for the year. James had left their money in the market after the fall plunge, and he'd been right not to panic. There it was: the reward for waiting.

Oh, come on: she wasn't a character in *Godot*.

She left the newspaper, towels, and suntan lotion on the lounge and went into the hotel. She took the elevator to her room, which had still not been cleaned. She peed, then eyed the bed, thinking of pulling the curtains and taking a luxurious afternoon nap. She never napped. James loved to nap, but she never did. It kept her awake at night. She stretched out on the bed, certain that the bright sunlight would keep her awake. With her arm thrown over her eyes, it was pleasant to lie there. Much nicer than being on a boat. As a child, her mother had told her to count sheep if she had trouble relaxing, but sheep were actually interesting creatures—maybe not so fascinating that they'd keep you awake, especially pre-Dolly—but more interesting than boats. If she really wanted to fall asleep, she could probably imagine charter boat after charter boat—white boats of a particular size, not boats she'd seen, but generic boats. Sort of sail-in-the-bathtub boats. Boats out on the water, fishing lines thrown over the sides, bail buckets by people's feet, buckets filled with gray wriggly worms.

She sat upright. What a hideous image. What a thing to think of on Christmas Day. She was doing it again: seeing something simple and examining it, zeroing in, zeroing in, until it became ugly. The shiny finish on a wood table? She'd see the scratch. She even knew what the damnable tendency was: she was always probing her own inadequacy. She was still convinced of her own inadequacy. So, okay; she'd been to a good shrink, she knew that. See the tendency, stop it. Say out loud to yourself, if necessary: Stop it.

"Stop it," she said, so loud she ended up choking. She sat up quickly, fighting to catch her breath. As the paroxysm ended, she straightened her back, catching sight of herself in a mirror hung from the back of the bathroom door. Her eyes were tearing; her hair, first blown in the wind, then tangled underneath her as she lay in the unmade bed, made her look like a cartoon crazy lady. She wiped her eyes with the palms of her hands and smoothed her hair, then got up and found her brush and brushed her hair for a long time before checking her image in the mirror again. She decided that even at her worst, she did not look forty-nine. Early forties, but not almost fifty. Maybe mid-forties, if she was having a bad day, but still attractive. And James had come back to her. As he pointed out, he had never left. He had slept with some woman at work a few times—a few times, meaning exactly three—three times, and the last time, according to him, he had begun to cry and had broken it off, and as soon as the unnamed woman—she did not want to know the woman's name—as soon as the woman stopped calling and hanging up two or three or, sometimes, four times a night, their life would be back to normal. She would be a woman who worked as a docent at the art museum and who taught needlework workshops on weekends and who sometimes stretched out on a hotel lounge while her husband fished. She thought that they had "retired" to Florida too early. Yes, the climate was nice, but the whole state was full of malcontents, dropouts, oldsters she had nothing in common with . . . except that, sadly, she did have something in common with quite a few of the women: women who developed myopia defensively, perfecting their techniques with needle and thread as someone, or something else spun a larger web in which they struggled. Since everything that happened happened whether or not she was the center of the universe, it was a waste of time, and verged on paranoia, to personalize everything. In a grand drama, you could always claim the central role, but if you saw life more realistically, as being a parade of extras who'd reported routinely for work, always a little too early in the morning, your own suffering, and even your triumphs, were not so significant. Applause did not routinely follow the acts of one's life. That tired old idea of life as a play. The only problem was that there was a script, but you might be assigned to play any role at any time. You might have a different role depending on the day. One day, a young woman who got involved with married men. The next, the middle-aged wife whose husband slept with younger women. Well, that script was pretty well thumbed. Also, the theme music always played in your head. At the moment, it was in conflict with the music coming from one of the maids' radios. Christmas music was playing as the maid opened the door, quickly said, "Sorry," and backed out of the room. The music had been "Frosty the Snowman."

Three o'clock. Just the time for tea. Or four. Four o'clock. Did people drink tea into cocktail hour? Or was five o'clock a little early for cocktails? When she checked again at five, Aunt Rose was neither inside the restaurant, nor outside, where tables and chairs faced the gulf. Maybe at the last minute she'd decided to join the men on the boat. Why would she want to have tea with a total stranger, any more than that stranger would want to have tea with her? She might be out on the boat, pulling in grouper, yellowtail, rebaiting her hook. Why assume that Aunt Rose was a little blue-haired lady teetering along for the trip? Maybe she had better sense than to hang around a half-empty hotel on Christmas, watching people in antlers serve tourists iced tea with candy-cane swizzle sticks. Maybe she was enjoying a slug of Jack Daniel's—that was Hetherly's drink of choice. Maybe, instead of being an arthritic hobbler, she was as adventurous as a one-legged pirate, come aboard to make mayhem and to over-throw the party. Roy Lichtenstein does Classic Comics: "Stand back or I'll halve you with my sword!"

Across the restaurant she saw the blond boy, asleep, leaning on his mother's arm. The mother and another woman were having something to eat at one of the booths. Here were tired people at the end of the day: parents and children; insignificant moments that nevertheless tugged at the heart, played against a backdrop of hotel employees, already foreign to these shores, metamorphosed for a day into harmless animals cavorting among easily amused tourists.

She debated between ordering a glass of wine or a pot of tea and decided to have the wine. What was all this preoccupation with tea? She never had tea. She preferred coffee, but it was too late in the day for coffee. She ordered white wine, making her selection on the basis of which wine was most expensive.

When Aunt Rose came into the restaurant through the sliding glass doors that opened from the pool area, she recognized her immediately. For one thing, there was a strong family resemblance with the high brows and the hooded eyes, but most of all, she recognized her from her fatigue. The sleepy eyes might have been part of it, but both Hetherly and Aunt Rose had the same slumped shoulders atop ramrod-straight spines. It was as if they were larger people than they should be, so they had found a way to accommodate.

"I was having a facial. Forgive me if I'm late. Also, forgive me for appearing without makeup. I couldn't see the point in having all that steaming, just to put on foundation," Aunt Rose said.

No hello? No explanation of how she'd decided to approach this table, instead of the one where a small blond woman ate alone, no clue about how she knew what she looked like?

"There was a time when I thought you'd be my niece," Aunt Rose said. "I imagine there was a time when you thought that, too, though no one really thinks about families when they're joining lives with another person, do they?"

She wanted to think that the woman was astonishing, but actually, once past her initial surprise, it seemed she had known her forever. It was as if two old friends had gotten together to communicate with gestures and brief expressions.

"I tried to find out what room you were in. You didn't leave me your room number. And I'm embarrassed to say that I don't know your last name," she said.

"You don't? It's Cornwell. That why he calls me 'Corny.'"

"He's always called you 'Aunt Rose' to me."

The woman shrugged. "Well—he's not much on establishing intimacy, and if he does, I suppose he doesn't let anyone else in on it," she said. To the waiter, she said: "Earl Grey tea, please, no milk, and I'm not English, but I'd appreciate it, anyway, if the water was boiling, not just hot."

The waiter nodded his antlers and walked away.

"The English can really be insufferable," Aunt Rose said.

"Have you spent a lot of time in England?" she asked.

"I married an Englishman," Aunt Rose said. "Much ado about the tea."

"Oh. You lived in England."

"No. They all love to live elsewhere. Meet them all over the place. We had a small place in Devon that we went to for a few months in the summer. A lovely old stone house. I miss it and I miss my husband, although I'd appreciate it if you didn't offer your condolences. It's all I can do to get through Christmas in the first place. It's been twenty years since he died."

"Hetherly—" She corrected herself: "Did Miles visit you in England as a boy?"

The woman looked at her. She was studying her, but not in an unkind way.

"He came once and it was a disaster. He's come to like the water, apparently, but when he was young you'd have thought every raindrop was there to bring him personal misery."

The waiter put the teapot and the unasked-for pitcher of milk in front of Aunt Rose. He placed a little sugar bowl carefully between them. She had not touched her wine, beyond taking the first sip. As he walked away, Aunt Rose said: "You know, I think there was a real-life story about a woman wearing white gloves who went out to hang up her wash and got shot by trigger-happy hunters, but it might be like the dog in the microwave. An urban legend, I mean. Some of the people who live in my building believe all of them. They think their son really knew someone who tried to dry the toy poodle in the microwave. Things like that."

She took a sip of her wine. "I feel terrible if you stayed away from the pool all day just because you thought you'd intrude on my vacation," she said.

"I needed a facial," Aunt Rose said, gesturing with her fingertips to her cheeks. "That, and talking on the phone to relatives and friends. Very difficult to get connected on Christmas."

"It is," she said.

"I promise not to dwell on this, but I've always been so curious: was he always just carrying a torch for you, or was there a real possibility you might have become a couple?"

So James—James, whom she wanted to disbelieve; James whom she wanted to disregard—had been right. She looked into Aunt Rose's eyes. "What makes you think he was carrying a torch?"

"He wrote you so many letters. I'd visit him, when I still flew places, and there would be letters in progress all over the place. Don't tell me he didn't at least mail some of them."

"Letters? Only in answer to mine. During the war," she added.

"It's still going on," Aunt Rose said.

"Writing me letters?" she said. She spoke to him two or three times a year. She never even got a postcard. He'd never sent a birthday card.

"Oh, that. No, I wouldn't know about that. I meant the war. In a manner of speaking, only, of course. Anyone who'd been there would take as much offense as the Holocaust survivors take when the Holocaust is brought up as a metaphor for general inhumanity," she said. "What I meant was: look at that parachute coming down over there, over that odd little island that seems to be nothing but trees, and the waiters—" She lowered her voice. "The waiters in their silly costumes, which they're wearing because they want to keep their jobs, of course. They'd do whatever they were told, poor things. And all those sirens. Have you heard them? They've been incessant, like the whole town's burning."

It was true. She had heard them all day, far in the distance.

"I've always liked that expression, 'for the sake of argument.' No Brit ever says that, you know. They just argue. But Americans always try to diffuse the animosity by claiming they're just doing something for the fun of doing it. Anyway: *for the sake of argument,* though it's peacetime, there are certain things that seem to be there as reminders: the parachutes and all the boats in the water and the young people I saw coming into town, wearing combat boots and camouflage outfits. With blue hair, I'll grant you, and they've pierced their bodies themselves, but still: it does remind one of terrible things that can happen during captivity."

"There was never anything romantic between us," she said. "I was engaged to someone else before James and I got together. I was engaged in college. All during the war. During the time I wrote to him."

"You were? He never told me that. Of course, what I know is just what I learned from Maude. She was so bitter toward the end. They were trying to adopt, and there he was, having an affair, right under her nose, with the same college girl she'd hoped to hire to help her care for the baby. Babies, as it turned out." Aunt Rose finished her tea. "I know that problems in a marriage are never caused entirely by one person, but it was hard for me to understand what he wanted, if he didn't want Maude. She'd gone back to school to get her master's degree, and she was such a hard-working, nice person. I came right out and asked him what he wanted, if he didn't want Maude, and do you know what he said? He told me that he wanted to sleep without anybody's cold feet touching his legs. I would have taken a fistful of ice cubes to bed and rammed those into his you-know-what, if my husband had been carrying on that flagrantly."

"He probably couldn't explain himself."

"He was so bitter when he came home and people weren't throwing themselves at him, giving a big parade for him for being such a hero. I know you must remember that. He drank a lot, and I'd never known him to drink before the war. Apparently Maude hadn't been opposed to the war, like so many people her age. I think that was one thing that attracted him to her, but at the same time, I think he deeply resented it."

"I didn't know Maude very well. James and I were living in Chicago during most of their marriage. I think we had dinner together a couple of times, when we got to New York. The four of us."

"She was a nice woman. She behaved very decently, I think."

"And by now your grandchildren must be . . . what? Seven or eight?"

"Nine and a half."

"That's good," she said, realizing that she sounded inane. She had never gotten to know the children at all.

"Maude remarried. A man with a child of his own. An older child. In college now."

"That's good," she said again.

"She always thought that when they separated, he was going after you."

"Me? But he was having an affair with someone else."

"Maude thought that was just Miles's way of passing time until he could get the real thing."

"Well," she said, "there was never anything like that between us."

"I certainly believe you. Anyway, after all this time he'd be crazy not to realize you're a happily married woman."

"I'm not," she said. "My husband is having an affair." She did not use the past tense. She did not even think before she spoke. In the moment she spoke the words, she was again an unhappily married woman whose husband was having an affair.

Aunt Rose leaned into the table. "Unless he's incapable of telling the truth, that's over," she said.

"Excuse me?"

"Miles reported to me that he said it was over and that he regrets it very much."

"He told Miles?"

"Well, they're close friends, aren't they?"

"No," she said honestly.

"They aren't? But he has something to say about James every time I talk to him. He always has news of James."

This was puzzling information. She caught sight of a parachute and watched the little black figure against the blue sky, drifting. From where she sat, the boat that pulled the parachute was not visible.

"He says you're all going to London in the spring. Surely, people who aren't close don't get together to spend a week in London and then go on to—"

"Wait a minute," she said. "Wait a minute. I don't know anything about London."

For the first time, Aunt Rose looked flustered. "Oh, I'm awfully sorry if I've ruined some lovely surprise. I must have, but nobody told me it was a secret. *Please* don't let on that I've told you—or would that be asking too much?"

"London?" she echoed. "But I teach. I do volunteer work. The work can't be dropped whenever I want just because I volunteer. I wouldn't have time to go to London."

"Oh, dear," Aunt Rose said. "Wash my mouth out with soap."

"Rose—you're sure that I'm part of these plans?"

"Well, I *thought* so," Aunt Rose said.

They looked at each other. In the distance, sirens wailed. From the booth, the mother she had seen earlier at poolside rose, holding her sack-of-potatoes son, her purse clasped against his back and walked bow-legged out of the restaurant, struggling with the boy's weight.

"The dead," Aunt Rose said, looking over her shoulder.

"Excuse me?" she said again.

"My war analogy," Aunt Rose said. "It looked like that woman was carrying someone who was dead."

"But it was just her son. Sleeping," she said, her voice going a little shrill on the last word.

"Well, I know that, dear. I'm just following through with my analogy."

"But if we see it as a war . . . I mean, earlier today I was thinking of life as a play, but to me, that's a warning that I'm spinning out of control, that I'm seeing things in a particular way to make all the craziness more containable."

"I suppose that's exactly what I'm doing," Aunt Rose said, pouring more tea into her cup.

"But it's just—it's just inside our heads. We can't take charge of the chaos. You're right: this place is strange and noisy, and it doesn't seem like Christmas, it doesn't seem *at all* like Christmas, and what you've just told me, really, is that my husband and my friend are a lot closer than I ever imagined, and I don't know what to make of that."

"I'm awfully sorry," Aunt Rose said quietly.

"But what *does* it mean?" she said.

"In wartime, strange conditions apply, I've always been told."

"I don't understand what you're saying," she said. "This isn't wartime."

"Oh, dear, I really have upset you. I'm really so sorry. I never for a moment thought I knew anything you didn't know. Maybe it's been planned as a surprise. Don't you think?" Aunt Rose put her fingers to her chin, lowering her voice. "He finds your husband quite remote, he was telling me. He thinks he's becoming more and more withdrawn, and of course no one likes that. Then again, maybe he's just exercising restraint. What should a friend say to Miles, when there's too much drinking. Too many women. Too much time off from work. I don't kid myself about his being a dutiful nephew; if I didn't live in Florida, he wouldn't be so keen on seeing me. He never visits all summer long, from May until November. As I'm sure you know, he rarely sees his own sons, in Minnesota."

"Why do you think he agreed to go through with the adoption?" she said, eager to focus on some issue that didn't pertain to her. "It seemed wrong of both of them to proceed, when they knew they were going to end the marriage."

"Maude is an heiress. She bought him off," Aunt Rose said. "She couldn't have children, so she got things in the works and then she bought him off."

"An heiress? An heiress to what?"

"What on earth would that matter?" Aunt Rose said.

For the first time, she had the feeling that she was being too gullible. She thought it was perfectly possible that the woman was having a little malicious fun, seeing how credulous a listener she'd found. Her intuition suddenly told her—a lightening of her heartbeat told her—that something wasn't right.

"An heiress to *what*?" she persisted.

"Well, since I don't understand machines, I don't really grasp what exactly the family did. Something with microchips. Something patented back in the sixties, I think."

Take it easy, she told herself. Don't ask too many questions, but don't stop talking, either. She had read, somewhere, that that was a helpful tactic for victims of kidnapping. She thought she recalled that you were supposed to follow the kidnapper's lead, though you should try not to ever stop talking entirely.

"So you see Maude fairly often? Maude and the grandchildren?"

"Not all that often, but we talk on the phone."

"I'm sure you'd like it if they lived closer," she said, after a long pause.

"What grandmother wouldn't," Aunt Rose said.

"Wouldn't you technically be their great-aunt?"

"Yes, I would, technically. But since I had so much to do with Miles's upbringing, he's always said he considered me a second mother. So when the children came along, I was given the honorific of 'grandma.'"

"How did you happen to have so much to do with his upbringing?" she asked.

Aunt Rose put her teacup down. There was sudden hatred in her eyes. "Because I went to them, when they didn't come to me," she said. "I intended to have some semblance of family life. My own husband was infertile due to radiation exposure. That was the worst heartbreak of my marriage. But I made the best of it. I gave my love to my sister's boy, and it was a good thing I did, because I was able to guide him away from some of her bad influences. His mother, Harriet. You knew she was an alcoholic."

"Really?" she said. If she was wrong—if she was way off track—it was cruel of her to have persisted with the old lady.

"She certainly was," Aunt Rose said. As she picked up her teacup, her hand wavered slightly. "It's traumatic to remember those years. Though they keep coming back to me, whatever I do to try not to relive them."

"Post-traumatic stress disorder," she said. She took a certain bemused pride in continuing the old lady's war analogy. "Nightmares. Feeling caught in a time warp."

"How do you know about such things?"

"Everyone's read about the aftereffects of war," she said.

The waiter appeared at their table. "Anything else for you ladies?" he said.

"No thank you. That's all," she said. As she spoke, she realized that she would have to converse with Aunt Rose, now, until James and Hetherly returned. She was going to have quite a few questions for James when he got back. How much she wanted to confront Hetherly with she would have to think about.

"It was delightful to meet you," Aunt Rose said, clasping her hand, suddenly formal. "I hope you'll forgive me for ruining their surprise. People get old, and they just blunder along. Half the time you don't even know you've done something wrong."

"It wasn't wrong. They should have told you, if it was a secret."

"Merry Christmas and happy New Year," the waiter said, dropping a few red-and-green foil-wrapped Hershey's Kisses on their table with the check.

She opened the folder and signed the bill. "Shall we?" she said to Aunt Rose.

"I think I may have another cup of tea, but you go on," Aunt Rose said.

Could she really be free? "You're sure?" she said.

"Oh yes. I like to watch it get dark. Quite the opposite of

what our troops think, fighting a war," she said. She raised her eyebrows slightly, smiling. "The dark gives the enemy better opportunities," she said.

On the way to her room, she thought that the old lady didn't know anything more about war than she did: what she read in the paper; what books told you; movies. Or, in some cases, first-hand reports. She, herself, had no first-hand report on Vietnam because Hetherly, alone among her friends at the time, had been the only one who'd volunteered. He'd volunteered, though every other boy she knew, every single one, had somehow dodged the draft.

In the elevator, listening to "O Come, All Ye Faithful," she wondered, for the first time, why he *had* volunteered.

The room had been made up, but the curtains weren't drawn. She went to the window and looked at the darkening sky. No more parasailers. No stars, either. It was a very black sky. She stared at it for a while. James was off having his fun. Buddy-buddy with the person he always took pains to remark was *her* friend. London? Surely Aunt Rose would know that if that was a total fabrication, with one single question she'd be found out. So who would risk lying that way? What if they really were going to London?

It seemed more likely, though, that the two of them might be going to London alone. But how peculiar. Why not meet in New York and see some plays? Pubs, theater, museums—New York had everything London had. Except that it wasn't far, far away. If it was New York, of course she could arrange for a weekend away. That would be no big deal. That was it: not that London, itself, was so important, but that they could ditch her. *Completely* paranoid, she told herself, sitting on the bed. Just because he had a fling with a woman he now admitted was obnoxious, she'd concocted a scenario in which a casual friend of hers and her husband were going off together to carouse and to act like silly boys together. They were both too dour, really. Weren't they both a little dour—Hetherly with his defeated, stooped shoulders and James with his self-containment? Not seeing the family at Christmas was a big liberation for James. Going fishing was a major thrill.

Fishing in the dark?

She drew the curtain, so the darkness wouldn't seem so insistent. It was perfectly possible that Aunt Rose was confused. Like the rest of the world, she'd probably gotten some things right and some things wrong. Maybe Hetherly had hatched the London plan and she'd been misled, thinking he'd communicated everything to her, and to James. Or maybe it was someone else: maybe someone else she knew would be going to London.

She found the room depressing. It was dark, though, so they'd be back any minute. She got up and picked up the remote control. She did not click on Power, though; she sat back on the bed. What if Hetherly had secretly carried a torch for her all these years? What if he was waiting? And if he led her husband astray, if the marriage collapsed, if James fucked one more person one more time . . . but that would be Machiavellian. Horrible. And why would he think she'd run into his arms, anyway? It made no sense. She was thinking of her friend, *her* friend, as he was so often called with a trace of annoyance, as monstrous. He wouldn't do a thing like that, would he? Might someone who'd been to war—might someone who saw life in terms of actions fought, battles won or lost—might Aunt Rose have been picking up his preoccupations, rather than reciting her own? Thinking of the world as a war zone would be peculiar, for a little old lady. Is that why she was preoccupied with war? Because Hetherly was? Vietnam was the one thing you knew never to bring up with Hetherly—but maybe he was like a fat person who only ate in private. Maybe, alone, he wallowed in the war, relived it, had flashbacks, so that the last thing he'd allow his friends to do would be to intrude on his private hell, his hermetically sealed nightmare. He appeared one way, but in private, he was another. How unusual was that? Any more unusual than not telling your best friend, not telling your mother, that your husband had had an affair? It was easy to radiate STAY AWAY. You just had to forcefully communicate your desperation to people, making sure you masked it as certainty. You had to let them know that you'd take no prisoners.

She sat a while longer. She tried to imagine the boat docking. If it wasn't, what was it doing? Out of fuel? Sprung a leak? Her precious husband, endangered? Right. Like he'd been endangered those times he was ostensibly staying late at work. The woman's name was Ellen. How pathetic to pretend that she didn't know her name. She'd even met her, briefly. Met her husband, too. The four of them, being introduced on the sidewalk outside the building. Ellen. Ellen. Ellen.

She went down to the lobby—almost ran from the room, as if the room, itself, was poisoning her thoughts. A fat man and a thin woman were checking in. In the corner, a Christmas tree decorated with pink and white lights glowed. Tinsel was draped from the branches. At periodic intervals, the white lights blinked. On one of the rattan chairs, an older man, wearing a bright red tie and a straw cap, sat reading a magazine. "A very happy Christmas to you," he said brightly, as she passed. "Thank you. You, too," she said.

There was no one behind the concierge's desk. Outside, a taxi was discharging an Asian couple. The woman was short and had on stiletto heels. The man wore a navy blue suit. The cabdriver held open the door of the hotel for them, in the absence of a busboy, the lights of his cab blinking in the driveway.

"Excuse me," she said to the man behind the desk. "The charter boats—do they leave from some particular place?"

"Which one you thinking of?" the cabdriver interrupted, putting down a Vuitton bag at the Asian man's feet. In her hand, the woman held a hatbox.

"Which boat? The *Treasure Trove*." She remembered, because there was a jewelry store she liked by that name near the museum. She had once bought a watch strap there.

"Garrison Bight," the cabdriver said. "The *Treasure Trove*'s a local boat. The private ones that come in this time of year, I don't know the first thing about them," he added.

"How far is that?" she said. "That's where the boats come in? Garrison whatever?"

"Bight," he said. "Bite, like a dog." He bared his teeth. "Eight minutes."

"Great," she said. She followed him to his cab.

"Garrison Bight, comin' up," he said. The cab needed a brake job. The brakes squealed when he stopped suddenly as a bare-chested man in a Santa beard cut him off.

"My fuckin' brother," the cabdriver said. "He sat me down before I was old enough to toddle away and gave me the low-down on Santa."

"He told you he didn't exist?"

"That's what he told me. You got any information to the contrary?"

"No," she said. "Can't help you there."

"Well, that bastard went to jail for embezzlement," the cab-driver said. "He wasn't really my brother, anyway. He was some kid that lived with us for a while when my mother took a shine to the owner of the gas station."

She said nothing. The houses were decorated with tiny lights that looked like icicles. Across the rails of the top porch of a Victorian was the outlined shape of a jumping shark. A block or so later, she noticed red lights outlining a huge cactus in someone's front yard.

"I never ask my passengers where they're from," the cab-driver said. "My girlfriend says that's strange. But they tell you, and it's probably a place you've never been, right? Somebody tells me, 'Reno, Nevada,' what should that mean to me?"

"You don't travel much?" she said.

"I belong to the greatest frequent flyer program of all," he said. "Astral projection." The cab went through a yellow light. "Yeah, that's the way to travel."

In another minute or so she saw a boatyard on both sides of the road. "That slip right there, by that *Dusty Dancer*? That's where the *Treasure Trove* docks. Out late tonight. I presume you want to disembark?"

"Yes," she said. She paid him and got out. A strong breeze was blowing. There was a wooden sign on a post sunk into the cement marked *Treasure Trove*. In the space next to it, another boat bobbed in the water. It didn't seem that anyone was on any of the boats, though she didn't know what she'd say if she did see someone. *Hey: Can you tell me the truth about my husband and a friend of mine? Do you tell fortunes, or are you just standing around on a boat?* The light changed and a motorcycle zoomed onto the road, voices screaming into the wind. She turned to see the two riders disappear. She walked forward and sat on the grass behind the sidewalk, feet stretched in front of her. Five minutes or ten minutes passed, and then, eventually, in the distance, she saw lights, and not long after that, what she assumed might be the *Treasure Trove*. As it grew larger, she felt sure that it was.

Unexpectedly, it emitted a low bleep—fast and rude, like a fart. Voices floated over the water. Laughter. Wild, merry laughter. It was a good-size boat.

She sat there all the time it took for the boat to slowly pull in. She watched men moving around on deck. In some ways, the scene in front of her didn't seem to really be happening, though it was vivid, like a movie. What boat materialized almost instantly, as if her wish was its command? It was a variation of her wondering, as she sometimes did, such as when she'd caught sight of herself earlier, in the hotel mirror: *who is this person?* She could hear everything everyone said. She could see the squealing, squirming dancers: bright-haired women dressed as mermaids. The costumes were made of green sequins that flashed like neon against the black backdrop of the sky. One woman was not dressed as a mermaid: she wore only a Santa hat, pasties on her nipples, and a G-string. Someone was laughing loudly, grabbing her around the hips. "No more room at the manger! Let's relocate this party elsewhere, my friends," a man's voice called. Music was turned on and quickly turned off. People began to disembark. People paid no attention to her. It was as if she'd become invisible. "You need a ride? Hey, you need wheels?" one man called. "Meet you at Teasers! Hey! Meet you at Teasers!" came another voice. James and Hetherly were not among those who were screaming. Between them, they half dragged, half held up a drunken mermaid. If the mermaid had been Hetherly's war buddy, he would have been accomplishing a noble, noble deed. Though James helped him—as much as he was able; he was stumbling almost as badly as the mermaid—Hetherly bore the brunt of the load. Out of the battle, into new territory. Across the field she'd later realize had been filled with fire ants—in the moments before she realized she'd been swarmed, that they'd attacked so quickly, there was nothing she could have done—in those moments, she'd been so focused on asking the two drunken fools in front of her whether they ever intended to take her with them to London that she'd tuned out her own pain.

What did they expect from her, standing there, bobbing like they were still aboard a wave-tossed ship, the mermaid so drunk that in spite of their support she'd gone down on her knees? Here was the treasure of the *Treasure Trove*. Here they were, taken aback for a second in the midst of their midlife crises.

Hetherly's eyes were wide with horror. He was sure that he had met the enemy. And James looked . . . leering. He leered so peculiarly that she was transfixed by his slack-jawed expression, though when his eyes went out of focus his expression changed entirely. She watched as Hetherly grabbed the mermaid more tightly, tipping her body toward his. The mermaid flopped life-lessly. And she might have bought it—she might have believed that it was Hetherly's mermaid, except that, with an unexpected surge of strength, the woman wrenched herself the other way, reaching out to James. Worse even than that was that he let her go. Let her slip to the ground. Was going to leave Hetherly to deal with it, while he began his lying explanation to her, trying to explain away what she'd seen. Hetherly, at least, had the decency to pull the mermaid up. He stayed to see that the mer-maid was settled in another passenger's arms.

The hazard lights blinking at the side of the road belonged to the same cabdriver. He got out and gestured, waving his arm for them to come into the cab. "Whew," he said, as they approached, and told them to keep the windows down in the back. What he thought of her predicament—why he'd come back, what he thought of any of it—she could not imagine. As she sat squeezed between James and Hetherly, increasingly conscious that something was very wrong with her—that she hadn't just gotten a few bug bites, that there was something terribly, painfully wrong: a fire that had begun to consume her from the legs up—she found herself concentrating on what the cabdriver had said earlier. He was right, and she believed him totally. It didn't matter if this was happening in Key West, Florida, or in Reno, Nevada.

Cat People

Mrs. Eugenie Nestor and her husband, Old Nestor, live next door to us in Key West, behind a tall bamboo fence with several shoebox-size rectangles cut in it so their cats can prowl in our yard. Key West has changed a lot during the twenty years my husband and I have been renting a winter house here. For one thing, these days you can throw away your alarm: if it's not the crashing clatter of the recycling truck twice a week—this beast can come at three in the morning, by the way—it's the daily whine of buzzsaws. No one needs an alarm anymore. The renovation has drowned out the roosters, machines screech more piercingly than any of the birds, and motorcycles let you know how frustrated the riders feel, having to zig and zag through so much traffic. The main street, Duval, is, during the height of the tourist season, entirely blocked off, being bulldozed and jackhammered. Everyone takes the next street over, Simonton, which means traffic pours by day and night. My husband refuses to drive the car and has even abandoned his bicycle because of the many ruts in the road, and because tourists have recently been reaching out their windows to try to topple the cyclists. It's a new sport, malevolent, but a direct response, people think, to the number of cyclists who frighten them by riding at high speeds on the right and sideswiping them or cutting them off. Yesterday I saw a woman in a convertible using a shopping bag like a big flyswatter. You used to see amusing, interesting things in Key West: men riding along in bikini trunks with their dogs in baskets on the front of their bikes, or adults pulling other adults in wagons on the sidewalk. And the gay people were quite flamboyant; leftover masks from Fantasy Fest might appear pushed to the top of their heads like one of those old lady pancake hats, or they'd wear masks on the street, nothing particular going on except that they were escorting some friend in chains down Duval, and the one who wasn't bound in chains would have on a miniskirt with a tee-shirt with something outrageous written on it, and over his eyes, a mask made of peacock feathers. AIDS took its toll in the '80s, though, and now most of the birds are in the trees, or snatching expensive goldfish out of people's little garden pools. Yesterday my husband saw a crane walking up the steps of a recently opened gift shop. Amazed tourists were giggling and gawking and photographing it. The storekeeper said, "Let it come in. Maybe it has a credit card."

Inevitably, the Conch Republic has changed. Even the conch is now imported. The tourists still come in droves and hurtle around the island on a big caterpillar with an awning called the Conch Train. My husband and I hear the punch line of a recorded joke as it passes, about every half hour. One of the drivers moonlights for my husband, coming on Monday and Wednesday nights to stand in our pool with some other models, clothed and unclothed. He recites the canned jokes to make them groan, and they roll their eyes or splash water on him. My husband understands that modeling can be very boring, and he expects to be talked to, but pretty quickly the models understand they won't be getting much feedback except for an occasional "Pardon me?" or "You think so?" Inevitably, the models who have been in analysis come to love my husband. If he could remember ten percent of what they tell him, I could spend my whole life amazed by people's bizarre lives and problems. Lem Rupert is not only a Conch Train driver, but also a weekend waitperson, as well as part-time model. Lem grew up in Wales, in a little place called Hay-on-Wye, which he calls Ham-on-Rye. Apparently the place is famous for its bookstores; some shops are so large they spill out onto the street and only awnings keep the books from getting rained on. Lem's mother was a maid in one of the inns and his father was away at sea for most of the years Lem was growing up. Lem has a sister, Daphne, who also models for my husband when she needs extra money. Like her mother, she works in a hotel, but it's the Hyatt in Key West: quite large and new and grand. Daphne has auburn hair and a ruddy complexion that my husband has speculated may be protective coloration, a way of disappearing while working in a big hotel that is primarily pink.

Last Wednesday night my husband had the two of them posing in the pool, Daphne on a raft, Lem holding a palm frond and pretending to be fishing out leaves, when Old Nestor had what my husband calls "an episode" with one of the cats. The cats seem to disappoint him in many ways. They do something that makes him bang a spoon on a pan—that is the very worst cat punishment for all of us—though other times the Nestors throw fruit or simply clap their hands and curse. But this night the orange cat did something that really set Old Nestor off. Even from inside the house, I could hear distinctly the metallic beat of the tom-tom, with Old Nestor's wife shrieking in falsetto. A banana was the first thing to end up in our pool, followed by the orange cat's darting through one of the shoebox holes in a state of wild agitation, making a mad dash so intense that it overshot the yard entirely and ended up in the water. An apple and several starfruit flew after it, and the apple smacked Daphne on the head, causing her to scream as she toppled off the raft into the pool. To make matters worse, the orange cat was terrified and attempted to scramble up Daphne, which was the first time anyone realized quite how afraid of cats Daphne was, though anyone might have been afraid of some wildly circling animal in fear for its life, with its eyes bugging and its claws extended. As I understand it, Lem was immediately possessed of enormous strength—such a surge of power that he dismantled part of the fence with his bare hands, and clomped into the Nestors' yard cursing every bit as obscenely as Eugenie and Old Nestor. Meanwhile, Daphne was shrieking in the pool, and the cat was swimming in circles around her like a shark, so my husband peeled off his shirt, stepped out of his sandals, and rushed into the water, swatting the cat toward the shallow end with the palm frond, where it quickly found the steps and clambered out. Daphne was in tears, really going crazy. She started whacking at Andy, accusing him quite irrationally of "offering no protection" or something like that, her hand on top of her head where the apple had hit it, the string on her bikini top having broken, so that she clutched one little triangle of fabric over one breast, while trying to elbow the other triangle over the other breast . . . well: it was pandemonium, and furthermore, the orange cat had run right through Andy's pallet, and there were blue pawprints everywhere. The cat's mad dash had triggered the other neighbors' new security system, so suddenly, amid the three-way cursing at the Nestors', a voice you knew did not originate from a human being, announced: "You have entered a secured area. You have five seconds to leave the premises." If the neighbors had been home, they could have come out to investigate, but they weren't home, so the alarm system went off, resulting in ear-splitting noise which only ended when the police arrived. They obviously knew the code and had no trouble deactivating the alarm, but in their haste, in the dark, they knocked over the birdcage, and the door opened and the Minichiellos' parrot flew off into the night, which made one of the cops completely exasperated and furious, as his partner laughed and laughed, grabbing hold of our back gate to keep himself upright. Then his eyes drifted to Daphne, with the string and triangles dangling around her neck, standing and screaming after Andy, because by then he, too, had disappeared into the Nestors' backyard. Though none of us knew it that moment, he had embarked on a plan to uproot every bush and tree he could find there that was without thorns.

"Fucking idle rich!" Daphne screamed, climbing out of the pool. "It's exploitation! Seven dollars an hour doesn't entitle you to slam-dunk me. I want that monster arrested. I want to press charges because he could have bloody well killed me, him with his rabid cat and his stinking bloody violence, I want whoever threw that rock *arrested!*"

"You miserable lowlife," Eugenie Nestor screamed. Which one of them she meant, I had no idea, but when an enormous bird-of-paradise plant was heaved over the fence into our yard, Old Nestor followed after it, through the newly broken fence, and as he attempted to scoop it up, Lem kicked him from behind and he went sprawling, and that was when the police finally did intervene—with the parrot staring down from high up in the palm tree, calling out: "Margaritaville! Margaritaville!" Like the bird, the laughing cop only got out individual words, but the address did get through, and within a matter of seconds there were sirens in the distance, and two police cars converged in front of our house, where Daphne now stood, topless, screaming that someone had tried to murder her. The upshot of it was that Old Nestor and Lem had to be restrained, and it took Andy quite a long time to disabuse the cops of the notion that a porn movie was being shot in the backyard. "Why do you keep asking when you don't see any camera?" Andy said repeatedly to the cop. "Look at this. Look here. This is what was happening, when our neighbors began throwing things after their cat. I was painting a painting. That's what I do for a living. I've been coming to Key West for twenty years. I'm a painter. I'm a painter." If he weren't so tall, he could have been mistaken for Elmer Fudd, jumping up and down. I was a great help in giving a balanced view of the whole situation. By ten P.M. they were gone—with Lem in custody, and Daphne weeping in a chair on our front porch, dabbing her eyes with a tee-shirt, saying that it was their father Lem had gotten his ungovernable temper from, and hadn't he been wonderful, going after the people who had tried to kill her? The Minichiellos' parrot had flown away. When Daphne stopped sniffling and put on her in-line skates to follow after Lem to the police station, we put on the evening news and took comfort in hearing how cold it was elsewhere.

On Thursday, quite unexpectedly, Eugenie Nestor appeared at the door, carrying a paper plate covered with Saran Wrap. "Father Donegan said you would let me in," she said. It took a moment to register. First of all, though I'd heard her screaming and beating pans for years, I'd rarely seen Eugenie Nestor, and when I had, she hadn't been wearing black wraparound glasses and a big sun hat with a calico bow. "Father said not to drown the kittens. To ask if you would take one. To ask all my neighbors," she said.

It registered. She had been to see the priest. He had told her—

"Bless you for enduring our struggles with the cats," she said. "I would like us to be friends. People should be friends with their neighbors, as Father says. He says there's a chance you might want one of the kittens. The Key lime cookies are a present, whether or not you care to take a kitten."

"You know, this is very nice of you, Mrs. Nestor," I said. "Please come in. Would you like an iced tea?"

"Do you have Coca-Cola?" she said, handing me the cookies. They slid around on the paper plate. There seemed to be only a few of them.

"Yes, I think we do. Come into the kitchen."

"This is a rental house, isn't it?" she said. "Very nice. I've looked through the fence. Of course, today that wouldn't be any problem, would it? My husband says the hole reminds him of *Ghostbusters*."

"We rent from a couple in Vero Beach."

"How would you feel about a cute kitten?" she asked, changing the subject.

"We don't have any pets. It would make it too difficult to travel," I said.

"Without ice, please," she said.

I poured the Coke into a glass. I poured some Perrier into a glass for myself.

"Father has taken one of the kittens," she said. "My husband's dentist might take one for his daughter. One way or another, I have to find people."

"An ad in the paper?" I suggested.

"He already drowned four. My husband, I mean. He said that regardless of what Father said, the cat was as much his as mine, and what he wanted to do with his four kittens was drown them." She cleared her throat. I moved toward the front porch. She followed. "Of my four, one has been spoken for, and there's a chance the dentist might take another."

I nodded.

"You wouldn't take one?" she said.

"I really can't, Mrs. Nestor. My husband and I travel a lot. It's very difficult to find places that will—"

"You can sneak them in," she said.

"Mrs. Nestor, I'm really not going to take one of the kittens. I realize you would like me to do that. But I'm not going to be able to."

"The Minichiellos are heartbroken about the parrot," she said. "They haven't heard about any sightings of it. They had that bird for years. They think it will die."

"That would be a shame," I said.

"I asked them to take a kitten, but she doesn't feel a kitten is a good replacement for a parrot that could count to fifteen. It always said good morning to her. She's heartbroken."

"I can understand that," I said.

"Father put up a note on the church bulletin board. It's been up for a week," she said. She had never taken off her black sunglasses. She had pushed the hat back on her head. She had drained her glass. She said: "The mother cat was upset he'd drowned the kittens. She knew it was him. She peed in his hammock."

"Perhaps we can talk another time," I said. "I have some things I need to do before it gets any later."

"Housework," she said.

"Errands," I said.

"If on your errands you think someone might be interested in a kitten, could I give you our phone number?"

"Absolutely," I said.

"We're in the book, but people are too lazy to look. You'd have to give the number to them," she said.

"Let me get a piece of paper," I said.

"And a pen," she said.

I went into the kitchen, forcing myself to be patient. Soon she would be gone.

"I was a lapsed Catholic," she said. "I regret those years away from the church."

"Just jot down your phone number," I said. "And thank you for the cookies."

"Do you think there's any chance you'll change your mind?" she said.

"No," I said.

"Because if you do, you could call over the fence. Or just walk through the broken part and let me know."

"I won't change my mind," I said.

She put her face in her hands and began to cry, using the piece of paper she'd written her number on as a tissue. "Nobody ever changes their mind," she said. "My husband hasn't changed his mind once in forty years. He said he hated cats when we got married. I gave away my cat. Then when we moved to Florida a cat followed me home one day and I thought he'd change his mind, because it was such a pretty cat. But he didn't change his mind about that cat or about any of the others. For forty years, he's drowned kittens. What do they say? 'Always a bridesmaid, never a bride.' With me, it's always a cat, never any kittens." She wiped tears from her eyes. She said: "I agreed with that woman who was screaming the other night. She came here to give us a message, do you realize that? She was sent from on high with a message. It's true: no one protecting anyone else. It's my right to have kittens if I want them, but would anyone protect my rights? Nobody would. Father says give away the kittens because my husband will drown them. I don't even know if they're alive now. I could go home and find them all in a bucket."

"Mrs. Nestor," I said, "this is not anything I can help you with. Do you understand?"

"You're a monster," she said. "Some people aren't cat people, they're dog people. I can understand that. But you—you're just selfish. You just want to travel. It's what that woman said. That woman was an angel, who'd come to speak to you. Did you hear her say that you were the idle rich? You are. You and your husband are monsters. You have friends who go on rampages, and you turn them loose like wild beasts, like other people's yards were the jungle. My plants were all pulled up. The same day he drowned the kittens, my whole yard was destroyed. You are horrible, violent, selfish people. I never want to see you again."

"That's wonderful," I said. "All you'll have to do is leave, then."

"Where can I find that angel?" Mrs. Nestor said.

"Cleaning rooms at the Hyatt, as a matter of fact. Go home and call the Hyatt and ask to speak to the angel Daphne Rupert. She works the afternoon shift. You can reach her."

Which she did, and here is what followed: Daphne exited a recently cleaned room, having no idea Eugenie Nestor was the one who had left three kittens in an Easter basket with a towel draped over the handle. It was there, wedged between the miniature shampoos and the rolls of toilet paper: a purple and pink wicker basket with three kittens curled inside. She took it to the manager's office, and the manager of course couldn't understand it, except that she knew a dirty trick had been played on the hotel. Daphne felt there was some suspicion that she knew more than she did—that perhaps they were even *her* kittens, which she was trying to foist off on the Hyatt. Well: thank God it was not a baby; they had all agreed on that. Really, it could have been much worse if a baby had been abandoned on the cleaning cart. The whole episode upset Daphne so much she blurted out the whole story to Andy, who had given her an extra two hours pay for the trauma she had undergone and who was therefore now back in her good graces, painting her floating in the pool in a new bikini he had reimbursed her for—a rather nice little blue-and-white checked cotton suit. He was able to be amazed, and to listen sympathetically, because I had told him nothing about Eugenie Nestor's visit. He'd been teaching at the community college, and when he came home I was on the phone, and by the time I was off, Daphne was in place in the pool, and I could hear, through the open window, that she was telling him a story that wasn't all that surprising to me. She thought something had been fated, though she barely understood what. Just a sense she had, she told Andy: first the cat jumping in the pool and circling, circling. Then, coming out of a room and seeing something on top of her cart that turned out to be kittens. She was no kitten lover, but one of the cooks at the hotel had taken a fancy to one of them, and the manager had taken the other two to her vet, who had agreed to try for a week to place them, before turning them over to the animal shelter. On and on Daphne went, about how peculiar she found life in Key West. "I want to go to Tortola next year instead of coming here," I heard Andy say wearily. The fence had been repaired by the gardener, who was very handy. Things were again calm at the home of Eugenie and Old Nestor. He was probably in his hammock, the orange cat having forgiven him—where else was she going to live?—curled in his lap. Eugenie was probably in the kitchen, baking another three (it turned out to be only three) cookies. I thought about the many places Andy and I had traveled during our marriage, and how many of those places had seemed magical, for a while. Key West lasted longer than most: the Atlantic breezes, the lush foliage, the amazing light that Andy captured so well, painting paintings that sold for enough money at the New York gallery that represented him that, by ordinary standards, we really had become the idle rich.

As I mulled over our good fortune, Lem passed by, driving the Conch Train. Once again, as he sped by, I caught the tail end of a joke dissipating in the breeze, like the string of a kite blowing quickly out of reach. I opened the front door and stood on the porch, looking at the bougainvillea spilling off a balcony across the way. Then I looked at two young men skating in sync, with their arms around each other, their bodies toned and tanned. Key West was a place that encouraged people to be childish, and I found that atypical, and delightful.

I was startled from my reverie when the Minichiellos' parrot began its countdown from the royal palm in the front yard. It was there! It had returned—or at least it taunted with the possibility of its return. It looked well, and seemed to be enjoying its freedom. Counting "one, two, three," it spoke looking directly at me, and then—though I may have seen too many Walt Disney movies—I would swear that it winked. The moment it said "fifteen" it flew away, having a more distinct idea than most of us when it should leave and perhaps even where it should fly.

The Women of
This World

———

THE DINNER was going to be good. Dale had pureed leeks and salsify to add to the pumpkin in the food processor—a tablespoon or so of sweet vermouth might give it a little zing—and as baby-girl pink streaked through the gray-blue sky over the field, she dropped a CD into the player and listened matter-of-factly to Lou Reed singing matter-of-factly "I'm just a gift to the women of this world."

Nelson would by now be on his way back from Logan, bringing Jerome and Brenda—who had taken the shuttle from New York, after much debate about plane versus train versus driving—for the annual (did three years in a row make something annual?) pre-Thanksgiving dinner. They could have come on Thanksgiving, but Nelson's mother, Didi, was coming that day, and there was no love lost between Didi and her ex-husband, Jerome. Brenda didn't like big gatherings anyway. Brenda was less shy than she used to be. She used to nap half the afternoon—Jerome said because she was shy—but lately her occupation as a gym teacher had become glamorous and she had quit teaching at the middle school and become a personal trainer, and suddenly she was communicative, energized, *radiant*—if that wasn't a cliché for women in love.

Dale turned on the food processor and felt relieved as the ingredients liquified. It wasn't that the food processor hadn't always worked—assuming she placed the blade in the bottom correctly, that is—but that she always feared it wouldn't work. She always ran through a scenario in which she'd have to scoop everything out and dump it in the blender, and the old Waring

149

Blender that had come with the house didn't always work. With blenders so cheap, she amazed herself by not simply buying a new one.

Jerome was not Nelson's father, but his stepfather. Nelson was forever indebted to the man for appearing on the scene when he was five years old, and staying until he was sixteen. Jerome had seen to it that Nelson was spared going to Groton, and had taught him to play every known sport—at least every ordinary sport. But would Nelson have wanted to learn, say, archery?

Nelson wanted to learn everything, though he didn't want to do everything. He wanted to do very little. He liked to know about things, though. That way, he could talk about them. Her mean nickname for him was No-Firsthand-Knowledge-Nelson. It got tedious sometimes: people writing down the names of books from which Nelson had gotten his often esoteric information. People calling after the party was over, having looked up some strange assertion of Nelson's in their kid's *Encyclopedia Britannica* to discover that he was essentially right, but not entirely. They often left these quibbles and refutations on the answering machine: "Dick, here. Listen, you weren't exactly right about Mercury. It's because Hermes means 'mediator' in Greek, so there *is* an element of logic to his taking the souls of the dead to the Lower World"; "Nelson? This is Pauline. Listen, Rushdie did write the introduction to that Glen Baxter book. I can bring it next time and show you. He really does write introductions all the time. Well, thanks to you both for a great evening. My sister really appreciated Dale's copying that recipe for her—though no one can make butterflied lamb like Dale, I told her. Anyway. Okay. Bye. Thanks again."

They would be twenty or thirty minutes away, assuming the plane landed on time, which you could never assume if you knew anything about Logan. Still: there was time for a quick shower, if not a bath, and she should probably change into a dress because it seemed a little oblivious to have people over when you were wearing sweats, even if you did have a cashmere sweater pulled over them. Maybe a bra under the sweater. A pair of corduroys, instead of the supercomfortable sweats. And shoes . . . definitely some sort of shoes.

Nelson called from the cell phone. "Need anything?" he said. She could hear Terry Gross's well-modulated, entirely reasonable voice on the radio. Only Nelson and Terry and her guest were talking in the car: all passengers silent, in case Dale had forgotten some necessary ingredient. *Yes, pink peppercorns. Try finding them on 95 North.* And of course they weren't really peppercorns, they were only called peppercorns because they looked like black peppercorns. Or: purple oregano. An entirely different flavor from green.

"Not a thing," she said. She added, disingenuously: "Thanks for checking."

She was wearing black corduroy pants and a white shirt. Keeping it clean would preoccupy her, give her some way to stay a little detached from everyone. In her way, she was shy, too. Though she wore bad-girl black boots.

"Brenda wants to see the Wedding Cake House. I thought we'd swing by. Would that mess up your timing?"

"I didn't cook anything," she said.

Silence, then. Mean of her, to set his mind scrambling for alternatives.

"Kidding," she said.

"I thought so," he said. "Well: what about it? Want to see it, yourself?"

"I've seen it," she said. She had toured it soon after they moved to the area. It was a yellow-and-white house in Kennebunkport, huge, with Gothic spires like pointed phalluses. Legend had it that it was the creation of a sea captain for his bride, to remind her of their wedding when he was off at sea.

"We'll be back around four."

Protests from Brenda. Someone else, talking to Terry Gross in a deep, earnest voice. "See you soon," he said. "Hon?" he said.

"Bye," she said. She picked up two bottles of red wine from the wine rack near the phone. A little too close to the heat grate, so no wine was kept on the last four shelves. Not a problem in summer, but a minor inconvenience come cold weather. She remembered that Brenda had been delighted with a Fumé Blanc she'd served last time, and bought the same bottle for her again. Jerome, of course, because of his years in Paris, would have the St. Emilion. Nelson had taken to sipping Jamison's lately. Still, she'd chilled several bottles of white, because he was unpredictable. On the top rack lay the bottle of Opus One an appreciative photography student had given her at Christmas. Two nights later, she planned to serve it to the doctor who had diagnosed both her hypoglycemia and her Ménière's disease, which meant, ironically, that she could no longer drink. If she did, she'd risk more attacks of the sickening vertigo that had plagued her and gone misdiagnosed for years, leaving her sweaty and trembling and so weak she'd often have to spend the day following the attack in bed. "Like taking acid and getting swept up in a tidal wave," she had said to the otolaryngologist. The woman had looked at her with surprise, as if she'd been gathering strawberries and suddenly come upon a watermelon. "Quite a vivid description," the doctor had said. "My husband is a writer. He sometimes stops me dead in my tracks the same way."

"Is he Brian McCambry?" Dale had asked.

"Yes," the doctor said. Again, she seemed surprised.

Nelson had been the one who speculated that Dr. Anna McCambry might be the wife of Brian McCambry. Dale, herself, had read only a few pieces by McCambry, though—as she told the doctor—Nelson had read her many others.

"I'll pass on the compliment," the doctor said. "Now back to the real world."

What a strange way to announce the transition, Dale had thought, though for her, her symptoms sometimes were the real world, crowding out any other concerns. What was more real than telescoping vision, things blurring and swarming you, so that you had no depth perception, no ability to stand. The doctor talked to her about alterations in her diet. Prescribed diuretics. Said so many things so fast that Dale had to call the nurse, later that afternoon, to be reminded what several of them had been. The doctor had overheard the call. "Bring your husband and come for drinks and I'll go over this with you while they talk," the doctor had said. "Drinks in your case means seltzer."

"Thanks," Dale said. No doctor had ever asked to see her out of the office. She wondered how common that was.

She opened the Fumé Blanc but left the bottle of St. Emilion corked. How did she know? Maybe Jerome would decide to go directly to the white French burgundy. What hadn't seemed fussy and precious before now did, a little: people and their wine preferences. Still, she indulged the vegetarians in their restrictions, knew better than to prepare veal for anyone, unless she was sure it wouldn't result in a tirade. Her friend Andy liked still water, her student Nance preferred Perrier. Her mind was full of people's preferences and quirks, their mystical beliefs and food taboos, their ways of asserting their independence and their dependency at table. The little tests: would there happen to be sea salt? Was there a way to adjust the pepper grinder to grind a little more coarsely? A call for chutney. That one had really put her over the top. There was Stonewall Kitchen's Roasted Onion and Garlic Jam already on the table. She had sent Nelson for the chutney, since Paul was more his friend than hers.

She went into the downstairs bathroom and brushed her hair, gathering it back in a ponytail. She took off the white shirt and changed back into her cashmere sweater, giving it a tug she knew she shouldn't give it to make sure it fell just right. She looked at her boots and wished it was still summer; she'd be more comfortable barefoot, but it wasn't summer, and her feet would freeze. She remembered that Julia Roberts had been barefoot when she married Lyle Lovett. Julia Roberts and Lyle Lovett: not as strange as Michael Jackson and Lisa Marie Presley.

Brenda entered full of enthusiasm about the trip to the Wedding Cake House. It was *amazing, beautiful,* somehow sort of *weird*— a little creepy, some woman living inside her wedding cake like the old woman who lived in a shoe. Then Brenda began apologizing: she had insisted they drive down the longest dirt road in history, to get a basket of apples. Nelson put the basket down on the kitchen island, which she'd soon need every inch of to do the final dinner preparations. She could no longer eat apples, or anything excessively sweet. She was sick of explaining to people what she couldn't eat, and why. In fact, she had started to say she was diabetic, since everyone seemed to know that that meant you couldn't eat sugar. There was also the possibility that the apples might be Brenda and Jerome's, to take back to New York, so she said, "Nice," rather than "Thank you."

It was a rented house, but the owners must have loved to cook. The kitchen was well laid out, with the exception of the dishwasher being to the left of the sink. Dale had become so adept at using her left hand to load the dishwasher that she thought it might be amusing to be both diabetic and left-handed. By the time she left the house, she might be an entirely different person.

"It's great to see you. Did you get my note? You didn't go to a lot of trouble, did you?" Jerome said, squeezing Dale, then letting go.

Brenda was still in a dither. "We didn't mess you up, did we?" she said.

"Not at all," Dale said.

"I shouldn't ask, but I've been cooped up in the plane, and then in the car. Would there be time to take a walk? A quick walk?"

"Sure," Dale said. She had just put the roast in the oven to bake. There was plenty of time.

"Would you mind if Nelson and I take a look at that wiring problem? I'm much better when there's natural light," Jerome said.

"Oh, he's on his kick again about how he can't see or hear!" Brenda said. She added, as if they didn't know. "He's *sixty-four*."

"What wiring problem?" Dale said. She wanted to be bare-foot. She wanted to be Julia Roberts, with a big, dazzling smile. Instead, she could feel the skin between her eyebrows tighten-ing. *Wiring problem?* The way Brenda talked got into her brain; in her presence, she started thinking in concerned italics.

"I was trying to hook up speakers in the upstairs hallway. I can get one of them going but not the other. Might be a bad speaker," Nelson said.

Nelson had spent a good portion of his book advance on new

sound equipment. Their compromise was that when people arrived, there would be no music. So far, the day had consisted of bluegrass, Dylan's first electric album, Japanese ceremonial music, an hour or so of *La Bohème,* and Astor Piazola. Dale had listened to the weather report and one cut from a Lou Reed CD that she imagined might be Jerome's theme song. She was fond of him, but he did think he was God's gift to women.

"You'll come, won't you?" Brenda said. She was wearing shoes that would have been inappropriate for a walk, if she hadn't been Brenda: brown pointy-toed boots with three-inch heels. This year's hip look, while Dale's had become the generic. Brenda had shrink-wrapped herself into a black leather skirt, worn over patterned pantyhose. On top was a sweater with a stretched-out turtleneck Dale thought must be one of Jerome's. He had kept his collection of French handknit sweaters for twenty-some years.

"Just down the road?" Dale said, gesturing to the dirt road that went past the collapsed greenhouse behind the garage. She liked the road. You could usually see deer this time of the evening. Also, because of the way the road dipped, it seemed like you were walking right into the sky, which had now turned Hudson River School radiant. Dale's friend Janet Lebow was the only year-rounder at the end of the road. When the nasty summer people left, taking their Dobermans and their shiny four-wheel drives with them, Janet was happy not only to let Dale walk the No Trespassing/Danger/Posted/Keep Out road, she usually sent her dog, Tyrone (who was afraid of the summer dogs), out to exercise with her. Janet was divorced, fifty going on twenty-five, devoted to tabloids, late-night movies, astrological forecasts, and "fun" temporary tattoos, of things like unicorns leaping over rainbows. She was not a stupid woman, only childish and traumatized—Dale presumed, by the marriage she never talked about. Tyrone was a smart golden retriever, black lab mix. When he wasn't in the tributary to the York River, he was wriggling in the field, trying to shed fleas. The dog and the kitchen were the two things Dale felt sure she would miss most when they had to vacate the house. They had it through the following summer, when the philosophy professor and his wife would return from their year in Munich. By then, Nelson's book would supposedly be finished. She knew she was not going to enjoy the home stretch. Nelson had written other books, which inevitably made him morose because of the enormity of the task. Then the music selections would really become eclectic.

Dale reached into the flour bin of the "Hoosier" cabinet and took out her secret stash of doughnut holes, which she bought on Saturdays at the Portsmouth Farmer's Market. She did not eat doughnut holes: they were exclusively for Tyrone, who thought Dale had invented the best game of fetch imaginable. He would race for the doughnut hole, sniff through the field for it, throw it in the air so Dale could see he'd gotten it, then gulp it down in one swallow. She had taken to applauding. Lately, she had started to add "Good dog, Tyrone" to the applause.

"Is that *cigarettes*?" Brenda whispered to Dale, though Nelson and Jerome were already walking up the stairs.

"Doughnut holes," Dale whispered back. "You'll see." She plunged what remained of them, in their plastic bag, into the deep pocket of her coat.

"I keep peanut M&M's in my lingerie drawer," Brenda said. "And Jerome—you know, he doesn't think I know he still drinks Pernod."

"It's for a dog," Dale said.

"Pernod?" Brenda asked.

"No. Doughnut holes."

"What do you mean?"

"Come on," Dale said. "You'll see."

At dinner—during which, Dale could sense, Brenda had greater respect for her, both as a cook and as a crazy woman (like the last moments of the Fourth of July fireworks, she'd sent three mini-doughnut holes up in the air at the same time)—they discussed the brass sundial Dale had placed atop autumn leaves in the center of the table. Nelson informed everyone that the piece sticking up was called the gnomon.

"No mon is an island," Jerome said. Jerome very much enjoyed wordplay and imitating dialects. Dialect from de islands was currently his favorite. They had recently vacationed in Montego Bay.

"And this is the shadow," Nelson said, pointing, ignoring Jerome's silly contribution. "This is the plate, this the hour line, this the dial, or diagram."

"You are a *born teacher,*" Brenda said.

"I broke that habit," Nelson said. He had. He had resigned in order to spend his time writing books. She had left with him, retaining only two loyal students who drove hours each week to work with her in the darkroom.

"Groton or no Groton, he had such an interest in knowledge that we had nothing to worry about with Nelson. I wore her down, and I was right to have done it," Jerome said.

The time would never come when Jerome would not want to be thanked, one more time, for having saved Nelson—as they both thought of it—from the clutches of Groton.

"Which I thank you for," Nelson said.

"And, if I'd been around at your birth, I could have stopped her from naming you for a sea captain," Jerome said.

"Oh, Nelson is a *lovely* name," Brenda said.

"Of course, if I'd been around at your birth, people might have suspected something funny was going on," Jerome said.

"I thought you met Didi in Paris, when Nelson was five or six," Brenda said.

"He was four. He was five when we got married."

Didi had gone to Paris to study painting. Actually, she had gone to have an affair with her Theosophy instructor. That hadn't had a happy ending, though Didi had met Jerome at the Deux Magots. No snail-like dawdling; by her own admission, she had struck with the speed of a snake.

"I didn't understand what you meant, then, when you said 'If I'd been around,'" Brenda said.

"I was just saying 'if.' If things had been otherwise. Other than what they were. If."

"But I think you implied that you knew Didi when she gave birth. Didn't he?" Brenda said.

"Brenda, you were a child when all this happened. You need not be jealous," Jerome said.

"I know I should let this drop, Jerome, but it seemed sort of strange to suggest you might have been there," Brenda said. "Am I being too literal-minded again?"

"Yes," Nelson said.

"Well, no, I mean, sometimes I feel like something is being said between the lines and because I'm a newcomer, I don't quite get it."

"I've lived with you for six years, Brenda," Jerome said. He said it with finality, as if she would do well to drop the subject, if she wanted to live with him another six seconds.

Brenda said nothing. Dale gestured to the soup tureen, beside the sundial. Also on the table was a silver bowl of freshly snipped chives and a little Chinese dish, enameled inside, that

Dale had found for a quarter at tag sale. People in the area did not value anything they were selling that was smaller than a beachball. The Chinese dish was an antique. Inside, there was a pyramid of unsweetened whipped cream.

"Fabulous. Fabulous soup," Jerome said. "So when are you going to let me bankroll your restaurant?"

He wasn't kidding. He'd wanted Dale to open a restaurant in New York for years. She thought, in part, so he could entertain clients there. Jerome had all the money in the world, inherited when his parents died and left him half the state of Rhode Island. Since Jerome was a part-time stockbroker, he'd managed to invest it wisely. Back in the days before Dale showed at the gallery in Boston, it had been more difficult to dismiss Jerome's ideas.

"So how's the photography coming?" he said, when she didn't answer. Brenda was still eating her soup, not looking up. Dale suspected he must have realized he'd offended Brenda.

"I've got some interesting stuff I've been working on," Dale said. "The woman down the road—" She gestured into the dark. Only a tiny blinking light from the bridge to Portsmouth could be seen, far in the distance. "There's one woman who lives there year-round—heating with a woodstove—and I've taken photographs . . . well: it always sounds so stupid, talking about what you're photographing. It's like paraphrasing a book," she said, hoping to elicit Nelson's sympathy.

"Just the general idea," Jerome said.

"Well, she does astrological charts for people, and they're really quite beautiful. And she has amazing hands. You'd think she was a musician. Very long fingers. I've photographed her hands, as she works on the charts. The books she consults are quite beautiful, too. The clutter on the table. All the stuff involved in doing a chart."

The longer she talked, the more stupid she felt.

"Have you had your chart done?" Jerome said. The stiffness of disapproval registered in his voice.

"No," Dale said.

"I had my chart done once," Brenda said. "I have it somewhere. It was apparently very unusual, because all my moons were in one house."

Jerome looked at her. "Didi believed in astrology," he said. "She thought we were mismatched because she was a Libra and I was a Scorpio. This apparently gave her license to have an affair with a policeman."

"I'm not Didi," Brenda said flatly. She had apparently decided not to let Jerome relegate her to silence. Dale was proud of her for that.

"Will you carve the roast?" Dale said to Nelson. "I'll get the vegetables out of the oven." She felt a little bad about leaving Brenda alone at the table with Jerome, but Nelson was much better at carving than she was. She stood and began collecting soup bowls.

"Does that woman with the earmuffs still see you?" Dale said to Brenda as she picked up her bowl. Very off-handed. As if the conversation had been going fine. It would give Brenda the excuse to rise and follow her into the kitchen, if she wanted to. Brenda said: "Yeah. I've gotten to like her a little better, but her worrying about losing body heat through her ears—you've got to wonder."

"All the world is exercising," Jerome said. "Brenda has more requests for her services than she can keep up with. The gym stays open until ten at night now on Thursdays. Do you two exercise?"

"There's an Exercycle in the downstairs bedroom. Sometimes I do it while I'm watching CNN," Nelson said.

Jerome gave his little half nod again. "And you?" he said to Dale. "Still doing the fifty sit-ups? You're looking wonderful, I must say."

"She can't," Nelson said, answering for her. "The Ménière's thing. It screws up her inner ear if she does that sort of repetitive activity."

"Oh, I forgot," Brenda said. "How are you doing, Dale?"

"Fine," she said. Things were better. The problem would never go away unless, of course, it spontaneously went away. Things had been so bad because the hypoglycemia complicated the problem, and that was pretty much under control, but she didn't want to talk about it.

"Remind me of what you can't eat," Jerome said. "Not that we wouldn't be too intimidated to have you to dinner, anyway. Better to reciprocate at a restaurant in the city."

"You don't have to reciprocate," Dale said. "I like to cook."

"I wouldn't be intimidated," Brenda said.

Dale looked at Jerome, who was seated facing the kitchen. "You wouldn't," he said. "I stand corrected."

"It can be a problem, when you're really good at something, that you never have people even try to do that thing for you," Brenda said. "There's a girl at work who gives the best massage in the world, and nobody will touch her, because she's the best. The other day I rubbed just her shoulders, and she almost swooned."

"Taking up massage, also?" Jerome said.

"What do you mean, *also?*" Brenda said. "This is about the fact that you don't like me working late on Thursdays, isn't it? I might remind you that if a client calls, whatever time it is, it's nothing for you to be on the phone for an hour."

"No fighting!" Nelson said.

"We're not fighting," Jerome said.

"Well, you've been *trying* to provoke a fight with me," Brenda said.

"Then it was unconscious. I apologize," Jerome said.

"Oh, honey," Brenda said, getting up, putting her napkin on the table. She went around the table and hugged Jerome.

"She likes me again," Jerome said.

"We all like you," Nelson said. "I, personally, think you saved my life."

"That goes too far," Jerome said. "I just wasn't one of those stereotypically disinterested stepfathers. I considered it a real bonus that I could help raise you."

"If only you'd taught me more about electrical problems," Nelson said.

"It's toggled together, but it should hold until I get my hands on a soldering gun," Jerome said. "But seriously—Dale—what do they think the prognosis is about this thing you have?"

Roasted vegetables cascaded into the bowl. Dale put the Pyrex dish carefully in the sink and opened the drawer, looking for a serving spoon. "I'm fine," she said.

"It's complicated," Nelson said. "She eats nothing but walnuts and cheese sticks for breakfast. You think she looks good? Will she still, if she loses another fifteen pounds?"

"Cheese is full of calories," Dale said. It was going to be impossible not to talk about it until everyone else's anxiety was alleviated. She lowered her voice. "Come on, Nelson," she said. "It's boring to talk about."

"Cheese? What's with the cheese?" Jerome said.

"Honey, you are *cross-examining* her," Brenda said.

"So—here is some fresh applesauce, and here are the vegetables—I'll put them by you, Jerome—and Nelson's got the roast," Dale said, going back to her chair. The chairs were Danish Modern, with a geometric quilted pattern on the seats.

Apparently, the professor and his wife had also had a sabbatical in Denmark.

"Oh, you already had apples. I *knew* you would," Brenda said.

"She won't touch the applesauce. Pure sugar," Nelson said.

"Nelson," Dale said, "please stop talking about it." She said: "Does anyone want water?"

"I think, if you don't mind, I'll have that Macon-Lugny 'Les Charmes' Nelson told me you laid in," Jerome said.

"Absolutely," Dale said, getting up. Nelson walked around her with the platter.

"She has some wine called Opus One for the doctor, who's coming to dinner, what is it—Thursday?" Nelson said. "We were supposed to go there for drinks, but Dale countered with dinner. Talk about being grateful."

"What year?" Jerome said.

"It was a present," Dale said. "From a student who's married to a wine importer, so I suspect it's good."

Nelson held the platter for Brenda to serve herself.

"Has it been properly stored?" Jerome said. "That could be an excellent wine. We can only hope nothing happened to it."

Dale looked at him. As interested as he'd ostensibly been in her health, the concern about the wine was far greater. She had thought, to begin with, that being so solicitous had actually been Jerome's way of pointing out her vulnerability. Poor Dale, who might have to be stretched out on the floor any second. It fit with his concept of women.

Nelson moved to Jerome's side. He was holding the bottle. "Nineteen eighty-five," he said.

"You know, that is a very elegant wine, indeed. Let me see that," Jerome said. Jerome cradled the bottle against his chest. He looked down at it, smiling. "As the person who once saved your husband's life, what would you think about my opening this to go with dinner?" he said.

"Jerome!" Brenda said. "Give that back to Nelson."

Nelson looked at Dale, with an expression somewhere between perplexity and pleading. It was just a bottle of wine. She had no reason to think the doctor or her husband were wine connoisseurs. There was the bottle of St. Emilion, but it would have seemed churlish—at the very least, to be playing Jerome's game—to mention it now. "Absolutely," Dale said. She pushed her chair back and went to the cupboard and took out their own stemmed glasses with a wide bowl that they had brought with them, along with her duvet and the collection of cooking magazines.

Dale put a glass at everyone's place. Jerome was smiling. "We can only hope," he said.

Brenda was looking at Dale, but Dale did not meet her eyes. She was determined to let them all see that she was unconcerned. Jerome was usually so polite; the thing that had surprised her doubly had been his blunt request.

"Tell me," he said, wine bottle clamped between his legs, turning the corkscrew. "Surely you aren't going to decline one small glass of this, Dale?"

"I can't drink," she said.

"Then what is that glass for?" he said.

"Perrier," she said, pronouncing the word very distinctly.

Jerome looked attentively at the bottle as he slowly withdrew the cork. He picked up the bottle and sniffed. Then he put a finger inside his white linen napkin and worked his finger around the top, inside the bottle. That was the first time it came clear to her that he was doing what he was doing out of anger. She picked up her fork and speared a piece of eggplant.

"You've fallen quiet, Dale," he said. "Is everything all right?"

"Yes," she said, trying to sound mildly surprised.

"It's just that you're so quiet," he persisted.

Brenda seemed about to speak, but said nothing. Dale managed a shrug. "I hope there are enough spices on the vegetables," she said. "I roasted them without salt. Would anyone like salt?"

Of course, since they had all now turned their attention to Dale, whatever she said sounded false and shallow.

"I appreciate your laying in Macon-Lugny for me," Jerome went on. "In most cases, white would go well with pork roast. But an '85 Opus One—that, of course, is completely divine." Jerome sniffed the bottle. It might have been snuff, he inhaled so deeply. Then he sat the bottle on the table, near the sundial. "Let it breathe for a moment," he said. He turned his chair at an angle, feigning closeness with Dale.

Dale picked up a piece of carrot with her fingers and bit into it. She said nothing.

"You had Didi to dinner last month with some friends of yours, I hear," he said.

Who had told him, since he and Didi didn't speak? Nelson, obviously. Why?

"Yes," she said.

Jerome took a bite of meat and a bite of vegetable. He reached for the applesauce and ladled some on his plate. He said nothing about the food.

"I understand you've made a portrait of her," he said.

Brenda was chewing slowly. She knew, and Dale knew, that Jerome was warming up to something. Didi was Nelson's mother. Dale didn't much like Didi—in part, because they seemed to have little in common. On top of that, she condescended by acting as if Dale was the sophisticate, and she—the world traveler—just a poor old lady. Dale had thought that photographing her—in spite of the momentary imbalance of power—might ultimately get the two of them on a more even footing.

Jerome said: "I'd be curious to see it."

"No," Dale said.

"No? Why ever not?" Jerome said.

"You don't like your ex-wife," she said. "There's no reason to look at a picture of her."

"Listen to her!" Jerome said, jutting his chin in Nelson's direction.

"Jerome—what's wrong?" Nelson said quietly.

"What's wrong? There's something wrong about my request to see a photograph? I have a curiosity about what Didi looks like. We were married for years, you'll remember."

"I don't want to see it," Brenda said.

"You don't have to. If you don't want any of the wine, you don't have to have that, either." Jerome twirled the bottle. As the label revolved in front of him, he picked up the bottle and poured. A thin stream of wine went into the glass.

"I don't quite see how not wanting to look at a photograph of your ex means I don't want wine," Brenda said.

"You prefer white. Isn't that so?" Jerome said.

"Usually. But you made this wine sound very good."

"It's good, but not great," Jerome said, inhaling. He had not yet taken a sip. He swirled the wine in his glass, then put the glass to his lips and slowly tilted it back. "Mm," he said. He nodded. "Quite good, but not perfect," he said. He cut a piece of roast.

Nelson kept his eyes on Dale, who was intent upon not looking at Brenda. Brenda was doing worse with Jerome's behavior than anyone. "May I talk to you in the kitchen?" Brenda said to Jerome.

"Oh, just take me to task right here. In the great tradition of Didi, who never lowered her voice or avoided any confrontation."

"I'm not Didi," Brenda said. "What I want to know is whether you're acting this way because you're pissed off I have a job I enjoy and that means I'm not there to answer your every whim, or whether there's some real bone you have to pick with Dale."

"Forget it," Nelson said. "Come on. Dale has made this wonderful meal."

"Don't tell me what not to say to my husband," Brenda said.

"Let's take another walk and cool off," Dale said to Brenda. "Maybe they'd like to talk. Maybe we could use some air."

"All right," Brenda said, surprising Dale. She had thought Brenda would dig her feet in, but she seemed relieved by the suggestion. She got up and walked through the kitchen, into the hallway where the coats were hung. In the dark, she put on Dale's jacket instead of her own. Dale noticed, but since they wore the same size, she put on Brenda's without comment. Outside, Brenda didn't realize her error until she plunged her hand in the pocket and felt the doughnut holes. "Oh, this is yours," she said, and began to unzip the jacket.

"We wear the same size. Keep it on," Dale said. Brenda looked at her, making sure she meant it. Then she took her fingers off the zipper. As they walked, Brenda began apologizing for Jerome. She said she'd only been guessing, back at the house: she didn't really know what he was so angry about, though she assumed they knew that he was more fond of them than his own family—this being the ex-wife and daughter he'd had between Didi and Brenda, and the son he'd had by a married woman. "He had a couple of beers on the plane. They took a bottle upstairs when they went to fix the wiring, too. Maybe he just had too much to drink," Brenda said.

"It doesn't matter," Dale said. She pointed at the Portsmouth light. "I like that," she said. "In the evening I like the colorful sky, but at night I like that one little light almost as much."

Dale tried to see her watch, but couldn't. "Too late to round up Tyrone," she said. She knew that it was, even without being able to see the time. In the distance, wind rustled the willows. They were walking where the path turned and narrowed, between the divided field. It was Dale and Nelson's responsibility, as renters, to have the fields plowed so the scrub wouldn't take over. In the distance, you could hear the white noise of cars on the highway. That, and the wind rustling, disguised the sound of tires until the headlightless black car was almost upon them. Brenda clutched Dale's arm as she jumped in fear, moving so quickly into the grass in her high-heeled boots that she lost her balance and fell, toppling both of them. "Oh, shit, *my ankle*," she said. "Oh, no." Both were sprawled in the field, the hoar's frost on the grass crunching like wintery quicksand as they struggled to stand. A car without headlights? And after nearly sideswiping them, it accelerated. It didn't slow down. The big shadow of the car moved quickly away, crunching stones more loudly as it receded than it had on the approach.

Brenda had turned her ankle. Dale helped her up, dusting wetness from her jacket, wanting to delay the moment when Brenda would say she couldn't walk. "Some God damned maniac," Dale said. "Can you put pressure on it? How does it feel?"

"It hurts, but I don't think it's broken," Brenda said.

Dale looked into the distance, Brenda's hand still on her

shoulder. "Shit," Brenda said again. "I'd better take these things off and walk home in my tights. You know, if I didn't know better, I'd think that car had been Jerome, zeroing in for the kill."

Kill. With a worse chill than the night air explained, she had realized that the car must have been speeding away from Janet's house. That they would have to go on—she, at least, would have to go on—and see what had happened.

"It's something bad—" Dale began.

"I know," Brenda said, crying now. "But the worst thing is that I'm pregnant, and I don't dare tell him, he's been so shitty lately. It's like he hates me. I feel like he'd like it if my ankle was broken."

"No," Dale said, hearing what Brenda said, but not quite hearing it. "Something at the house down there. Janet's house."

Brenda's hand seized Dale's shoulder. "Oh, my God," she said.

"Wait here," Dale said.

"No!" she said. "I'm coming with you."

"I've got a very bad feeling," Dale said.

"We don't know," Brenda said. "It could have been kids—drunk, playing a game with the lights out." From the tenuous way she spoke, it was clear she didn't believe herself.

Slowly, helping her to walk, Brenda's boots in one of her hands, the other around Brenda's waist, the two of them walked until the little house came in sight. "Not exactly a wedding cake," Brenda said, squinting at what was hardly more than a clapboard shack. There was one light on, which was an ambiguous sign: it could be good, or it could mean nothing at all.

The front door slightly ajar was the worst possible sign. Dale surprised herself by having the courage to push it open. Inside, the wood fire had burned out. A cushion was on the floor. A mug lay near it, in a puddle of whatever had been inside. The house was horribly, eerily silent. It was rare that Dale found herself surrounded by silence.

"Janet?" Dale said. "It's Dale. Janet?"

She was on the kitchen floor. They saw her when Dale turned on the light. Janet was breathing shallowly, a small trickle of blood congealed at one side of her mouth. Dale's impulse was to gather Janet in her arms, but she knew she should not move her head. "Janet? Everything's going to be okay," she heard herself say dully. She meant to be emphatic, but instead her voice was monotonal. Her ears had begun to close—the warning that she would soon have an attack of vertigo. But why? She had drunk no wine, she had eaten no sugar. Panic attacks had been ruled out when Ménière's had been ruled in. *"You must learn the power of positive thinking,"* she heard the doctor saying to her. *"I know it sounds ridiculous, but it works. I'm not a mystical person. It's more like biofeedback. Say to yourself: this will not happen to me."*

The room was quivering, as if the walls, themselves, were about to slope into italics. She repeated the words, silently. She could see Janet's chest rising and falling. Her breathing did not seem to be labored, though whoever had been there had tried to strangle her with a piece of rope. From the color of her face, it was obvious she had been deprived of oxygen. The long fingers were balled into fists. Blood oozed from a cut on her arm. An ankh cross dangled from one end of the rope. *The Dictionary of Symbols* lay on the floor, a blood-smudged chart beside it. Beside that, torn from the wall, was a photograph Dale had taken of Janet's hand holding the fine pearwood brush she used to draw symbols. The photograph had been ripped so that the brush was broken in half. Remembering, suddenly, what she must do, Dale went to the wall phone and dialed 911. "Someone is unconscious at the end of Harmony Lane," she said. It was difficult to tell how loud, or soft, her words were. Harmony Lane—was that what she had just said? What ridiculous place was that? Some fake street in some ridiculous Walt Disney development? But no—they hadn't gone there. They had rented a house in Maine, that was where they were. She squinted against the star shining through the kitchen window, like a bright dart aimed at her eye. It was not a star, though. It was the light from Portsmouth.

The woman who answered told Dale to stay calm. She insisted she stay where she was. It was as if all this was about Dale—not Janet, but Dale, standing in Janet's kitchen. For a second the voice of the woman at 911 got confused with the voice of the doctor: *this will not happen to me.*

There was a shriek of sirens. They sounded far, far away, yet distinct: background music that portended trouble. Dale was so stunned that instead of hanging up, she stood with the phone in her hand, imagining she'd hung up. She had seen Janet two days before. Three? They had talked about squash. The squash Janet would appreciate Dale buying for her at the Farmer's Market. "This is her neighbor, Dale," she said, in what she thought was an answer to the question the woman was asking, faintly, on the opposite end of the phone. Why didn't the woman ask about Janet? She should mention her, if the woman was not going to do it. Where to begin? "We saw a car," she heard herself say, though her mouth was not near enough for the 911 operator to hear.

That was the moment when Tyrone burst out from underneath the two-seat sofa, charging so quickly he overshot Dale and toppled Brenda, who screamed with fear long after she might have realized it was only a dog. Tyrone was as afraid as they were; everything was made worse by Brenda's high-pitched scream.

"Oh, God, I'm so sorry," Brenda said, apologizing to the cowering dog, its back legs shaking so pathetically, Dale could not see how he remained upright. "Oh, God, here," Brenda said, inching closer, reaching in the jacket pocket with trembling hands for a doughnut hole and holding it out to the dog who did not approach, but stood shakily leaning into Dale's leg. No one looked at Janet's body. Wind rattled the glass, but the louder sound was that of sirens. Dale saw Brenda cock her head and turn, as if she could see the sound. Brenda turned back and threw the doughnut hole, missing by a mile.

"It's okay," Dale said, moving her leg astride the dog and edging the doughnut hole toward him with the toe of her boot. It was a powdered sugar doughnut hole that left a streak of white on the floorboards. By Janet's hand had been a streak— no: a puddle, not a streak—of blood. Dale did not look in that direction, she was so afraid Janet might have stopped breathing.

She looked across the room at Brenda. Brenda, dejectedly, was about to throw another doughnut hole. Dale watched as she tossed it slowly, repeating Dale's words: "It's okay." Then she took a step forward and said to Dale: "Make him forgive me. Make him like me again."

The dog stayed at Dale's side, ignoring the doughnut hole that had fallen just short of its paw.

Dale was stroking Tyrone's head. Tyrone had become her dog. Brenda and Jerome's child, she thought, would become Brenda's child. All of Jerome's women had wanted babies, and he had bitterly resented every one: the son born to the married woman in France, whose husband believed the child to be his; the daughter born as his marriage to his second wife was disintegrating. Nelson had been the only one he wanted. Well— if you had what you already considered the perfect child, maybe that made sense. Nelson was intellectually curious, smart, obedient, favoring his stepfather over his mother, a loyal child.

The two of them would be at the table, finishing dinner, Nelson having found a way to excuse Jerome, Jerome's passive aggression subsiding into agreeableness—as if, by the two women's disappearing, any problem automatically disappeared, too. Without them, Nelson and Jerome could move on to the salad course. Drink the entire bottle of Opus One. Nelson would probably have brought down the photograph of Didi, her face deeply lined by years of having kept up with Jerome in his drinking, as well as other bad decisions she had made, and of course from the years at St. Tropez, enjoying too much sun.

Too much sun. Too much son. Jerome would like to play with that.

Though what Jerome was talking about, having already told Nelson he was seriously considering separating from Brenda— was the story of Baron Philippe de Rothschild: the baron, being a clever businessman, and more importantly, a visionary, realized that much might be gained by joining forces with the California winegrower, Robert Mondavi. Mondavi was summoned to Baron Philippe de Rothschild's, where he dined on fabulous food and drank great wine. It was a social evening: business was not discussed. It was not until the next morning that the baron—at this point, genuinely admired by Mondavi for his taste, elegance, and good manners—summoned Mondavi to his bedside, like a character in a fairy tale. The possibility was discussed of combining their efforts, and sharing the profits fifty-fifty. Mondavi suggested producing only one wine: a Cabernet. Did he say this tentatively? The baron agreed. Would he have said the same? The wine would be made in California, where the baron's winemaker would visit. Mondavi, flattered, was thrilled, as well. His name, linked to that of Baron

Philippe de Rothschild! The baron also triumphed, realizing that by embracing his would-be adversary, both men could profit. Nothing remained except for the ceremonial drinking of a one-hundred-year-old Mouton, followed by a very cold Château d'Yquem: a perfect deal; a perfect meal—it even rhymed, as Jerome pointed out. A brilliant label was designed, providing the perfect finishing touch.

The talk back at the house was about perfection. In a perfect world, all wines would be perfect. Ditto marriages. All books brilliant (a toast was drunk). Superior music (again, glasses were raised) would be listened to, keenly. In that fairy tale, which was not Dale's, and which was not Brenda's, either, no woman would lie badly wounded on her kitchen floor.

Brenda crossed the room and stood at Dale's side. "Doughnut hole," she said quietly, looking down, then picked it up, at the end of its trail of powdered sugar, as if plucking a shooting star from the darkness.

This time, Tyrone showed interest. Dale picked up the other two. The dog was definitely interested. There was no dirt on the doughnut holes, Dale and Brenda could see, as they examined them closely.

"Why not?" Dale said, giving voice to what Brenda was thinking. They could pretend to be people at a cocktail party, eating pleasant tidbits.

But sirens pierced the night.

They signified a problem for someone, Nelson knew. Another problem, Jerome also thought.

The sound overwhelmed Bartók on the stereo. The sound was shrill and constant: a sound you might say was annoyingly like a woman's voice, if one could still say such things, which of course one could not.

Then the crescendo of sound, demanding their attention.

One preceded the other out of the house. That door, too, was left open to the wind.

A police car, a second police car, an ambulance, a fire engine—the full militia leading the way.

To what? The two words were like a heartbeat: *to what; to what.*

Down a dirt road in a country far from France.

Down a narrow road across from a rented house.

The meal left behind, one or the other having remembered to extinguish the candles.

The Infamous
Fall of
Howell the Clown

"It was 1954, and it just wasn't done. You didn't have an unsupervised birthday party for a seven-year-old, presided over only by a gentleman friend dressed up in a polka-dot jumpsuit with an organdy collar and red lipstick and blue eyeshadow, wearing beach sandals with pink socks. Well—go ahead and laugh: it turned into a disaster, didn't it?"

"How old was Cousin Charlie?"

"It was 1954. Charlie was seven, Steven was six. I should also add that your mother was twenty-five, but because women in those days wore almost as much makeup as the clown, she looked like a more mature woman than she was. She was only twenty-five, one year younger than your aunt Sylvie, who had never been put on God's green earth to supervise the upbringing of children, so of course who did Sylvie marry but Parker Winkleman, the most irresponsible, pig-headed boy for miles around. Nine months from the day they married they had Charlie, and he was no more than brought home from the hospital than the two of them had the bassinet on the back porch and were out in the street riding their bicycles, telling anyone who asked that they were 'keeping an ear out for the baby.' Why, the woman who lived next door would have to go out on her front lawn and flag them down, when she got too worried about the crying. There they'd be, riding in bigger and bigger circles, ringing their bells at each other like a couple of bears in the circus. No one could believe such irresponsibility. When she went in to have the second one, Sylvie's mother took her aside and told her: 'Tie your tubes.' She would never have listened, except that she had two babies, and suddenly Parker Winkleman had lost his job at the bank."

"And when he disappeared, no one went to look for him?"

"What do you think it was, the Wild West? Somebody saddled up his horse and galloped from town to town, inquiring about mysterious strangers? Nobody could take time off from work. Private detectives weren't heard of in those days, or at least I never knew anyone who'd heard of them. We thought he'd find himself a job and send for the family. We certainly didn't think he'd disappear. Every time the phone rang, we'd all leap for it. Every occasion, we'd expect to see him return: somebody was always sure to announce a scenario in which he'd suddenly appear, with birthday presents for his child, or bringing flowers on their anniversary. You have to understand that we had no frame of reference for Parker Winkleman. Even Mrs. Winkleman never understood him. She raised him the same as his brother, but he threw spitballs in Sunday school and aimed his slingshot at songbirds, and when he married Sylvie, he had plans to move to Paris, France, and turn her into a fashion model, though how he thought having two children in two years would help her form, I don't know."

"How long was he gone before Sylvie started the affair with Howell?"

"First of all, I'm not walking along this street with you today saying that any such thing happened. At least, we never thought in terms of 'affairs.' Laugh if you want, but in those days, we thought two people could be friends. I don't have any stories about Howell creeping out of her house early in the morning, and no one ever so much as saw him put his arm around her shoulder, even when they stood at the funeral of Mrs. Winkleman. They behaved very properly. Friends of Sylvie's often went along if they went to the movies, or for a sundae. His father accompanied them, before he became so ill. I think, frankly, that a lot of men in the neighborhood felt sorry for the two boys left without a father and rallied to Sylvie's side. I don't know that they had an affair. Maybe he felt sympathetic toward her and the boys."

"Then why was it so wrong to leave him in charge of the birthday party?"

"You tell me, please, why Sylvie had to go shopping when she had a party full of children. For clothes, it was—not even groceries. Oh, I see your look. You think it was liberated of her to go off and do what she wanted. But think of the position it put poor Howell in: you can't be an adult doing your job of supervising when you're also disguised as a clown and going around making mischief. You can't be two things with children at one time, or they'll stop believing. Can you imagine Santa Claus placing presents under the tree and muttering, 'Where did the stains come from on this carpet?' The most important thing was to convince the children he was a clown—I think he had a curly red wig and those bushy eyebrows attached to a big red nose, as well—anyway, if he hadn't had the bad reaction to the medicine the doctor had given him, he would have stayed put in his tree, but the medicine poisoned him, in combination with the glass of beer he had before he was in costume, when he and Sylvie were stringing crepe paper from tree to tree. He was not a drinker, and it turned into a very hot day, and he must have been twice as hot inside that clown suit, and then the penicillin he'd been given for his throat must have reacted with the beer, so that after he climbed up in the tree to pretend to be Juliet calling to Romeo, which is not something I'm very clear on, or ever was— from up in the tree, he just opened his arms like a big red-haired, red-nosed angel spreading its wings and Bam! He crashed down, and if it had not been for the birthday presents on the ground that cushioned his fall, Howell would have hit into the earth like a meteor. They think he fainted from the heat, and that he was a little delusional when he got into the tree because the medicine had already started to interact with the beer. Apparently he'd been frustrated because the children had never heard of Romeo and Juliet; that was going to ruin his clown routine, so he had to stand there in the hot sun, feeling sicker and sicker, explaining the story, and by the time he started to climb he was already sweating, and more than a little anxious, because he'd seen Sylvie's car pulling out of the driveway, and where was she going? Surely the poor man never in a million years thought his Juliet would open her arms and then black out and take a dive into boxes filled with animal toys and erector sets and Mr. Potato Heads. He fell with such force they found a baby manatee under an azalea bush outside the porch one week later, and some piece of the Mr. Potato Head stabbed his forehead, so he looked like the Frankenstein monster with its screw when they turned him over. We can only laugh because they fixed him at the hospital, but that day no one was laughing, and some of the children stayed so frightened they didn't even want to have birthday parties when their time came around. They started going to matinees with a few friends, seeing *The King and I* over and over. I, personally, consider that a fate worse than death. I never could stand Yul Brynner, but I think that other bald actor, Sean Connery, is extremely handsome. Of course, it helped that he played James Bond, and didn't have to stalk around a palace singing 'Et cetera, et cetera.'"

"And that night Steven's nightmares began?"

"Yes. Before he fell, he'd picked out Steven to be Romeo, and he was speaking directly to Steven when he hit the ground. You can see that would be traumatic for a child. All through school, every play by Shakespeare made him terribly nervous.

When they were the lesson, he wanted to stay home, whether it was *All's Well That Ends Well* or *Macbeth.*"

"Well," I said, "I thought he spoke beautifully at the service. Maybe in spite of that crazy day, years ago, Howell still inspired him to be an actor. When we were kids, he was always so shy. I didn't expect him to be so dynamic."

"If you're so curious, I don't know why you've never asked," Violet said, suddenly. "When we get to Steven's apartment, why don't you ask him before Sylvie shows up and stop bothering me about things I don't know the answer to."

"I'm not sure he or Charlie would tell me the truth. They were always a little distant. They always kept secrets from me, you know."

"You're a girl. I don't think they knew what to make of you. They were used to teasing girls, being attracted to them but trying to pretend they weren't. They saw you as their responsibility, but they weren't sure how to act toward you because you were also a family member. They were eleven and twelve when you went to live with them, and you were thirteen years old and acted much older. They both had crushes on you. Or at least Steven did."

"Violet."

"I'm not saying he wanted to marry you. There are other kinds of crushes." She frowned at me. "You were always too hard on Steven. Do you realize that? When you were little children, playing together, you'd sometimes explain to people who came into the room that Steven was just there because he was tired of playing outside. You'd find some way to explain that he didn't really want to be with you, it was just the lesser of two evils. Why have you always been so hard on Steven?"

"I'm not hard on him. Didn't I say he was the best speaker at Howell's memorial service?"

"Oh," Violet said, "it's so hard to believe. Howell was doing fine until he went for that new treatment, and it poisoned him just like the beer and the penicillin did. He never had a strong constitution. I hope he was her lover, you know. Because if he wasn't her lover, I don't think he would have been anyone's. At least, not much of one, spending all his free time with Sylvie and you and the boys, and the rest of the time living at home with that cranky old father."

As we talked, we had walked from the church up Sixth Avenue to Sixteenth Street. A few tulips had poked up in the tree boxes, but either someone had picked the blooms or they had not blossomed; the anemic green leaves, dust speckled, curled like banana peels as they drooped to the ground. A single marigold bloomed in a squiggle of foliage. Next to it lay a baby's pacifier. Farther up the street, we saw one high heel. It was spring in New York, the trees budding, pollen like yellow chalk dust on the steps of the brownstones, vibrant red tulips in a vase offering proof that indoors, at least, tulips prospered. We both saw them through the iron bars of someone's ground-floor window. I had once lived in the Village behind similar bars and screens—lived far enough downtown that Sixteenth Street seemed like uptown, which it did not seem at the moment. Compared to Fifty-fourth Street, where the hotel I was staying in was located, this was still quiet, pastoral New York. I had come into the city the night before from Pennsylvania for Howell's memorial service, meeting Violet in the morning, as she got off the Metroliner from Washington at Penn Station. There she had stood, five feet tall, carrying an overnight bag patterned with roses, her good Georg Jensen pin, a stylized, sterling silver maple leaf, pinning her scarf to her wool jacket. She was as alert as a bird, bright-eyed, attuned to the roar of the trains, the noise of the PA system, the crowd. But she had never understood

New York. She didn't know if Penn Station was uptown or downtown, and furthermore, she couldn't remember where uptown became dangerous or at what point downtown turned into Wall Street. She understood, in theory, how the avenues ran, but alone, she would turn a corner and find herself on another avenue, not a cross street, and how was that possible? She understood there was some mysterious benefit to crossing a street to catch a cab much of the time, but when those times were, or which streets ran uptown or downtown, she could never remember. Now, she hopped along at my side, her practical leather-laced shoes stuffed with two layers of Dr. Scholl's cushion inserts, part of her money folded in a slip pouch, other money pinned inside her bra, a crisp twenty dollar bill and all her change in her wallet, in case someone demanded her purse. In the last few years, she had begun coloring her hair, which had not become predominantly gray until well after her sixtieth birthday. Whoever was doing the dyeing was good: a few streaks of gray were left, waving away from her temples; it gave her hair a look of motion, made it look as if the wind had uncovered unexpected ripples of gray. Violet had always been my mother's best friend, as far back as I could remember. The two of them had spent so much time together they had often come to use the same expressions, accompanied by many of the same gestures as they spoke. But the way I had been supposed to see it, my mother had been a practical, down-to-earth person, Violet something of a dreamer. My mother was the organized, determined woman who had looked adversity in the face and triumphed over it, becoming a dental hygienist when my father divorced her, whereas Violet talked about going to college but never enrolled, even though the handwriting was on the wall about her husband's job. Whether my mother had meant to present this concept of Violet deliberately or not, I have no idea, but she had consistently planted seeds of doubt about whether Violet was, at all, a practical person. Since they told each other almost every thought and desire, and since my mother repeated many of those things to me, there were always a lot of things to hope, or even to pray for, on Violet's behalf, whether it be that she find her missing cat, Bugle Boy, or that her husband get a much-needed raise, or that she be selected to sing a solo in the church choir. My mother gave me to understand that Violet always wanted things—the implication was that she was constantly at odds with the way things were, that she was sadly dissatisfied—and while my mother would say to me that she wished all Violet's dreams could come true (finding the cat or singing a solo were, equally, "dreams"), that was not very likely for Violet, or for anyone. What I think now is that my mother, so dissatisfied and disappointed by life after her divorce, which forced her to get a job she hated ("Another day of carving the pumpkins," she would say in the morning, opening her mouth wide and jutting out her jaw as she examined her own teeth in the bathroom mirror), needed someone she could consider more troubled and insecure than she. In her resolute, but world-weary disparagement of Violet, my mother rose to more heroic heights, the way a person reading a fairy tale will nod knowingly and cue a child to anticipate disaster from the moment the wolf appears. When I was young, like every other child, I accepted my mother's version of everything; then, of course, I saw that she did not predict things perfectly, that her sister—my Aunt Sylvie—took something of the same attitude toward her that my mother took toward Violet. Perhaps because back then people did not often directly contradict others, as is common now, people relied more on gestures, such as an upward roll of the eye or a raised eyebrow. Throughout my childhood, I began to observe a domino effect of skepticism that tipped so gently it did not knock the person down but that nevertheless passed like an electric current from my grandmother to her oldest daughter, from the oldest to the youngest, from the youngest to her best friend. And no doubt part of the reason I was so fascinated was because the falling dominoes did not extend to me; though I was next in line, I was displaced by Violet—unwittingly, just because of her constant presence and because of the place she occupied in my mother's affections—Violet became the recipient of my mother's sotto voce concern, the person we of course wished well, though her ideas were quite unlikely to materialize. What a shocking thing it must have been for my mother when she realized she, herself, was dying—that the cancer Violet had assured her would stay in remission had recurred, that she would in all probability be leaving her beloved only child to the care of none other than Violet, a woman who adhered to predictions from psychics, who believed doctors did not pay enough attention to exceptions—to those few patients who inevitably survived unlikely odds. Over coffee, when I was present, my mother gave Violet the bad news. The wolf just sat in the bed and stared. Whatever Violet thought, in its own good time the wolf was simply going to devour its prey, my mother would die, and that, and only that, would now be the end of the story. Of course, my mother had a sort of love-hate relationship with Violet—she was the voice of my mother's own hopeful, unspoken optimism: how could she not?—so toward the end my mother complicated matters by arranging for Sylvie to take me, though she made Violet swear that she would oversee my upbringing, made Sylvie promise that Violet would be a second mother to me, made the two of them all but promise that they would bake alternating layers for my birthday cakes and sing to me in unison. Fortunately, Sylvie did not dislike Violet, or resent her intrusion. She had seen so much of her through the years, she considered her a member of the family. It was also a rather lonely life, difficult enough economically and emotionally before I joined her household of two increasingly wild boys—and because I withdrew so completely after my mother's death, Sylvie was no doubt happy to have someone else shoulder part of the burden: someone to share the task of driving me twice a week to the psychologist's office; another person to confer with about her decision to take out a loan and settle me, eventually, in another school; someone to confer with as she tried to learn the proper but always shifting signals of when to approach me and when to leave me alone. Though Violet was married, I have only the sketchiest memory of her husband, who worked a night shift and slept most of the day, so that even when my mother was alive, he rarely appeared in our lives. Also, by that time, something had happened and it had been decided—or had it simply turned out?—that Howell Jenkins would not join Sylvie's household. He stayed with his parents, nursing first his mother, then his father, through long illnesses. When I first went to live with Sylvie his mother was very ill, and in part because of guilt (his mother was ill, but my mother was dead)—because of the numbing grief we had in common, and because there was such turmoil when I first tried to settle in with Sylvie and the boys, Howell began to visit infrequently, though a few times Violet came to stay at Sylvie's house on the weekend, to take care of the three of us, while—we were told—Sylvie stayed at the Jenkins's house. Or maybe she didn't: maybe he left his parents to fend for themselves, and he and Sylvie went to a motel and had wild sex for two days. Maybe they watched *Casablanca* on TV and ordered steaks from room service and drank champagne and planned their future, in the happier times sure to come. They could have, because somewhere along the way Sylvie had gotten

divorced from her runaway husband, eventually Howell's
mother died, and in the last year of his life, Howell's father was
moved to a nursing home when Howell could no longer lift
him, so finally Howell had the house to himself. Then she could
have gone there any time, snuck over in the afternoon, during
her lunch break, detoured there on her way back to her house
after work. . . . All my information about Sylvie's divorce, and
about Howell's parents, I found out in bits and pieces from Violet, when we were shopping for new school clothes or eating
lunch at a downtown tearoom or—those times the psychic
guaranteed Violet would not break any bones—ice skating
together in the evening, at Parker's Pond. Violet didn't suggest
the romantic scenarios; I thought of them myself, admiring my
grown-up imagination, sure that someday I, too, would lead
whatever secret life was necessary to fulfill my every desire.
When I was the age my mother was when she married, eighteen,
I was living in the East Village with a drug-dealing cabdriver
who was married to a woman in Mexico City. That summer I
left him, left New York for Vermont, though that may have been
a preemptive strike, because he'd begun missing his wife in
Mexico. When I was twenty, the age my mother was when she
had me, I had dropped out of school and was working as a waitress, proud of myself, in those years of pinwheel eyes and paranoid, incantatory fixations, for not using anything stronger than
grass. I was mugged on Avenue A by two teenagers who said
"Peace and love" as they jumped my back, got arrested for
shoplifting, applied for a student loan and went to another college which I flunked out of at the end of spring semester, had
an abortion, wrote half a novel, was arrested for rioting, finished
the novel and abandoned it, dramatically, on the IRT, hitched to
California, went with a man to London, broke my ankle dancing in a nightclub, and through it all—though I can't picture it

and I don't want to remember the particulars—I apparently wrote letters to Sylvie and to Violet, as well as calling Violet, drunk, from a pub in Wales, asking that she send me my blue jacket which, as I described it, she realized was a jacket I'd had when I was eight or nine years old. A boy I'd broken up with maliciously called Sylvie and said I'd OD'd and was dead. During that same period, Violet phoned a friend in London and asked her to come to my flat and take me to dinner, and when the woman got there, though I'd been hungry, and therefore receptive to her proposal on the phone, I refused to go to the door and told my boyfriend to tell her I'd left London that afternoon. I think she saw me in there, behind him, sitting in one of the two canvas butterfly chairs, smoking a joint, listening to the Rolling Stones. I think I remember her going on tiptoes and waving, at the same time I was waving a cloud of marijuana smoke away from my watering eyes. But that's pretty much the story of my generation. Maybe a little different in the particulars, but similar in content to so many other people's lives. Sort of the counterpart of Violet's: *"It was nineteen fifty-four, and it just wasn't done."* It was nineteen sixty-seven, and it was done every day.

The big surprise, once we were inside Steven's loft, was that Charlie had rushed to the airport, hoping to make it back to Boston before his wife gave birth. He called her at the end of the service, and the outgoing message on their answering machine said, "Charlie, come home. I've gone into labor. It's twelve-thirty and I'm leaving for the hospital."

"Gracious!" Violet said. "I suppose that was the sensible thing to do, but I can still remember when a woman never referred to her condition. Women stayed inside the last months of their pregnancy. They certainly wouldn't have broadcast the news to the world."

"We all need a drink," Steven said, steering us toward the front of the loft. "A friend from work's tending bar. Tell him what you want, and have something to eat. He's brought beautiful things to eat." He pointed toward his friend, and the few people who had preceded us, so strongly backlit they'd become shadows.

"Even I need a drink," Violet said, as I helped her out of her coat.

"How are you, sweetheart?" Steven said to me, kissing the side of my head.

Damian, Steven's assistant, was sitting on a stool, leaning on the drawing table, propped on one elbow. Though he had on a suit at the service, he had changed into jeans and a pullover. "Because there's a reception here now following a memorial service," Damian said, in his thick English accent. "What do you think: we should let you test the security system and maybe at the same time we could turn on the radio and hope for a test of the emergency broadcasting system? Maybe run the Kentucky Derby through while we're at it?"

"They're very officious," Steven said apologetically, as if we were on the receiving end of Damian's sarcasm. "It's about my new security system" he said. "They want to test it right this minute. It's no time to do it, is the point."

"The point is," Damian echoed, "this is not the time."

"So *officious*," Steven hissed to the ceiling.

"Love, can you understand what I'm telling you? We don't want to activate the cross-beams because people are standing all over the place. Grieving people. We're here mourning the dead," Damian enunciated slowly.

This is when it occurred to me that we were not. We were

shaking off our coats, anticipating socializing with one another in a more private setting out of the church, relieved that the service was over: annoyance at life's absurdities began creeping in; hunger was gnawing.

"Security system?" Violet was saying to no one in particular, as I put my arm around her shoulder and moved her toward the far end of the loft. "I hope he hasn't been robbed," she said. "I guess it's just a precaution." Then: "I couldn't live like this."

"How are you?" Steven's friend from work said warmly, reaching across the table to shake Violet's hand, then mine. "We met briefly last Christmas," he said to Violet. "I was going out as you were coming in."

"Oh, yes. You had your dog, on a leash."

"Didn't seem proper to bring him today," the man said. "I usually take him everywhere. They started a day-care center where we work, you know, and now I drop the dog at day care. He loves children. They said that if one more person wanted to bring a dog, I'd have to leave mine at home. But do you know what? Nobody wants to. I'm just lucky. The dog and I got lucky."

"A dog in day care," Violet said. She didn't seem surprised. Perhaps it might have surprised her if she hadn't already had her quotient of surprises hearing about the way Charlie found out his wife had gone into labor and learning that a security company wanted to conduct a test which would catch all of us in a kleig light of sound. Somewhere down below, a car alarm was set off, whirring a repetitive, mechanical shriek, as though the woman on the phone had exacted revenge, haunting us with the possibility that obnoxious sounds might yet move closer. As Violet requested a Bloody Mary, I looked past Steven's friend who was bartending, seeing the sky darkening with rain clouds, the wall of sand-colored buildings facing our building from across the street. In the high shine on Steven's floors I could see shadows of the clouds reflected, and for a minute it reminded me of Parker's Pond, the blurrily indistinct shapes cast by one's legs and feet and skates. When I looked up, Steven's friend was holding out two glasses: one, a wineglass; one, a glass filled with ice, silently offering me two possibilities. "White wine, thanks," I said, but my interest was in the stack of cubes in the other glass. Like the world in miniature, they reminded me of the surface of the pond, the pond into which Violet had been promised she would not slip, one of the many places I followed her believing that if she was safe from harm, of course I was safe. Now, through the years, things had changed: it had begun to work the other way, so that Violet followed me: uptown, downtown, a silent accomplice in the mysterious ritual of how to get a cab that would take off in the right direction.

When Sylvie came in, she was wet from the rain. With her hair plastered to her head she looked like a woebegone little girl, though the mist on her face had enlivened her cheeks, at least . . . she was so pale in the church. She blew us a kiss and—shoes slipped off—hurried into the bathroom, probably to towel dry her hair, to reapply lipstick. What could it be like, to lose someone you had such a close relationship with for forty years? What would it be like to go to that person's memorial service and hear people praise the person's unfailingly unique virtues, allude to intimacies, offer gentle jokes the deceased would presumably smile to hear? So many private thoughts in public places. What would Sylvie's private thoughts have been? Why didn't he marry her? Or was the answer clear, and only outsiders didn't intuit it?

I looked around the room. The people were family friends—or they were Steven's friends, like the man tending bar, like

Damian—people who barely knew Howell. Though many of Howell's friends had been at the memorial service, as I looked around the room I saw that only two people who seemed to be Howell's personal friends had come to Steven's loft. And those two, a man about Howell's age, wearing a too closely fitted dark suit he looked uncomfortable in, and a younger man with badly dyed blond hair and nervously hunched shoulders, who either did not have, or who was deliberately not wearing, the sort of clothes everyone else had on—even those two, I realized, were gay. There had been such an assortment of people in the church—people he'd worked with; people from organizations he'd given his time to; neighbors—that until the core group assembled, the obvious never occurred to me. As much as this gathering was for Sylvie—for her children, her niece, her sister's one-time best friend . . . as much as it was Steven's gesture toward his mother, it was also his gesture toward the two men, who seemed hardly to know one another, yet who stood close together, silently, awkwardly, the younger man finally helping the older man off with his jacket and adding it to a pile of coats on the chair by the entranceway, exchanging a few pleasantries with Damian, the older man so contrite it was almost possible to read his mind, to understand that what he really wanted was to bolt. Then the younger man went back to his side and gestured toward the table set up by the front window. I had been staring at them—I hadn't meant to, but when my thoughts locked, my eyes must have, also—so of course as they came nearer they pretended not to notice me, or my stare. The older man walked right past me, but as the younger man passed he turned, then walked back to where I stood, his shoulders hunched, as if he were trying to fold into himself. "Ladies," he said, ducking his head and raising it again. It was the first time in what seemed like hours that I realized Violet was at my side, that she was all but clinging to me, her glass empty, her expression slightly worried as she looked in the direction of the still-closed bathroom door.

"You don't know who I am," the man said as he approached, "but Howell often spoke of you. My name is Justin DeKalb. The surprising thing is, I would have recognized you anywhere, because I used to skate at Parker's Pond. Howell described you both to me many times, but the minute I walked in, I realized I actually knew you. Not exactly that I know you, but I used to be there when you were. At Parker's Pond." As he said this, he clasped Violet's hand, smiling at her and then—more tenuously, it pained me to see—at me. How long had I been staring at this man? How long had I been rooted to the spot, oblivious of Violet, of Sylvie's long disappearance, of the man's discomfort? With the floor gleaming around us, I had the giddy feeling we were, all three of us, back there—back at the big pond Mr. Parker had dredged one winter on his front fifty acres that had seemed to all of us the most miraculous thing, the most wonderful gift. The memory made me spontaneously reach out to take Justin DeKalb's hand, the way so many of us had locked fingers on those winter nights, at times to tease someone who was skating too slowly into action, or to coax someone into being our partner, or simply for the fun of making contact, seeing if fingers could communicate an idea: figure eights, or a race, or a conga line.

"I can't believe it," Violet was saying. "That crowd of people, and you remember the two of us? Well, I guess that says something, but I don't know that I want to know what." She smiled, her eyes glittering.

"I liked the way you skated together," he said. "You were beautiful skaters."

"I never was," Violet said, though she did not protest too strongly. "I was scared to death," Violet said, still gaily, but lowering her voice. "Scared silly, and you'll laugh, but I always paid a psychic before I got out on the ice to tell me if I was going to make it. One time she advised against it, and I didn't go. I pretended to be sick. Here's something I never confessed until now: I pretended to have a terrible stomachache—you may even remember," she said to me, "because you were so disappointed. I knew you'd be angry at me if I told you we couldn't go because the person you called 'Madame Money' said the ice might crack." She turned to Justin DeKalb. "Then I felt terrible, because it was always a way to get her out of herself, because she was so hopelessly sad her mother had died, and none of us who loved her knew what to do. Skating always did the trick, but that time I just lost my courage. Now I look back and wish we'd never missed one night at Parker's Pond."

This heartfelt confession so surprised me that I just stood there. As Violet was talking, Justin DeKalb had let go of my hand, and I looked at it, as if perplexed by the emptiness of my own hand. Because as she talked—up until almost the end of her confession—I had been on Parker's Pond. I had felt that freedom again, the exhilarating, numbing cold, and the sensation had cleared something in my head. Without Violet—without the approval of anyone else—I could, and should, simply proceed with my life.

"Yes," Justin DeKalb said, nodding. "It was a tragedy that your mother died so young. My condolences."

"And mine, of course, about the death of Howell," I said.

"Oh, we have got to get more cheerful," Violet said. "At the very least, I need another drink to bolster myself."

"You were scared?" I said suddenly. "Every time?"

"I was," she said, "but it was a good kind of scared. I only feel bad that I let you down that one time. Sylvie was—" she looked toward the closed bathroom door "—considering the things that had happened in her life, of course she was traumatized, but she always took her responsibilities very seriously. She wouldn't skate herself, you know, and she refused to let you go there without adult supervision. So I just got so I'd hold my breath and do it. After the first few minutes, it wasn't so bad." She smiled. "And look," she said. "We survived."

Sylvie left on the last shuttle for Boston. "Off to the birthing room!" Steven said to his mother. "Straight life is so hectic," he sighed, hailing a cab. Sylvie embraced us: first me, then Steven, not caring that the cabdriver had started the meter when he stopped, or that he was looking impatiently out the window. As she got into the cab, I thought how much Sylvie looked like my mother. The rain had twirled her hair into soft curls. Like my mother, she was wearing a heavy coat of lipstick that glowed the unnatural pink-purple of phlox, though she wore no other makeup. In the cab she looked as small as Violet, like someone who could also use a little protection in the big city, though I knew she knew where she was going, and also that the news from Boston had been a sort of exciting ending to a difficult day. I was still not sure if she had lost a friend or a lover, though it began to seem strange even to me that I was still fixated on that. Maybe I had just wanted to live vicariously; maybe, like most other adolescents, I had wanted to think her totally in my control, while at the same time I had an urge for her to have escaped me, to have a secret life. And perhaps she had, though she probably did not silently contain the conventional secret I had suspected it would be.

"What was it Tiny Tim said?" Sylvie said, rolling down the window as the driver waited to move into traffic, "'God bless us, each and every one?'"

"I think Tiny Tim *sang* it," Steven said. "I think he sang it, and it was 'Tiptoe through the tulips.'"

She sniffed, with a look of mock exasperation. As the cab pulled away, Steven stood at the curb, playing air music, strumming an imaginary ukelele close to his chest, looking as wild-eyed as he could. The rain had also made his hair curly, which helped. That, and his shirt hanging out of his pants, the dark circles under his eyes at the end of this long day. "To the gaaaaaarden wall," he was singing in falsetto, as the cab pulled away.

"That's 'La Guardia,'" I said to him.

"Good one," he said.

"You're not going to believe this, but it wasn't until tonight that I realized Howell was gay," I said to Steven.

"What did you think?" he said.

I said, "I didn't think anything."

"But you know what was interesting?" he said, opening the inside door with a key, walking toward the elevator. "What was interesting was that he knew about me before I did. Remember that party when he got drunk and fell out of the tree? Don't even bother to answer, because I know you remember. A perfectly ordinary accident, and it's become family lore. Somebody got a little out of control, and nobody's ever recovered from it. Think about it: divorces are never mentioned, my father took off and was never heard from again, but all Howell did was get a little tipsy and take a tumble, and for all eternity, everybody's been fixated on his bizarre behavior. The infamous fall of Howell the clown. I'd bet money that even though nobody brought it up at the memorial service, it was on a lot of people's minds. I look back now, and you know what? I'm still the only one who understands why it happened. That stuff about Romeo and Juliet. His playing Juliet to my Romeo. He knew then that I was gay, and I didn't."

"Steven—weren't you six years old, or something?"

We got onto the elevator. He pushed five. "Seven, wasn't I?" he said.

"He never—"

"Jesus," he said. "Of course not."

"What about Sylvie and Howell?" I blurted out.

"That's an interesting question. My guess?"

I nodded.

"My guess would be that when Dad took off and when your mother died, when Sylvie had to get that job she always hated, and when—don't take this wrong—you came to live with us and for so long you were so goddamn inconsolable, by that time, Sylvie felt like she'd pretty much seen it all come and go. I think for most of his life, Howell couldn't *wait* to see it go so he could get on with his life, but that somewhere in between his wish for things to change and her certainty about how life was going to be, they got attached to each other. That if there was no going forward, there wasn't any going back, either."

The elevator doors opened. What he'd said was very astute, but I wasn't fully concentrating. What he was saying had just reminded me of something. It had reminded me of years ago, the first of the many times I'd left New York, when I'd been living with the man in Alphabet City. He said the only way out of New York was to make a run for it, because if you thought about it, you'd be like everybody else who was trapped; you'd weigh the pros and cons, and the bottom line would be that you'd never get out. It made me wonder, now, if it was easier to leave a lover, or to leave a city—though of course so many times the two are so interconnected you can't be sure what you're turning your back on. Or maybe you do find out, but not until you're really out there, on the road. Then, if it feels like the road's stretching toward something, you find out you've still got horizons, but if all you can see, in all that space, is a person, that person's no mirage. He won't recede. You just have to turn around and find him again.

I was thinking these thoughts not so much because of the man I ran away from when I was eighteen, but because at the moment, I was for all intents and purposes in limbo, the labyrinthine yet familiar limbo of New York. It wasn't my home in Allentown, and it wasn't whatever I'd go toward next. The day before Howell's memorial service, my husband had said there was no use in pretending, no point in his going to a memorial service and sitting at my side as if we shared a life; we were going to separate, and it was only a question of time before one of us was gone.

As soon as Steven turned his key in the lock and opened the door, I glided past everyone, hurrying across the huge expanse of shiny floorboards to the windows, the big glass windows that fronted on lower Fifth Avenue, and stared outside with such concentration tears rose in my eyes. There were stars in the sky; I could see them where the rain clouds drifted apart, and though there were only a few, they still seemed as wonderful as they had seemed scattered everywhere, long ago, above Parker's Pond. There were the stars and, far below, there was steam blanching the night, rising from below ground, where, on the subways, distances were being traversed, people were in transit. I saw through to that. I saw it as clearly as Violet had seen inside Sylvie's mind earlier in the evening, and as clearly as I had seen into Howell's gentleman friend's mind when he stood in Steven's apartment and hoped to disappear in a crowd that was not crowded enough, having no idea whether it would be more painful to be acknowledged or to go unnoticed. I suddenly felt as though I could see through anything, much the way Madame Money had claimed to Violet she could see the

future. Like her, I knew at the very least how to make an educated guess. Keep pressing your luck and eventually your luck
won't hold: ice will crack, subway cars collide. At some point,
accommodate fear, because otherwise fear will subsume you.
But it was difficult to think cynically that minute. Across
Steven's loft, Violet was talking with Damian, a fresh drink in
her hand, and the man with yellow, yellow hair was waiting on
the fringes, eager to approach. At Howell's memorial service,
and at the reception afterwards, Violet was flirting, cocking her
head in mock disbelief at whatever Damian was saying to shock
her, and as strange a feeling as it was to have, I envied her. I
envied her because in all probability she was playing a game she
did not even know she was playing. The farther I moved away
from the glass, the more clearly they were reflected. I knew
them so well, I cared for them or sympathized with them. I
appreciated their good intentions in difficult circumstances.
Eventually I turned toward the windows, almost nose-to-the-
glass, so I felt the outside coldness through the windows almost
as an ache. Then I simply stood there to spy on the world that
had nothing to do with them. As I looked down to the wide
open spaces of the city—though it's true those spaces existed
primarily as corridors between buildings—I could have been
Howell in the tree, intentionally myopic, a little dazed, wishing
to be a little daring, but unlike Howell I had braced myself to
stand firm, taking in everything that was not the life inside this
room, this claustrophobic room that had become a repository
for people's good intentions, for their attempts at understand-
ing, this loft above Fifth Avenue that most of them would never
stand in again, which had suddenly become the place where
they could understand what was not understandable, where
they could have a drink, meet the people they'd always wanted
to encounter, where they could forgive at the same time they

were forgetting. Though I looked at Violet reflexively for my love to be beamed back, I knew I had already begun a journey outside her parameters. Nose and fingers to the glass—because who was watching, who cared?—there was all of New York. Outside there seemed, amid steam and stars, to be nothing but space.

See the Pyramids

T HE STONE rabbit's ears stand completely upright, a reminder to Cheri that for perfect posture, you should imagine someone pulling your head straight toward the sky, as if a piece of string is attached to the center of your head. And if you don't care about perfect posture? Grab the string and loop it around your neck, then let him pull. The big marionette manipulator in the sky: God, who wants you to stand up straight. His celestial voice filtering through Anders's barking baritone: *I've told you and told you to stand up straight; you're going to get curvature of the spine, be a stooped old woman before your time.*

Cheri considers what a disappointment she sometimes is to Anders. She is pretty, but not regal; talented, but not with an unusual talent; nice, though given to sulking. The stone rabbit, which Anders has corrected her about—it is a cement rabbit, not stone—stands in the center of the back-porch picnic table, a deity waiting for its nightly offerings: small windup toys from the local drugstore positioned at its bunny feet; a bough of lilacs from the garden; a contemporary update provided by the addition of a woven friendship bracelet tied over the bunny brow as an improvised sweatband. They love to joke, Anders and LaValle; it's something men of that generation seem to do, Cheri has noticed: have big plans and enjoy small jokes. The vintage Farrah Fawcett poster from someone's garage sale has been laminated to become a dartboard for suction-cupped arrows; Anders has obtained drinking glasses at a flea market that are illustrated with Jughead and his friends Archie, Betty, and Veronica; there is a moose doormat that says WELCOME TO

THE CAMP. Though Cheri disdains retro for the sake of retro, some of the old jokes—including fashion—seem to make more sense than all these proliferating adolescent jokes.

They have rented this house on the Maine coast for July. The situation is that the owners, with ever increasing property taxes to pay on their waterfront property, now rent out their house for the last two months of summer and move back to their apartment on Beacon Hill. Cheri is occupying the house with Anders, LaValle, and Erin. She and Erin bankroll the place with money from modeling. Anders does the inventive, sporadically presented cooking. LaValle is a complete deadbeat who doesn't even wash his own clothes, though he does have some interest in "motoring," as he calls it: having them all pile into the car with a picnic Anders has packed and driving somewhere nice to eat it. Erin, Cheri's best friend, loves LaValle, which is why he's part of the picture: Erin's "agent"; her "driver"; a willing "assistant to photographers" (which means that he has the smarts to point out where it's sunny). Erin herself is a very capable person, but lazy. She'll occasionally toss LaValle's clothes (silk underwear; shorts; tacky tourist-shop tee-shirts; sweatpants) into the washer as a little kiss of domesticity; in exchange, he takes care of what he calls "the details." This can include going to automatic teller machines for cash advances on Erin's Visa card, renting movies to watch on the VCR, phoning around until he finds someone who will give Erin a cervical cap, sending orchid plants as special thank-yous to particularly nice photographers or stylists. Anders and LaValle generally keep a certain distance from one another, like two male dogs who know that once they make eye contact, it perpetuates the necessity of marking the territory. When Anders is on the porch, LaValle tends to be in the yard. Therefore, when Anders starts in on Cheri's posture, there's no one to rescue her.

Erin is having her afternoon nap, lying on the bedroom floor on top of a Styrofoam surfboard, with a wet sheet stretched over her and a fan going full blast. Cheri and Anders are alone on the porch. They're both fading in the heat, slightly out of sorts, nagging each other a little, at loose ends until Erin wakes up and they can set out on an afternoon adventure. Short of a strong, cool breeze, only a movie animator could bring them to life, and the animator would probably opt first for the flamingo on the face of the clock; start the cement rabbit jumping; take the candles, in the shape of penguins and have them waddle fat-lady-in-a-girdle style across the tabletop. Farrah could step out of the poster and be there, with all her fabulous, fabulous hair and her pearly white teeth, to join in the fun. Scratch that, though: it's the middle of a heatwave, and nothing is moving, the air is stultifying and still. Anders has been on Cheri's case all day: the necessity of eating something, at least a spoonful of something, for breakfast; the advantage of speaking along with the French language tapes when the instructor tells you to; the lecture on bad posture and the evils implied therein. *Jeez,* Cheri thinks; after a certain point, even most parents aren't so diligent about the necessity of their children's self-improvement, are they? Don't they run out of steam? Cheri didn't stay around in California to see how family life would play itself out. She ran away from her father and stepmother when they had the second squaller in two years, hit the road directly after visiting Janey in the hospital (a courtesy call with Dad, who stayed until the end of visiting hours). Cheri had a nylon suitcase packed with her clothes hidden in the trunk of Dad's Mercedes. Made it to Seattle, courtesy of a nice trucker, no hands-on-knee stuff, no probing questions about how young people today felt. By the next evening, she'd proceeded to the safe house she'd been to a couple of years before when she escaped from her mother's place in Topanga, got a new ID from a vending machine set up in the bathroom: a rigged-up photo booth in case you wanted to have your ID picture look like you, instead of selecting from the photo box, then using the old Royal typewriter on the little desk that had been put up under the window to fill in whatever information was necessary (depending on what you took: driver's license; student ID), a photocopy machine on the vanity next to the sink, sign on the dotted line, and presto, you had credentials which would look highly professional when you slipped the card in your wallet after using the three-step laminating machine that stood on top of the toilet tank. There were no towels and wash-cloths in the bathroom, and if anyone showered in there, Cheri would have been surprised. There was another bathroom downstairs for that; the upstairs bathroom was the manufacturing plant, the first step toward your journey out into the world as someone else, with a different . . . what would you say? A more advantageous social profile. The house belonged to some second-tier studio type in L.A.; it was rumored he'd given it to his teenage son who was blackmailing him. It was also said to have once served as a retreat for Robert Redford. Back when the heated pool got filled. In the days when not so many people crashed there. Anders's brother maintained the house, and his lips were sealed about who actually employed him.

Cheri had met Anders the morning after her arrival, when she was on her way out to look for a waitressing job. He was helping his brother change a tire. It was love at first sight, though what Cheri had stopped to fall in love with was the car: a voluptuous red bullet car, shining in the rare Seattle sun. There she stood: scrawny, too-tall little Dorothy Weston, having just dyed her hair auburn and plucked her eyebrows into skeptical high arches, wearing chandelier earrings she'd found in the "giveaway" box, her only makeup some Princess Di electric blue on the inside of her lower lashes, the perfect girl to ride in such a perfect car. "Cheri Sandler," she said in response to Anders's smile. And she had the papers to prove it.

For years, Cheri has felt that she's gotten away with something. Judicious people might want to talk about good health or even good luck, but the something Cheri thinks she's gotten away with has more in common with the red sports car. She thinks that because of her looks—her hair now back to blond, remuneratively photographed good looks—people are attracted to her as a sort of keen machine. Envious people can easily be discounted; people who look at a hot car and know they're not the type—that's unfortunate for them, but good for what's being appraised. For a while, what she thought she was getting away with was Anders—his connections; his bright ideas; his vigilance about what she deserved, and what she could get. But then she realized that he needed her more than she needed him, so she started thinking that what she was getting away with was living without love. In other words, with Anders she could have the same things people in love had—companionship; attention; affection—more than that, though, she could have the appearance of being part of the status quo, so fewer people would hit on her, fewer people would ask her to explain herself, less speculation would go on generally—but he didn't think she loved him, and she didn't think he loved her, so if things fell apart, at least it might be less emotionally devastating. The downside of her relationship with Anders was that not being her lover, or in love with her, he had free range to take the positions lovers are not supposed to take toward one another: bullying father toward daughter; teacher to pupil.

"When is she ever going to wake up?" LaValle says, coming onto the porch and sniff-sniffing the air, in which he's caught the scent—the unmistakable Dove soap scent—of Anders. Anders's own nose twitches slightly, as he starts his approach-avoidance dance, moving behind the plant stand to snap off a dead fern frond, then circling forward until he's out from behind his protection. Erin—now there is a person Cheri loves. Cheri often reminds herself that if she was fucked-up because her mother, predivorce, and pre–Topanga Canyon, ran away to join an ashram when she was five, Erin had it worse, because her mother moved her so-called spiritual advisor right into the house to follow her like a shadow, intoning speculative questions about the yin or yang of what Erin's mother was doing. The advisor's husband came and went—mostly went—but when he was in residence he had clients come for Rolfing, and Erin, who had spoken to some older friends about the situation, got the mistaken impression that the deep moans she heard were the sounds of people in childbirth, so that of course she was frantic, absolutely desperate, when she herself got pregnant at twelve. Then she had the baby and the spiritual advisor appropriated it, moved to Montana, leaving behind the husband, who still came and went, though after his wife's departure he and Erin's mother began long nights of drinking frozen vodka together and eventually had a baby of their own. Babies. Women of every age were always having babies. The girls at the agency always talked about getting their bodies in shape for childbirth, which meant trying to overcome bulimia. Every magazine was full of advice about pregnancy and raising children. Cheri had zero inclination to have sex and insisted on seeing a doctor's report that the person had tested negative for HIV and had no sexually transmitted diseases before she'd sleep with him, and except for unavoidable business reasons, she wouldn't sleep with anybody, anyway. She had an IUD, and Erin was going to be fitted with a cervical cap as soon as she could get back to the private clinic in Chelsea. Meanwhile, Erin was not sleeping with LaValle, who had begun embracing and winding around her like an octopus. She was probably just taking afternoon naps to get away from him.

"I'm going to make sandwiches for us," Anders says, skirting the imaginary line that divides his porch space from LaValle's. "Diet mayo? Anyone?"

"Plain bread, toasted, please," Cheri says.

"Would you like me to help you?" LaValle says.

"No, thanks," Anders says. "But perhaps it's time to rouse the Sleeping Beauty?"

"I'm wide awake," Cheri says, trying out a Farrah smile.

Both of them let it pass and turned toward the kitchen door. What are women supposed to love about men? Cheri suddenly wonders. Their butts and their shoes. That was what you usually heard: their butts and their shoes. LaValle is so thin he doesn't have a butt. Anders she's seen naked so many times that denim-covered, there's absolutely no mystery. His butt is covered with fine, corkscrewy blond hairs that grow in a haze from pores large enough to make his skin look pocked, like a pincushion. He has the same hairs on his legs, with oblong patches chafed away at the front of each thigh. His hands are very nice, but the way he gestures bothers her; he's always declaring something, then moving his left hand as if throwing a Frisbee. His right hand is used to slap something into the ground—an imaginary pole, perhaps. Or in the arcades, those games where they give you a rubber hammer, and you have a split second to mash down the head of some Muppet or whatever it is that keeps popping up. Frisbee, Muppet bashing: the self-righteous stupidity of the military (left hand); the declining interest rates (right).

Erin comes downstairs in briefs and one of LaValle's white shirts. She has one black toenail, from stubbing her toe on a rock when she stumbled in a brook the week before. Also one nail painted red: an experiment with color. She sinks into a wicker rocker and crosses her legs, pushing her hair back from her sleep-puffed face. Cheri reaches out and clasps her hand, swings it back and forth a few times, drops it.

"Today is my mother's birthday," Erin says. "You know how things come to you in dreams? I dreamed I came downstairs and Anders had made a huge cake, only it was a wedding cake instead of a birthday cake, and my mother was there in the kitchen, eating it. I thought that if she wasn't saying anything to him about making the wrong kind of cake, I certainly wasn't going to. It didn't exactly come to me in a dream that it was her birthday—I was wondering about whether it might be before I went to sleep, but once I saw the wedding cake, I was sure it was her birthday, instead. She got married on Valentine's Day. That's hard to forget."

"To your father?" Cheri says.

"Well, to my knowledge she never married Yannos."

"Sri Sensitivity," Cheri says, under her breath: her variation of the Rolfer's Hindu name.

"Sri Stolichnaya," Erin sighs.

A brown rabbit with a white tail emerges from the underbrush at the edge of the property, where the land begins to slope toward the meadow that leads to the dock.

"Look at that!" Erin says.

"And the robin!" Cheri says.

A robin is dive-bombing the rabbit. The rabbit hops forward, then zigzags, springing closer.

"Open the door for it!" Erin squeals, bringing Anders, slice of bread in hand, onto the back porch. He almost collides with

Cheri, who's jumped up, amused at the idea that she controls the gate at the finish line. "Come on, Mr. Rabbit!" she hollers, throwing open the porch door, and surprisingly, the rabbit, instead of retreating from her voice, hip-hops toward the door, fast, veering off to scurry under the chokecherry bush just as the danger of being pecked equals the terror of finding himself inside, among vacationers. The swooping bird circles for a last, desperate dive. Suddenly, on the stereo, Patsy Cline begins to sing: "See the pyramids. . . ." When they first got to the house, LaValle hooked up small speakers with amazing sound quality, which he placed horizontally on the overhang above the kitchen door; as Anders makes lunch, LaValle, freed from the constraint of silence while Erin was asleep, has turned on some music. "See the pyramids. . . ." Problem is, the CD's damaged. Where is LaValle? This excitement between the bird and the rabbit has been going on while Patsy Cline sings the same three words over and over. Is that the shower Cheri hears? "See the pyramids. . . ."

"LaValle!" Anders barks. Then he turns and takes the back stairs three at a time. The CD player is in LaValle's room. LaValle has put on one of his favorite singers, then gone to take a shower.

"Along the Nile," Patsy Cline sings. It's a relief, like sneezing after keeping still and waiting. "See the . . ." But again the music stops, and apparently it's stopped for good, because Anders is running down the stairs, while up above, water is still pelting down in the shower.

"That was our nature lesson for the day," Erin says.

"That rabbit didn't have good posture," Cheri calls to Anders. "Did you see that its ears were just flopping? Not like its head was being pulled up by an imaginary string."

"Do you know," Anders says, coming back onto the porch,

"that this is the forty-third day of flooding in the Midwest? People have lost their homes, they don't have drinking water, they have nothing to eat, they're sleeping in shelters, their crops are ruined, they don't know where to turn—and what you want to do is tease me for caring about your posture. I don't care so goddamn much about your posture. I feel like joining the relief effort, going out there and laying sandbags, because that would be more constructive and more meaningful than trying to help you, when you've got a charmed life and not even the sense to be thankful. You're a wiseass who nags anybody who cares about her."

"Really, Anders?" Erin says. "You're taking a plane to Illinois or someplace like that to stack sandbags on the levee, or something like that?"

But the damage has been done. Cheri is crushed, and Anders isn't budging. He's turning to go back into the house, but he isn't budging. To add insult to injury, he calls over his shoulder: "Erin, at least you know a big word. You know what a levee is."

Tears roll down Cheri's cheeks as the rabbit hops out from under the bush, then makes a mad dash for the underbrush.

"Maybe it got too near the robin's nest," Erin says, looking off to the middle distance, trying not to embarrass Cheri by noticing the tears she's trying to wipe away.

"Maybe it'll go back in the woods and get bitten by a viper, like I've been," Cheri says.

"You're clever," Erin says. "I don't know why he picks on you."

"Clever? I'm clever but I'm not intelligent, am I? That's what he thinks, too."

"I live with a moron. How intelligent is that?"

"He's not a moron. He's nicer than Anders a lot of the time."

Erin shrugs. This is generally true, so what can she say?

"I don't have to be with him," Cheri says.

"Of course you don't," Erin says.

"But you think I do."

"I don't think that. I think you could be with anybody."

"Anybody. Like who? Henry Kissinger?"

Erin's eyes flash with surprise. "Kissinger," she says slowly. "What would make you think of him?"

"Because maybe I listen to NPR. Maybe I see his name when I read the newspaper occasionally, when LaValle throws it on the bathroom floor."

"Isn't he a slob?" Erin says. "I mean, he really is. He discards the newspaper first, then lets things pile up on it, like socks and stuff from his pants pockets when he's emptying them, and then he picks up the newspaper like he's going to carry everything off nicely on a big silver tray, and he's astonished when everything falls all over the floor." Erin sees that Cheri is still crying. "Don't let him make you feel insecure," Erin says quietly. "Life's not one big improvement lesson. You're a beautiful girl, you've got friends who love you. . . ."

"What friends? I've just got you, and you'll probably marry LaValle. It'll be like my father marrying Janey. Suddenly Cheri is no longer number one. I'm not feeling sorry for myself, I'm just telling you the way things are. Or are going to be."

"He has been bugging me about marrying him," Erin says.

"Yeah? Well, I just knew he was. He doesn't like Anders at all, and he'd probably like it better without me, too. Just the two of you in this house would be better. You could get married, go on a honeymoon, see the pyramids."

"And what? Come back to the United States and sit with him all alone in some big house on the Maine coast, watching the birds and the bunnies? Get real."

"What's the difference? We're sitting here watching the birds and the bunnies."

"Well," Erin says after a long pause. "I'm sure we should be saintly like you-know-who and go throw sandbags in front of flooding rivers."

"You're going to marry him, aren't you?"

"I don't know," Erin says. You can hear the squirm in her voice. "He's not so bad," she says. "We're used to each other. I don't want to keep experimenting. I see where that's gotten everybody else: married to people who are sort of right for them and sort of wrong for them. But they spend so much time getting into relationships and getting out of them. I don't know anybody who found anybody perfect, do you?"

Cheri doesn't answer. She's going through the list of her friends, which is small, indeed. Once Janey was her friend. Janey confided in her that she didn't want a second child, she was just doing it because it was what Cheri's father wanted. She was afraid he'd leave her for someone else. Cheri had seen him in a car once with a woman—at a drive-in hamburger place out by the beach, on a day when she was skipping school; she'd seen him and ducked down to the floor of the car so he wouldn't see her, but she made her boyfriend pull in near her father's car and describe the woman. "Now he's kissing her," her boyfriend had said, and she had felt physically sick, crouched on the floor of the car. The baby wasn't six months old. "I was kidding. I was just kidding you," her boyfriend had protested later, but he'd said it so intently, with his eyes narrowed, that his earnestness had been a dead giveaway he was lying. So: Janey—but why stick around to see Janey get hurt?—and another girl she some-times wrote letters to, a girl from grade school who lived in Santa Fe now, and an ex-boyfriend who felt he was her friend, though she didn't feel the same way; he was just someone she'd once slept with a few times. Still, she sometimes called him, late at night, because she was on the East Coast, and he was back there in California time. Though that wasn't it: she called late because she didn't want Anders to know she was calling. The boy was sentimental and loved to play Remember When. Remember When I won you that prize on the Santa Monica Pier. Remember When we did it in the elevator at the Chateau Marmont. He was in law school. He seemed maudlin, earnest, and trapped in the past. She was a little afraid, finally, that he'd depress her more than he could help her. So that left Anders— who did like her, let's be honest—who liked her, but who couldn't stop himself from criticizing, and Erin, who'd been her best friend since they met in Seattle at the safe house, and then there was no one else, unless you counted LaValle, who was ambivalent. She didn't think he liked her or disliked her; he was ambivalent. A word Anders had taught her.

There the two of them stood: LaValle freshly showered, his long hair combed back with a wide-toothed comb, wearing white bermuda shorts and a Banks Beer tank top, and Anders, gripping the canvas carryall that held their lunch, looking slightly chagrined at the direction the day had taken.

Cheri quickly scanned the woods, looking for the rabbit. Gone, and likely to stay hidden for a while.

On the way to the car, Anders reached out and took her hand.

The house LaValle had them "motor to" was half an hour away, a historic house once owned by a shipbuilder, down a paved road so rutted and dusty Cheri thought at first it was a dirt road. For a second, beyond the tall trees, she could see only the second story of the house, which reminded her very much of the way the safe house peeked through the woods in Seattle. What a thing to call a house: as if, like the rabbit rushing onto the porch, once over the finish line you were inside, *safe*. What did that mean? That the wolf wouldn't dare huff and puff? That the cops couldn't come with a search warrant? That it could remain a well-kept secret, even if half the teenagers in Santa Monica knew about its existence? Or that Robert Redford, with all his money, might not decide to buy the place, just pick up the phone and have his attorneys work it out: *Oh, there's a laminating machine and fake ID forms so kids can get a new identity? Well—maybe that could be relocated to the pool house.* Redford wouldn't shut down an important, *safe* place, would he? After all, hadn't she read somewhere that he built a building at Sundance around a tree?

The lawn was scorched because it hadn't rained much this summer, but the bushes and trees were green, and the gardens off to the side, with iron garden benches placed here and there to face the tiered lawn that stretched to the bay, were blooming with white phlox and morning glories and begonias— more flowers than Cheri recognized, more than necessary to make a lavish garden. LaValle is preening: everyone likes the place he has discovered. He leads them through the garden, down a path to a small house that sits below, and they cup their hands to the windows to look into the empty rooms, seeing through the French doors on the opposite side the bay, glistening in the sun.

"It's so wonderful not having to pose," Erin says, standing on tiptoe next to Cheri, to see the highest reaches of the little room inside.

"I know. It drives me crazy when everything in the world turns into a backdrop for a pose," Cheri says.

Anders and LaValle have walked ahead, around the corner of

the house, looking for the ideal picnic spot. Cheri sees their profiles as they pass the last window, and thinks, briefly, that Anders is cuter. When either one of them is in trouble with Erin, or with her, they draw together. They've organized into a team now, sniffing out new territory.

"I wonder if this is a caretaker's house, or whether it's just here, empty. It doesn't seem like anybody lives inside," Erin says.

As they're staring in, taking in the very un-California wideboard floors, the fireplace and mantel in the room Cheri would make her bedroom if she lived there, a little girl comes around the corner and stops, seeing them there. She's pretty, about four years old, holding a small toy horse. Cheri looks at her Velcrofastened running shoes and her white anklets, her grass-stained knees protruding below the pleated skirt of her short jumper. In ten years, she's the person who'll look at Cheri and Erin posing for the camera—if they last in the business. Right now, though, what they have in common is that they're all three a bit rumpled on a summer day, all three strangers to a place that seems to be empty except for them. Then the little girl's mother comes on the scene, snuggling into the side of an older man, who has a baby in a Snuglee on his back—a sleeping, bonneted baby. It's instantaneous, the woman's sudden look of recognition, and Cheri sees that Erin sees it, feels the wheels turning in Erin's brain, writing the whole scenario before the woman speaks: they look familiar; are they in the movies? On TV? Cheri senses Erin's irritation; her determination to be polite; her desire to move on. Just as Erin smiles, the woman says, quietly, "Dorothy Weston."

Jesus; it couldn't be worse if the woman had said Rumpelstiltskin. Better if she'd said Rumpelstiltskin, in fact. It's somebody from California, some friend of Janey's, isn't it? The midwife Janey had for the birth of her first baby, or . . .

"Dorothy. Honey," the woman says.

The little girl runs to her mother's side and does what Cheri wants to do; she hides, shyly. She puts her horse in front of her lips and gazes over the top of its mane, waiting to see what will happen next. What happens next is that the man looks puzzled. "This is a friend's daughter from California," the woman says to the man. Couldn't there be a hint of doubt in her voice, Cheri wonders? She certainly isn't responding to the woman. Erin, taken aback at hearing Cheri's real name, has frozen.

"I'm afraid you've made a mistake," Cheri says.

"You're Carl and Janey's daughter," the woman says. The doubt in her voice, Cheri can tell, has only to do with why Cheri won't acknowledge this.

"I'm not," Cheri says: a mere half-lie; she's Janey's step-daughter, maybe, but not her daughter. The woman's persistence is unnerving, though: she looks friendly, and slightly puzzled, but she keeps eye contact with Cheri. The next thing Cheri blurts out is ridiculous: "I'm her sister," she says, gesturing toward the dumbstruck Erin. Even though Cheri is tall, Erin towers above her. She is dark, and Cheri is fair.

"Excuse us. Our husbands are waiting," Erin says.

"Your husbands! But my God—you can't be married," the woman says. "Janey told me you were in school. Private school. In Boston. Or Baltimore, did she say?"

Francine. The woman's name comes back to Cheri. The woman was in Janey's book discussion group. It's the woman who was studying ballet, who wore pretty ballet flats she let Cheri walk around in when she was a little girl. What is Francine doing in Maine?

"Excuse us," Erin says again. Erin takes Cheri's hand.

"Mama, who are they?" the little girl asks.

"Dorothy," the woman says, half in answer to the child, half trying, still, to engage Cheri. "Are you afraid I'll tell them I saw you, and you weren't in school?"

"Come on, darling. Let's let these ladies get on with their day," the man says, putting his arm around Francine's shoulder.

"Do you want to pet my horse?" the little girl calls to them, when it's clear they're really leaving. As if caught in the glare of headlights, Cheri simply stops moving. It's Erin who turns and pets the horse, murmurs that it's nice, smiles at the man—he's their best hope, except for Anders and LaValle, and where are they? Where are the husbands, the two men who would be proof that they're married women? Erin says, "It's summer. School's not in session in the summer."

Francine seizes on this, as if it's an admission. "Then," she says, "you're afraid I'll say I saw you here?" Her voice is gentle now.

"Really, darling," the man says, trying to steer both Francine and the little girl past them, around the corner of the house. The woman almost lets herself be directed away, then stops. "Janey has missed you," she says. "All you have to do is say the word, and I won't mention that I've seen you. I have the feeling—I get the feeling now that everything isn't all right."

"It's fine," Erin says.

Cheri nods in agreement with Erin. The little girl has bent over and is galloping her horse through a patch of dry grass, making clicking noises with her tongue as its hooves touch the ground. Then she raises the horse to soar into the air. Showing his frustration, now, the man reaches in his wallet and hands Cheri his card: James Q. Rosenberg, Attorney-at-Law. An address in Amherst, Massachusetts. Fax, telex, phone. "If either of us can help you, please call," the man says.

"What can you help with, Daddy?" the little girl says. "Do you want to help me get the horse to fly?"

This goes unanswered, but finally, under pressure, Francine smiles a hesitant smile, looks down, and follows the man. Cheri brushes her hair behind her ears, pretends to be busying herself examining a hangnail. Erin is a wreck; she looks after the people as if Bigfoot just stepped into their path, roared, and stomped off.

"What can they do?" Erin says, thinking out loud. "The worst they can do is call them and say they saw us at Hamilton House. They don't know where we're staying. There's no way they can find us."

"Hamilton House?" Cheri says.

"That's where we are, stupid. Didn't you see the sign when we pulled in saying 'Hamilton House,' and some date?"

"Jesus, Erin," Cheri says, exploding with all the rage that has been smoldering since Anders put her down earlier in the day. "Jesus, please forgive me if I didn't know the name of some deserted house I've never seen before that was lived in by somebody I've never heard of. I mean, we're not exactly at the Washington Monument, Erin."

"I didn't mean 'stupid' as in 'stupid.' Don't get mad at me just because your boyfriend's a prick."

"He's not my boyfriend," Cheri says.

"He's not? What is he? He's just somebody you happen to hang out with? Somebody you ran into, like you just ran into those people, only he was more like a stray dog, you decided to keep him?"

Cheri is about to scream, to really let go, when suddenly a feeling the exact opposite of rage comes over her. A stray dog isn't a bad description of Anders. And wait: wasn't Erin herself saying earlier that it was just as well to be with one person as another, because no one ever came up with the perfect person?

Erin looks sheepish; she can no doubt read Cheri's mind.

What she wonders, though, is what trouble the woman might cause Cheri, whether there isn't something, anything, they can do to get the woman to entirely erase any memory of them. In a fairy tale; that's about where that could happen. Or if Anders and LaValle were their bodyguards, maybe: big, threatening types with karate skills or guns. Where are Anders and LaValle? Are they eating alone, rudely, without them, Erin wonders, as she rounds the house. But no: there's the canvas carryall on a bench. And far, far in the distance—that might be them, of course it's them, cavorting in the water, naked. Forget the near disaster that almost happened on shore: run off, pups of boundless energy, newfound friends that you are, drop your clothes and splash into the water, swim far out until you're just two specks.

Side by side, they watch them. Suddenly the day has unexpectedly divided into Us and Them, and Erin and Cheri, still quaking, are sitting on a bench in a place that has once again become totally quiet, except for the occasional call of a bird, or the faint sounds of the men's voices drifting off the water. Erin, still slightly abject at being snapped at for using one wrong word, reaches into the bag and unwraps a sandwich without offering one to Cheri; instead, she settles the bag between them. Let her fish out her own sandwich, she's thinking, as she opens the foil and bites into hers.

In the distance, they hear a car door slam. The ignition is turned on. It's at that point that Erin looks down and sees the horse, jumps up without thinking, drops the sandwich back in the bag, and rushes toward the car, hollering: "Wait!" Cheri, seeing what Erin has scooped up from the dirt just beneath the bench, jumps up and runs alongside, her hair flapping in the breeze, their dual screams resulting in the car's ignition being switched off. The man is frowning as he looks at them out the slowly lowering window. They've arrived at the car together—

sisters in spirit, if not in fact—Erin holding the horse above her
head like a trophy, bending to hand it through the lowering
back window to the surprised and happy child. "Thank you
very much," the man says. "I didn't know she'd dropped it."

"Daddy, I got my horse!" the little girl squeals.

Now that we're heroes, can you please just forget all about us? Erin
silently wishes, looking past the man to the woman, sitting in
the passenger's seat, holding the baby.

"Those people," Cheri says, breathlessly. "Those people you
thought I knew. Who are they? Did anything happen? I mean,
would a child of theirs being off at school really upset them for
some reason?"

Francine looks at Cheri. "Well, they've had some bad times
recently," she says. "They separated a few months ago. My
friend, though—Janey. I always suspected she was covering for
her stepdaughter, or going along with what her husband told
her to say, because the daughter ran away. That was the rumor,
but no one repeated it to Janey. I think Janey would like to be in
touch with Dorothy. I'm sure she always felt closer to her than
she does toward her own little boys."

"Probably that girl should get in touch," Cheri says.

"I hope she will," Francine says. "Also, my husband is an
attorney, if anyone needs any help. About anything," she adds
lamely.

"They know I'm an attorney," her husband says. It's too
halfhearted to really sound grumpy; by now, he's figured out
Francine isn't mistaken. He nods to the two of them as the window rolls up.

"She's not going to say anything," Erin says, watching the
car drive away. "You really took a big chance, but you could see
it in her eyes: you said you'd get in touch, and she believed
you."

"Somebody who knew them was bound to see me some-time," Cheri says.

"Well, it's completely amazing they haven't seen your face in the magazines after all this time."

"They don't read anything but *Time.*"

"She gets her hair done, doesn't she?"

"Lucky," Cheri says. "So far, lucky."

"I really don't know what I'd do if our family fell apart," Erin says, her voice suddenly tremulous. "Because of what? Because of some technicality? I mean, after all this time, what if they found you and made you go back?"

"What are you talking about?" Cheri says. "If he'd hired private detectives, don't you think I'd have been found? They find everybody, let alone somebody who's working, who's got her picture in magazines. His friends must read magazines, don't you think? You don't think anyone ever pointed me out? You really don't think he'd know how to find me?"

"Then what?" Erin says. "He knows, but he doesn't want you back?"

"As you'd say to me, that's right, stupid."

"But she does," Erin says haltingly.

"Maybe she does," Cheri says. "Apparently, until recently, she was still living with him. I always wished her good luck, she always kept quiet about what was really going on with me. She knew how he could be; if I was going to get out, I'm sure she thought I was entitled."

As they walk, a bird lights on the rim of an empty fountain; another swoops down and the two birds hop in, pecking at something, before rising together, in sudden flight.

"Maybe that guy could help you, if you ever needed help," Erin says.

"Don't go mushy on me, Erin. Some high-priced lawyer is

going to get involved in my wanting to live on my own? Because my father was a bully who made it a point *not* to rape me or beat me up, just to scream in my face until I started hyperventilating?"

Erin is looking after the car, which is long gone. "He didn't seem like a bad guy," she says. "Don't lose his card."

"Just what the guys tell you when they're dying for you," Cheri says. "'Don't lose my card, baby.' Praying you'll call. Praying they'll get laid."

"So she left him," Erin says after a long pause. "You must be glad for her sake that she left him."

"Doesn't mean that much to me," Cheri says.

"It doesn't?"

"I mean, that all seems like such a long time ago. You're my family now, you know?"

Erin nods. She knows, exactly. Now all they have to do is stick together for one more year plus one month, and it will be too late for the law to do anything about it. In August 1994, when Erin is nineteen years old, Cheri will turn sixteen: no longer a minor, no laws about statutory rape to worry about; no fake ID ever needed again. Can't buy liquor at sixteen, but Anders and LaValle take care of that anyway. And maybe you can't get married in every state, but there are some you can get married in at sixteen, places where you show your ID, your real ID it could be then, and they give you a marriage license. The two of them could have a double wedding, elaborate or simple, whatever they chose. *Oh, please, time. Please go fast,* Erin silently prays. Because Cheri is her best friend in the whole world, and more than anything—or at least as much as she would like the assurance that the four of them will always be together—she would like to think of her as safe.

In Irons

———

MISS MAY was baby-sitting. Derek was at a Cuban restaurant, breaking up with his girlfriend, Marcia Ryall. Two sips into the first beer, he had blurted it out; by the time he finished the bottle, she had excused herself to go to the bathroom and gone out the front door, instead. That was what a waitress told him, when he finally got up and knocked on the bathroom door and a deep-voiced man told him to hold his horses. "Was she crying?" he asked the waitress. "I didn't notice," she said. She noticed a woman, five foot six, with short brown hair and glasses, wearing a white tee-shirt and jeans, but she couldn't say whether that totally inconspicuous person was crying? He went back to his own uneaten dinner, and Marcia's. He ate his fried porkchops, as well as her fried plantains, drank her untouched glass of sangria (sweet!), then asked the waitress to put the leftovers in a box. Miss May might want a late-night snack. He bought himself a cigar, but tucked it into his pocket with the toothpick instead of smoking it. That might be his own late-night snack.

He was in the doghouse with everybody: Sallie, his ex-wife; Miss May, his ex-wife's aunt, who had raised her; his second wife, who was in the process of divorcing him; his girlfriend, who had listened to what he had to say without comment, before excusing herself to go to the bathroom. He was not yet in the doghouse with his daughter, Hillary. Then again, she was four years old: too young for the bathroom trick, even if she'd been inclined. If she said she needed to go to the bathroom, she needed to go to the bathroom. Right now, she was home watching *Frasier.* Her favorites were Daphne and the dog. Every time Daphne spoke, or the dog came into the room, she would laugh. Her bedtime was usually nine o'clock, but an exception was granted—even by her mother—for *Frasier.*

He stopped at In Irons, his favorite bar down by the waterfront. "I suppose that's some S&M place, where dominatrices rap your knuckles when they put down your overpriced drink?" Sallie had said to him sourly, when he invited her out for a drink several nights before—the night she flew into Key West from Lake Charles with Hillary and Miss May. Sallie no longer lived in Lake Charles; she'd moved to Houston, but she had stopped in Louisiana to round up Miss May, who was expected to be Sallie's eyes and ears during the week mother and daughter were separated. He'd always liked Miss May and, if truth be told, he'd been a little uneasy about entertaining his daughter for an entire week. Marcia would have helped him, but it seemed dishonest to ask her to take care of Hillary for a week, then dump her, so he'd decided to level with her the first night she could get free from her job. She'd been expecting to meet Hillary at the restaurant. She'd even bought a bracelet for Hillary that spelled out her name in pink painted letters across smooth glistening shells. He didn't know that. Wouldn't know it until some time later. He crumpled the cellophane that had been wrapped around his cigar. The cellophane looked sad to him: the cigar animal's shed skin. He held the cigar to his nose and sniffed. A big bruiser on the barstool next to him shot flame from a lighter in his direction. It was a small silver lighter. One that no doubt had a history.

"Thank you kindly," he said through clenched teeth, turning the cigar slowly in the flame.

"*De nada,*" the bruiser said. The man was drinking something the color of brass. On the jukebox, Dean Martin was singing "That's Amore." Down the bar, a boy and girl who looked too young to drink were making out, rubbing noses. Their noses were so mobile, it didn't look as if they contained any cartilage. On the TV over the bar, a weatherman gestured at a map of the United States, across which rolled various streaks and marks: clouds jerkily passing over the northeast, followed by diagonal slashes signifying rain. The weatherman's pointer dropped to Florida: the big pee-pee (Hillary's term for male genitalia) of the United States. The state of Florida began to pulsate with excitement, the sun spreading a nimbus that glowed the length of the state. Eighty-five degrees, it said at the tip. Everywhere else, the weather was lousy. In Aspen, where Lolly, his second wife, had relocated with her cinematographer boyfriend, it was snowing—but of course that made everyone very merry in Aspen. He had spoken to her on the phone in November, and she had told him to call back any time he was feeling blue. He supposed he was, though he wasn't sure why, since the relationship with Marcia hadn't been either exciting enough or a good enough fit that it might at least have seemed comfortable. But to just walk off like that. . . . He took out his money clip—a present from Lolly: Scrooge McDuck jumping in the air, looking deranged, money floating all around him. The wad was slim—he had no desire to see if any big bills were at the bottom, or if the best he had was twenties—but he extracted enough to pay for his beer and leave a tip, then walked out, still half expecting that the guy who'd lit his cigar would say something to him, though no one said anything. There was a pay phone around the corner, but he thought: what for? A melancholy call to Lolly, while a nice fire crackled in her fireplace and her two golden retriever puppies ran in circles, the cinematographer probably sitting there in his Eames chair, or whatever the hell it was, his *Mission* chair, thinking how visual it all was. The guy was eight years younger than she was. All those hair extensions and stomach crunches paid off for Lolly.

Sallie, on the other hand—if he believed what she said—hadn't dated since their divorce. She hung out with a bunch of rich divorcées in Houston, but the ranks were getting depleted, she complained (he heard this from Miss May), because all the embittered doctors and lawyers' wives who'd been turned in for this year's model had become lesbians or, possibly, were playing at being lesbians. Sallie sat in on a Monday-night lesbian poker game, which a priest who'd weaned himself away from blackjack also came to, as well as a ballerina with osteoporosis, who was writing about the group in her memoir. Miss May loved, in particular, to gossip about people she'd never met—and she loved any wisp of tragedy or scandal. By day Sallie worked in an advertising agency, but by night she gambled, when she wasn't studying foot reflexology with a Mr. Chinn, who went ballistic if anyone wrote his last name with just one "n." One night a week she, and some woman she worked with drove miles and miles to go bowling. His daughter often imitated her mother's bowling as she stood in line waiting for him to buy something. She'd bring her clasped hands to her face, take three steps forward, while slowly swinging one arm behind her, then bend her knees deeply to roll the imaginary ball, always declaring a strike and giving a cheerleader leap before returning to his side.

He got into his old yellow Mustang convertible and started it. Leonard Cohen, on the tape deck, was singing "The Future." What he liked about the song—aside from the lyrics—was that except for the girl chorus, he could believe that Leonard Cohen might just be singing to himself in the shower. It was the sort of song that made you feel that the singer might have dropped a bar of soap in the middle of a verse, but gone right on singing.

There was never a parking place on the small lane where he lived. Most of the houses had driveways just big enough to hold a car, but the two parking places on the street that belonged to no one had been claimed by a madwoman who put trash cans in the space she considered hers, to keep other cars out, and by a giant: a seven-foot man with a shaved head and a third eyebrow tattooed above and between his real eyebrows. He had hung a sign on a ficus tree whose roots had broken through the asphalt of the second parking place, making it almost impossible to park in, anyway, that said PARK AND BE KILLED. If you thought the police would go around and talk to the person who displayed such a sign, you didn't know anything about Key West. So between the trash cans and the subtle warning, he never even tried to park on his street anymore. He usually found a place two blocks away, near where Roy Scheider used to live. Then there was the nightly internal debate about whether he should try to wrestle the top up; only the left side could be secured, and the zipper only closed over a fraction of the back window, but still: it was some help if it started to pour—especially if done in conjunction with spreading the old shower curtain in the back trunk over the front seats. But tonight he was too tired; even if he triumphed over bad weather, that wouldn't mean he hadn't still fallen down on the job about everything else—the look Sallie gave him at the airport had communicated that, beyond a doubt—so he chose to believe the man with his pointer: all through the night his car would be dry, and the next day, radiant Key West would continue to beam with sunshine.

Miss May was eating an ice cream on a stick as he came in, carrying the leftovers. It was like bringing a lump of coal, when the recipient already had an amethyst-filled geode. The TV was on low. Miss May had been painting her nails: several little bottles were sitting on top of an *In Style* magazine she had carried off the plane. The aroma of acetone filled the room. Miss May said: "Oh, darlin', I do hope you had as good an evening as the girls. Your little beauty has pink toenails and red fingernails, which she promises never to bite again. We had a tea, and I found the most adorable things in your cabinet. That beautiful etched glass decanter was our teapot, and for a strainer we used the toe of one of my ripped nylons, stretched over two chopsticks I found, and the tea itself was vanilla almond, which I brought with me from the specialty store in my neighborhood. We thought the little Japanese dishes were nicer than coffee mugs, so we took out those pretty square bowls and used them as our teacups, and then Hillary had the idea of going outside to get some lovely bougainvillea to put in the tea because she said—can you imagine?—she said: 'Mommy's friend Father Donovan puts an olive in his martini, so I need to put a pink flower in my tea.' I went to Houston in September and he came to dinner. He's quite the man about town. I don't think he's spending his time praying and making jelly . . . though I guess that's the monks. I doubt if they're playing poker!"

As she talked, he sat in the wicker chair draped with a serape. He had found the chair on the street, the first of the year, when the landlords loaded out the possessions of their evicted tenants. The serape had been left behind—he had had Marcia clean it for him in Woolite—when a truck crushed a tortoise crossing Route 1, and he had almost slammed into the back of the truck that had stopped abruptly, but not abruptly enough. The woman in the truck's passenger seat had jumped out and thrown a serape over the turtle, wailing something in Spanish that he couldn't understand. The man had then become involved in getting the woman back in the truck. He had succeeded, leaving the serape behind, which Derek had slowly unfolded, as if he were inspecting a wound that had been under bandages for days. He had stood in the breakdown lane, considering the pulpy turtle, then the serape, and then he had placed the turtle several feet off the road, near a mango tree, placing a few fallen leaves over it, then folded the serape and put it in the backseat of his Mustang. The sofa Miss May sat on had come with the "furnished" apartment: meaning that there had been a mattress, sofa, and metal kitchen stool, as well as an overturned wooden crate draped with a tablecloth commemorating the state of Idaho. When Sallie sent Hillary's drawings, he began to use the nails that were already in the walls to put them up, sometimes puncturing the sun, or the roof of a house, or some enormous bird or plane in order to hang them. The antique Turkoman prayer rug had been a Christmas present from his uncle George, in Istanbul. The club chairs he was storing for a computer repair person who either would, or would not, eventually return to Key West, depending on her guru Rama's advice. His friend Tad, who was an electrician, had gotten the chandelier rewired, cleaned, and working. There was even a dimmer switch, which Tad had pulled out of somebody's trash the day after Christmas, still in its package. The TV was something Marcia had loaned him, because it took up half the space in her bedroom, which was eight by twelve. He imagined that soon she would be repossessing it.

"Did you and your friend Grant ever finish that screenplay about the lady who was abducted by space aliens?" Miss May asks.

"He was working on that alone. I wasn't part of that project."

"Wasn't Troy Donahue interested in it?"

"I don't remember that."

"What is that box on your lap, darlin'?"

"It's yellow rice and beans. I thought you might want it. There's some garlic chicken, too."

"Oh no, anything with garlic is not for me," Miss May says.

"There was a great bit in Grant's script about one of the spacemen giving Troy Donahue something that looked like a root, and Troy reaching in his pocket and taking out a little packet of Gummy Bears. Then it went into a fantasy sequence in which the root began to sprout and to wind around everything in the room, like kudzu, while the Gummy Bears came to life and were acting sort of like the June Taylor dancers, doing these bizarre kicks in sequence, while the kudzu kept slowly strangling everything."

"Sometimes when he was wound up, I could see that Sallie didn't think he was proper company for a young child," Miss May says.

"Miss May, how did you raise somebody as conventional as Sallie?"

"Well," Miss May says, "I never did think she was a bit conventional, but in high school, you know, there were gangs and there were sororities, and she had to choose between them, and she chose the sororities. They all talked the same way in the sorority, and she began to talk the same way they did, which was sort of arch, if I had to describe it any one way. They used words to ward things off, the way the gang girls used spiky jewelry and the pointed toes of their black boots—all those girls in those ugly, expensive boots they spent their last dimes for. Of course, now I suppose they'd have guns."

"Tell the truth, Miss May. Didn't you think she was being very conventional, getting married to an AAA travel agent who wore chinos and oxfords and volunteered at the soup kitchen on Friday nights?"

"I thought you were a nice person. I still think you're a nice person. You and Sallie both changed so much, it would have been a miracle if you'd stayed together."

"You know what, though, Miss May? I put her back in the position she was in in high school. I made her choose between the uptight world we were living in and the almost total freedom Wendell represented. She took one look at the craziness, and for the second time in her life, she opted for self-preservation, as she told me so many times. She had to rejoin the sorority, so to speak."

"Your friend Wendell I never took to, as you know," Miss May says. "But it serves no purpose to speak ill of the dead. And if he might have known he had that disease, and lured you into his employ when he actually knew he'd be getting worse and more and more dependent, then I really do not think he was a good person at all." She looks around the almost empty room. "How long is the money Wendell left you going to last? You were always a very energetic, self-motivated person, but I don't see much of that anymore. You came here to . . . well, as I see it, you moved to land's end. You might have come for Wendell's sake, but he's dead, and you're still here. You're going to have to settle on a job, eventually. It's like you're on an overnight camp out in your own home, Derek. Sleeping on an inflatable mattress . . ."

"That's gallantry. I'm giving you and Hillary the bed."

"I'm sorry if I've antagonized you," Miss May says. "It just seems to me that a man who once created a lovely home outside Atlanta . . ."

"Things!" he says. "They'd started to proliferate. It was like Grant's script: one little root that expands like speeded-up time-lapse photography. You see the tentacles begin to creep outward. . . ."

"Derek, dear, furniture does not grow in your house. You may decide that you've brought in too much furniture, but . . ."

Actually, the divesting had been inspired by Wendell, whose own passing on of possessions began in the months before his death. He wanted to see that predictable mixture of anguish and appreciation on his friends' faces. Even the washing machine was loaded off, their garbage man returning at night, with a borrowed truck, smiling gratefully. Wendell swore that that night he dreamed of diapers agitating, and that he saw them as beautiful: art in motion. In the cases where there were thank-you notes, he even divested himself of them, sending a husband the thank-you the man's wife had sent and scrawling in the margin what a gracious, wonderful person the husband had married; forwarding the thank-you from a famous musician to the man's agent, so he would be sure to see the musician's elegance in writing, as well as in playing violin. It was a crazy time, but far more inspirational than John Lennon's singing about imagining no possessions. Wendell hadn't wanted to give things away in order to get rid of them; he had wanted to think that he had relocated them in the world where they should be, as if they were friends who would offer other friends new possibilities. In the Fantasy Fest parade the month he died, Wendell rode in a gondola atop a float of fan-agitated roiling blue-crepe-paper water; he was dressed as a mermaid, with his silver-gold sequined body padded with Bubble Wrap inside, because he was so thin. From the float, he threw small plastic fish he'd bought, as well as his entire collection of silver demitasse spoons. "If we were really in Venice, and people weren't waiting on Duval Street to snatch them up, they'd sink to the bottom of the canal and over time they'd metamorphose into the things our civilization really prizes, like sneakers and beer cans. Or they'd be a miracle for some drunk who'd lost a shoe: he could dip his hand in and pluck out a mate. It would be a reverse fairy tale; instead of people getting silver, which nobody cares about anymore, they'd get Keds that could be dried out and worn, or beer cans the truly creative could make mobiles out of. Imagine the pyramids done over, built with Budweiser cans," Wendell had said.

Derek had met Wendell in Atlanta, where Derek had been a travel agent with a large national company. Wendell had been planning a trip to Venice, and when the plans were concluded, he had asked Derek: "Would you like to accompany me?" "I have a wife," Derek had said. "The invitation extends to her, of course," Wendell had said. "What did you have in mind?" Derek had asked. "Traveling with young, attractive, companionable people," Wendell had said. "Spreading the wealth. It's my mother's money that I inherited. She would have been *scandalized* to think I'd take my travel agent and his wife!"

Off to Venice. Even Sallie had been charmed by Wendell at first. If their child had been a boy, they'd intended to make him Wendell's namesake. For a year, Sallie had cooked and kept house, and Derek had done Wendell's bookkeeping and travel arranging, kept the social calendar, responded to requests from charities for Wendell's time and money. Then he had begun driving Wendell to doctors. He had filed health insurance claims, written vague responses to charities hoping Wendell might appear at their fund-raisers, installed an answering machine so no one would have to immediately contend with the constant calls from friends and acquaintances, wondering why Wendell had simply disappeared on them. He had arranged for the move Wendell wanted to make to Key West. He had begun to read books on Wendell's disease; to set up appointments with specialists; even to inquire about alternative medicine, other forms of healing. After the move, it was not too long until Sallie left, claiming, against all medical evidence, that she wasn't going to risk having her baby become ill. "You're the couple—you and Wendell. Not you and me. And forget the accident of Hillary!" she had screamed at him. "Are you really such a do-gooder, going from your one-night-a-week at the soup kitchen to assuage your liberal guilt to daily duty with a dying man, or do you just like the good life? Or maybe you think that when the end comes, you'll be the beneficiary, because of all your damned benevolence. Look into your heart for the real answer," she had railed. He had tried to look, actually, but he found his heart had turned to stone. That had started to happen as he read more and more about the disease. It had intensified in doctors' waiting rooms, begun to shrink and to solidify during various trips to the hospital. So first Sallie went crazy and jumped ship, and then Wendell became truly demented, settling into his gondola for his last ride down Duval Street. Then Wendell had died, leaving him as one of the beneficiaries. He had met his second wife at the funeral home. Her father had died, and she was his only survivor. They had their grief in common. Also a love of kayaking, an interest in reading mysteries, a taste for Mexican beer, a desire to engage in sex as a way to mitigate pain. Those things would not a marriage sustain, as he quickly realized. Add to that the fact that she was from California and felt like she was living in a petri dish in Key West. How could people stand to creep around the little streets with all their stop signs, when there was a big world of freeways? Why did people aim spotlights on their perfectly ordinary palm trees at night? What was all the self-congratulation, as if people were getting away with something? There was great weather elsewhere in the world. People bedazzled with the weather? She was gone in a year.

"Now tell me, darlin', and I will never ask again," Miss May says. "If there was a chance that you and Sallie could start over—both of you in a neutral place, I mean—isn't there still some little part of you that says there's still some real love between you? I cannot believe it doesn't say something that Sallie will give no other man a ghost of a chance, and that you've gone in the exact opposite direction and let anyone who wants to be your girlfriend go out with you, though you refuse to have that mean anything emotionally."

"What I can't believe is that Sallie would have put you up to that question."

"She didn't. I'm asking because I think a reconciliation might be possible."

"Miss May, you never married, yourself. How come you think marriage is such an important institution?"

"That makes no more sense than asking me how I believe people can jump high hurdles when I can't jump high hurdles."

"How *do you* think Sallie and I could jump high hurdles, Miss May?"

"Well, I think you both care for each other, and I think you found yourself in very unfortunate circumstances, where you had to devote all your attention to a dying man, instead of to your wife and little child, and now that that's over, I don't see why you couldn't start again."

"What if I resent the things she said about my character? What if I resent the attitude she took toward the dying man? What if I discovered something about Sallie that would make me too skeptical of her ever to get back together?"

"Well, darlin', what else is ever going to be like that again? If you had it to do over, I can't believe you'd do the same thing. Wendell took you in, darlin'. We've all had people take us in, but then we learn from our mistakes."

"You and Sallie have always insisted that Wendell knew the

day he met me he was dying. I know that isn't true. I made his first doctor appointment, Miss May. We both found out together."

"He might have known without admitting to himself or anyone else that he knew," Miss May says. "But a person intuits things. You'll never tell me he didn't intuit it. He hadn't spent his whole life doing impulsive things, had he? His mother was dead and buried twenty years before he came to think it was so important to spend as much of the money she left him as he could. He had a lifetime in which he could have moved to Key West—why did he have to take the first offer he got on his house and give away his things and get to Key West as fast as he could? You know the answer as well as I do. It was intuition."

He thinks about it. "Do you intuit that I see your point, Miss May?"

"I do, actually," she says. "But a fat lot of good that's going to do me."

His friend Tad comes with his truck, so the TV can be returned to Marcia. Marcia hasn't asked for it—in fact, she's never answered the phone when he's called—but the big TV seems to reproach him, so he wants to give it back. He has the key to her apartment. He also has another TV that Hillary can watch just as well—though she has little interest in anything but *Frasier.*

While Hillary and Miss May swim at the beach, he and Tad load the TV onto the truck. Tad covers it and secures it. They set off, listening to Tiny Tim's Christmas album on Tad's CD player. When Tad says, "Poor fucker," Derek at first thinks he's sympathizing with him: another girlfriend gone; even the big TV disappearing. Then he realizes that of course Tad is talking about Tiny Tim's recent death.

Outside the house in which Marcia has an apartment, they see Buddy, the landlady's son. He's shooting an airplane from something that looks like a hypodermic needle: aiming into the hibiscus hedge. Buddy is too old to invite the tragedies he invites; he's ten, and he should know better than to bring home stray kittens his mother will toss out, or to aim fast-flying toys into thick hedges.

"She's gone," Buddy says.

"Your mom?" Derek says. "That's okay; Marcia gave me a key to let myself in. We've got a TV here we need to return to her."

"Not Mom. Marcia," Buddy says.

"Gone? Marcia's gone?" Tad says.

"She went to Tallahassee," Buddy says, releasing the spinning plane. It falls to the cement in front of the hedge.

"When's she going to be back from Tallahassee?" Derek says, turning to help Tad lift the TV.

"Never," Buddy says. "She sold Mom her brass bed, and now it's mine." Buddy is preening. He loves this one-upmanship.

"And what's she doing in Tallahassee?" Derek says, trying not to let on how rattled he is.

"Same thing she was doing here," Buddy says. "She's gone to be a nurse at the hospital there, and she can still use her pussy."

This provokes a moment of stunned silence. Then Tad starts laughing. He nearly doubles up, bracing himself on the side of the truck. "That so?" Tad says. "She took her pussy with her?"

Buddy nods, a self-satisfied smile on his face. There: he said something dirty.

"How'd she find a job so fast?" Tad asks Derek.

It remains a rhetorical question. Buddy snaps a hibiscus

from the hedge and tucks it behind his ear, swaying his hips and pouting, dancing a satirical dance.

"What are we going to do with the TV?" Derek says. It's more a question to himself, which he happens to ask aloud. Both Buddy and Tad answer at once: "Smash it," Buddy says. "Take it home," Tad says. Derek looks at the TV, under its gray cover. He can see it smashed, all over the ground; he can imagine it back in his house, making him feel even more guilty.

"Hey, you guys got any pot?" Buddy says. He picks up a Frisbee from the ground and pretends to sail it toward them. Tad ducks. Derek, who's still trying to take in what Buddy said, sees the Frisbee, but doesn't much care if he's hit. What's one more thing?

"Hey, man, let's go," Tad says to Derek.

"I'm going to tell Mom you came here and that when I told you Marcia was gone, you cried and cried," Buddy says to Derek.

"Why are you going to do that, Buddy?" Tad says. He's started back to the driver's side of his truck, but he looks over his shoulder to ask the question.

"So she'll think he's a sissy," Buddy says.

It isn't until he's seated in the truck and it pulls out from the curb that it occurs to Derek that Buddy might have made it all up. "Turn around," he says to Tad. "I don't trust that little bastard. I want to see with my own eyes that she's gone."

"Really?" Tad says, slowing. "That didn't even occur to me."

"It just occurred to me," Derek says.

They go around the block and return to the house. Buddy is nowhere to be seen. Tad puts the truck in park and keeps the motor running. Derek jumps out and reaches over the side gate, undoing the latch. He walks through the side yard, littered with Buddy's toys and rotting lawn furniture, and climbs the stairs to Marcia's apartment. He puts his key in the lock and turns it.

Inside, Marcia's sofa is where it always was. The pictures have been taken off the walls. The shades—were they Marcia's?—have been removed from the windows, so the room is very bright. He walks into the tiny bedroom. Nothing there, except a pillowcase thrown on the floor. The shades are also gone from the bedroom windows. He's almost out of the room when he sees something in the corner: a piece of clothing, or something. But it isn't that. It's a doll. A voodoo doll, pins stuck in its cloth body, small charms sewn to its upper arms, black bull's-eyes drawn on forehead, stomach, and thighs—one thigh pierced with a small metal stick. There is a tiny puff of real hair on its head. Around its waist is the thing he can't stop gawking at: HILLARY, spelled out in pink paint on its seashell belt, some curlicues of lavender paint spiraling away from the last three letters. A large safety pin runs down its spine, more of the purple curlicues flying away from the head of the pin. Below the pin is stitching with black thread. Piercing both feet are tiny gold balls: Marcia's earrings. The gold studs she always wore.

He puts the doll in his back pocket—pushes it in, though he knows that most of it protrudes. Like a child eager to show something he has drawn to Mommy—not a good analogy: this is most certainly not something he has created—he thinks about showing it to Tad. To get corroboration that the thing really exists. That he could possibly have found such a thing.

Tiny Tim is warbling on the tape deck. From somewhere, Tad has gotten himself a Diet Coke. He raises the can in greeting as Derek approaches.

"Something really awful," Derek says. "Something you are not going to fucking believe."

"She's dead?" Tad says immediately.

"No, she's not dead, but I think she wishes Hillary was, for some reason."

"What are you talking about?"

"This," he says, reaching behind him and extracting the doll.

"What the—"

Tad reaches for the doll, but hesitates. It's clear he doesn't want to touch it. "God almighty," Tad says. "This, from a nurse?"

"I don't think she was thinking along the lines of helping mankind when she made it."

"No. I can't imagine she was," Tad says slowly. "I tell you," he says, "you've got to road test them for a good long while before you get in deep. There's more crazies out there than you can ever imagine."

"Does this seem like anything Marcia would do?" Derek says.

"My point, exactly," Tad says, after a moment's silence. "God almighty," he says again.

"Do you know anything about this stuff? Do you have any idea whether we should . . . I don't know: is this something most people would tell the cops about?"

"Most people like us don't think of cops as our saviors," Tad says. "Just to remind you," he adds, after a long pause.

"But what if she's violent? This is *really* off the wall."

"I'll say," Tad says. He puts a finger tentatively on a bull's-eye, as if he's touching a little bruise; he still doesn't reach for the doll. He stares at it. "Did she ever even meet your kid?" he asks.

"No."

"Well, that's the way people really get even," Tad says. "They go for what you love the most. They lynch your dog, if they know you love your dog, or—hell—even the Mafia plays dirty now: they've started killing people's wives, people's sisters.

That Getty kid—remember, years ago? They kidnapped him and cut off his ear and sent it to the old man, to get the money. Remember?"

"I'd just as soon not," Derek says.

"It happens all the time. Fingers in the mail . . ."

"Stop talking about it!"

Tad looks at him. "You don't really think this thing has any power, do you? It's a stupid doll that a psycho made—forgive me for casting aspersions on one of your girlfriends." Tad takes the doll, a look of disgust on his face. He holds it in front of his face and begins to wave his fingers, moving his hand from the tip of his nose to the face of the doll. "Booga, booga," he says, in as ominous a voice as possible. He looks at Derek. "You should certainly be bummed out that you found such a lunatic, but hey: good riddance, huh? I say we unload her TV so she won't have any reason to come knocking on your door."

Derek nods. He most certainly does want to return the TV and never see the inside of the apartment again, never see Marcia again, never see snotty little Buddy again either, for that matter. He gets out, and the two of them wrestle the TV off the back of the truck. Supporting the TV one-handed, Tad fumbles for the gate lock and unlatches it, and the two of them proceed through the littered lawn, up the stairs, into the apartment Derek, in his shock, left unlocked. They leave the TV in the middle of the living-room floor. They both leave immediately, and this time Derek locks the door, then drops the key through the mail slot.

Back in the car, Tad takes the doll off the passenger's seat and tosses it on the dashboard, where it lies on top of a small clipboard. There is also a dirty bandanna and a crumpled Dove Bar wrapper.

When Derek gets home, he stuffs the doll in his back pocket

again. He feels smarmy, as if he's sneaking in pornography. He's glad that Miss May and Hillary aren't home. He goes quickly to his bedroom and puts the doll on a shelf in the closet, slamming the door instead of gently closing it.

He believes they are at the beach. Why wouldn't they be? How could he know they'd be at the emergency room: that Hillary is being treated after being stung by a sea nettle?

By the time Miss May and his daughter are ready to leave, the swelling and pain have all but disappeared. Because he wasn't at the beach, Sallie can't even pretend to blame him. Hillary was in the care of Miss May; he was off doing an errand when it happened.

He says good-bye to them at the airport. He buys Miss May a big bottle of aloe lotion and the new issue of *People* magazine, and Hillary a painted wooden fish from the airport gift shop, as well as a bag of Hershey's Kisses and a water gun shaped like a flamingo. As he bends to embrace his daughter, he notices how substantial she feels: her rib cage; her sturdy hands grabbing his shoulders; even her hair—long, and sleek, cascading below her shoulders. "Ow!" she says, as his shoulder clamps her hair to his chest. "Ow, Daddy, watch my hair!" He kisses Miss May, and she smiles and turns her head and offers him the other cheek, as well. Kiss, kiss: then they're both on their way. He waves at them in the departure area. Miss May waves him away, and eventually he goes—back outside the airport where the pink cabs wait for arriving passengers.

Just to make sure—call it superstition; call it simple silliness—he isn't going back to Key West, though; he's going to Sugarloaf, where Dr. Frankel Hidburt lives. Dr. Hidburt is not a medical doctor, but a doctor of philosophy; a professor of

Jungian studies formerly connected to the Church of St. John the Divine, in New York City. Several years before, Derek met Dr. Hidburt when he was researching hospices in Florida. In his retirement, Dr. Hidburt worked with a well-known holistic healer in Boca Chica, giving additional information and counseling to patients who consulted the healer for homeopathic treatment, as well as volunteering at the hospice founded by the healer and his brother. The hospice no longer exists, but through St. John the Divine, he had been able to track down Dr. Hidburt who, he was pleased to hear, still lived in the area and was writing a book about his years at the hospice. Hidburt remembered him at once: the young man who had persuaded him he must take one more patient, when the place was already Old Mother Hubbard's. "Yes, certainly, come and have coffee," Hidburt had said to him when he called, without even asking why he wanted to see him again.

The directions Hidburt had given to his house were precise. Hidburt's house was high up on stilts, flat-roofed, starkly modern, with a few small palms dotted around the lawn. The most incongruous detail was a window box, filled with red geraniums. An old black Lab got up and jingled his collar and wagged his tail. "In the house, in the house," a woman called to the dog, as Derek got out of his car. The dog looked at her as if she was crazy. It thumped down and rested its chin on the sand.

"Are you afraid of dogs?" the woman called to Derek.

"No," he said. "I hope I don't have any reason to be."

"I never know if people might be afraid," the woman said.

As he passed the dog, it thumped its tail. It was such an unthreatening dog, it was ridiculous.

"There aren't any pets inside," the woman said. She had still not said hello, or said her name. He felt that he should introduce himself, so he extended his hand and told her his name.

She shook his hand firmly and said that her name was Casey Carswell. "I have a brother named Derek," she said. "I don't meet many people who have that name." She added: "Where I grew up, in Maryland, Casey was a very common name. Down here, I haven't met anyone named Casey, but maybe it's just coincidence that I haven't met them. What do you think?"

"What do I think?" he said, not sure how to answer her.

"Casey, let the gentleman in," Hidburt called. "You're standing right in the doorway."

"Dr. Hidburt has a new pool table," Casey said.

"Hello, Dr. Hidburt," Derek said. When he raised his hand in greeting, Casey flinched and recoiled. He frowned, taken aback. Then, as Hidburt walked toward her, she backed up so that she stood against the wall. Hidburt seemed not to notice. He smiled at her, and then at Derek. "Nice to see you," he said, extending his hand. "Nobody ever told me a writer's life was so lonely. I guess that not knowing that is why so many get taken in."

"Will you be playing pool?" Casey said.

"No, dear," Dr. Hidburt said. "We'll be having coffee, as we discussed a short time ago." He looked at Derek. "That is, if you'd like coffee. We also have juice and tea."

"That's Dr. Hidburt's pool table," Casey said, pointing to a very new-looking pool table on the front porch.

"It's wonderful," Derek said.

"Can we offer you something to drink?" Dr. Hidburt said.

"Is there orange juice?"

"There is," Dr. Hidburt said.

"One orange juice, one coffee," Casey said, nodding. She turned and walked down a hallway.

"Isn't my fiancée the perfect hostess?" Dr. Hidburt said. He smiled. "You look surprised. Didn't think the old man had it in him? I met Casey three years ago, when she was recovering from an automobile accident. She had no short-term memory for almost a year. Today she's an example of what the human will, coupled with rehabilitation, can accomplish."

"Wonderful," he murmured, not having any idea what else to say.

"She doesn't have any brothers. She had a husband whose name was Derek," Dr. Hidburt said. "But come into my study. By which I mean the room with bookcases. You hardly ever see real bookcases in Florida—at least, where I go, I don't see them."

The room was filled with built-in bookcases. There was a long wooden table Hidburt used as a desk, and a leather chair with a mashed blue pillow leaning against the back. There were clusters of framed photographs at both ends of the desk: some were of smiling people; others showed people propped up in bed, some with cadaverous heads, lips parted as if in a smile.

"Who knew how much healing would be needed?" Hidburt said. "I look back, and I see that for so many years, I was just a gentleman philosopher. Though I don't imagine anything prepares you for the battlefield. You know, Sugarloaf itself was once set to become the sponge capital of the world. Did you know that? Surgarloaf was purchased by two brothers who had a dream, but like many dreamers, they also made a miscalculation: they didn't realize what a slow process it would be, breeding sponges. And they ran out of money, and eventually they had to declare bankruptcy. They were going to grow sponges on disks, as I understand it: no problem with sand—none of those bothersome facts of nature intruding. But they ended up bankrupt, because the sponges would only grow so fast. Whereas you look at the things in our world that proliferate when we don't want them to, and you see them everywhere. There are epidemics of so many things, and there are those who'd call some of them progress. There's even an epidemic of roads, when you think about it. Too many roads leading too many places."

Derek nodded. Hidburt gestured for him to sit in a chair, as he sank into his own leather chair, adjusting the pillow behind him. On the desk, the light of an answering machine blinked. There were several coffee mugs on the desk. Derek was trying not to look at the desk, because so many of the photographs, which he could easily see from the chair he'd been asked to sit in, were upsetting.

"What brings you?" Hidburt said suddenly.

"What prompted my call . . ." He stopped, not sure where to begin. "I have a four-year-old daughter. She was just an infant when I knew you, and her mother left not long afterwards, so I'm not even sure if I ever mentioned my daughter to you."

"I'm not sure myself. Is it your daughter you've come to talk about?"

"Well, indirectly. Yes. I mean, this is probably not something you have any direct experience with . . ."

"Don't outguess me," Hidburt said. "Also, it would help if you weren't so damned vague."

"My daughter was visiting me. She left today, to rejoin her mother in Houston."

"The roads there!" Hidburt said. He frowned with consternation.

"A woman I used to date . . . a nurse. This nurse, Marcia, put a curse on Hillary. Hillary, my daughter. She was bit by a sea nettle the same day I discovered the voodoo doll."

Hidburt nodded.

"I remembered at the hospice . . . you once made the comment that there was a real bond between the patients and the toys, not just because the toys were comforting, but because as death came closer—I think this was your point—the line of distinction began to disappear between animate and inanimate objects. You said that it would be foolish to assume that only human beings had souls. That various things had—I can't remember, anymore: that they had their own qualities. Was that the word you used?"

"I don't recall."

"But you do remember our conversation?"

"Yes. You were sobbing outside in your car. Your friend had dropped his monkey, or whatever it was, on the floor, and you had picked it up and had been about to return it to him when you realized you were inclined to bolt with it. Which you did, as far as the car."

"Yes," Derek said.

"The symbolism was obvious. You couldn't rescue your friend, so you were rescuing *his* friend, the monkey."

"Right. But you'd said to me before that you thought . . . didn't you think the toys had the equivalent of souls?"

"I might have talked about how we mythologize things," Hidburt said. He sat back in the chair. "But exactly what does this have to do with the voodoo doll?"

"Well, I wondered . . . do you believe in them? In their power, I mean."

Hidburt reached for one of the mugs. He swirled the liquid inside. "Yes," he said simply.

"I have it in the car. I didn't know whether I should bring it in or not. To tell you the truth, I didn't know exactly how to bring it in. I suppose I could have put it in a bag, or something, but I couldn't . . . after all these years, what would you have thought if I'd walked in with a voodoo doll?"

"I've seen stranger," Hidburt said.

"Could I get it?"

"Yes, of course. Go get it."

"If you saw it, you could tell more about it."

"Are you asking, or trying to reassure yourself?" Hidburt said. "Go get it."

He got up and walked out of the room. The house was quiet. There was no aroma of coffee; he had never been brought his orange juice. Outside, the dog again beat its tail, but didn't stand. It didn't turn its head to watch him walk to the car. He opened the car door and took the doll out of the glove compartment. He'd put it there, as if in a little coffin, because he hadn't wanted to look at it on the drive. Now, the doll felt slightly damp and warm. He held it in his hand and started toward the house. In one of the windows, he thought he saw Casey's face, but as he came closer, he realized it must have been a shadow cast from a downspout.

He was lost in thought, so he was surprised when the dog suddenly rose and trotted up to him, collar jingling. The dog was interested in the doll. He no doubt thought it was a dog toy. Or it might have been some weird, New Age bone. Derek snorted and looked at it from the dog's perspective. Which made it look at once curious and harmless—a silly thing, created by a silly person. It embarrassed him that for days, he had been so sure it had an awful power. He gave in to the dog's curiosity and held it lower, for the dog to sniff. The dog sniffed and sniffed, like a cat with catnip. When he raised his arm, the dog gave a little leap in the air.

"Don't give him anything that could splinter inside him, like a turkey bone, because it could cause internal bleeding," Casey suddenly said. She was standing again in the doorway. She had on a cap turned backwards. She was wearing glasses.

"Oh, no, this isn't for the dog. It's something I brought to show the doctor," he said, feeling suddenly very peculiar.

"Please don't feed the dog," Casey said again, as if he hadn't spoken.

He raised his hand, meaning to show her it wasn't food. As he did, the dog lunged, got the doll, and began to run, bolting across the sand.

"No!" Casey screamed. "He could die!"

This brought Hidburt immediately to her side. She began to speak to him urgently, whispering, pointing to him all the while, real hatred in her eyes.

"The dog!" he heard Casey say, but Hidburt was turning her away from the door, quite forcefully, disappearing with her inside the house. Should he follow them in? The dog had almost vanished; it had moved much faster than he'd thought possible. He had misjudged the dog's abilities. The dog had run fast and far, disappearing in the direction of swampy mangroves. What had he caused now? More confusion and unhappiness. He never anticipated anything: not that his wife would leave him; not that his girlfriend could be truly malicious and crazy; not even that a dog would jump for a toy and dash off with it. Everything was a big surprise to him. Just as Sallie had said when she told him she was leaving: everything came as a *biiiiig* surprise.

He walked slowly up the steps. Casey was crying. He could hear her, even over the classical music that had been turned on. He heard the doctor's voice in the distance, and eventually, as Casey's crying subsided, he heard him more clearly, consoling her as one would console a child. He knew he was overstaying his welcome, but still, he sank back into the chair he'd sat in earlier. Surely Hidburt would understand—or could be made to understand—that the dog's getting the doll had been a simple accident, and really: it was not his fault if Casey was out of control. He had not intended any of it. Hidburt had been quite willing to see him. In fact, he had all but said that his was a lonely life.

But as time passed and Hidburt did not return, he began to feel more uneasy. Should he leave a note of apology? Would it be best to get back in his car and drive away—was that the way things could return to normal? He was just about to do it—he saw blank paper in Hidburt's printer—when the doctor returned, shaking his head in embarrassment.

"One step forward, two steps back," Hidburt said. "I apologize. She sees that she reacted excessively, but she doesn't have perfect control over her emotions. She'll be bringing my coffee and your orange juice."

"I'm awfully sorry. It all happened so fast that I—"

"What doesn't? Except those things that we wish would pass quickly," Hidburt said.

"I guess we can assume the doll's long gone, and I don't have to worry about that anymore," he said.

Hidburt's small smile faded. "Oh, its being gone doesn't mean you don't have to worry about it," he said. "It does simplify my removing the spell, though, because without seeing it, I can do what you might call a generic banishment, though that will probably work just as well. But in order to be very specific, I'd have to know exactly how it was marked."

He could imagine it, being gnawed in the boggy ground under the mangroves. Just when he had convinced himself it was harmless, the doctor was telling him that its power would still have to be diffused.

"You won't mind that I don't speak the words out loud?" Hidburt said. He opened the top drawer of a filing cabinet pushed under his desk and removed a box. He rummaged around in it and took out something dark and small. Then he reached in the box and took out a book of matches. He looked around and reached for a coffee mug, poured its remaining liquid into another mug, and turned it upside down on the desk. He placed what turned out to be a little cone of incense on the mug and lit it, fanning the match slowly until the tip of the incense glowed orange. Then he closed his eyes and blew it out, squeezing his eyes shut even more tightly, moving his lips as he spoke silent words. A smell something like jonquils filled the room. In the background, music ended and was replaced by silence. He could not hear Casey anywhere in the house, though he imagined that as soon as anything upset her, they would both hear her immediately.

"Please. No negative thoughts," Hidburt said quietly, opening his eyes and looking up. As Derek looked at him, surprised, Hidburt bowed his head and began moving his lips again. "There," he said after another minute. "I can tell because of the change in the air that it's already taking effect. Can you feel it yourself? Sometimes people can."

"Then there really was a spell? All this time, the spell was on?"

"If you'd told me on the phone what your concern was, I'd have invited you to come out that day."

"But Hillary's all right? Nothing's happened to her?"

"Well, these things usually aren't timed to keep coming at a person like balls from a pitching machine," Hidburt said. "In all probability, she's fine." He pushed his phone forward. "Please call and put your mind at rest," he said. "The curse has been undone. Would that it was always so easy."

He nodded in agreement. He reached for the phone. He looked at it and concentrated, but the Lake Charles number kept popping into his head; he couldn't remember the newer number.

"I'm afraid to ask if you're psychic, because you probably are," Derek said. He added: "I'm afraid I haven't memorized my ex-wife's new number."

"Too many things to remember," Hidburt said. "That's what Casey and I wrestle with every day." As he spoke, he seemed to deflate, slightly. Hidburt frowned. "Not only am I not psychic," Hidburt said, "but if I might overstep my bounds and ask you a personal question? I'm a little surprised to find that during the period I knew you, you had a wife and a daughter. I assumed that you were his lover. Not that it's any of my business if you were or you weren't."

"Why did you assume that?"

"If I recall correctly, he told me that."

"Well, it wasn't true. I worked for him. I wasn't his lover."

"I see," Hidburt said. "Well, people say many things, some of them true, some of them not."

"I know he wanted me to be his lover, but I wasn't," Derek said.

"Near the end, quite a bit of pretense often goes on. People think that the dying see things so clearly, but even the ones who are in their right minds . . . in my experience, even then men remain dreamers and writers of fiction. You take my example of the brothers who intended to grow their sponges; they just wouldn't believe they couldn't prevail."

"It drove my wife crazy that I was so devoted to him, but it wasn't sexual. I was only devoted to him as a friend."

"My dear man, I hope you don't think I'm doubting you," Hidburt said.

"No, but I think she believes that to this day. That there was something else. I think she was very jealous of him."

"As would be natural, if she believed that."

"And she thought I was hanging around for his money. She only thought the worst of me."

Hidburt shook his head sadly. "I'm not a marriage counselor," he said. Hidburt stood. "I'm afraid if you'd like a glass of orange juice, we should proceed into the kitchen ourselves," he said. "I'm sorry not to have at least provided you with a beverage."

"No, think of all you've done for me. Really. I can't thank you enough. May I give you something—"

"Absolutely not. Your intuition brought you to me again, and my skills allowed me to fulfill your request."

"Your dog will come back all right, won't he?"

"Plenty of life still left in him. I was glad to see that," Hidburt said, smiling.

"Should we look for him?"

"Why? Gnawing on his treasure out under some tree, happy as a pig in shit, as they say."

At the door, Derek held out his hand. Hidburt clasped it with one hand and patted his shoulder with the other. "You take care of yourself," Hidburt said. "Life's bad enough when you do, so there's no point in not."

"I really appreciate this. I can't say how much—"

But the second time Hidburt patted his shoulder he also saw to it that Derek stepped onto the landing outside the door. Raising his hand in silent farewell, he quickly closed the door.

He was halfway back to Key West before he began to wonder whether Hidburt might not have trotted out a few tricks as a sort of salve. Whether the whole afternoon hadn't been something of a put-on. Did an educated man really believe in the power of voodoo? Or, as a Jungian, was it a belief in symbolic power? Perhaps he'd seen so much he hadn't expected to see that he came to accept everything. And if you could accept anything, why couldn't your own charade—your own exorcism charade—be part of that?

Still, he felt that some spell had lifted. He felt relieved, wanted to remain impressed, not to seriously consider the possibility that Hidburt, himself, was some crazy old man. As well as what he might have done in removing the spell, he had also listened and believed—surely he'd believed—what he had told him about his relationship with Wendell.

Wendell who, near the end, had said to him: "I'll float back like an old trout, belly-up. I'll be reincarnated as the most banal thing you've ever seen—and since there are sure to be so many of them, you'll have to wonder every time whether it isn't me. Every time the trash is knocked over. Every time a branch falls on your car. Every time you get a piece of junk mail. It might be me in the envelope. You just keep right on, without me, rowing in that big, grand cesspool of a canal, past those beautiful palaces, underneath those starry skies, but all that flotsam and jetsam—you're going to have to wonder, with every piece that floats by, whether or not it's me."

Well: Wendell certainly never would have come back as anything so dramatic as a voodoo doll. That was a crazy woman's curse, whereas, in his dying, filled with spitefulness and envy for the living, all Wendell had wanted him to be haunted with was the dingy ordinariness of life. If he did reconcile with Sallie, would Wendell blow a cold wind from the great beyond, sending a shiver up her spine on the night he proposed? Would he take a ghostly walk, preceding them, all the way upstairs, to become—if not his lover—at least the gritty sand on the sheets?

Coydog

F RAN reached between the car seats, hauling the insulated nylon bag onto her lap and unzipping it. Inside were airplane peanuts she'd saved from her most recent business trip, and celery sticks, apples, plastic spoons, and a jar of peanut butter. Hank had run into a convenience store to buy crackers, but had grabbed cookie wafers by mistake. Back in the car, all the time she laughed, Hank had done a slow burn. She bit into an apple and offered him another, with her free hand. He shook his head no.

"You seem a little down," she said. "What about a pep talk? Should I give my husband a pep talk?"

He shrugged, looking in the rearview mirror as he passed a small white car. Across the top of the rearview was an additional mirror that allowed you to see four other views of the road. It was like one of those fashionable series paintings she'd been seeing in the downtown galleries: paintings that imitated photographs, or rather snapshots, of inconsequential things. One of the mirrors magnified Hank's blue eyes; another provided a view of Hank in profile.

"If your sister asks her usual elliptical questions, why don't you think about what she probably wishes she could ask directly, and answer the implied question?" Fran said.

"I don't want to be doing this. I don't want to be doing this. I don't," he said.

They were riding in a borrowed car. Their car had electrical problems. Cars were loaned by friends these days the way furniture used to float around in the sixties. This one had been borrowed from a man visiting their neighbors in Morristown. He had driven to New Jersey from Los Angeles, and his idea of the perfect vacation was to spend one week being driven by others or taking cabs. The car was a big navy-blue Buick the man had won in a blackjack game in Lake Tahoe.

"Dreamy Dora," Fran sighed.

"I know what you're going to say next," he said. "You're going to say that if there's a pause in the conversation, it isn't my responsibility any more than hers to fill it."

His hand, rubbing a lock of hair off his forehead, was magnified in one mirror and appeared clawlike in the next. The mirror made her unhappy. She stopped checking it. She put the apple core on the dashboard. A truck passed them on a curve, hissing its brakes. Gravel flew backwards, plinking their car. Their car. It was not their car. It was a car a stranger had won gambling.

This would be the group at Hank's parents' summer gathering: Georgette, Hank's mother; Winston, Hank's stepfather; Aunt Hettie, who was not actually an aunt, but the local Amway dealer; Uncle Macklin, Aunt Hettie's boarder, who had recently become engaged to her, thereby earning the honorific "Uncle"; real Aunt Georgia, eighty-four; Dreamy Dora, Hank's sister; Myra, Dora's constant companion. Myra was a recovering alcoholic who had been in Dora's therapy group. She replaced mufflers for a living.

Every year, there was a Fourth of July party on June 28, so the family wouldn't have to be on the road on the Fourth. Similarly, Christmas was celebrated the first weekend in December, and Winston's mid-January birthday was combined with the Christmas celebration. Georgette would allow no mention to be made of her birthday, though she sent cards to others. She tucked handkerchiefs into every card she mailed, so they always arrived marked "postage due." It was funny. Everybody's family was funny, except on the day you were driving toward them.

At the gas station, Hank pumped and Fran got out to stretch. After only a few months without running, her body felt lax and permanently stiff: those two descriptions, which might seem contradictory, were actually two distinct, troublesome things. She had stopped running on her doctor's advice, to see if her periods would resume. She was twenty-nine. She and Hank had decided they should have a baby.

A few miles past the gas station, they saw the sign pointing to Route 676, and Hank heaved a sigh as they turned in the direction to North Lake. "You know what I feel like every time I come to see them?" he said. "I feel like I'm not really an adult. Like I don't have a job. Like where I work is just an illusion. I also feel like I've never gotten it up in my life. I feel like my anatomy doesn't exist." He looked at her. "And after that un-adult outburst, would you care to share any of your innermost thoughts with me?"

"I feel that I don't have breasts," she said.

In spite of himself, he laughed. He reached over and patted her knee. "I know I say this every year," he said, "but I really see no point to visiting on June twenty-eighth. Next year I'm not going to do it."

Through the side window, she saw rowboats tied to big tree trunks near the lake. And someone . . . someone pedaling an enormous duck, or swan. Someone sitting atop a swan, skittering erratically on the bright blue water.

"God almighty," Hank said. "It's Macklin. Isn't that Macklin out there? That's his lamb's-wool hat, I swear it is."

A duck, not a swan. It zigzagged out of view, but as she squinted into the distance, she remembered that Macklin had

for years been carving wood to make what he called "folky art."
Now, one of his big creations was apparently floating around
North Lake.

"Remember when he got Georgette to plug in her hairdryer
so he could demonstrate the windmill he'd made out of cereal
boxes?" Fran said.

"I'm not riding in that thing," Hank muttered.

She said, "You're lucky my mother is dead and my father
lives in England."

"Only child," he said. He pretended to taunt her. "Only
child. Only child."

"Only child," she echoed, as the car swung into her in-law's
driveway. She flipped down the visor and examined her face.
There was no makeup to fuss with. Her hair had just been cut
and curled, and the new hairstyle pleased her. She flipped the
visor up, noticing, as she did, several large wooden animals on
the front lawn. There was a pig, a greyhound, and a genuinely
alarming bear, reared up on its hind legs, fangs bared. "Also
birdhouses," read a hand-lettered sign nailed to the bear's leg.
"Ask at door." An arrow pointed toward the house, as if whoever read the sign might miss the ranch house with brown
shutters that sat ten or fifteen feet behind it.

Dreamy Dora threw open the door and waved; Georgette,
in her jumpsuit and apron, ran past her daughter and threw
herself around the greyhound's neck, honking its rubber nose
as Hank and Fran got out of the car.

"Hello, darlin'. Both my darlin's," Georgette called.

"Quite the menagerie, Georgette," Fran said, embracing her
mother-in-law.

"What is it doing at your house?" Hank said. "Why doesn't
Macklin have this stuff over at Hettie's, or at her store?"

"He does, darlin'. Macklin put some in our front yard to

spread the wealth. Aren't they the funniest things? And they work, too. One goes in the water."

At sixty-seven, Georgette was still smiling and slender, but her hair was noticeably thinner, and almost entirely gray. Her older sister, Aunt Georgia, dyed her hair silver-blue. Fran tried not to stare at Georgette's hair as they broke their embrace. Georgette smelled of talcum powder and hot chocolate. No one in the family drank coffee anymore, since Dora had decided to give up caffeine.

"Well, put 'er there, pardner," Hank's stepfather said, wandering out of the house. "And let the pretty girl kiss my cheek, if she will."

"Home, home on the range," Georgette said, as Fran went on tiptoes to kiss her father-in-law.

Dora, on the front stoop, called out, "This is not a television series. It's our life." Though she gestured toward the carved animals, everyone stopped whatever they were doing, slightly perplexed. Dora often had the ability to completely stop conversation.

Hank raised a hand to his sister, offering a silent hello. "When's Hettie and Macklin's wedding?" he said to Georgette, as they all started toward the house.

"Well, I don't think that's anything we asked when you two were living together!" Georgette said.

"I'm not asking them. I'm asking behind their backs." He held the door open for Fran, who was already biting her nails.

"Okay. It's not important. Don't tell me," Hank said.

"August first at three P.M., by a justice of the peace in the garden of the Café Domani," Georgette said.

"Come on down to the shed and see my restoration work," Winston said. "Keeps me busy. Keeps me off the streets." He turned to Georgette and winked.

Over the winter he had kept Hank and Fran posted on the progress of the bicycle-built-for-two he was fixing; he had also sent Polaroids of a carriage cabin he was working on, though the carriage lacked the framework. It was something Macklin had promised to work on with him now that summer had come. Winston loved puttering around the shed so much that he wore battery-powered socks and double layers of thermal underwear so he could work there all winter long. More than a dozen flashlights mounted on brackets that swiveled toward his projects greatly augmented the wan New England winter light. Winston's invitation to the shed was only meant for Hank; it was understood that Fran would stay in the kitchen with the women.

Another of whom appeared, suddenly. Myra came in the back door, wearing the twin to Georgette's apron over her plaid shirt and stirrup pants. Her feet were in paint-spattered tennis shoes, with poked-out toes. She wore her socks bunched at her ankle like a teenager, but she was forty-three, and six feet tall. Fran extended her hand. Myra's handshake was resounding.

"Myra, darlin', I don't want you weeding my garden for another moment," Georgette said. "I do not think you are a gardening service, Myra!"

"We came yesterday," Dora said to Fran. Her voice was dull; Fran couldn't tell whether this was meant as subtle criticism, or as a fact even Dora was bored to announce.

"What does my girl say?" Georgette said to Dora. "Does she say that she will have a cocoa with chipped ice? Because there's fruit juice if cocoa isn't wanted."

"I don't want anything," Dora said.

"Will it be a big wedding?" Fran said, feeling the sudden need to speak and jolt herself into sociability.

"Will what be a big wedding?" Dora said.

"Uncle Macklin and—"

"Of course!" Georgette said. "Seventy people is a *big* wedding. When Winston and I married, we had ten family members and his best man and the woman who stood for me, and oh—we would have had the dearest girl as ring bearer, but she had such a bad cold she couldn't come, and do you know, now that little girl is engaged herself."

"My marriage was a disaster from start to finish," Dora said. "This everybody knows." She went to the refrigerator and found a Coke. "You didn't say you had Cokes," she said to Georgette.

"I just assume my family knows I always have Coca-Cola," Georgette said. She opened the cupboard and offered Dora a tall glass. Dora waved it away, opened the can, and drank.

"I was thinking that I might go out and sit in the horseless carriage, to try it out," Georgette said.

"It's a sexist thing to say, but I don't see why we don't just leave the men alone," Myra said.

"It's true, though. They'd hate it if we barged in," Dora said.

"—And I," Georgette said, breaking into the middle of her own thought, "I do mean to sit like a princess in the carriage eventually, now that nice weather has come."

This early in the visit, the time had already come when Fran began to replay the past to convince herself she had a life apart from these people, whose conversation jumped from subject to subject like the ever clicking minute hand of the kitchen clock. She thought of some things from the day before: going to the doctor so he could take a blood sample; dinner at the Chinese restaurant with Hank. Hank had worn a hat in the rain, instead of carrying an umbrella, and she had joined him, plopping on her canvas hat with the lavender bow her best friend called her Mr. Ed hat. With their spring rolls, they had ordered champagne to celebrate her promotion. In this kitchen, jobs would never be talked about, let alone promotions. And, in fact, she didn't think she had much to be proud of. The person the store had wanted to promote to chief window dresser—a nice man named Stone Franklin, who had once built a Lego Ferris wheel in the front window, which he'd studded with dangling bikini pants and brassieres he'd made it appear the Ken dolls placed in the cars of the Ferris wheel had discarded—had left for Hawaii, and she had been their second choice. Perhaps third.

The cocoa had not entirely dissolved, Fran saw, as Myra helped herself to cocoa. It spread like moss on Myra's teeth. Everyone was running out of things to say and Georgette, who could never stand a silent moment, announced that she was going out to the shed.

"Just once," Dora said, the minute her mother was out the door. "Just once, I wish she would come back and say something brilliant. Do you know what I mean? That she might come through the door and have discovered something."

"What would she discover?" Myra said.

Dora had gone to the big picture window. She frowned. "Aunt Hettie and Uncle Macklin," she said.

Fran was always anxious around Dora because Dora was so fractious, and she could never anticipate what Dora would talk about. It was the opposite of Dora's problem with Georgette— Dora's histrionic fatigue with Georgette's predictable responses.

"Myra," Fran said. "Do you like to come here? Do you mind coming?" It was out of her mouth before she could stop herself.

Myra snorted. "Of course I don't like to come," she said.

"It's really none of my business," Fran said.

"You have a right to ask any question you want," Myra said. "Have the courage of your convictions, Fran. It's absolutely necessary in this family."

The storm clouds were so heavy, and the rain so imminent, that the idea of a front-lawn picnic disappeared as a possibility. As Fran sliced tomatoes, Winston and Macklin arm wrestled on the kitchen table; each time Macklin won and they locked hands again, Winston accused Macklin of rising out of his chair. "I'm buns to leather," Macklin hissed, through clenched teeth, and Fran was surprised that he would call the plastic chair covers leather. From earlier in the afternoon she had retained the conjured-up image of a stopped Ferris wheel, and now she envisioned various family members—for all intents and purposes, everyone here was family—stopped at the top. Then she imagined their expressions. Most of them instantly appeared, but Hank's expression was not decipherable. She tried to imagine his strange look as frightened, but that didn't seem right. She tried to imagine him scowling, and that came a bit closer. He was out of the room, pulling up croquet stakes from the side lawn that Georgette was worried sick would get rained on and warp. Again, Fran tried to conjure up a more believable image of Hank atop the Ferris wheel, but the bemused look he had, coming back toward the house with the disassembled croquet set in his hands, couldn't be superimposed on the image of him scowling.

"Put a bit of lemon juice on the tomatoes so they don't discolor," Dora said to Fran. She had been standing beside Fran, stirring brownie batter.

"Tomatoes don't discolor, Dora."

"Of course they do. They're just like apples," Dora said.

"Too many cooks spoil the broth!" Georgette said, looking over her shoulder from where she was stirring a pot on the stove.

"Mother, we're dealing with factual information here," Dora said. "I don't want this to get blown out of proportion, though, so I'm going to take three deep breaths and say no more."

"That's wonderful, darlin'," Georgette said. Georgette looked around the kitchen. "Where is Myra?" she said.

"Weeding," Dora said dully.

"Weeding! But poor Myra's done enough."

"She doesn't cook," Dora said, "so she's gone out to weed."

"Well, we aren't here doing penance!" Georgette said. "If one of us doesn't cook, there's no need to find another activity just to keep busy."

"That's what the whole human race does, Mother," Dora said.

"Sloth. A day of sloth for me," Winston said. "After much expenditure of energy, sloth."

"The day you didn't get the television fixed was the happiest day of my life," Aunt Georgia said.

"I'm not of that opinion myself," Winston said, "but Georgette decided we'd see what life was like without the television."

"I did watch every minute of the Los Angeles earthquake's aftereffects," Georgette said.

Dora snorted.

"Please let us not talk about upsetting things on the Fourth of July," Georgette said.

"It's not the Fourth," Hank said.

"I hope you're not on the roads that day," Georgette said, putting a lid on the pan and wiping her hands on her apron. "It won't be because of me if you're out on the highway July fourth."

"Rain," Dora said, as the first raindrops began to fall. She opened the front door. "Come inside!" she screamed shrilly to Myra.

Fran looked out the window and saw Myra, holding a trowel

and running fast, her tall body hunched. She bolted over the greyhound and raced between the bear and the pig. Hank reached past Fran to close the windows, then ran to the back door, which had blown open in the wind, and slammed it shut. Winston rolled in the windows by the table, looking out at his "folky art," made intermittently bright by flashing lightning. As he stepped back, his elbow knocked over the vase of daisies on the table, and Aunt Georgia jumped in fright, as Winston reached forward, too late, trying to steady it.

"Spilled milk," Dora mumbled, pouring batter into a large greased pan. She wiped her forehead against her large, fleshy upper arm.

"Someone in the royal family gardens in the rain," Myra said, taking the dishtowel off the refrigerator handle and drying her hair. "Which one is it, Dora?"

"Myra gave me a calendar with month-by-month pictures of English royalty, and suddenly she thinks I know everything," Dora said. She was speaking into the sink, but quite distinctly, as if the spout were a microphone. "Myra, you're probably confusing the queen taking walkabouts in the rain with her corgis with gardening in the rain," Dora said. "That was the April picture."

"A feast for royalty, that's for sure," Winston said, coming up behind Georgette and hugging her. Then he quickly undid her apron bow and jumped back, laughing. "Gotcha!" he said.

"Married for many a long year, and as happy as teenagers," Aunt Georgia said.

Fran looked at Hank, who was mopping up spilled water on the table. Outside, a strong wind had come up. Sheets of rain lashed the house, sending rivulets down the windows.

"Henry," Georgette said, calling Hank by his given name. "Darling, you know—I say this to you, too, Fran—your father and I would like it very much next Fourth of July if we could see your lovely house in Morristown and change things around a bit. About where we visit, not move furniture in your house, I mean."

"This is not an important occasion to me one way or the other," Dora said. "Myra and I were saying, coming up here, that it's just a summer visit. We don't know why there's this pretense of celebrating the Fourth."

"You young people are so busy, we thought it might make it easier," Winston said. "We could stay at a motel. We're very adaptable people."

The notion of their adaptability was so far-fetched that Fran, Hank, and even Aunt Georgia snorted along with Dora. Dora, though, stopped peeling carrots and pointed her finger at Georgette, laughing until tears came to her eyes. Then, abruptly, she stopped. "They don't want us," she said.

Fran quickly contradicted Dora, but her voice was so insincere it embarrassed her. Everything she said came out in a rush: how they'd meant to entertain them at Christmas, but then she'd had to fly to Cleveland for business; that they'd thought so many times of inviting them, but work, horrible work, always got in the way. . . . As the words rushed out, Fran found herself talking more than she intended. Suddenly, she was ordering Dora not to contradict what she was saying. She was telling Dora she was very unpleasant when she made her constant, negative comments, and that Dora was not to rush in anymore and contradict everyone's thoughts. Fran said, tremulously, "If you think it exhibits your superiority, Dora, you should know that it does quite the opposite."

Wide-eyed, Dora again began to pour tears. She scooped up a pile of carrot shavings and threw them at Fran, though they were so light they fluttered to the floor just beyond Dora's outstretched hands. Dora and Fran stared at the orange curls on the floor. Fran was aware that all eyes were on them. She kept her head bowed.

"You're a spoiled snot. You don't know anything about family dynamics," Dora said. "I have every reason to resent them. They made me have an abortion when I was in high school. There happens to have been a boy who wanted to marry me, but no one in this house would hear of it, Miss Hettie the Queen of Propriety included, and I decided after that—"

"Be quiet, Dora," Myra said.

"I will be quiet," Dora said, speaking very quietly and emphatically. "I will be quiet to honor my chosen one."

"Please, ladies," Winston said.

"I've become a lady?" Dora said to Winston. "When did I become a lady? After my insides were scraped out?"

Hettie pushed her chair back from the table. "Macklin," she said, "I think we had better take a stroll."

"Oh, now, our discussion's all over," Winston said. "Push your chair back into the table, Hettie. It wouldn't be July Fourth without you two." He looked at Macklin with a worried expression.

"I think we might borrow an umbrella and take a little walk," Macklin said. "Rain's eased up. I say we stroll out among my animal kingdom and breathe a breath of fresh air and continue with what is sure to be a lovely dinner."

"They'd never talk about it from the minute it happened, right through my marriage and divorce from Dan Kramer, until last year when I was in the hospital," Dora said to Fran. "They still don't want to think it happened, or that they had any part in it. His name was Richard Mayhall, and he'd given me his grandmother's engagement ring, but Georgette and Winston intimidated me and made me have an abortion, and every time he called me, they hung up the phone. I missed all the rest of the year at school. They kept me back a year because they wouldn't let me go back until he'd graduated."

"We did what we thought best," Winston said.

"I'm not familiar with this issue," Macklin said. "I do know that life is filled with sadness, but I think we have to move forward and forgive."

Georgia's face rested in her hands, her elbows propped on the edge of the table. Myra had disappeared some time before. Not sure what to do, Fran said to Dora, "I'm sorry," and bent to pick up the carrot scrapings.

"That's what they didn't mind doing to my insides," Dora said to Fran, as she carried the stringy carrots to the garbage disposal.

"Enough!" Hank said. "Macklin, get an umbrella out of the hall closet and take your walk. Look at that: it's brightening over the field."

"He knew all about it," Dora said to Fran. "That's why he doesn't feel the way you feel now."

Fran frowned, looking at the pile of carrot shavings she'd just dumped in the sink. Why had Hank never mentioned it? And how many other secrets did she not know? She looked at the sun, peeking out between fast-rolling clouds. The field was beautiful—glossy in the rain. It was the field they'd crisscrossed in the past on cross-country skis, and on the Arctic Cat, driving in figure eights, making themselves dizzy roaring through the snow. After the graphic image Dora had just conjured up, she could not throw the switch for the garbage disposal. Instead, she stood there, looking out the window, sensing that Hank had left the kitchen. Then she was aware that someone else—it turned out to be Dora—had also left the room. As she turned and looked at the people who remained, she had an afterimage of Macklin's absurd animals on the lawn, and thought for a second that it would be wonderful to join them and sail off on Noah's Ark. As soon as that thought formed, though, it was followed by another: the family would probably climb aboard with her, and also, they would float forever, and nothing would endure, because everyone was old, except for Dora and Myra, who were gay, and among Macklin's animals, there was only one of each. She had seen three doctors, and only one held out a slight hope that she might become pregnant eventually. Which made her unsure whether it was sad, or tragic, that species might disappear. And as she looked out the window again and saw Hank walking with his arm around Dora's shoulder, she wondered whether he was sympathizing with her, or trying, as his family had once done, and as he himself had just recently done after her disappointing doctor's visits, to persuade her that things almost always turned out for the best.

Only the women were in the kitchen late at night, except for Hettie, who had left with Macklin right after dinner. They could all have been elsewhere, because for hours they had drifted in many directions, sitting beside their husbands, finding excuses to help each other (Georgette explaining to Fran how to roll her hair in a French twist, once it grew), making phone calls (Myra, more upset by the discussion than Dora, had phoned one of their friends from the support group and talked to her for an hour). But though they could have retreated, they did not, straggling into the kitchen one by one, for real reasons or on some pretext, so that by midnight Aunt Georgia was uncharacteristically wide awake, knitting, and Georgette was humming, rearranging food on the refrigerator shelves. Myra, Dora, and Fran sat at the table. Myra was drinking wine, which Dora said she wasn't even tempted by, and Fran was enjoying a Coke—Coke Classic, full of calories she usually wouldn't consider ingesting. She had told Dora about the miscarriage she suffered the year before she and Hank married, and about their subsequent inability to conceive. Myra, seeming much milder than usual, occasionally touched Dora's wrist and said they could adopt children, if that was important to Dora. Georgette and Dora darted looks at each other, but only connected when they talked about very general things: cooking, and gardening, and the fact that summer seemed not to have come yet, with such rainy and often cold weather. The implication was that there was still much fun to be had when summer really began. The windows by the table had been rolled open again, and a mist of rain glistened on the windowsills.

"Let me show you what Winston did," Georgette said, throwing a light switch by the cabinet. He had hooked up a floodlight, which beamed intensely, lighting up Macklin's animals. "He'd heard reports of prowlers," Georgette said, "but you know, I think men just like to install things. They're reassured by lights and alarms."

The bright patch of lit-up lawn was mesmerizing to Fran. Around the border, where dark grass gradually brightened to white in the illuminated circle, something was happening, Fran saw: something was moving, some shadow was darkening the light. At first it was just a flicker in her peripheral vision, but gradually she realized that her eye kept being drawn back to one spot. Dora, still with an eye on Fran, followed Fran's line of vision, and Georgette turned and looked, too. She was the first to whisper that there was something out there. Myra stood, towering over them, staring. "It's a dog," Myra finally said.

"It's a coydog," Aunt Georgia said, her needles in the air, blue yarn coiling from thumb to needle. "I heard about them down at Hettie's store. Since spring, the woods have been filling up with them."

"People call mutts that, darlin'," Georgette said, "but they don't really exist. It's like the unicorns. Wild coyotes mating with people's pet dogs is just . . . it's a way people upset themselves, Georgia."

"I know about coydogs," Myra said. "They were in the Southwest, where I grew up. People would say you could tame them, but I never knew anybody who did. You were supposed to keep away. They were worse than wild dogs, except for wild dogs in a pack."

"People should bring in their dogs at night," Georgette said, ignoring Myra's remark. "Nowadays there's more traffic. They should have them on leads if they don't want them run over."

"Look at it nosing into the light," Dora whispered.

Whatever it was, its pointed ears, backlit, stretched enormously as the creature cast its shadow. Then the shadow retracted, and everything was still. Aunt Georgia was the first to react, letting down her guard by heaving a great sigh, sure it had gone away. From the bushes close to the house, though, it began, once again, to approach the periphery of the light. It must be mistaking Macklin's animals for a real menagerie, Fran realized. It must be trying to get a scent to find out whether it was encountering friends or foe.

"Look!" Dora said, grabbing Myra's arm, toppling her glass of wine. "It's got the bear!"

For the second time that day, liquid—red wine—spilled on the table and pooled in a puddle, quickly seeping through the tablecloth.

"Salt. Salt will stop it from staining," Myra said. But she didn't know where the salt was, and for some reason everyone sat paralyzed, staring at the spilled wine. The coydog, finally backing off from the animals, suddenly darted into the darkness, and was next heard bristling through the hedge of forsythia outside the kitchen. Aunt Georgia drew back and Fran looked at the wine-soaked tablecloth, the wine moving in a rivulet toward a magazine, heading toward the vase of daisies. The second hand of the clock dropped and ticked, dropped and ticked.

"What do you not like about our coydog, Mother?" Dora said, pulling up the tablecloth, wadding it in her hand, wine spattering her blouse as she squeezed the wine-sodden cloth into the sink. "Just the idea offends you, so it shouldn't exist?"

Tick-tock, tick-tock, he loves me, he loves me not, Fran thought, looking from the clock to the vase of daisies, a few heads dangling, a few petals shed, once again in place on top of the table.

Much later, alone in the kitchen when everyone had gone to bed, Fran turned on the spotlight and waited. Eventually, as she thought might happen, she did manage a final look at the coydog. Near its tail, its coat was missing big patches of fur, and its ribs protruded. But there it was, still smitten with its wooden compatriots, or sick, perhaps: it was probably moving in circles and seeming disoriented because it was sick. As with so many things that were at first terrifying, Fran thought, it was also sad. It approached the pig, but went only so close. Then it hung its head and sniffed close to the greyhound. If she hadn't been exhausted, she would have watched it longer, but she was tired, and simply turned off the light.

She would be married to Hank for four more years. In that time, though the family convened regularly in Morristown, all of them would inevitably talk about this day. Other things would be omitted. The stories told could be summarized as follows: I remember the day the poor lonesome coydog got a broken heart when it went and fell in love with animals not quite its kind.

Perfect Recall

UNCLE Nate was estranged from the family for many years—a period during which, my mother told my sister and me, Nate intended to be a loner and misbehaved if anyone forced him to do anything for the family. He was her only brother, and I know it made her sad that he had moved to Maine and gone into what she could only see as self-imposed exile. I must have been seven when my mother, sister, and I spent the first day with Nate I could really remember at a small cove beach not far from his house. We were not invited to his house, though. "A total mess, nothing I could do with it," Nate said to our mother, who seemed to blithely accept this information. We had hot dogs and lemonade for lunch at a small shack near the beach where Nate's girlfriend, Kate, worked. Kate had a teenage daughter named Cindy Sue, and she also had a large husky named Prince Valiant. The dog could balance a hot dog on his nose. He would scratch the sand to smooth the ground when he saw Kate coming toward him with the hot dog. Then, after he was done scratching, Kate would step forward and center the hot dog on his nose, vertically. Prince Valiant would move slightly to the left and right to keep it upright for several seconds after Kate's hand was removed, his blue eyes crossed, and then he would give the hot dog a little toss in the air, catch it, and eat it in two bites. The dog was delighted when this trick had to be repeated for my sister, who had run off while he was still scratching.

The summer we went to Maine my sister, Elizabeth, was fourteen. In another four years she would be married to Donovan McCallister, who told us he was twenty-five when actually he was thirty-five, and one year after her marriage, Elizabeth would open her door to find a woman standing there holding a small boy by the hand: the reputed son of Donovan McCallister. She then became the mother to four-year-old Banyan McCallister, so named because he had been conceived behind the wall-like roots of a banyan tree in Key West, Florida, when Donovan was stationed at the navy base. The woman had been a waitress. She later married a private investigator, who, on their honeymoon, tracked down Donovan McCallister so he could assume responsibility for his son. The introduction was not very successful, because Elizabeth almost fainted, and Banyan burst into tears the minute the door was opened, and Banyan's mother, the former waitress, while not crying, was apparently not coherent, either. Though that preliminary encounter did not go well, Donovan was forced to go to a lawyer, who ordered a test to ascertain parentage, which came back after what seemed an excessively long time saying that Donovan McCallister was the boy's father, unless you were going to argue about .0000001 percent, which would of course make the lawyer richer but get little sympathy from a judge. How exactly Banyan came to move in with my sister and her husband was never clear to the family. Obviously that had been Banyan's mother's intention all along, but why this came to be was either not talked about, or perhaps not even questioned. Even before the test results came back, Banyan had been ditched. He was left by his mother with a hotel-provided babysitter who, when Banyan's mother and the private investigator did not return by three A.M., called the phone number she had been provided with, which turned out to be my sister and Donovan's home phone. It was the day after the woman's initial visit, and after a night of arguments and acrimony, my sister was packing her suitcase to move back home. Why she stayed is not clear.

That day at the beach, Kate—who had apparently facilitated the exchange of letters that resulted in Nate's picking up the phone and telling the family exactly where he was—took my mother aside and told her that Nathaniel, as she called Uncle Nate, had proposed and retracted his proposal three times in the three years she had known him. Each time he proposed had been the day after Valentine's, and the third time it happened, and she accepted, and then he called on February 16 to say he'd just as soon put it off for a while, she realized that the reason Nathaniel proposed the day after Valentine's Day was because the large satin hearts filled with candy were fifty percent off. "Too conventional to propose on the day itself," Uncle Nate had apparently told her. She'd believed the proposals the first two times, but the third time he proposed, she'd agreed without any hope that there would really be a wedding. Her reason for confiding in my mother—who told us the whole story that night, on the way home—was to try to elicit her help. Kate's idea was a little vague, but basically it involved assembling the family for dinner at her house, and then mentioning that for three years Uncle Nate had proposed to her and then rescinded the offer. She thought she might embarrass him by telling everyone what he'd done, sort of anecdotally, but she also hoped for the family's support: a chorus of chiding voices. My mother told Kate she doubted such a strategy would work. But Kate pleaded with her to bring us next Valentine's, as well as our mother's mother and grandmother. My mother, more to find a way to end the discussion than anything else, said that she would think about it, though she didn't think she would ever get Mother Brink to Maine in the winter, with her arthritis, and of course my father had simply disappeared from the face of the earth over three years ago, so Kate could hardly expect *him,* since my mother no longer expected him, herself. That would leave only Grandmother Huntlowe, Mother Brink's mother, but everyone knew she would go absolutely anywhere, as long as someone drove her.

I have to interrupt at this point to say a few things about how my sister, Elizabeth, usually conducted herself on car rides. She reverted to being babyish: a whiny brat, who kept up a constant routine of chatter, singing songs off-key as she interrupted her questioning to recite a limerick, grandstanding as if the car were a stage. She would call out "deer crossing!" when we passed a sign that depicted a leaping deer; she would change the stations on the radio so often that my mother made her ride in the backseat. On that particular car ride, she had demanded to know *everything* about Kate, and about Kate's daughter, wanting to know why Kate's daughter was called by her first and middle names, wanting to know why the South lost the Civil War, wondering aloud about all the missing men in everyone's family. She was singing along with the radio, "Lovely Rita, meter maid . . . " when a deer jumped across the road and my mother swerved into the breakdown lane. We found out later that she had slammed on the brakes harder than necessary to also avoid a family of possums, which is what made the car careen off the road and hit a tree that stopped our skid down the incline. There was serious damage to the right side of the car. Nothing happened to our mother, except that it provoked an asthma attack. She got her inhaler out of the glove compartment, put it in her mouth, and squirted. My sister, Elizabeth, although she had only the teeniest cut from where her hand hit the window handle, became hysterical, hollering for Grandma Huntlowe, instead of Mother, which really offended Mother. I was in the front seat, and the Beatles were still singing. All that had happened to me was that I got a headache the second the car hit the tree, but between Mother's asthma attack and Elizabeth's personal drama, I was the most coherent person when the first of many motorists who'd stopped reached our car. One of them, a man in a pickup truck, was the person we later lived with for many years, but that night he was just a tall red-haired man in a blue shirt and blue jeans, who had trouble figuring out what had happened because his glasses had flown off as he ran down the incline. When he first arrived, he was breathing as heavily as my mother. He was also more full of questions than my sister. "All right, everybody, take it easy. Who's hurt?" he said. My sister, when he opened the back door, unfastened her seat belt and scurried into his arms. By then, a man and a woman had arrived on my side of the car. I remember the woman saying, "My God. They were listening to the same song we were."

Uncle Nate was called to come get us, as my mother talked to the police and we watched the car slowly towed back up the incline. My mother was weak-kneed and tearful, constantly saying how glad she was that the tree stopped us. She kept trying to cuddle us, wiping away her tears and my sister's and telling me what a brave girl I was. After the accident, as we waited for Nate and for the tow truck, she and I shared the front seat of Dennis Trellis's pickup, bumping each other's hips to try to get more room. We would sit in that seat many more times, as it turned out, but that night it seemed a continuation of our adventure, sitting in such a large, unfamiliar vehicle as our mother talked to the police.

Uncle Nate came for us in Kate's station wagon. Kate was in the passenger's seat, her hair uncombed, no makeup . . . and I thought that no, he would never marry her, whether or not the family said he should, because without makeup her eyes almost disappeared, and she had no top lip at all. I was wrong about her prospects, as it turned out, because riding back to his house he began to declare how very glad he was we were all alive and miraculously unhurt, and before we got to his house he said the accident made him realize that life was full of terrible surprises, and that the one thing he wanted to do was to be wedded to Kate, which my mother quickly agreed would be a wonderful idea. Kate took what he said seriously because it was not the day after Valentine's.

Uncle Nate's house was as much of a mess as he'd said it was, but it was also more interesting than just any messy house. The kitchen counters were flecked with congealed food and caved-in Chinese take-out cartons. The ceiling was peeling so that the surface matched the shag carpeting in the living room. The only furniture was a sofa and two pole lamps hung with drying socks and a coffee table made from a lobster trap, with a piece of glass on top that had seashells glued around the edge. There were more cartons, and TV dinner containers, on the coffee table, as well as empty milk cartons and tools. In the living room were posters of Elvis and Jim Morrison held to the wall with yellowing tape. There was Elvis in one of his sparkly white jumpsuits paired with Van Gogh's *Starry Night*. Leaning against the walls were old tires decorated with the oddest things: forests fashioned out of bent metal hangers that had been painted green were on some of them—little plastic animals glued to the tires helped the illusion—and others had boats sailing on them, the tops of the tires painted blue and white to look like ocean waves, while another one had the Eiffel Tower made from broom straws, with little plastic dollhouse figures walking toward it. My mother, preoccupied as she was, began to squint at them with curiosity almost as fast as my sister and I did. "Nate . . . whatever are these?" she said.

"They're what I do to relax," he said.

"There's no champagne, but there's grape juice," Kate said, surveying the refrigerator shelves. "Who will drink a toast to my marriage to Nathaniel?"

"I should just lie down," my mother said.

"The sofa folds out," Kate said, sounding disappointed.

"I'm sleeping with Mom. I was almost killed," Elizabeth said.

Everyone looked at Elizabeth. I continued to look at Uncle Nate's tires.

"You're an artist," I said.

"Well, yes, I suppose I am," he said.

"He's very creative," Kate said.

"This place is weird," Elizabeth said. "Mom, you're not going to have an attack because it's so musty, are you?"

"Shhh," our mother said.

"What's going to happen to our car, Mom?" Elizabeth said.

"I never thought they'd like it here. That's why I didn't have them in today," he said. "I'm not comfortable here myself, it's just that it's my house."

"That was so awful," Elizabeth said. "That was so, so awful. Mom, you said you saw possums? Do you think they were really there, or do you think you imagined them?"

"Of course they were there," our mother said.

"Did they have little shiny eyes?" Elizabeth said.

"Please stop talking so much."

Our mother looked at Kate. She said: "He gave me his phone number. He seemed awfully nice, but I don't know why he thought I'd have any reason to call him."

"Double wedding!" Kate exclaimed.

But Nate married Kate at the office of the county registrar, and though she eventually went to live with him, our mother never officially married Dennis Trellis. She couldn't have married him if she'd wanted to, because she had never divorced our father. But she started living with him a few months after the accident, after many late-night telephone calls. First my mother moved us to a little town half an hour away from Uncle Nate and Aunt Kate's that we moved out of that spring, when our mother moved in with Dennis. Elizabeth thought that our mother was "unstable," and that her relationship with Dennis was making her sacrifice her daughters' best interests for her own insatiable sexual appetite—meaning: tap dancing classes and elocution lessons with Mrs. Marieanne DuFarge, in my sister's case. My sister explained sex to me, in the rather histrionic way Mrs. DuFarge had encouraged her to talk when she had something of importance to say, using a broom and a dustpan to illustrate her point. So that was why we were living in rural Maine. That was what was going on with the creaking bedsprings at night: Dennis Trellis was sweeping our mother.

Elizabeth, not to be done in by what she called "rural isolation," began a program of self-improvement she hoped would make her a highly paid model. She was tall for her age—five nine and growing—and it was her ambition to walk the runways in Paris. She steered her sled into a tree to break her nose—she was successful—and came out of surgery with the bump on her nose gone, as well as two black eyes we worried would never disappear. She hung photographs of exotic models on her bedroom walls and examined their eye makeup under the lens of the school microscope. She padded around the house wearing ankle weights, to give her shapelier calves. When she was sixteen, my mother and Dennis gave in and let her join the gym. There, she took step aerobics and practiced jumping up in the air like a jack-in-the-box on the trampoline, as well as attending Saturday morning advanced workouts. She was lean and muscular, with long hair and her new, almost perfect nose, and she wore more makeup than anyone in town. It was the frustration of her life that our mother steadfastly refused to let her climb into the gym's tanning machine, but eventually she decided to opt for a look she described as "pale and perfect." "Mom, I am *trying* to look like Liz Taylor in *Cleopatra*," she would whine when criticized. *"This is an established look,"* she would argue, barely containing her contempt. Dennis Trellis just shrugged, trying not to take sides. I, because I saw the effort that went into applying so many colors and substances to her face, was admiring of anything that took so much work. Elizabeth let me squirt mineral water on her face from a plant mister turned to the finest spray, to protect her makeup. She taught me how to paint her fingernails, and then how to do nail art. For Christmas, she got what she most desired: a subscription to French *Vogue*.

She met her husband-to-be, Donovan McCallister, at the gym. She met him when she was eighteen, just after Eileen Ford turned her down because she didn't have the right look. She had taken the train to New York, neatly dressed in a shirt-waist dress and low-heeled pumps, carrying a small overnight bag (she was going to stay on Central Park West with an old lady who was a friend of Grandmother Huntlowe's). Inside the bag she carried what she really intended to wear to the interview: a tiny black skirt, sheer stockings painted with a viper breathing fire at the ankles, her T-strap patent leather high heels, and several scarves she folded artfully, then tied around her breasts, dropping a white sheer blouse over top and adding necklaces of varying lengths, dangling ristras and silver crosses.

She went to four agencies, but she didn't have the right look for any of them. She came home with her waterproof eye makeup a mess, having cried for hours on the train. She was convinced that the "unsophistication" of Maine had tainted her, in spite of her best efforts. "I look almost like Lauren Hutton, so why didn't they want me?" she asked, for weeks. The plant mister went back to misting the philodendron. She stopped "cleansing her system" with quarts of mineral water. The Cleopatra look was abandoned for a modified, early Cheryl Tiegs. And then she met Donovan, who came into the gym to deliver lobsters. Many places in Maine where you wouldn't expect to find lobsters had lobsters: the Midas Muffler Shop; the greeting-card store. Donovan's cousin owned the gym, and Donovan and his friend Billy kept the tank by the front desk stocked, making a dollar fifty for every lobster sold up to one and a quarter pounds, and two dollars for every lobster sold up to three pounds. Billy whistled at my sister as she was leaving the gym. Donovan apologized for his creepy friend. Elizabeth ended up buying a three-pound cul and bringing it home for the family. In a year, she was married to him.

I haven't said much yet about myself. I've been a tagalong all my life. I was the youngest in my family, and it inhibited me. I looked to my sister to explain things, and to my mother to deny most of Elizabeth's explanations and substitute her own ideas. From their two ways of thinking, I arrived at a compromise, which I ran past Dennis Trellis, who had his own axe to grind, though I didn't know that then. He was large and affable and sincere, and I thought he was the most objective person in our family, though now I know that he was bitter he hadn't succeeded the way he'd hoped to in life, and that he always expected the worst. He had been sure, the night he went off the road, that when he got to us, somebody in the car would be dead. He had feared Elizabeth would be killed on her trip to New York City. He had thought Grandma's friend would have forgotten her arrival, and that she'd have to sit all night in Penn Station. He also thought that indeed she would become a model, and that that guaranteed a life of drugs, sex, exploitation, and overwork, while she associated with the smarmiest of characters. So, along with sweeping, these were the things he would discuss with my mother at night, which reinforced her own fear of the world. Leaving aside her problems with us, she already had a brother she considered crazy, or at best, a wild eccentric; her sister-in-law was fixated on the fact that Uncle Nate might leave her, because since the wedding, he had never again celebrated Valentine's Day with the half-price candy-box hearts; Aunt Kate's daughter, Cindy Sue, had gone to college in Roanoke, Virginia, and dropped out to become a Moonie, and she had been married in a mass ceremony in Madison Square Garden. Even Prince Valiant was a worry: "a homosexual"—it was the first time I'd ever heard the word—because when a male collie moved into the neighborhood, Prince became infatuated with it to such an extent that one time, chained to the doghouse, he dragged it half a mile to the other dog's property, to visit. They preferred to kill sheep together—it was the dog catcher who first alerted Uncle Nate and Aunt Kate to the dog's alliance—but when both dogs were tied up, Prince still found a way to make a visit, and together the two of them dug a large hole in the lawn, which they stuffed themselves into, dragging their chains down with them. My mother also began to worry more and more about Grandma Huntlowe, because she wouldn't eat anything but devil's food cookies and Fritos, and about Mother Brink, who had become agoraphobic (though we didn't know the term in those days), and who watched daytime soap operas and confused the characters' problems with Mother's. To his credit, Dennis Trellis tried to deal with all these problems, buying groceries for Grandma, phoning Mother Brink's doctor; taking Uncle Nate aside and telling him the wisest thing, the day after Valentine's, would be to buy his wife a box of candy. He was also reading a book about intervention (Cindy Sue) and how sensitive men could best deal with menopause (my mother), though he preferred reading the Sunday comics. He was stumped about what to do with the problem of Donovan McCallister—not only did they both consider him unsuitable for my sister, but Donovan had become so involved in various self-protection classes that he was always shadowboxing the walls. Still, some part of him felt that he and Donovan were similar, or at least he wished he could also be a hustler, filled with confidence about himself, pulling lobsters out of the water after finishing his day job, working out at the gym on weekends, taking judo classes and boxing. But he also thought Donovan was a smooth talker—he did not believe he was only twenty-five and asked for proof, which Donovan showed him by way of a fake ID he'd made at an amusement park—and he worried, as he probably would have worried about any suitor, that he would take advantage of Elizabeth.

About this time, what my mother called "the doubling up" began to take place. Mother Brink moved back in with Grandma, to be taken care of (meaning: an odd diet that forced her to cook for herself, and no more daytime TV). Prince Valiant was given to our family when he wouldn't stop running away, but we only had him a few months before he died of a broken heart, on the same day he refused, for the first time, to do the hot-dog trick. Then that summer Elizabeth got married to Donovan, and soon thereafter—as I've already mentioned—

Donovan's son, Banyan, showed up at the door, which made an instant family of three. People shifted around, the dog died—it was a little as if we'd been tinged by magic, except that nothing was straightened out at the end of the evening.

An amazing thing that did happen, though, was that Nathaniel Jasper Brink—my Uncle Nate—became a sensation in the art world.

In the summer of 1979, a new gallery opened in Belfast, Maine, run by a former New York City art dealer. Lula, the owner's wife, had been a friend of Kate's in high school, and when she moved to the area, she called Kate. Kate had her over, and she saw Uncle Nate's tires. She not only saw them, she flipped for them. She had Kate take her out to the garage, where by then Nate had set up a workroom, to see the pieces he was working on. She came back another day to photograph them, bringing her husband with her. He offered to have a show. Uncle Nate said he didn't think so—they were his hobby. Private. But Aunt Kate prevailed. He would have done anything to console her after Prince's death and Cindy Sue's disappearance.

The night of the show, Uncle Nate put on his nicest jacket and pants, and Aunt Kate wore a dress she had ordered from Frederick's of Hollywood. Outside the gallery was a big white limousine. There were also motorcycles and a Jaguar convertible, and someone was filming the opening for the local news. The limousine turned out to belong to Tony Curtis, who was already inside the gallery. Alex Katz was there. Aunt Kate overheard Tony Curtis telling Ada Katz that the woman getting her plastic champagne flute filled was Johnny Carson's wife. Aunt Kate was struck by all the celebrities. It took her a while to notice that Nate's tires had all been placed on white cubes that sat in front of enormous blowups of Lula's photographs. The show had a title: TIRED ART. It flew from two white flags leaning out from wall anchors. Fans tilted upward sent the flags billowing. They were large and silky; they reminded Nate of sails that had caught the wind. He thought they were the most beautiful things in the show, he told us later, including his art.

The photographs that provided the backdrops were, for the most part, highly editorial. The tire with Polynesian figures sat in front of a photograph of a woman in a grass skirt, bare breasted, silver rings piercing the woman's dark nipples. The tire with the farm animals and windmills stood in front of a photo of a crowded parking lot. The tire glued with toy cars going every which way had as a backdrop a heap of compacted metal in a junkyard. Uncle Nate had thought of his tires as whimsical; in the gallery, people regarded them with serious expressions, nodding and whispering. Three tires sold, and the penguin tire with spray-painted snow was put on hold.

I stood at Uncle Nate's side as he moved around the gallery. All the tires had been placed in front of photographs, except for the one that had been sunk. Wires attached it to the corners of a large fishtank. It was Nate's sea-life tire: metal waves, sprayed various shades of blue, plus little rubber fish, including a shark that seemed to be pulling fish backwards. Among the fish was a drowned woman, about a quarter of an inch tall, in a blouse and skirt. There was a small bicycle on its side, and a tiny tire Nate had gotten from a toy truck. The photograph behind the tank showed a shark zeroing in on a decapitated corpse, a cloud of blood spreading smokily through the water. The tank was on a higher pedestal than the other tires, so that the photograph showed through when you looked at it at eye level, wavery and distorting. That was the photograph that prompted Kate's shocked question, which elicited the information that that particular photograph came from a service that supplied photos.

"Powerful," the woman standing next to Uncle Nate said.

There was seaweed. There were real fish: little neons, darting above the tire as if it were a reef.

My mother, biting her lip, turned her head away.

"Cool," Elizabeth exhaled in a hushed whisper.

"God," Dennis said, turning and walking away.

Who could have guessed that Uncle Nate was soon to move out of the garage, into a studio he'd put up on his property with the proceeds he'd make from the show? Or that a monograph would exist the next year that featured pop-ups of the tires? Aunt Kate was soon to have a new puppy and a sapphire ring, and for a brief time there would be exciting vacations for all of us. In my own case, I would also have a computer, which Nate thought I needed because of the journal I'd been keeping about what happened to members of our family. He, himself, would be getting a new Jeep, and Kate a new Volvo. In their future were trips to St. Bart's and to Virgin Gorda. Uncle Nate's clothes would come from L.L. Bean, instead of being things he found at the kidney foundation shop.

Lula Rahv came up to Uncle Nate and stood at his side, beaming. "Champagne?" she said, holding out a glass.

"You'd probably like it better if there was a photograph behind me of a cork flying into somebody's eye," he said, taking the glass.

"Is this person by any chance the artist?" a smiling man with a red face, wearing suspenders and white pants, said. He had just bought the Polynesian tire. The red dot was being placed on the wall by Lula Rahv's husband.

Though Uncle Nate didn't know it then, the smiling man was the ticket to his future: Andrew Kingsley. "You must come to Boston, to see my art collection and to meet my aunt," Kingsley said. "You'd be interested to meet my aunt." He paused, then said, significantly: "My aunt is Willa Walker."

Uncle Nate looked at him blankly.

"The landscape painter," Andrew Kingsley said. "I've started to keep my own expanding collection in her dining room."

Aunt Kate knew who Willa Walker was. She had seen her paintings at the Museum of Fine Arts, and she remembered them: lovely, lyrical little landscapes. She looked so pleased to be introduced to the woman's nephew that Nate just could not refuse. This was before Uncle Nate carried a Day-at-a-Glance book, though, so he jotted down the time and place of the meeting on a cocktail napkin. Kate had seen landscape paintings that moved her that much? She'd spent time at the museum? She was a constant surprise to him.

One week to the day, they owned a Willa Walker. They had gotten it—a silvery painting of the Charles, at dusk—in trade for Uncle Nate's "Desi Chasing Lucy" tire.

Miss Willa—that was what her nephew called her—said the tire was something that would bring both her nephew and her much pleasure. It would be a great addition to what she called her nephew's "annex." I wasn't there that day, so the rest of what I say is from Kate's report. Uncle Nate and Aunt Kate stood in the doorway, taking things in. On one wall was a photograph of tree branches—was that what they were?—that looked like it had been shot many times, then torn in half and jaggedly patched together. A plaster bird was on the floor beneath it, in a puddle of feathers. The companion piece was a cement birdbath. The cement birdbath was in the shape of a bird. Miss Willa turned on the spotlight by touching a special wall switch. Music also filled the room at the touch of another button: *La Traviata.*

"Miss Willa has the most interesting dining room in Boston," her nephew said.

"I didn't use it for years," Willa Walker said. "I was delighted when Andrew proposed an art gallery. I heard once that Joan Kennedy never cooked in her kitchen. That she put her scarves and hats in the kitchen drawers. We don't live our lives in particular rooms anymore, do we?"

While Uncle Nate was certainly the dominant figure in our family when he was alive, after his death everyone looked around—sort of like birds looking for a few more grains of food, I guess—and without consultation, it was mutually agreed that the next person most deserving of our attention was Banyan.

Banyan had perfect pitch and played the piano beautifully. He also excelled at field sports and t'ai chi. He slept at night absorbing language tapes playing softly. He helped his father prepare his taxes, and he helped Elizabeth, whom he called "Mom," cook dinner. He was a brilliant mimic, whose repertoire included Ingrid Bergman in *Casablanca* and question-and-answer sessions with Ronald Reagan that would leave even Republicans laughing helplessly. To put it mildly, Banyan was an unusual child, who got a lot of positive feedback. People always wondered aloud at his natural talents, and they commended him for being so interested in his schoolwork, in which he excelled. For years, Banyan was inclined to be a historian, though his facility with languages made him think, also, of becoming a translator.

He appeared on *College Bowl* (Duke). He went to the first two years of medical school (Yale). Then he spent a year in Paris, because that was a city his father particularly loved when he and Nate and Kate had gone there. There, he studied art. He soon began to be less interested in painting than in performance art, though. One of his most popular routines had to do with re-creating an entire hockey game while standing in the same spot. Girls adored him, because he was handsome as well as talented. When he returned to the U.S., he had a wife, Marie Catherine.

I thought Banyan was the most self-assured, interesting person I'd ever met. I had gone to the University of Maine at Orono and become a librarian, and I lived just a few miles down the road from my mother and Dennis. I saw them often, and sometimes Elizabeth drove from Cambridge, where she managed a store that stocked soaps and perfumes that were so harmless you could feed them to fish. She still had the same car Nate had bought her, which had well over 150,000 miles on it, but which she wouldn't get rid of for sentimental reasons. Sometimes Kate joined us for dinner. She had a dog that did no tricks at all, and that would not even respond to "Lie down." It was quite a comedown after Prince Valiant. All it did when you told it to lie down was cringe a little, then get all misty-eyed.

On the Saturday I'm going to tell you about, Elizabeth reported that she had gone to have Miss Willa Walker's landscape appraised. The Museum of Fine Arts had suggested someone in downtown Boston—a very nice man, she thought. The landscape should probably be worth about a hundred thousand dollars, she said, disguising her smile.

"No!" my mother shrieked.

Years before, Banyan had selected that particular landscape because he thought it was the most wonderful. Even as a child, Banyan's excellent eye had been respected. Going through the slides Andrew Kingsley had sent, Banyan had picked out his favorite, and Uncle Nate—who felt that in making the trade, he was atoning for the discounted Valentine hearts—simply deferred to Banyan's opinion. When Nate died, though—working on a final tire, before a planned trip to Santa Fe—the Willa Walker painting he had given her as a gift had made her sad. She willed it to Banyan, but gave it to Elizabeth for safe keeping. Elizabeth kept it in a box in her closet for a long time, but eventually, when our aunt died—also unexpectedly, while opening a can of Campbell's soup—she took it out to get it appraised.

"You can't sell that. It was promised to Banyan," Dennis said. "A hundred thousand . . . can that be right?"

"Well, we wouldn't sell it out from under him. We'd tell Banyan about the appraisal," Elizabeth said to Dennis.

"Banyan's not money hungry," my father said.

"Dennis, people don't have to be *money hungry* in order to part with something," my mother said.

"He grew up in a family where his aunt sold everything her husband ever made as fast as she could after his untimely death, including the man's Day-at-a-Glance book. Think of it: she sold his personal calendar to a Japanese businessman! She'd have sold his socks if anyone wanted them," Dennis said.

"You mean you wouldn't be interested if something you owned was worth a hundred thousand dollars?" Elizabeth said.

"There's too much thought given to money in this family. If you ask my opinion, it contributed to Nate's death. All the money did for Nate was enable him to buy rich food that gave him a heart attack. As if running around the world the way he did wouldn't have killed him soon enough."

"What do you mean? St. Bart's isn't exactly a Third World country, Dennis."

"He died because he was out of his element."

"Ridiculous!" Mother said. "Who could believe that people

who travel abroad return home and die because they've been out of their element?"

"Jim Morrison," Dennis said.

"What about Jim Morrison?" I said.

"He died in France, didn't he?"

"This is utterly ridiculous," Mother said. "You embarrass yourself, Dennis."

"Amelia Earhart," he said.

"I think we should call Banyan and let him decide what he wants to do," Elizabeth said.

"Where is it?" Dennis said.

"I don't think we should tell you. Who knows what you might do with it," Mother said.

"Wrapped in Bubble Wrap in my trunk," Elizabeth said.

"You locked the car?" my mother said.

"Yes, Mother. And I also pick up the kettle when it whistles."

"I wasn't questioning your common sense, Elizabeth. There have been radios stolen out of cars around here lately. That's something new. When Dennis and I moved in, as you know, we never locked the door."

"The world has changed," Dennis said.

"It sounds like you mean to dig in for the rest of your life," Mother said.

"The so-called good life killed Nate," he said belligerently. "That, and letting people convince him he was a genius when he was just a tinkerer."

"*Never* say such a thing," my mother said. "*Never, never, never.*"

"Dennis, people who tinker fix broken locks, or whatever. Nate was an artist," Elizabeth said.

"You grew up in this family, and you're true to their beliefs."

"But Dennis—you're part of the family, too."

"I know it. I don't know why people didn't pick up any of my beliefs. Everybody just wants to chase after fame and fortune. Banyan is genuinely gifted, and he's still maturing. Why corrupt him with money?"

"Banyan has always been a real favorite of your father's," Mother said. "He leaps to his defense, when I've never heard him defend—"

"Defend what? Elizabeth's ill-advised idea to marry when she was eighteen? Jane, with her talent for writing, deciding to become a librarian and recommend other people's books all day? She never even gets in the sunshine. You look unhealthy, Jane," he said, turning to me. "It's important that you take care of yourself as the family scribe."

"You can be a mean person sometimes, Dennis. I hope you realize that," Mother said.

"I give credit where it's due. Jane has perfect recall. I could ask her what I said at Sunday dinner three weeks ago, and she'd tell me. I don't know—maybe having a memory like that will serve you well one day, Jane. At least you think about other people."

"I think it's in Banyan's best interest to tell him what the painting is worth," Elizabeth said.

"Let's face it, Elizabeth. It's sad but true: Dennis has never forgiven me for not legally marrying him, because it makes him feel like an outsider. And the only other outsider, in a way, is Banyan—because he joined up late, and might not have joined up at all. Poor child: imagine that his own mother took him by the hand . . ."

"What's done is done," Elizabeth said, making a motion as if to disperse cigarette smoke. Or perhaps the past seemed to dangle in front of her, annoying, like a cobweb.

"Maybe Banyan will take us on a trip," Elizabeth said. "He

was so lucky to be left that landscape in Uncle Nate's will—won't he want to share the wealth? Those trips were so much fun."

"Donovan provides you with stability," Dennis said. "He's been a good provider. A good father, too. He should have a say in whether you tempt his son with that amount of money."

My sister glowered at him. It was the same expression she had on her face the day he said, "You most certainly will not become a model." Soon after that, she'd taken the glass off the frame that held the formal photograph of Mother and Dennis and misted Dennis's face with the plant sprayer. She already had the short-short skirt. Even the viper stockings, if I recall correctly.

Years passed, though, before I drove with Elizabeth to tell Banyan about the value of his inheritance. The day we set out, Miss Willa Walker's painting was still wrapped in Bubble Wrap, in the trunk. Elizabeth had swaddled it in towels and placed it in a box. Banyan and Marie Catherine lived in a small town in Vermont no one has ever heard of, called Cray. Banyan drove over two hours to play piano at the big new Sheraton in Burlington on the weekends. He was again enrolled in medical school—though a less prestigious one—and Marie Catherine, during certain periods of the year, helped collect sap to be made into maple syrup. She worked mornings making flower arrangements for the local florist.

"When he sells it, I'm going to consider that closure, of a kind, and stop writing about the family," I said. "Mysteries are what sell, anyway."

"You're just depressed," Elizabeth said. "You need a boy-friend."

"Well, you met Donovan accidentally, didn't you? I'm waiting to meet someone accidentally."

"I was done up like a whore. And I was *young.*"

"Thanks a lot," I said.

"I'm not saying you're old. I'm just saying that I was *young*. I didn't know what I was doing. I'm amazed they didn't put up more of a fight when I said I wanted to marry him."

"I think she was traumatized, being left with the two of us, you know? I think she wanted to believe there was stability in marriage."

"Hm," my sister said.

"I mean, I think she was also hoping against hope our father would show up again, though maybe that was just so she could have it out with him. I think she cared about Dennis, don't you? I mean, that she still does."

No answer from Elizabeth.

"I don't think he was just a convenience," I said.

"I guess I think he was," she said. "They fight all the time."

"I don't know," I sighed. "I admit that people's marriages don't look so desirable to me. My friend Karen Quinn actually got kicked in the butt by her husband and broke her rib crashing into the kid's snowman. I mean—"

"There are always bad marriages. Donovan and I have had a pretty good marriage, don't you think?" Elizabeth said.

"It's none of my business."

"You don't think so?"

"You and Donovan don't even speak half the time."

"Honey, after that many years, you've heard every opinion," she said. "Ask me his opinion on anything, and I'll tell you."

"Whether you should tell Banyan about the painting," I said.

She shifted in the seat. "I didn't mention what we were doing on our trip to Vermont," she said.

We drove in silence for a while.

"But if Dennis is right and Banyan's not materialistic, he'll be glad to give you a cut, won't he?"

"Well, he has a wife. I find it hard to read Marie Catherine." She looked at herself in the rearview mirror. "And he and I had that big fight when he dropped out of Yale, and I don't think he's ever quite forgiven me. After all, I'm not his mother. I'm just some woman his father—"

"Didn't screw behind a tree," I finished.

"You can be so horrible. Why can't you just forget unpleasant things?"

I smiled my best Mona Lisa smile.

Ahead of us was the steep hill that led to Cray. It crested and then the road swung to the right and we drove the narrow route that had once been a logging road, recently paved because the head of the volunteer fire department lived on it. In another mile or so we turned down Banyan's street, Crabapple, and drove slowly through the ruts to the last house on the dead end.

Marie Catherine, always happy to have visitors, ran on tiptoes to the car. Ballet flats in Vermont? But there she was, in a swirling skirt and a little tube top with a sweater thrown over it, and her pearls and her little black shoes. Behind her, I could see dried flowers lying in piles, like brush, on the front porch. The morning glories were in bloom. Most things in this part of the world had about a ten-day growing period, and everyone went around gaping, as if they were stoned.

Elizabeth embraced her daughter-in-law. I bowed from the waist; it was something that just occurred to me, for no special reason, except that Marie Catherine had never assimilated herself into American culture and she never knew what to expect from anyone, so why shouldn't I do something a little different? On her tiptoes, she hugged me hello.

"Banyan goes to get ice cream and cookies!" she said. "You did not see him coming down the road?"

"No, and thank heaven," Elizabeth said. "That road is impassable. I'm always afraid the car will slip down the incline."

"Because of that terrible accident when you are only children," Marie Catherine said, solemnly.

"Well, yes," my sister said. "Has that passed into family lore?"

"He tells me it was very romantic, that you met the man who was to be your father when he was protecting you two young girls because the car had fallen into some tree."

"That was the night everybody got so shook up, it changed us for all time. It's when she"—Elizabeth indicated me—"decided to write the story of that, and everything else, though she's never shown anything to us to this day. It was also when I realized my mother was just as fragile as I was, so I'd better have a plan to look out for myself."

"But it works out well, because you gain a father," Marie Catherine said. "Come on the porch and see what I am making. Wreaths, for autumn."

"We didn't want to move to Maine," I said. "Her, particularly."

"I had my eye on Paris, but I couldn't even make it in New York," Elizabeth said.

"You wished to go to Paris?" Marie Catherine said, a little surprised.

"Look at me. Once I thought I'd be a model."

"Yes, but you are *très jolie,* you know. And you do not go to Paris?"

"No," Elizabeth said. "It was all a young girl's dream."

"A dream because many pretty girls model in Paris?"

"Yes."

"Mm. *Oui,*" Marie Catherine said, eyes downcast.

"Look at those purple flowers. They don't even look dried. What are those, Marie Catherine?" I said.

"Statice," she said. "And over here, these dry very purple, too. Heather. But those buds are very delicate. You have to handle carefully, because they are very fragile."

"What would you most like, in the world?" Elizabeth said.

"*Moi?*" Marie Catherine said.

"Yes. If you could have anything. You know—the way I wanted to be a glamorous model with a glamorous life, when I was young."

"But still, you know, you are *très jolie,*" Marie Catherine said.

"What would it be?" Elizabeth probed.

"I don't think about this! I am happy, *oui,*" Marie Catherine said seriously.

"You wouldn't even like a new car, or a dog, or a boat to go out on Lake Champlain in the summer?"

"Dog?" Marie Catherine said to me, tilting her head.

"We don't really understand people from your generation very well, Marie Catherine. A lot of our friends moved to remote places, or they joined the Peace Corps or something like that. It's just that you and Banyan seem to be *very* unmaterialistic."

"If I make a pretty wreath, I don't need to hang it for myself," Marie Catherine smiled.

"*Would* you like a boat?" Elizabeth said.

"Maybe Banyan," Marie Catherine said, helpfully.

"A boat, a car, maybe your own studio, where you could make your wreaths? If you had a hundred thousand dollars, wouldn't you think of something to do with it?" Elizabeth said.

"Why one hundred? Why not ten?"

"Only one. One hundred thousand."

"Well, that is very nice, but probably I will not think of what I want until I have so much money."

"What did you want when you were a child?" Elizabeth said, sinking into a blue butterfly chair. I jumped up on the porch railing. Marie Catherine stood there on the wide wraparound porch, as if alone, on stage. She seemed slightly perplexed, but eager to please.

"A castle!" she said. "And a dragon to breathe fire against enemies, if the drawbridge"—she gestured with her hands— "might be stuck. And of course many flowers, and rabbits, and no foxes, and beautiful birds."

In the distance, we could see Banyan's car bumping toward us. There was something wrong with the suspension; even the Vermont roads were not so bad they would account for the car bouncing like a seesaw.

"Listen, darling, your mother has come today with the idea of our having very, very much money," Marie Catherine said as Banyan got out of the car. "I am telling her we will move to a castle like the one in the book. The castle, *n'est-ce-pas?*"

"Cherry Garcia?" Banyan said. He slammed the car door behind him, clutching a brown bag to his chest.

"Hello, Banyan," I called.

"Hello, Jane," he said.

"Hello, sonny," Elizabeth said. She was needling him; he hated to be called anything except Banyan.

"Hello, nonwicked stepmother," he said, coming up the porch steps. He kissed her on the cheek. He leaned over to kiss the top of my head. He put his arm around Marie Catherine. "You two look very well," he said. "Tan and fit."

"Practicing your bedside manner?" Elizabeth said. Her remark seemed to deflate her. "Maybe I am sort of wicked," she said. "I was wicked to Jane in the car. She needs a boyfriend.

But maybe I'm not being realistic about how difficult it is to find one."

"The family curse. A belief in the advisability of getting together with just anybody," he said.

"Banyan! *C'est terrible!*"

"It's right on target," he said. "When they make their choices, they range from impulsive to irresponsible."

"But you are very lucky that you find a mother who truly loves you!" Marie Catherine said. "She chooses to love you. That is even more of a compliment."

"Put 'er there, Ma," Banyan said, leaning his cheek toward Elizabeth. She kissed it.

"He is mischief," Marie Catherine said.

"The ice cream's melting," Banyan said. "Let's dish it up."

As we followed them into the dark house, Elizabeth whispered: "Is this a big mistake? I shouldn't say anything?" but there was no time for me to answer. Marie Catherine was gesturing toward the kitchen table, where white linen place mats and punchwork white napkins had already been placed. She had Grandmother Huntlowe's silver flatware, as well as her silver pitcher, which sat on a trivet in the center of the table, filled with pink phlox. Banyan pulled out Elizabeth's chair. He moved to pull mine out, but I beat him to it.

"How's Donovan?" he asked.

"When last heard from, he was exactly the same," Elizabeth said. "He was deploring television violence and wondering whether he should take early retirement."

"What did you tell him?" Banyan said.

"He just wonders aloud. He doesn't accept any incoming information."

"That's true," I said.

"She thinks that your father, and some man who kicked his

wife from behind and sent her crashing into a snowman, represent modern marriage," Elizabeth said, sucking on a spoonful of ice cream.

"This is terrible! You know a man who is so violent?"

"I'm sorry I asked," Banyan said.

"Do you think he should take early retirement?" Elizabeth asked Banyan.

"No. He doesn't have enough interests," he said, between bites of ice cream.

"Do you think I should make more of an effort to get a man interested in me?" I asked.

"Absolutely. I see it all the time: guys who burned out in their first marriage get into their forties and realize the errors of their ways. No more fanning the flames. They want a neat little bonfire to warm their hands over. They're willing to try again."

"And do you think we should get a dog?" Marie Catherine suddenly interjected, looking Banyan right in the eye.

"No," he said. "We've already been through this."

"Because he doesn't realize, it could be a nice dog like that funny dog that was in your family that did the tricks." She looked at both of us, in turn. Elizabeth looked noncommittal. I looked off into space like I'd missed the comment entirely.

"Well then, if I can't have a dog, maybe one hundred thousand dollars, like your mother mentions?"

Banyan shook his head. "There was an old TV show called *The Millionaire*. The money only brought unhappiness. Some guy went around ringing doorbells—this was really the Dark Ages; now, he'd get blasted away, or at the very least they'd look through the peephole and tell him to beat it or they'd call 911. Anyway, he'd go into people's houses and announce he was giving them one million dollars. From then on, it was nothing but misery."

Elizabeth frowned, pursing her lips. Her expression was clearly not the result of sucking on a bitter cherry. "Wasn't that show before your time?" she finally said to Banyan.

"We used to watch it on the VCR when I was at Yale. I think the joke to some of them was that it was just a million bucks," he said, snorting.

"A soap opera," Marie Catherine said, having decided what sort of a show it must have been.

Driving to the inn where we'd spend the night before continuing the drive home, I remarked on the obvious: Banyan and Marie Catherine seemed happy, but not foolishly happy. Why add anything to the mix—dog, castle, money—that might ruin anyone's equilibrium?

"Well, that's exactly what old stick-in-the-mud Dennis was arguing earlier, in case you don't remember," she said.

We rode a while in silence. Sometimes she sounded like our mother. More often—it was true—I tended to sound like Dennis.

"So what are you going to do about it?" I asked, finally.

"Hold on to it and see what happens," she said.

"Like a spell you don't cast?"

"Like a spell I don't cast."

We didn't talk anymore until we pulled into the driveway of the inn. We'd stayed there other times when we'd visited Marie Catherine and Banyan. The owner knew us now; last time, for the same price, he'd given us the honeymoon suite, which had a Jacuzzi. We sat in it together, bubbling, amused at the many strange places we'd found ourselves, individually and collectively, over the years: moving to Maine; visiting Europe; the summer I went tubing with a man I thought I'd marry, except

that it turned out he was already married. Also, the time we visited Miss Willa Walker's Boston apartment, which was the
grandest place we'd ever seen in real life. We'd gone there with
Uncle Nate to trade a tire for her landscape. It had of course
been inferior to the house Elizabeth planned to live in when
she made it big as a famous model, but still: we couldn't believe
our eyes. In retrospect, the strange stalky plants must have been
orchids. The music, which we'd never heard anything like
before, had been the voice of Teresa Stratas. And so many
strange things, all in one room: later, we would realize we'd
been looking at Alex Katz cutouts, John Martini sculpture,
Cornell boxes. We were with Uncle Nate, and he was deliver-
ing his tire, walking down the street from the expensive lot
we'd eventually had to park in when he couldn't find a parking
place. The tire was in a plastic garbage bag. We'd been so
excited, and Miss Willa Walker had been so nice to us. As soon
as we arrived, she phoned her nephew and he came over and he
and Uncle Nate drank champagne. Miss Willa Walker had iced
rose-hip tea, which we drank, too, with heaping spoons of
sugar, and absolutely loved. It was served to us in the same
stemmed glasses the men drank from, congratulating each
other on their trade: the landscape for the tire. But Uncle Nate
got the better of the deal, and Miss Willa Walker's nephew
missed his guess: after Uncle Nate's death, the tires didn't
appreciate in value. In fact, when they went up for auction, few
were even bid on.

"You get the bags, will you?" Elizabeth said, handing me the
keys to unlock the trunk. She was primping; though she had no
real interest in the owner, she still compulsively made herself
attractive when meeting any man she'd met before.

He was happy to see us. Real honeymooners were in the
upstairs suite, he said, winking to us, but he had set aside a

lovely room with twin tester beds that overlooked the pond. We must come down and have whatever drink we'd like from the sideboard set up in the library, and then he would tell us about the special dishes the chef had prepared for dinner. Though he offered to help, we had only two small overnight bags, one of which was slung over my shoulder. The bags, and the Bubble Wrapped landscape, which I had taken out of the trunk not because I thought there was any danger of its being stolen, but simply because I wanted to see it again.

The room was pretty: Laura Ashley wallpaper and white lace curtains. As he moved in front of us, still expressing his joy at seeing us again, he touched a button that activated the stereo: some very lovely music, probably Chopin. Then he moved around the room, turning on a light on the desk, using a dimmer switch for the recessed lights near the large bay window that looked out to the field and the pond. With everything about the room just the way it should be, he turned to us as happy, as satisfied, as Miss Willa Walker had been that day years ago, standing in her private museum. I felt like a little girl again, someone who barely knew what was going on—that was the truth; you could be a grown-up and know less and less about what was going on—but nevertheless experiencing a vague, happy anticipation.

"I never thought about it until now, but wasn't it strange Miss Willa Walker had none of her own artwork hung on the walls?" I said, looking around the room once the owner had left.

"I think artists are like that. Musicians might be an exception. They don't mind playing their own compositions. But think about it: writers talk about other writers' books; painters hang work by other artists." She sat on the side of the bed. "And anyway, are you sure?"

I knew because Dennis had been right in what he'd said during the argument about getting the painting appraised: I did have perfect recall. Uncle Nate had asked whether any of her work was hung and she had said no, once she'd painted her landscapes she didn't want to think about them anymore. Meanwhile, her red-faced nephew had placed his new acquisition on a wooden cube that had been put in the room in anticipation of the new piece. He adjusted the lighting until the tire was its blackest black, and the hula girls and the cavorting tigers sparkled. Then he stood there and he did the most amazing thing: he laughed. It was a spontaneous laugh that was as surprising as an opera singer when she reached the highest note, though it lasted nowhere as long. I suppose it could have been an explosion of exhilaration, except that it was not. It was not a mean laugh, but a loud, surprisingly neutral laugh—and it deflated Uncle Nate as surely as a knife would deflate a tire. On the way home, we had sat quietly in the seat. Aware of the black cloud of Uncle Nate's mood, we had both climbed silently into the backseat together.

"You see that the family keeps that painting we just got no matter what happens, and you hold it until it's worth a fortune," he finally said, as we crossed the border into Maine. "You mark my words. Whatever that cocky guy thought, I got the best of that deal. You girls see that that painting is taken care of, whatever you do."

I could hear his words as I took an Audubon print of a bird down from above a reproduction Chippendale table and leaned it against a chair. I unwrapped the landscape and looked at it a minute, then lifted the wire onto the picture hook. I touched it lightly at one corner to balance it, then stepped back.

Hanging there, the landscape was luminous under the spotlight. It was almost as if the lighting had taken the painting into consideration. It was much more impressive than I'd remembered. It also looked perfect in the room: elegant and unique. Surely anyone would prefer this to a long-necked bird sweeping its beak toward insects. Anyone would be fascinated by the play of light on the water, echoed by silver molecules of mist. The figure of the rower suggested action: the curve of the paintbrush indicated a body moving forward. Around the bend, the painter had somehow managed to suggest, would be more of the same: open space; more water. You didn't need to wonder what the front view would be like—what the rower's expression would tell you. The rower was purposefully moving through water, moving through time, our last glimpse of him as definitive as anything we would see if we really stood on shore, watching him round the bend.

Elizabeth had been looking out the window, but as she turned away, she saw that I had hung the painting. She looked slightly perturbed for a second, seeing the Bubble Wrap on the floor. But then she came toward me. She backed up and stood at my side and saw it from my perspective, and eventually a slow smile spread across her face. As sisters, we had had so many unspoken agreements, and now she saw my point: maybe this was the perfect room through which the small silver-blue river should pass.

The Famous Poet,
Amid
Bougainvillea

———

HOPPER caught the ball the second time it was tossed to him; a victory, of sorts, since the day before the ball had gone through his fingers as if it were breeze passing through cobwebs. He caught with two hands, the way little kids try to catch. That was because the disease had made him a little kid: a little kid and an old man. Much of the population of Key West wasn't doing even as well as he was, of course—the ones with AIDS, though surely there were other people on the island who, like him, had MS. And if not on the island, there were the much reported on Hollywood people: Annette; Richard Pryor. Well—at least nobody was writing stories about him, saying how goddamned courageous he was, interspersing the stories with little photos from his past, showing him wearing his Mouseketeer ears. Then again, he wasn't famous, though his employer was. Until the disease began to take its toll, he had worked for fifteen years as the studio assistant of Carwell Craig Bowman, the expatriate British figurative painter whose murals hung in the hippest restaurants and private homes. In Komae City, outside of Tokyo, Carwell had painted a faux aquarium as the entranceway into a real aquarium, with a faux flood and faux broken glass marking the transition between the outer room and the inner reality. Hopper and Carwell—it was the same year Hopper met him—had been invited to the opening party where, at a sit-down dinner for twenty, they had dined on sashimi cut from living fish, held in a plastic press that allowed the insertion of a thin sharp knife. Afterwards, trying to make light of the ghastly evening, Hopper had suggested to Carwell that he inquire whether the host might not like to leave everything just as it was, and he would return, to paint the shocked American man who had fainted, lying on the floor near the not-at-all faux banquet table.

Hopper thought: you remember the past when you feel bad. Awful things seem remotely amusing. Amusing things seem remotely sad. Most of all, things seem at the same time vivid and remote.

"Going to keep that ball all to yourself?" Randy says.

"No," Hopper says. "I thought I'd get out of the wheelchair and get in some batting practice. Enough of this Toss-the-ball-to-the-feeb; I'm going to get into a crouch, take that palm frond over there, strip it, and use it as my bat. Spring training commences." As he speaks, he tries to throw the ball back. It goes about halfway, rolling several feet short of Randy's foot. Randy is sitting at the side of Carwell and Modello's hot tub. Randy can go in the tub, but Hopper can't because of a new medicine he's taking. It isn't as if the tub could do anything for Randy— he had a stroke almost two years before that he recovered from as much as he is ever going to recover—but it feels good. The hot water feels good. At any given moment, tub or no, Randy feels better than Hopper, he'd be the first to admit.

The two of them have become the odd couple. Odd in all ways, because although both of their employers, Carwell Bowman and Mark Modello, are gay, Hopper and Randy are straight, yet they have become a sort of couple by default. A couple joined by adversity. After Randy's stroke—which left him in a coma for two days, and in the hospital for almost a month, followed by another month in rehab—he had looked at Hopper (he had looked *at everyone*) in a new light. That was just before Hopper had to give up the canes and go into the chair. On the afternoon of Randy's stroke, he had been on the telephone ordering from Office Max when he had slowly, dizzily realized that he was lying on the floor, listening to a woman say, "What quantity of Post-it notes, sir?" repeatedly, though his mouth would not move to shape an answer, let alone beg for help. Modello—the famous Italian furniture designer, whose pieces were, earlier in the week, shipped to the Sultan of Brunei—had returned from an afternoon at the Pier House Beach Club to find Randy unconscious, the phone emitting off-the-hook beeps, Giles the dog alternately growling at the phone and licking Randy's forehead. "I was so disoriented, I thought Giles had rabies and had gone mad, or something," Randy could remember Modello saying to him in the hospital. But on what day? A week into his stay? Two? When had Modello begun to make light of everything, accepting their changed lives with a shrug, invoking his own ineptitude, rather than referring to Randy's obviously disastrous state? There had never been any question of shipping Randy back to Kansas; Modello let it be known immediately that he planned to hire another gofer, and a nurse for as long as necessary. They would proceed as always and hope for the best. The best turned out to be: no mental impairment; regained speech, with slurring no worse than many of Key West's functioning alcoholics; coordination better than the witch in rehab had predicted; and—for amusement value—the male nurse had run off with the male gofer, the two of them leaving a note and disappearing into the night like love-struck teenagers. When he had his stroke, Randy had just celebrated his fifty-first birthday. He did not smoke or drink (except for the occasional cold sake on a summer day), was not overweight, bicycled everywhere, and had always felt, as a Gemini, that he could not only conquer the world, but many worlds. Suddenly he found himself discussing the various pros and cons of hardwood canes with Hopper, aged thirty-seven. Previously, he had not exactly looked down on Hopper, but until he had his stroke, he'd had little in common with him, except for their subsidiary positions in their respective households, and who wanted to acknowledge that?

Randy had grown up as the eldest son of a doctor in Kansas City. He'd flunked out of med school, and then he had lived for a few months (it was supposed to be a few days) with his mother's "bohemian" sister in Greenwich Village. He'd gotten a job at a bookstore, and he'd been told to deliver several architecture books to the Gramercy Park Hotel for Mark Modello. He had never heard of Mark Modello. But Modello had struck up a conversation with him, standing in the doorway of his room in his bathrobe, and to his own surprise, Randy had agreed to leave New York to chauffeur Modello to Miami, where they might both decide whether permanent employment might be mutually beneficial. Modello couldn't do anything except make furniture: he couldn't drive; he couldn't make a sandwich. But he knew about things: he knew about the places he'd traveled to; he knew about food and wine, opera, architecture, books, writers, painters. All of which made more sense than knowing the routes of the vascular system, presided over by the heart, which was a hollow muscular pump, surrounded by the pericardium. It had been November in New York. The idea of sunshine—of Miami Beach, which was where Modello would be working for the next six months, or so—had been irresistible. "Is he homosexual?" his aunt had asked him. "I don't know," he had said. "Should I ask?" He could still remember the expression on her face, both quizzical and myopic, as if she could only squint hard enough, by looking through her own puzzlement she could visualize the answer. "If you don't care, then I don't see why you'd ask," she had finally said. Now, he could see that she had raised the question as a warning—though it was also possible that she might have been actually wondering if he, himself, was homosexual. These were the things that in the not-so-distant past weren't directly spoken of—except, perhaps, by black-stockinged "bohemians" who lived far from Kansas. He could still hear his father calling his aunt, so long dead, "the bohemian." Later, he found out from a younger brother that "bohemian" had been his father's polite term for "Communist."

Hopper's background was quite different. He'd grown up in different times, and in a different world from Randy. He graduated from Hollywood High and was raised by an independently wealthy father who spent his life working on screenplays that were never made into movies, although he made a good profit from his hobby; he sold the vintage motorcycles he refurbished to some of Hollywood's finest, Steve McQueen among them. Harper was his given name; Hopper was his nickname, for "all hopped up," because even by the standards of Hollywood High, he smoked so much pot. He quit cold turkey, though, during the period when he studied Scientology, and by the time he'd quit both drugs, he was twenty years old, a moderately talented surfer and photographer with the requisite tragic vision—meaning that he took intensely close-up photographs of bums in Santa Monica, which he cropped so that their ravaged faces seemed to be abstract relief maps. These he showed to girls to lure them into sex with a man who was both hard-boiled and sensitive (a persona he'd picked up as an impressionable youth from watching the movies of Steve McQueen). He met Carwell Bowman when he valet-parked his car at an L.A. restaurant. The car was a rented BMW convertible. It started to rain just as Carwell picked up the car, but he had no idea how to get the top to latch. Hopper stuck his hand through the window and latched one side, then moved to the passenger's side and sat to latch the other. He saw that Carwell's finger was bleeding. He saw this because Carwell was staring at his own finger, transfixed. "I can't stand my life," Carwell said to him—or something close to that. Hopper took off the bandanna he wore around his neck—the lucky bandanna that had once served as an ex-girlfriend's hamster's hammock—and wrapped it quickly around the bleeding finger. "But where is La Cienega?" Carwell had said. "Where is fucking *anything*?" The other carhop honked; the couple who had just gotten into the Cadillac behind them didn't want to have to pull around them to pull away. "Where is *one moment of common courtesy*?" Carwell asked. When the occupants of the Cadillac honked again, Carwell sprang from the car, a fierce frown on his face, wrapped finger pointed like a gun, whereupon he was set upon by the other carhop, who jumped on his back and brought him to his knees. This all happened in seconds. There was a sudden pileup of bodies on the sidewalk, and the woman had gotten out of the Cadillac and was screaming—standing there in her white miniskirt and go-go boots and her little silvery jacket, screaming. Somehow, out of those few disastrous minutes, it had been decided that Hopper would drive Carwell back to his hotel, and subsequently that he would serve as his savior, flight arranger, phone answerer, and general handyman. Girls flocked around Carwell; it was no longer a problem to attract girls, because Carwell filtered them down to Hopper. This was in the not-so-distant past when girls were girls, and not women. They didn't want to be women; they wanted to be girls, looked out for like kids, tolerated like kids if they needed cab fare to get home, if they had to be bought new earrings because they'd lost one of a pair and they were so, so sorry. It was like they wanted their hymens back, Hopper had said to Carwell. Carwell considered Hopper a creative thinker. He had not hired just any assistant, he told people proudly: don't just look at his accomplishments; wait until you hear the way this young man expresses himself.

And then flip forward fifteen years to the time when Hopper started to be cold. He never turned on the ceiling fan in Key West, even on summer nights. Sweaters, extra shirts . . . nothing kept him warm. The tropical breezes were no longer refreshing, they were icy. At first it was a joke. He had a broken thermostat. But alone, worried, he would sit on the side of his bed and rest his head in his hands, and some nights his fingers would tingle, but he made a distinction between that sensation and being able to feel. He heard something about mosquitoes—maybe not mosquitoes, exactly, but some tropical insect that stung you with numbing aftereffects. Then he heard that the effects lasted a day or two. Maybe three. A year later, things began to waver and to go out of focus. At first it took one or two blinks to bring the world back. Soon it took not seconds, but minutes—and blinking didn't speed things up. He went to an eye doctor and said nothing about the visual distortions; he said only that his long-distance vision didn't seem to be as clear as it used to be. The doctor examined his eyes and gave him a prescription for glasses, and he was so relieved, he almost hugged the doctor. He listened attentively: he would not need the glasses for driving unless that made him feel more secure; he might find it convenient to use the glasses on days when there was excessive glare; the glasses were not very strong, but he should find that they helped. He found that even with the glasses on—he filled the prescription that day, and never took them off, even to sleep—the world looked, increasingly, the way air looks as it rises out of a heat grate. A year later, he couldn't open a jar. Actually, he sometimes succeeded, but one time the effort took the skin off the pads of his fingers and—

full circle, in an odd way—he didn't know his hand was bleeding until he saw the glistening red streaks around the top of the pickle jar.

Even though they had been friends most of their adult lives, Carwell and Modello had grown closer as they increasingly extended themselves, altering their own plans to accommodate the shocking and unexpected limitations of their friends— Hopper and Randy had become their friends long before their health failed. Who knew what Carwell and Modello really said to each other. Who knew whether they cried on each other's shoulder on those forays to South Beach, or whether they were the silly, lighthearted trips Carwell and Modello presented them as. Who knew whether they might not be covertly inquiring about alternate arrangements for that time when things might get worse. Yet who was going to face them down and demand to know what they really, truly thought—especially when they were so heartbreakingly upbeat ("Well, it's *time* I learned how to open my own pickle jars!"). For years Hopper and Randy had gratefully accepted their continued employment—if that was what it was. They made a pact not to suffer bouts of excessive self-pity in the older men's presence, and to the extent that they were able, they still did whatever they could around the houses. Telephone answering machines had taken some of the heat off long before they became sick—that is (thank you, rehab witch), *physically challenged*—and Randy could still cook, those nights he wasn't too exhausted from getting through the day. Hopper could still shake Carwell out of a funk by making acerbic remarks. Each had also had a hand in selecting and training his replacement: in Hopper's case, a young woman named Doris who had grown up in a family of six brothers, who prided herself in carpentry and plumbing repairs; in Randy's case—being the Gemini he was—he had decided on two people: a Cuban chef/launderer/gardener, plus a former New York City model named Lisa Lee who had relocated to the Keys to be with her girlfriend, who worked at a lumberyard. Lisa Lee had great organizational skills and functioned in Mañana Land as if she were still in New York City, which surprised enough of the people enough of the time that they came through for her: she procured impossible-to-get plane reservations; last-minute bookings in fancy restaurants; out-of-print books. Her beauty neutralized her assertiveness, and people genuinely liked her. Randy was quite smitten, himself, but Lisa was interested only in her girlfriend—and the girlfriend proved invaluable in locating difficult-to-find wood.

Right now, Randy is back in the hot tub, humming a little song. Hopper is looking through a copy of *Entertainment Weekly*, checking the movie reviews. There is almost enough breeze, if he holds the magazine right, to turn the pages for him. Today is Friday the thirteenth of December. They are in the yard behind Carwell and Modello's houses, the yard with the enormous kapok tree the Clara Barton preschool children are taken on annual trips to see, waiting for the arrival of the Famous Poet. The Famous Poet will be picked up at the airport by Lisa and transported to his good friend Modello's house, where they will all enjoy a late dinner of Cuban-style paella. "Just wait until I stumble in on my last legs, and you bring up the rear in your wheelchair," Randy says. "The last time he saw me, I was doing fifty chin-ups and a hundred push-ups a day, and we got drunk and he told me he'd always felt he had to overcompensate because so many men assumed he was gay because he was a poet—that until recently he'd lifted weights and run twenty miles a week, but that lately all he wanted to do was to find people who *were* gay, so the heat would be off and he could just drink with them. Then he got all upset because he was worried he'd somehow offended me—God knows how, unless he was thinking that I thought he'd implied I was gay. . . . In any case, I got out the cognac and we went at it, and as I recall, we both got very sentimental about the dog. He's always been so proud of giving Giles as a gift to Modello. He started to feel sad because Giles was getting old, and he should be given a very special Christmas. This was December, so that did make some sense. Anyway: we started imagining T-bone steaks for Giles, and then slow-running cats, cats that couldn't get away. . . . I don't know why it seemed so funny, but we woke Giles up to tell him all about the slow cat Santa would be bringing him, and the Famous Poet was down on all fours, meowing and pretending to barely move at all—just inching forward and meowing over his shoulder. Modello had gone to bed hours before. But suddenly there he was. We'd made too much noise, obviously. Suddenly he was standing there in that monogrammed blue silk robe of his, and those awful terry-cloth slippers he won't get rid of. And through clenched teeth, he said—he almost spat it!—he said: *"This is not a good environment for the dog."*

"Oh, man, I can hear him," Hopper says. "That same archness Carwell has. That *'Where is one moment of common courtesy?'* mode I told you about. I think they caught it from each other, like measles, and they reinfect each other all their lives, so when they least expect it, they're standing around in a silk robe, fretting like old queens."

"You miserable monster!" the old woman next door screams at her cat. She throws something and goes inside, slamming her door. Carwell and Modello are eagerly awaiting the death of this neighbor, so they can buy the adjacent property and expand their compound. Hopper and Randy look briefly toward the fence. There is a small peephole, about the size of a marble, that the Cuban drilled, which Carwell subsequently painted around, transforming it into a bullet hole through the forehead of Andy Warhol's blue Mao.

"I'm worried about what will happen when he comes," Randy says. "I asked Modello what he'd told the Famous Poet about me, and he said, 'Nothing.' I think he meant it. I have such a pallor, and I look like I'm years older than Modello, now. You'd think he would have prepared him."

"Oh, he'll just feel even sorrier for you," Hopper says. "Let me give you some coaching on how that goes. The person gives you a pitying look, but not too much of one, and you return the look with an expression that has to communicate, in less than three seconds: yes, I'm ruined, but I'm valiant, and things will get worse before they get better, though in my own case, since I don't believe in an afterlife, things really won't get better, and P.S. I don't believe in reincarnation, and don't even think of talking to me about vitamin supplements, let alone acupuncture, which should be left to porcupines defending themselves in the wilderness."

"That look takes five seconds," Randy says.

"Practice makes perfect," Hopper says. "We have the rest of our lives to work on this."

"But you wouldn't rather be dead, would you?" Randy says.

"What makes you ask that? It always shocks me when you say something plaintive."

"'Plaintive,'" Randy says. "I wouldn't have known that word when I met Modello. I think it was part of my charm that I barely knew the English language."

"Don't be ridiculous. He was attracted to your looks. You could have been a thesaurus, or you could have been mute."

"He didn't intentionally employ the handicapped," Randy says. "I can assure you of that."

"No, I know he didn't," Hopper says, "but did you ever wonder what both of them were doing hiring straight guys? Don't you think maybe they wanted to torture themselves, just a little? And that this is the way it boomeranged on them?"

"You're in a hell of a mood," Randy says. "For one thing, they're two very different people. I've admitted to you that for a brief period, more years ago than I can really remember, Modello thought he could wear me down. But it wasn't like he chased me around the house, you know. Sex was never an issue. I mean, it was, but that was because he was pretending to be so relentlessly heterosexual. All those women. Those lovely women wearing his pajama tops as nightgowns, using champagne flutes as bathroom glasses."

"It was sort of decadent, wasn't it?" Hopper says. "Their bisexual period, I mean. I'd find the girls' panties under the pillow after they'd gone, as if the sex fairy, instead of the tooth fairy, had left a token of appreciation."

"They've gotten older," Randy says. "Now when women come they don't bother to pretend. And when men come, they're just friends—people from the past. Do you think they've both given up sex so we won't feel left out?"

"No," Hopper says. "I think they got tired. Tired, and worried."

"Maybe the Famous Poet will shake things up. He still magnetizes women, doesn't he?"

"I don't know. But he wrote a letter saying that what he most wanted was a quiet couple of days," Hopper says. "I asked whether I should take some WD-40 to my squeaking back wheel—just joking, but Carwell seized on it; said it was my house and that I shouldn't feel in any way inhibited. That the Famous Poet was just a visitor."

"So what are the plans?" Randy says. "All I've heard about is tonight's dinner. Something must have been set up. I should have asked Lisa."

"Lisa told me that the guy's reputation precedes him, and she wants as little to do with him as possible."

"That was the thing about us," Randy says. "Totally non-judgmental."

"Well, you can't be getting a free ride on the roller coaster and suddenly say, Excuse me: I don't think this ride is what it's advertised as, at all; I think it's House of Horrors."

"Did you feel that way?" Randy says, moving a small white plastic boat around in the bubbling water. "I never thought any of it was scary. I thought it was all sort of chaotic but tame."

"Well, you must admit, some of the parties got out of control. And some of the street trash the guests would bring home could be a little frightening. But you have to admire them: through it all, they were working."

"They still do work all the time, though it seems like a lot of the fun is gone. That now all they're doing is quoting themselves," Randy says.

"What do you mean, 'quoting themselves'?"

"Their style. Things get repeated. They've gotten locked into it. That, or they have to concoct something that isn't heartfelt, just so it will be new."

"Like a painter doing a painting in which another painter's painting is hung on the wall in the background," Hopper says.

"Sort of like taking a picture for your Christmas card, in which you're holding up last year's Christmas card and smiling," Randy says. He swishes his hands around in the water. He smiles up at Hopper: "All those jokes, being sent out to friends' refrigerators."

"Listen to us," Hopper says. "Here we go down memory

lane. One of us staggers, and the other rolls his squeaky wheel-chair."

"Well, now, those aren't our only distinguishing characteristics." When the little boat bobs close to Randy, he pushes it away with his nose.

"I guess it's the holidays. I'm feeling sorry for myself because Christmas is coming."

"Christmas always made you unhappy. It used to irritate me that you'd have nothing to do with the annual party. You'd do all that work, and then when the big night came, you'd go to the 801 and drink."

"Like I would have been the life of the party," Hopper says. "Witness the fact that I'm all but forgotten. He thinks that if he sits me out in the yard, I'm suddenly uplifted. Dazzled by nature. To say nothing of providing upbeat talk to entertain a person about a hundred times more sophisticated than I am, who's probably turning into a prune rather than leave me sitting here alone."

"Not so," Randy says.

"I take that as a compliment. But what, exactly, are you doing, bubbling up to your neck, by the hour?"

"Avoiding Felix. He acts like every mollusk he steams open contains a pearl."

"The Famous Poet requested paella, I hear."

"You know what they're doing? They're fattening him up for the kill. Since he got that fancy award, they've both been eyeing the possibility that he might want to go in on that real estate deal with them."

"An ulterior motive? You could believe of our distinguished employers that they might not be operating with the purest intentions?"

"It is their mutual intention to prosper," Randy says.

The back door of Mark Modello's house opens, and Giles the dog skitters out, under fire from a barrage of Spanish.

"Come here, Giles," Randy says, bumping through the water to the rim of the hot tub. Randy's voice is all concern. "Did that nasty Felix yell at you?" The dog runs in a wide circle around the hot tub, then catches the scent of something in the breeze and looks up.

A raccoon is sitting in the silver buttonwood tree. It has obviously been there the whole time, quietly waiting until that time when it will again have the yard to itself. Giles—perhaps in deference to the raccoon's size—continues to sniff, but does not approach the tree. Morons on motorcycles streak by, opening them full throttle. It is almost enough noise to shake the raccoon from the buttonwood. Everyone cringes.

Lisa comes out of Modello's house. She is wearing white pants and a hooded jade-colored sweatshirt, with the hood thrown back. She is carrying her big keyring. In the world of the ten thousand things, Lisa has keys to open a significant number of them: car keys; security alarm keys; her own house keys; keys to the shed; duplicate keys in case her girlfriend loses her keys.

"I'm off," she says. "Everybody seems sure I'll recognize him by his . . ." She searches for the right word: *"grandeur."*

She takes the Mercedes, driving it out after opening the gate, which is flanked by cascading pink bougainvillea, through which large gargoyle heads partially protrude.

"Good-bye, pretty girl being paid time-and-a-half for going to get the Famous Poet. Good-bye," Randy says, getting out of the tub. He waves the white towel he'd left on the hot tub railing like a big handkerchief, then wraps it around his waist. His knees feel suddenly so weak that he plops down on the fieldstone, right where he is. He's stayed in the hot water too long;

that can be counterproductive, as he knows, but he was frustrated by the kink in his back, determined to soak the pain away.

"You all right?" Hopper says, wheeling his chair to face Randy. Giles noses around Randy, sniffing the wet towel. His real concern, however, is with the raccoon. He keeps glancing behind him, like someone talking to a bore who's become smitten with another person far across the room at a cocktail party.

"Just a bit of fatigue," Randy says. He looks at his feet. He does look like a prune. A white prune. The skin will unshrivel—at least, why not pretend to have faith in your body and assume that it will—but inside, whatever narrowed and warped will stay that way forever. He puts a hand on the dog's rump, to steady himself. The dog stands still, obligingly, his now white muzzle further whitened by a small puddle of light aimed from a spotlight onto a royal palm.

"You've been depressed all night, yourself, haven't you?" Hopper says.

"Well, it's my own fault. I was more than capable of helping to prepare the dinner, but it just drives me crazy when Felix exudes goodwill in the direction of—well, basically in the direction of seafood. He can be all by himself, and he'll still be talking to the shrimp and marveling at their beauty, raising his hands above some steaming pot as if it's a magical infusion he's absorbing through his skin."

"I've seen him," Hopper says. "How do you think he got that disposition, when his family lost everything when they fled from Cuba? And his sister dying so young, and all?"

"Current research seems to indicate that people are issued their dispositions the way they're issued blue eyes," Randy says, though he isn't really concentrating on what Hopper is saying. The pain in his back has resumed, with more intensity;

the soaking did nothing, except perhaps to exacerbate it. For a few seconds in the tub, bubbling, he had felt pain-free and wonderfully buoyant. It was probably thumping down on the fieldstone that made the pain flare.

"What do you think they're doing, staying in the house all this time?" Hopper asks. When Randy doesn't answer, Hopper answers his own question: "They're continuing their bonding experience. Imagine having known each other almost forty years, living next door to each other, never even giving a formal dinner without inviting the other, but never—"

"Oh, we don't know that they weren't lovers," Randy says. "But really: what would it matter?"

"You think they might have been? I always take everything at face value, I guess. When Carwell told me he and Modello never got it on, I couldn't understand why, since they're so inseparable, but I believed him." He thinks about it. "I certainly believed him," he says. He reaches out to pat Giles as he walks past, but his hand seizes up and all he can do is plunk his fist on the dog's back. Giles looks back, briefly puzzled. Then he continues toward his water dish, beside the traveler's palm. "It would be naive to think that every homosexual would sleep with every other homosexual, I guess," Hopper finishes.

The pain in Randy's back is burning like a pilot light. He has an image of a tiny constant light inside him, and he wonders, for a second, whether he might temper its annoyance by thinking of it not as a pilot light, but as his spirit. His continually glowing spirit. Then he decides that no, there might have been a time in the sixties when that would have worked, but it would never work now. The wet towel is making him cold. But the truth is, he isn't sure he can stand up. He imagines himself a flea, hopping onto Giles's back, riding into the house, tiny and invisible, transported. When Giles finishes drinking water, he walks over to the back step and goes into the house, his dog tags jingling.

"I was just seeing if I could shake your confidence before," Randy says. "One time—I don't remember how—but one time it came up in conversation that they'd discussed the possibility of having some sort of a romance, but both of them agreed that the other just wasn't his type. And they're so much alike! Isn't that a riot . . . that *that* would be the reason they wouldn't do it?"

"Gets less funny when you're in my position, and you realize you'll never have a 'type' again. That you can have any type you want, I mean, but it's irrelevant."

Randy looks at him. He realizes—as he rarely does—that Hopper is years younger than he. He thinks about saying: "Could you wheel over here and let me see if I could use your chair to pull myself up?" Instead, he says: "How come you never got married? Just think the chase was the best part of it?"

"Yeah," Hopper says. "Seemed like it was a game that could go on for a pretty long time."

They sit in silence. More motorcycles whiz by. The raccoon looks down from the tree.

"Yeah," Hopper says again. "Lucky lady, the one who got spared marrying me, having to search her soul and then decide it was the best thing for both of us, after all, if she left."

Randy looks at Hopper. A blanket is stretched across Hopper's lap and the heavy sweater, like a shawl, that was thrown around his shoulders when he first wheeled out now seems appropriate, rather than excessive. Randy hears himself say, "I'm cold."

"You cold, man? I guess so, huddled with nothing but that little soaking loincloth to warm you."

"The thing is, I don't think I can get up," Randy says.

"Can't get up?" Hopper says immediately. His voice is

higher than usual. He turns the chair in Randy's direction and rolls over to him with a few quick strokes of the wheel. He looks at his hand, which is unclenched but also, he can tell, useless. Instead of extending it, he uses the ball of his hand, clumsily but quickly, to lock the chair. Then the scenario that moments before had seemed so desirable to Randy materializes: he shifts—uncoiling the pain from the pilot light into a burning corkscrew—and reaches for the top of the wheel. "That looks good. Grab on," Hopper says.

Randy looks at him. "See? It's not just Felix. You've got a good disposition, yourself. You think I'm going to be upright, after a little maneuvering, in just a few seconds."

"To tell you the truth, I don't really assume that," Hopper says. "I just feel bad that there's nothing I can do to help you."

"Don't pay any attention to me. I was just jazzing you because I needed to stall for time," Randy says. He shrugs. "Fifty-three fucking years old," he says. He brings himself to one knee and, ignoring the pain, moves his hand from the top of the wheel to the armrest. He can feel—thank God; he can feel—strength returning to his upper body. He tells himself: *Take your time; take your time.*

"Go slow. You're doing great," Hopper says, his voice again at its normal level.

"It's so pathetic. What can you do but laugh?" Randy says. He adds: "Also, I'm highly motivated. I've got to piss in the worst way."

As Hopper snorts a laugh, Randy brings himself up, unsteadily. He brushes his sides, as if he were cleaning something dusty. Then he adjusts, for a few seconds, to being upright. "Be right back," he says, heading for the kitchen at as good a clip as he dares, and the adjacent downstairs bathroom.

In the time he is gone, Hopper and the raccoon look at each

other for a long time. Eventually, the raccoon moves down a branch. You could even say the raccoon did this while staring. Hopper decides to let it win the stare-down—actually, he had been trying to calm down and to put the image of Randy on one knee out of his mind, so he hadn't so much been staring at the raccoon as simply spacing out, but try to communicate that to a raccoon—so he looks in the direction of the bougainvillea, through which he can see one of the gargoyle's protruding wings. The pair had been his birthday gift to Carwell the year they moved to Key West, before you saw the things in every gift shop. Obscured by the lushly flowering bush, he can now see only the stub of one's nose, and the wing of another. Which makes them seem a little nightmarish, because they're so effectively hidden.

Lisa is not yet back from the airport, a drive that at this time of night should have been no more than ten minutes each way, so there is a good possibility the Famous Poet's plane was delayed in Miami, or wherever he changed to a commuter flight. Only little planes are allowed onto Key West, setting themselves down like toys, little people ducking their heads and climbing out, their eyes ablaze with appreciation and wonder. The heat! The sun! The palms!

He imagines himself one of those people: a person who leaves his airplane seat, who walks jauntily down the steps to the tarmac. But the image dissolves; he doesn't even have a scenario for what he'd do first: jump in the air and click his heels, or simply stride purposefully into the terminal. What a simple wonder that would be: to walk across the floor to baggage claim, reach out and pick up his bag . . . he'd sling it over his shoulder; none of those rolling-wheel suitcases. He'd . . . oh, he'd stop for a Coke at the machine and drop the coins in himself, plugging in quarters with his thumb, the way he used to. . . .

Lost in thought, he closes his eyes, but even then, what he visualizes starts to vaporize. He opens his eyes, not surprised to see the yard, rather than the interior of the Key West airport, though he had not at all expected to see the raccoon, completely descended from the tree. It is sitting on its haunches, which makes it seem at once toylike and casual—if "casual" is a valid way to describe a raccoon. It's a big one: barrel round and bright-eyed. On the ground, it looks larger but, paradoxically, less imposing. It seems to have no clear idea about what to do next.

"Just don't turn out to be rabid and leap at my fuckin' throat," Hopper says.

As if shaken out of a reverie—is it sick? Could the thing really be rabid?—the raccoon draws itself up as if to say that it is in perfect health, perfect shape. It sniffs the ground. It takes a few steps forward. It really is big. Where does a thing that size keep itself? Under someone's porch? Then, as suddenly as it appeared, it runs off, darting quickly through the open gate.

It is only a matter of seconds until Hopper hears the sickening squeal of brakes. Why couldn't it at least have darted out in front of one of the Testosterone Pigs on their motorcycles— someone who might have been toppled? Why the banality of a car that will simply strike the big unlucky raccoon and keep rolling? But oh, hell. Goddamn and oh, hell: the poor bastard should have sniffed the ground just a few seconds longer. Then it might still be alive. He hopes it isn't suffering. That it has been killed instantly. The car has moved on, as if there was never a problem—but what else is to be expected in Key West? Friday night—and Friday the thirteenth, no less—it was probably struck by some drunk whose reflexes were shot to shit. It wasn't likely Mother Teresa would get out of the car and minister to the dying.

Was it the air, as evening moved toward night, that made

him suddenly so cold, or just the MS, screwing up his circula-
tion? More of the prelude to the nightly sweats and shivering?
Well . . . the poor bastard was probably well out of it. How long
was it going to last on a tiny island that was getting developed
inch by inch, day by day? But if that was so, why was he crying.
Because of the shock of it. The simple, unexpected reality of
something suddenly getting snuffed. It was awful. He remembered back when he drove, the things along the highway. The
little Key deer, hovered over by buzzards. The mashed turtles.

"Brr," Randy says, coming down the steps. "It got cold suddenly, didn't it?"

Randy has put on long pants and a beige turtleneck. He is
the picture of the casual male—the way the raccoon had been,
for a few moments, a casual raccoon. It is on the tip of Hopper's
tongue to blurt out what happened, but Randy has had enough
trauma for one night. He seems much better. Pulled together.
He picks up the pool cleaner and runs the net just below the
surface of the water, clearing it of kapok leaves.

"Come down, come down, wherever you are," Randy calls
into the tree, raising the blue netted pool scoop, seeming not to
care that the raccoon is no longer visible.

"Getting late. I wonder where Lisa and our charming house-
guest are?" Hopper says.

"You know, as much as I like Lisa, I always breathe a sigh of
relief when she leaves at night. That still leaves Felix, of course:
Mr. I-Work-for-Less-Señor-I-Live-in-Your-Downstairs-Bed-
room. Doris does her eight hours and there's no keeping her
after that, so she's out of your hair." Randy glances around the
yard. The lights that are on timers have come on. From the side
of Modello's house, they can see the end of the long lap pool,
lit from below, its green-painted bottom glowing. "The people
they hired—well: we *told* them who to hire—they're very good,

but it's a job to them, you know? Although Felix makes me nervous, sometimes. Telling Modello, who is the atheist of all atheists, forgive me, about how he implores God in his prayers every night to bless what he calls 'the family.'" Randy shakes his head. "Still, the bottom line is that they're being useful, and we're hanging out like any other Key West bums, except that we're not whiling away the evening with beer, since neither of us is supposed to drink."

Hopper picks up Randy's false elegiac tone: "Yes, here the two of us are, turned out into the Peaceable Kingdom with old Giles, on his last legs, watched over by our friends the gargoyles, and the koi over there in its little burbling pool, all draped with protective netting. . . ."

"And high up in the tree," Randy says, "Mr. Coon, looking down on all of it like that guy up on the billboard in *The Great Gatsby*—Dr. Ecklestein, or whoever he was—the eye doctor."

Hopper draws in his breath sharply, remembering his earlier visit to another eye doctor: the eye doctor who didn't know his secret, the nice man who gave him a prescription that might be useful on days when there was a lot of glare.

Randy hurries on, gesturing over his shoulder. "Up there with his big bright eyes, just hangin' out, taking it all in. Nothing to say about it, of course, but that doesn't mean he's not learning from our sad travails."

So why doesn't he look? Hopper wonders, suddenly irritated at Randy. Why does Randy take so many things for granted? What if they hadn't worked for people who were compassionate? What if they were in a ward, somewhere? Okay— the ward might have been more imminent for him than for Randy; but what if they were drugged, living with a bunch of crazies, nobody even to visit them? What made them deserve the good—the better than good, *excellent*—treatment they've gotten? One step outside the yard he, himself, had just been derisively thinking of as the Peaceable Kingdom was the driver who'd mowed down the raccoon and continued on his merry way. What luck was it—what incredible good fortune—that the two of them had been born men, instead of koi fish, their little ponds draped with insubstantial netting so the cranes wouldn't swoop down and slurp them into their beaks? What amazing DNA miracle had made them able to stand upright—well: in principle they could stand upright—without barrel bodies and striped tails, and a brain barely able to comprehend so-called civilization, let alone its dangers?

"Looking a little mashed down in that chair. Can I help reposition you?" Randy asks.

Yeah, Hopper thinks bitterly; you can put your hands under my armpits and pull me up. We can pretend you're the big puppeteer in the sky. You can reincarnate me, if you've got any hidden magic powers, and sit me in that silver buttonwood. I'll come back as the raccoon. Instead of saying those things, though, he says: "Do you think you could help me down those steps into the tub?"

"The hot tub?" Randy says. "I thought the doctor said you shouldn't go in."

"What you're really thinking is that we're both so pathetic, you couldn't help me in if you wanted to, and if you did, I'd drown," Hopper says. Part of him hates Randy. But another part of him comes close to loving him. All sarcasm about puppeteers aside, he wouldn't mind being lifted by Randy, and being placed in the relaxing water would obviously be the perfect finale. He eyes the water. It is the water that he most wants. If only Randy can be embarrassed into trying, the moment in the hot tub might be his. He prods just a little more: "You think five minutes is going to do me in?"

"Felix can stand on the sidelines and pray for you," Randy says wryly.

He has convinced him. There remains only the discarding of his clothes. Stripping down to his tee-shirt and boxers.

"Let me get that shirt unbuttoned," Randy says. "You're sure you're not going to freeze? I think I'd better go get some beach towels before—"

"No, man, don't do that. It might call attention to what we're doing."

Slowly, with less strength than he'd like to have, Randy helps Hopper out of the wheelchair. He reaches into the side bag and takes out Hopper's folding cane, snaps it open with two quick motions, and hands it to him. Hopper managed to unzip his pants while still sitting—he never fastens the button at the waist anymore—and he raises his legs as best he can for Randy to pull them off. Without his clothes, the breeze really cuts into him, but he can see the steam rising from the tub, just a few steps in front of him. He uses the cane, but lets himself lean on Randy. Why was he so angry at Randy just a few moments before? Randy is his friend—Randy wants him in the tub just as much as he wants to be in it. It would be a victory for both of them.

And so it is. He clasps the rail with his left hand, maneuvering with the cane in his right. He sinks into the water and bumps down the steps. On the deepest step, sunk almost to his neck, he grins up at Randy, who is standing in a proprietary way, almost like a tall lean crane himself, ready to swoop forward any minute. Realizing that he's hovering, Randy looks away. "You taking all this in, or have you already sprouted angel wings after you've flown the coop?" Randy calls up into the tree.

Angel wings? So Randy has known all along. He must have heard the tires, too. He might even have seen it, from the bathroom window. For some reason, he obviously intended to pretend, before, that it hadn't happened. But he knew it had. He knew all along, and he had just been pretending things were otherwise.

Hopper exhales, letting tension exit with his breath. His shoulders sag comfortably and he slides what he thinks is one more inch forward, then slowly leans back on his elbows. He is that way when Lisa drops off the Famous Poet, parking the Mercedes and saying something quickly to her passenger, waving to the two of them but not returning to the house herself—setting off, later than she wanted to, for another night with her girlfriend.

The Famous Poet stands for a few seconds, just inside the bougainvillea. He has only one small leather satchel: a suitcase that looks to Hopper—and he should know, he thinks grimly—all too much like a doctor's bag. But no: he has not come to minister to the sick. Just before his arrival, Randy impulsively stripped down to his underwear, too, to join Hopper in a final dip. So the Famous Poet stands there, not suspecting anything is wrong with them. In the twilight, he sees only the familiar faces he's seen intermittently through the years, smiling as they've always smiled, and he thinks—Hopper knows he thinks—that they will soon be at his disposal. My God—the time he sent me out for grapefruit juice, when there was already orange and apple, Hopper thinks. *He thinks I'll spring out of the pool and run off to get him whatever he might want,* Hopper almost whispers to Randy, he's so amused with what an impossibility that would be. At the same moment, Randy is thinking: *He thinks things are the way they've always been.* And he locks eyes with the Famous Poet to see whether that isn't so.

But look at him suddenly noticing the wheelchair, trying to put that together with the rest of the picture. Look at him searching the yard to see if maybe somebody else is present: some Christina—one of those pretty women from the past— down in the grass that isn't really grass, but fieldstone, reaching toward the house straight behind them—no house up a hill in the distance in Key West. But that's not it, is it? It's one of them in the hot tub—one of them, who's not letting on, since both faces have turned to him with pleasant, almost bemused expressions. It must be the older one, or could something have happened to the younger? He will write a poem about it, later; but for now, he can only imagine which one it is, never suspecting that for all intents and purposes, it's both. Meanly— childishly—neither is letting on. Through no prearrangement, they've become perfectly complicitous, hiding everything from him but their smiling faces, as if to say: *Here we are. As a prize-winning analyst of matters of the human heart, would you care to descend and join us?*